KAZAKH
PEN CLUB

КАЗАК
ПЕН КЛУБЫ

KALIKHAN ISKAKOV

Tall Cedars

Translated into English by Simon Geoghegan

Edited by Simon Hollingsworth

Published under the supervision of
President of the Kazakh PEN Club
Bigeldy Gabdullin

Cover design by Madina Niyazbayeva

Printed in the United Kingdom

ACKNOWLEDGEMENTS

The publishers would like to thank the Kazakh PEN Club for their continual support on this project. The project was initiated by Kazakh PEN Club President **Bigeldy Gabdullin**, designed to expose the best works of classic Kazakh writers to the global literary stage through their translation into the English language. Through the tireless efforts of Mr Gabdullin, the project gained the financial and logistical support needed from influential Kazakh state organisations and private companies.

The Kazakh PEN Club is most grateful to Akim of the East Kazakhstan Region **Danial Akhmetov** for his financial assistance in the translation and publishing of this book.

FROM THE 'WE ARE KAZAKHS'
SERIES OF PUBLICATIONS BY
THE KAZAKH PEN CLUB

KAZAKH
PEN CLUB

КАЗАҚ
ПЕН КЛУБЫ

KALIKHAN ISKAKOV

Tall Cedars

Published by The Kazakh Pen Club, © 2023

Translation copyright © Simon Geoghegan, 2023

Kalikhan Iskakov
Tall Cedars

TABLE OF CONTENTS

TALL CEDARS

1

Kazhimurat woke his younger cousin Almurat by holding his hand over his nose and running his bristly chin several times over his warm face.

'Hey, what's that? Ah, it's you?' Muttering sleepily, Almurat dressed hastily and followed his cousin out of the room, stumbling over the boots standing at the entrance as he went.

The moon was directly overhead. The diesel generator, which had been humming since the previous evening, giving light to the fifty-or-so homes in the remote taiga village, emitted a dull, spluttering sneeze like an old man before stuttering and falling silent. The bulbs on the lampposts began to fade, flickering rapidly and then going out altogether.

The sleeping world was barely visible in the twilight. The sky seemed to be veiled with a pale reflection of the long-set sun and the silently slumbering forest crept closer to the aul[1] as the shadows of the tall, spreading cedars soundlessly crawled across its inhabitants' deserted backyards. The bumpy uneven ground had been swept clean by the early autumn hoarfrost and resembled the surface of a lake. Cows lay in the centre of the enclosure in Almurat's yard like motionless boulders. From the thickets of nettles growing near the garden came the many voices of a feline choir.

---

[1] Aul – In Kazakhstan, the aul represents the very heart of the traditional Kazakh culture and community. In the 19th and early 20th centuries, the aul would typically consist of a migratory group of 50–70 yurts, united by household and family ties. But in post–soviet time the word came to mean village and the community that lives in it.

His encounter with his brother had immediately and magically shaken Almurat from his sleep. Kazhimurat walked ahead, dragging his right leg slightly and not turning around. A dark, winding trail followed him across the pale hoarfrost and Almurat strode along it swiftly in his oversized boots, crushing the thick frozen uncut grass and just avoiding stepping on his cousin's heels.

It was September — the end of the fast.

Old Batikha's yellow, pot-bellied samovar billowed steam as it sang its perennial victory song. The room was stuffy and the fat autumn flies were relentless. The old woman tried to swat them away with a tea towel, but they would simply rise up in a swarm, only to descend back down and become stuck in the wooden honey bowl with its carved handle. The yellow samovar, table and all three people ended up migrating to the open veranda in the hope of finding some respite out there.

As was her custom, Batikha spread her hands in front of her face in a gesture of prayer. At one time, she had been a tall attractive woman, with a ruddy face, shining black eyes and plump well-shaped calves that would barely fit into her *ichigi* boots[2]. The light in her eyes had dimmed and she had become sagged and crumpled like a ball of raw wool that has been squashed and flattened in the hands of a spinstress. The old woman's thin, drawn lips moved silently and weakly in prayer. She barely managed to pass her hands over her face again before dropping her arms helplessly onto the table and falling into thought.

---

[2] Ichigi boots – Soft leather boots, often decorated with leather inlay and stitching.

The moon had concealed itself behind the trees and the shadows cast by their leaves covered the *dastarkhan*[3] with a mottled pattern that crawled like giant beetles, gathering up the crumbs of *irimshik*[4] and *kurt*[5] that lay on it. A dung beetle flew onto the veranda with a loud buzz, hit the wall and fell to the floor. The commotion made a large dark-grey cat that was basking near the table wake up with a shudder. The sound of what was probably a stray dog gnawing on a bone could be heard nearby. Almurat frowned in disgust, grabbed a large, rough-hewn axe lying by the wall and threw it at its source. His aim was so accurate that a plaintive yelp immediately went up, followed by a red-haired mongrel racing past the rubbish heap and disappearing into the darkness.

'What did you do that for?' Batikha asked angrily. 'What a bunch of louts and ruffians you all are! The moment you see a dog, you can't help sinking to its level.'

'Let it gnaw bones in someone else's back yard!'

Batikha reluctantly poured tea for Kazhimurat and, with a cold expression, handed him a bowl. I thought you might want to share our joy, but, as always, you prefer the company of your precious Kerzhaks[6].'

---

[3] Dastarkhan – A richly patterned cloth laid out for guests on the floor, but in more recent times a table. In other contexts *dastarkhan* can refer to the food being offered on it and the hospitality of the hosts offering it.

[4] Irimshik – a sweet made from dried plums.

[5] Kurt – A kind of dried cheese and an extremely important traditional Kazakh staple that can kept for a very long time. As a rule, kurt is prepared for the lean winter months.

[6] *Kerzhak* – an alternative term used for the 'Old Believers' who split from the Russian Orthodox Church in the 17th Century. They were persecuted and fled to the most remote regions of Russia. In Altai, the Kerzhaks were among the first ethnic Russians to live in the region and referred to

Kazhimurat gave Batikha a short, piercing look as if to say: *Am I not here now, sitting at your table? What difference does it make when I come to see you?* He then took an unopened bundle of roubles from his pocket and placed it in front of her. However, his gesture didn't seem to placate her.

'It's not your money I need! All you had to do was show your face for appearance's sake. So that folks might think we're a family. Would it really have been so hard for you to sit down with everyone else for the wedding?'

'You're not going to give him any peace until you've aired all your grievances, are you?' Almurat smirked. 'I'm not the first or last person in the world to get married, you know.'

'Well, who else am I going to complain to if not him?!'

Batikha had been boiling *kazy* horse meat sausages in the samovar. She lifted the lid, took out the thick sausage, the size of her hand, glistening with fat, and placed it on a dish. She noticed the bottle of vodka that had appeared on the table, which until then had been hiding under Almurat's knee, and, groaning, straightened up.

'Oh, my poor back! Do you see, how old and tired I've become? Who, if not you, should be supporting your younger cousin now? You are the eldest, after all. We heard you'd been awarded the Order of Lenin — it was all the talk of the neighbouring auls. And we're very happy about your success too. But you... Well, you must have driven past the village many times and you never came in to see us once. Dear God! This back of mine will drive me to an early grave, it will...'

themselves as Kerzhaks to distinguish themselves from the 'Russian' settlers who arrived in Altai much later.

Almurat waited for his mother to go back into the house, poured two porcelain drinking bowls to the brim with vodka, stirred a spoonful of honey into each and pushed one over to his cousin. Kazhimurat glanced at the bowl absent-mindedly but didn't touch it. Almurat took his gesture to heart — maybe his brother really wasn't that well disposed towards him, after all.

'Perhaps you'll join me?'

Kazhimurat clicked his tongue and shook his head, but then nevertheless raised the cup to his lips. And so, they sat there like strangers, unable to converse and each sipping their vodka, without even raising a toast. Almurat was more convinced than ever that the past twenty years hadn't changed his elder cousin one bit. His appearance hadn't changed either: his face, with its rough scar resembling a horseshoe, was as stern as ever, almost completely blackened by the wind. The only difference was a few grey hairs around the temples. His cousin might be sitting next to him but he felt very distant. The years they'd spent apart had left their mark.

The moon gradually emerged from the thick curtain of leaves and its face brightened as it filled with light. The leaves seemed to crowd each other out on the branches and fell to the ground with a dry rustle. An early morning chill blew in from the mountains. It was quiet in the aul and the only sound came from the splashing of the nearby stream, which alternately grew louder and then diminished into complete silence.

A single light was burning far away, on the side of the mountain. By now, the herders had long left the mountain pastures and were all coming back down to the valley for winter. Someone was out gathering pine nuts, signalling the imminent arrival of autumn. The aul wore a clean coat of hoarfrost and the air was infused with that special autumnal aroma peculiar to the coniferous forests of the taiga. The moon rolled down behind the nearby mountain and the stars glowed and then melted away like dying embers in the sky, which was now becoming ever clearer in the grey morning light. Kazhimurat sat silently, gazing at the distant, forlornly flickering light. Perhaps he was thinking about the distant past when there had been none of the coldness that now reigned in his relationship with his family. Only when Almurat had filled the bowls for a third time did Kazhimurat finally stir and stroke his moustache. His thick, curly, bristling whiskers disappeared for a moment under his shovel-sized hand, before appearing once more from under his thick fingers.

Batikha reappeared, shuffling in her boots.

'I've made up a bed for you in the living room.' Then she turned to her son, 'Will you be staying the night too?'

'I have things to do first thing in the morning...' Almurat hesitated. 'I'd probably better be off.'

There was nothing stopping him from setting off for work from his parents' house. After all, he and his new bride didn't live very far away. However, the old woman understood that Almurat was afraid of upsetting his young wife, who did her best to keep him on a very short leash. Even if he spent a single night at his parents' home, she wouldn't let him near her for a whole week. *Oh, the times we live in,* the old woman thought bitterly. *Things have come to a fine pass when a young bride behaves towards her mother-in-law as if she's little more than a witch.*

The table was cleared and Kazhimurat went out into the yard. Almurat hesitated, not knowing quite what to do. He, too, ventured down the veranda steps and, for wont of anything else to do, he tidied the firewood, scattered around the hearth, and gathered up the tethers for the calf and lambs that had been left lying about. He hung them on the door, guessing that this was where his mother would want them. The old woman lived in this large holding all on her own now, but it still had plenty of livestock and didn't lack for anything. The house itself was surrounded by numerous outbuildings. There was an enclosure for the sheep, a barn for the cows, a stable and a hen house. There was also the forge and the workshop where Almurat's father had once worked but they stood empty now. As their only son and in accordance with Kazakh custom, Almurat should have taken over all this, but somehow things hadn't turned out that way.

'Well, I expect you'll be staying in the aul for a day or two,' Almurat remarked to his cousin apologetically, almost as if he were about to ask him for a loan. 'No doubt we'll be seeing each other again soon...'

He lingered hesitantly a little longer, not knowing how to invite his cousin over to his home as a distinguished guest. He was worried how his wife might react to the idea or, rather, what she would make of the inevitable expense this might entail. Kazhimurat sensed Almurat's discomfort and, in order to spare him, started to climb up the ladder leading to the roof of the forge.

'Where do you think you're going? Can't you see the frost?' Batikha shouted up agitatedly. 'Don't you go lying on that roof — you'll end up catching your death of cold!

15

Do you hear me? Here, Almurat, at least take him some blankets!'

In his youth, Kazhimurat had spent many a frosty night on this roof, greeting the early-morning blizzards with the dawn. A bit of autumnal hoarfrost wasn't going to bother him, just so long as there weren't any wretched fleas. The thought of fleas cast his mind back to the old, smoky bathhouse, where he had often spent the night in his childhood. The bathhouse was still standing, but, being superfluous to requirements, it had been dragged to the very end of the kitchen garden, where it looked more like a crooked old tombstone now, leaning over forlornly as if peering inquisitively into the sheep enclosure. The corner where it now stood was densely overgrown with burdock and spearwort and had now become a rubbish dump from which a heavy stench emanated. No one visited it anymore and now it stood abandoned.

The moon had disappeared behind the escarpment. The firmament seemed to have been split into two, the first part looking rather like frothy milk that has curdled on the fire, before darkening to reveal the entire Milky Way. The handle of the big dipper stretched out to the east — morning was approaching. It might have been because he had been looking at the sky so long but he felt as if the forge was rotating gently with the earth, and floating away somewhere. He suddenly realised how much he had missed this soft autumn season and its clear, sublime sky.

Kazhimurat cast back in his mind to the past and, from the depths of his memory, he recalled a pure, tranquil, autumnal sky just like this one. His childhood, a truly distant memory now he was forty, had been a time of rare joys and great sorrows. The first things to emerge from the twilight of his past were the ice-blue peaks of the Altai. Then, from out of the darkness of his memory, marched a familiar dense forest, its trees packed tight like the stiff, black braids of a woman's plait. Then he recalled a small village, which, seemingly unable to find a place for itself in that boundless woodland world, had buried itself in an impenetrable thicket of tall shrubs and bushes, its houses scattered in disparate directions, as if estranged from one another. They had been placed in a haphazard fashion, with some facing east, others west and others still, to the north. Nevertheless, the people who lived in this aul were all from the same clan and therefore related. Was it really this same sky that had witnessed his bitter childhood and his troubled youth, and was he really looking up at the same stars that had shared his grief all that time ago?

Once an adult, Kazhimurat had only looked in on his home aul once or twice. He didn't live a great distance away, so he couldn't complain it was too far; it was a matter of one-hundred-and-fifty kilometres, no more. It was simply that he resented his relatives for not leaving him alone and because of his own stubbornness, something he simply couldn't overcome. This time he had come against his will and because of his ill health. For several years now, Kazhimurat had been going to the Rakhmanovskiye Klyuchi centre for radon-bath treatments. This year he had completed his course of treatment, but his illness had taken a turn for the worse and he had been unsure if he'd even make it home alive. Therefore, Kazhimurat could not simply drive past and avoid dropping in on his family and native aul as he had on previous occasions. He was only a little over forty, hardly a great age for a man, but the trouble is that, as the years go by, people increasingly think about their roots, those who have gone before them and those that they are going to leave behind. As the Kazakh saying goes, don't expect even a thread's breadth of sympathy from a heartless son. Kazhimurat had no children to boast about to his relatives. The aul had plenty of children called Murat but he was not destined to call a single one his own.

His father Yelmurat was a dashing figure who had never spared either himself or others. It was widely claimed that he had made his fortune through raiding and robbery. And if the rumours were to be believed, there wasn't an aul in the entire district, or even beyond the Altai Mountains, that hadn't been the victim of one of his night-time raids. People said that Yelmurat was so strong that he could stop a horse at full gallop or bring down a bull by its horns. Kazhimurat couldn't really remember what his father had looked like. All he knew about him was that he would ride a light-bay stallion one night and then a raven-black one the next and that he left and returned home when everyone else was asleep. He was incredibly tall, as dark as night and with shoulders as wide as a barn door. Kazhimurat remembered him wearing a colt-skin winter overcoat that smelled of horse sweat and *kumis*[7]. On summer nights, his father would

---

[7] Kumis – A mildly alcoholic drink made from fermented mare's milk. The mare milking and hence kumis fermenting season traditionally runs between mid–June and October.

wake him up by tickling him with his short beard and, in winter, by shaking the frost from his whiskers onto his face. During the day, Kazhimurat hardly saw him... What else did he recall? Oh yes, he had overheard various conversations about his father, which in reality were nothing more than a combination of fiction and outright slander. There were times when certain folk had called him the son of a brigand. It was not for nothing that Batikha had just now referred to his side of the family as a band of thieves. And that was all he knew about his father, whose name had long since ceased to cause him either joy or shame. People were either proud to have known his father or simply cursed his memory. And there were plenty of them in these parts.

News of the October Revolution eventually reached the distant auls, having spread over the spurs of the Altai mountains and acquired a fair degree of speculation on the way. Those auls that couldn't get their minds around the new life on offer migrated with their herds to foreign parts, while those who did not have the strength to leave their native lands remained behind. Yelmurat left with those who went abroad, but his brother Tazhimurat, despite having no idea what the new government would bring, decided not to follow him. Not only did Yelmurat leave for foreign lands, but it was said that he forced hundreds of others to go there with him. Having led several auls abroad, he returned back to persuade and force more and more to leave their native homes. At first, Yelmurat lived with his wife and then four-year-old son Kazhimurat right next to the border, without crossing it, but later, when it was discovered what he had been up to, he was forced to fight his way out of the country. In the ensuing shoot-out, Yelmurat's wife was killed and the Red Army soldiers took little Kazhimurat from his dead mother's arms and brought him to Tazhimurat. After that unforgettable day, the boy found his fate left in the hands of his uncle and his wife Batikha. Soon after, an unprecedented famine descended on the auls and when it became clear that they couldn't cope with an extra mouth to feed in the house, Batikha didn't hesitate to hand him over to the local Soviet orphanage. Kazhimurat only returned to his native village during the war in nineteen forty-two, having travelled the world and experienced more than his fair share of grief and hardship. He lived in the aul for several years and then disappeared again and now he had returned to his kin for a second time.

The hoarse, sleepy crow of first one and then the rest of the cockerels resounded out over the yards across the aul. The grey morning light filled the sky. Like the solitary eye of the fairy-tale sorceress Sholpan — the morning star glowed a baleful crimson in the east. The cows in the middle of the enclosure stirred into life, breathing heavily and tangling their horns as they rose. Then they huddled up against the wattle fence, leaning and rubbing against it with such force that it began to creak, threatening to break under their weight. The discordant shrill barking of the dogs filled the air that had only just been hanging so peacefully over the aul, eliciting an involuntary shudder in Kazhimurat, like the sound of a ladle being scraped along the bottom of a cast iron Kazan cauldron by a disagreeable and thoughtless housewife. *Even the dogs have gone to the dogs,* Kazhimurat thought to himself. *There was a time when the village had real wolfhounds who could knock a rider from their horse in the blink of an eye. Where had they all gone? Evidently, as the size of the village's herds had shrunk, so had the size of its dogs...* He smiled to himself, pleased that his thoughts had so quickly and unexpectedly switched their focus onto the little details of aul life.

The tall branching cedars gradually shortened and gathered their shadows back under themselves. The morning breeze blew in from the mountains, carrying with it the smell of hoarfrost, which pleasantly tickled the nostrils. Unable to resist the early morning's soporific onslaught, Kazhimurat imperceptibly closed his eyes and dozed off.

First came the roar of a starter, then, with a choking sneeze, an engine rumbled into life. A *Belarus* tractor was nuzzled almost right next to the neighbour's gates, proof positive that now it was machines and not horses that people parked up in front of their houses. Not everyone is lucky enough to be endowed with such a prized possession, but being startled from your sweet morning slumbers by one is no one's idea of a blessing.

Too lazy to get up. Kazhimurat lay for some time luxuriating in the warmth of his blanket. The sky was hanging high above him and the birds chirped loudly and animatedly in the nearby bushes.

The familiar sound of a pair of wooden heels on the hard floor could be heard.

'Drop dead, you wretched animal! You can run away for now, but you're still getting the chop sometime today!'

Batikha was separating a dark grey gelded ram with a bald head and a huge fat tail from the flock and was trying to drive it into the barn. The yellow pot-bellied samovar was standing out on the veranda again, with a white porcelain teapot warming on its chimney. The tinkle of a silver bell could be heard coming from somewhere. Soon enough, an old man as thick-set as an oak, appeared out of the forest, driving a small herd of mares and foals into the village from where they had been sheltering in the night. The air was cold and as clear as crystal. A rare and unusual mist was forming next to the forest. A humid vapour rose from the thick clumps of green bushes and the wispy, pale-yellow ears of the tall grasses that covered the slopes of the hills.

'Hey, Batikha! Take your mare and feed her at home!' Old Kasen shouted as he rode closer. She won't get by on the bare stubble up there.

'Who's going to drink kumis in my house these days?' Batikha replied, breathing heavily and sitting down on the plank benches that had been knocked together next to the outer wall of the house. 'It's a lot of bother keeping a mare tethered up at home. Take her away with the herd, if you can.'

The old man was driving the herd at a good pace and didn't really listen to her. Seeing him hurry past on his bay gelding with its drooping belly, Batikha shouted after him:

'Hey, old friend! Spare me a minute to come in and slaughter my ram!' But at that moment, she caught sight of her red cow nursing her calf who was tethered in the yard. 'And you can drop dead too! What are you shilly-shallying about for? Get yourself off to the pasture! I haven't the strength to drive you out today, I can barely keep myself on my feet as it is...'

It really must have been a great punishment for her to have to live all on her own with no one to even sit down at table and share her food with. She could not find a soul even to dine with. Not a single person who might join her for the free food if nothing else... Kazhimurat recalled how Batikha had once spent an entire summer saving every last crumb of dried cheese and butter she could find, so that the family would have enough for the winter. And if she hadn't, they might all have ended up starving like so many others. But now, when the house was blessed with ample sufficiency, it stood empty, with no one to enjoy its abundance — her only son Almurat had left his old mother and built himself a separate house on the other side of the village. Despite the old Kazakh saying that *you can trust a wife in your arms about as much as you can trust the horse under your saddle*, in reality, there is no person closer or more important to a man than his wife... Looking at the old woman, pitifully hunched over on the plank bench, Kazhimurat made a mental note to have a word with his cousin.

Tazhimurat's house lay on the very edge of the aul, which stretched out along a long hollow. Far beyond the low-lying southern hills, the jagged snow-white peaks of the mountains sparkled, like frozen splinters of sun. The green forest that filled the gorges between them steamed as if it were breathing. Further down below, where it came to a stop, the lake gleamed like mercury between the thick underbrush and reeds. The milky mist and the waning moon gradually began to fade away in the dim light of the approaching dawn.

Kazhimurat passed through the hollow, overgrown with dense grass, where the air was drenched with the smell of horse sorrel, and came straight out onto the nearest lake. The still surface of the water was covered with birds. Slicing through the water with their plump chests, the white geese with their red beaks rushed for the safety of the islands of reeds and soon the small waves, raised by the birds, lapped against the shore. The serene early autumn sun was slowly rising across the sky, exuding a strange, drowsy warmth on everything below. Kazhimurat took off his shirt, pulled off his boots and sat down on the shore, exposing his back to the gentle rays. The din of the restless ducks resonated from the poultry farm on the opposite bank; it was evidently time for their morning feed. At the mouth of the small river flowing into the lake stood the blackened remains of a wooden mill, its winding wooden sluice stretching down from the mountain. The watering hole was silent. White feathers and down floated on the surface of the lake.

Not far off, the reeds rustled and parted, to reveal a punt, on which Almurat and a young red-haired woman with thick, shiny elbows were sitting. She was wearing an apron made from an old overcoat and, for some reason, it reminded Kazhimurat of his father's, saturated with the smell of horse sweat and kumis. Suddenly, the boat turned sharply and disappeared into the reeds. Either the young couple was embarrassed by Kazhimurat's presence, or they were chasing after the geese that had swum away from them in fright. After a while, loud, brazen female laughter came from the thicket before subsiding, as if it had been smothered.

Kazhimurat decided to move. He didn't want to swim near the bank, where the water smelled of mud and fish, so he headed off towards the old mill. He enjoyed a dip in the mill pond, recalling the old times with the familiar old mill. The blades of the wheel that used to turn in the water had now rotted and its four vertical supports had sunk into the mire, while the stone millstones were now half submerged under the ground, resembling ancient, dilapidated stone monoliths. The upper part of the structure leaned precariously towards the lake and had been propped up with a log. The whistling cries of the jerboas could be heard under the mint bushes by the millstones and the mesmeric cooing of the wild turtledoves came from inside the dilapidated building itself.

Flour had long been available for sale in the local store, bread was baked at the factory and the creaking mill, which had once fed the entire aul, was quietly descending into oblivion. Nothing lasts forever in this world. Not only had the mill been forgotten, but so had the name of the man who had once erected it with his own hands, lovingly hammering each plank into its proper place. People are rarely recalled and remembered these days, but it had been Tazhimurat who had built the mill. However, even during his life, Tazhimurat had seldom been called by his full name. More often, people referred to him as Murat the Blacksmith, Murat the Carpenter, Red-eyed Murat or Murat the Miser. True, he could skilfully construct an elegant, intricately carved wooden rosette or forge a thin steel needle, but he would never show disdain for the good work of others. Probably, from his many years of working with hot metal, his eyelids had become inflamed and red, adding a peculiar colour to a face that was dark and sombre as it was. In the old days, folk would have said of him that he had *neither a saintly nor a pretty face*.

According to the Kazakh proverb, cattle settle and breed where the farmer is bright of face. However, Tazhimurat was a remarkable exception to this rule. Evidently, either the wise men who came up with these old sayings were mistaken, or the cattle had gone blind. In any event, after Yelmurat had fled over the border, Tazhimurat's house was considered one of the most prosperous in the aul and all four types of livestock were bred there. People would come to pay Tazhimurat their respects and offer the strength of their arms in labour, sometimes begging and demeaning themselves for the sake of a horse, on which they desperately needed to go somewhere, or for the loan of a cow, without whose milk their children would not have been able to survive. He never joined the collective farm and did not depend, like others, on the workdays accrued at the end of the year. He preferred to be paid for his work directly upon completion, whether it was for cutting and sewing a saddle, bending and moulding the runners for a sled or shoeing a horse. Although no one dared say it to his face, there had never been an instance when Tazhimurat hadn't scooped off at least a cup of flour from the sack of grain that the unfortunate widows or orphans would bring to him to grind. Indeed, Kazhimurat thought, people sometimes fail to see the scar on the face of an honest man, but are quick to discern evil in that of a covetous one. This is the way of the world — there is always a mixture of bad and good. Evidently, the world we live in needed people like Tazhimurat. If there are no bad people, how can you see the good ones?

The punt emerged from the reeds again, but it carried only the red-haired woman. Almurat was no longer with her. Kazhimurat rubbed his chest and shoulders with his towel until they were red, his torso already covered with goosebumps. He felt the tight knot of his muscles moving and rolling, and he began to warm up. He put on his shirt, quickly plugged the toe of his boot, wrapped his once frostbitten and now toeless right foot in his footcloth and put on his boots. Every person has their faults, but, for Kazhimurat, his mutilated foot was the height of misfortune. Since his toes had been amputated, he had never taken his shoes off in front of others and had never felt at ease when invited into their homes as a result. He felt ashamed. On this occasion too, as soon as Almurat's head had appeared behind the gaps in the mill building's rotten planks, Kazhimurat immediately grabbed his right boot.

Almurat's face was flushed and beads of sweat glistened on the tip of his nose and his clean-shaven cheeks. His whole appearance betrayed the fact that, from early morning, he had downed two or even three bowls of distilled mead, which would be sure to set the blood coursing through the body's veins. He had also obviously just been in the company of a woman, as was evidenced by the two or three long strands of bright red hair that protruded from under the unbuttoned collar of his shirt. Catching his cousin's gaze, Almurat turned away, pretending to look at something on the lake, and brushed the hair off with a rapid movement.

'I can barely move my legs from those never-ending chores around the farmstead,' he said loudly. 'This post of calibration test administrator has proved a right pain.

It's been a whole year and I've barely had a moment to myself.'

The young red-haired woman had reached the opposite bank, jumped into the water, dragged the punt to the shore and began mooring it to a stake.

'How's the village going to learn how to raise poultry, if they don't even bother keeping an eye on the cattle?' Almurat remarked, blocking the view of the opposite bank with his back. 'I had to look for someone to work with the hens on the side. I ended up taking on Trofim the miller's young daughter. Of course, you know him, don't you...'

Two red-haired boys were playing boisterously next to a reed-thatched house that stood on a sandy promontory amidst a sea of white birds. Kazhimurat recognised old Trofim next to them, who, in the untucked shirt he always wore, was applying grease to the wheel of his cart. He remembered that the poor folk also used to go to Trofim to ask for favours sometimes — for grinding a single, partially filled sack of grain, the poor supplicants would have to fill the notch on the millstones up to ten times.

'This mill has stood here for ages until it was allowed to fall into disrepair. Now there's not enough feed in winter and the cattle perish by the hundreds, yet there are so many ears of corn lost on the field and in the barn yard. If they were harvested and ground at the mill, there would be enough food for both the livestock and the poultry. But all this is just hot air because there are barely any people left in the village... There's no one like you, a jack of all trades, who could repair and run the mill. I barely have enough time to keep these fifty households in the village going.

Already since the previous day, Kazhimurat had been trying to work out who in the aul was still around. The majority of the elderly residents had passed away, while the younger generation had mostly moved to other parts, either to study or simply to seek their fortune. The windows and doors of their empty houses had been tightly boarded up.

'If you haven't used all your leave up yet, maybe you could stay awhile in your native aul. You could relax a little among your own. Otherwise, you'll have turned into a complete hermit before you know it...'

They say the fish understand the language of the frogs. And, naturally, Kazhimurat understood what his cousin was driving at, but he didn't let on. He got up and silently walked back to the aul.

The smoke from the hearths had thinned and dispersed in the air. There was no trace of the tractor that had woken him that morning. It was that time of the day when the aul folk, not overly bothered about their chores, would sit around drinking their morning tea. For some reason, Kazhimurat suddenly felt empty inside...

2

Kazhimurat didn't have the heart to turn down his cousin's request and stayed for a while in the aul. Two and a half weeks had passed since he and old Trofim had demolished the old mill and then started rebuilding it. Kazhimurat had got out of the habit of doing a decent day's work after two months of idling in the hospital. His shoulders ached from the weight of the axe, and he wasn't even able to lift his end of a log beam. He reminded himself of an old draft horse, suddenly freed from its yoke but quite forgetting how to perform its duties. At first, Kazhimurat had counted on the help of the aul's pensioners, people who had only recently been working in production and who were supposedly more conscientious than others. However, his hopes proved to be unfounded. Those who only yesterday saw themselves as hard workers now wanted to focus on nothing more than their own personal gardens and holdings. From morning to evening, the old people would dote on their precious short-tailed mares, while others even became mullahs. It was as if they had swept their 'conscious' memories of the past under the mat and now, dressing up as Allah's servants, they wandered around the numerous nearby auls, flocking to any funeral and commemorative feasts and eating their fill like crows. *They only have to tether a half-dead old mare next to the house to imagine themselves the richest people in the aul!* Kazhimurat mentally scolded his people.

There was equally no point in placing any hopes on the truck and tractor drivers, for, during this hot season, they would be too busy bringing in the hay and ploughing the fallow fields for the steppe farms. There was no sight nor sound of Almurat since he'd gone in search of a truck crane. And so, it fell to Kazhimurat and Trofim to work together, relying on their former strength.

The floor and the drum were already standing on four supporting piles. All that remained was to fix the chute and put the millstones back in place. There was really nothing much to it — lifting the heavy millstones would be a piece of cake. However, they still needed to be dragged in place and set on their foundations.

Trofim had returned from his house extremely agitated, his face twitching as if he had a serious toothache. He smelled of onions, and Kazhimurat would have sat to the windward side of him, but the old man moved right next to him and, almost breathing right into his face, began to pour out his soul:

'That son-in-law of mine staggered in. The bastard finally remembered he has children. He was in a right state, ragged, hungry and reeking of the booze. A sorry state, he was. We kind of let it pass, but he was so drunk, he still gave us a mouthful. So, I gave him a hiding with the poker and threw him out. What a sorry excuse for a man! Our people are not as smart as they used to be...'

The old man's eyes, as clear as glass, were filled with sadness. He thrust his axe into a log, tossed the whetstone to one side and lay down on his back.

'I thought I'd better keep my distance from him. But, like some stray dog, he's learned to sniff out when something is going for nothing and nothing tastes sweeter than others' scraps... And as for my daughter, well, a woman is always a woman... She's started nagging me that she's finding it hard on her own and that she wants to get out more. She'd be better off finding some work and feeding her kids instead of throwing herself at one waster after another! God, forgive me!'

The sky was fathomless, empty and blue without a single thing to focus the eye on. The heat of the afternoon subsided towards evening, but the sun's rays were still warm, playing on the lake's smooth surface and flashing like sparkling needles that made the eyes hurt. The trees on the northern side of the hills were still a verdant green, which was especially striking in the evening. On the southern side, however, the leaves had already fallen, with only the dense conifers offering any cover, which made the hills look like old men with shaven heads and thick beards and whiskers. Weary from the heat, Trofim yawned and, without taking his eyes from the sky, continued to pour out his woes:

'I swear to God, when the mood takes hold, I'm also tempted to loaf about like a complete waster too! But my grey hairs and dignity won't let me and, anyway, Almurat wouldn't let me... He's made a name for himself, an example to everyone on the farm! The only thing is that he just doesn't know how to get the young lads on side and can't keep them from leaving the aul. So, he pins his hopes on the old men who still have a conscience. But what can we offer? We're about as useful now as a fifth wheel on a cart...'

The grasshoppers had come to life again by the evening, blithely chirping away, and the marmots whistled their startled calls to each other, predicting a protracted winter, even though the autumn had been a warm one. It is only those with no responsibilities in their lives who don't find that the end of the warm season elicits a certain uneasy sadness. It seemed that old Trofim lived in harmony with the laws of nature.

'The smelly ones always seem to live a long life.' Trofim said, as if reading Kazhimurat's thoughts. He peered at him and went on,

'Here I am, stinking to high heaven, and yet I still want to live. So, let's get this mill built and I'll bring my ragtag possessions over here and live by the water. I'll think about something other than death, God forgive me. Maybe that will be easier than keeping watch over my own daughter's hemline. 'So, you've nothing to say again, eh? Well, fair enough... You've been silent all your life. Perhaps you find it easier that way.'

Blissfully exposing his belly to the sun, the old man unhurriedly expounded his thoughts and ideas. To an outsider, he looked like a grizzled old wolf sprawled out on the grass after feasting the whole night on an entire yearling and was now full and content, and happily belching and reminiscing about that now distant evening. His thick, hairy arms, stained as if they'd been corroded by salt, lay limply by his side. Deep wrinkles, reminiscent of the folds on a ram's neck after its head has been boiled in a deep cauldron, ended at his temples. A large, unsightly nose roamed upwards on his broad face and his shaggy, greying beard began at the throat and, joining under his nose, extended right up to his ears. The once mighty muscles of his neck, testifying to a strong, indomitable nature, had been reduced to a mess of withered old tendons. It was only in his muscular, ox-like cheekbones that showed through his beard and whiskers, and in his eyes that shone deeply beneath his overhanging brows, that one could perceive something cold and stern. This old man was clearly still a force to be reckoned with.

Trofim suddenly began to snore and did not wake up again. Kazhimurat sat hunched over the sleeping old man, like an eagle guarding its prey. He had considered trimming the logs to save time, but he didn't want to wake the old man from his sweet dreams.

It was still quiet in the aul. Fat wreaths of smoke swirled from the stocky clay oven chimneys that adorned every yard and were used to make bread. Some thirty short-tailed mares stood tethered at a distance from the homes, huddled close to their foals and affectionately sniffing at them. The well-fed horses never stopped shaking their heads as if calling their masters — those same devout old pensioners, whom Kazhimurat had only just now been mentally berating. However, none of the men was in a hurry to take their bucket to the milking yard. They must have been still drinking their long, protracted, midday tea, pondering which aul might provide them with the best free supper and the most entertaining idle chit-chat that evening.

Previously, there had probably been a manager appointed for every head of cattle and all the men in the aul without exception would have been busy employed in some position or other ranging from manager to accountant — each shouting at their subordinates and waving their handkerchiefs for effect. In short, there wouldn't have been a single man in the aul who was not busy doing something. But now the only thing that kept them busy were their wretched dock-tailed mares, which had become the must-have feature of every yard, and a throwback to the idle habits inherited from their forefathers.

Kazhimurat chuckled: were a time suddenly to come when people would be served their food in dump trucks and their water in the buckets of industrial diggers, there would be barely one of his fellow aul folk who would consider such a lifestyle odd or an abomination. However well a man might live now, he is never likely to forget the most difficult moments of his past and that is why Kazhimurat found the current life of his fellow countrymen a little absurd, much like a white-haired old man taking up an old *kuruk* lasso and horsing around in a foolish game with his six-year-old grandson.

His throat was dry and he wanted a drink. He suddenly imagined the taste of the thick autumnal kumis in his mouth so vividly that it almost felt real. Kazhimurat got up, went to the spring and drank a few mouthfuls of water that reeked of iron, scooping it up in handfuls, before returning back to his original place. Trofim was still sleeping like a log. So, what was it that this once mighty and irrepressible old man dreamed and yearned for? Did he feel sidelined from a life in which he had been accustomed to feeling he was in charge? Or did he hanker for a peaceful old age, something he evidently believed he deserved in his later years? Why did he dream of solitude even though he had lived his entire life on the periphery? Kazhimurat himself knew only too well what loneliness was. If he was angry, he chastised himself and if he rejoiced, then he alone felt this joy. However, there was never a time when he blamed the Almighty or entrusted his innermost thoughts to the first passer-by. Once more, he recalled the old man's baritone voice, declaring, 'So, you've nothing to say again, eh? Well, fair enough... You've been silent all your life. Perhaps you find it easier that way.'

What did the old man find that was so enviable in Kazhimurat's life, for it was so one-dimensional and odious, a life where he could hear but not entrust his thoughts to another? People often complain that misfortunes befall them because they talk too much and, at times, they curse their lack of eloquence. Kazhimurat, however, had dreamed about the ability to speak with his own kind for as long as he could remember. He dreamed and, at the same time, bitterly cursed his fate for the merciless treatment it had meted out on him. The saying: *a man with a full belly will never understand a starving one* could have been coined with his situation in mind.

'Hey, there!' Kazhimurat heard from behind him, followed by the familiar sound of shuffling boots. 'What's keeping you so long? There's little use in cooking food if it isn't eaten when it should be. Oh, my poor back!'

Batikha, her joints creaking, knelt beside him and unfolded a bundle to reveal a bone of mutton with fatty pieces of meat and a cup of rich broth, to which, judging by the colour, sour milk had been added for piquancy. Having laid out the food, Batikha, startled by an unexpectedly loud snore, looked round and shuddered at the sight of Trofim, sprawled out on the grass.

'Oh, Allah! Laid out like a holy relic! Wake him up and give him some meat. He might be a wrong'un, but he's still your friend. Oh, my wretched back! It'll be the death of me, it will!'

Kazhimurat decided not to wake the old man. Trofim lay with his arms outstretched and his wrinkled forehead covered with beads of sweat. His face was twitching convulsively and painfully as if it were being pricked with a needle. Kazhimurat tore off a broad burdock leaf to protect his face from the sun's slanting rays. He took several slices of meat from the bone, chewed on them without much appetite, drank two or three gulps of the broth and then covered the food with the edge of his towel and moved it to the shade of a tall nettle bush in case Trofim might want something when he woke up.

'Perhaps I didn't add enough salt?' Batikha asked in a worried voice. 'Why did you eat so little? You don't like my cooking, is that it? I went to my daughter-in-law's and asked her to try the broth first, but she refused. She sits there, quite out of sorts. All it takes is for me to utter a word and she explodes in a rage. In the old days, folks would say that she's the sort who'd empty the ashes of the fire to spoil her own nest. But who's to blame? She couldn't care less that her husband hasn't a spare minute to rest his head on her pillow... There's only one thing on her mind and, Allah forgive me... My only son has become a scapegoat for the frustrations of some empty-headed woman, but what can I do? To think it's come to this.'

Everyone has their own sadness. They say that when someone weeps sincerely, then even an empty eye socket will shed tears. Kazhimurat could see that Batikha was suffering, but he had not yet decided what he was going to do about it. He felt a kind of ambivalence towards the old woman's current plight given that, in her youth, she had never been bothered by the misfortunes of others.

Batikha sighed sadly, wiped her tears with the end of her white *kimeshek* headdress and looked at the sun as if using it to calculate how long she still had to live. After all, it is the nomads' custom to count their days this way. The sunrise marks the beginning of a new day and the sunset the end of the latest day of a man's life. Batikha's dull eyes betrayed a certain resignation.

The percussive racket of a diesel engine drifted towards them from the east. Trofim came to as if he'd been stung, raised his head and listened.

'Thank God, it's still a good way off...'

'You poor man, how bloated you've become!' Batikha said, looking in horror at Trofim. 'Quick, get up, or you'll pop your clogs in your sleep and you'll have to reconcile yourself with your Christian God!'

'Or perhaps you think I'll end up going off with a bloated bang?' the old man grunted. 'Well, you can keep your caustic comments to yourself, Granny, and give me something to drink. And you can tell your son to get out of the habit of handing out undeserved tongue-lashings, while you're at it!' Trofim caught sight of the bowl in Batikha's hand and spoke in a mix of Russian and Kazakh: 'Hello! Is that broth, I see before me? Have you made it nice and bitter? Can I have a bit?'

'All you deserve right now, is the last rites and your last supper, you bloated old so-and-so! I can see you've already had your dinner!'

'That's going a bit far! I've still a way to go before my last rites, *baibishe*[8], a long way... What do you want me to do? Cross myself and intone *bismillah*[9] at the same time?

'Don't you take God's name in vain!'

---

8 Baibishe is a respectful address to an elderly woman.
9 Bismillah – 'In the name of Allah'.

'Oh yeah, and what is the Almighty going to do with me, then?' the old man replied, again slipping back into his native tongue. 'He's not going to let me in up there, that's for certain. I was talking to him in my dream just now. It turns out the whole lot of us are rejects. He stuck two fingers up at me and then kicked my arse back down here! So, why should I thank him for anything? So, I'll say *in the name of Allah* just to spite him. And, as the saying goes, *Allah versin!* — may Allah reward you... and me for my gratitude.' With that, Trofim emptied the bowl in one gulp and ran his palms over his sleep-swollen face.

'I hope it kills you, you old reprobate! There are people fasting out there and you've gone and desecrated my dishes. Are you incapable of trimming that unruly beard of yours? It looks like a dirty old piece of felt. You could fasten it to the ram's belly to stop it mounting the ewes.'

'My beard takes no responsibility for the wicked ways of rams and men,' the old man said, stroking his beard with his hand and then laughing out loud. 'It contains not only the angels, but a herd of demons a thousand strong. Ha-ha-ha! It is saturated with women's tears, for in my youth a good many of them were shed here... You see, Batikha, I was just dreaming about your husband. These devils had just crucified him and were then frying him in a large roasting pan. He was a sinner, during his life he took a lot of our grain against the rules. Well, Allah said to him, it's the devil made you such a miser and that's where you'd better go... Therefore, you don't need to believe in me, but you will have to feed the devil and all his greedy legions to make sure they do right by you in the next life. Ha-ha-ha!'

39

Trofim really did look like a man who had been inspired by a most unusual dream. His eyes had come back to life after the rich, sour broth and he had become altogether livelier, like a herder saddling a horse from the herd, ready to set out on a long and exciting journey, anxiously anticipating something new. Moments later, he was writhing around like an eel, his nails scratching away at his hairy, sweaty chest. It turned out he had been sitting on top of an anthill and the insects were now happily taking great bites out of him.

The rumble of the tractor deepened as if it were moving away from the aul. Batikha listened out to it and, finally convinced that her son would not be coming to hers that day, hurriedly began to clear away the dishes.

'Oh, my wretched back! I'd better be off. I only have the one cow and if I don't get to her first, she'll give all her milk to that calf of hers. And the herd must already be on its way back from the pasture.'

'Your son is turning off towards the field camp. So, I wouldn't wait up for him today, Batikha.' Trofim shook out his shirt, put it on and stepped towards the water.

To the west, the rays of the setting sun blazed, dissolving the boundary between earth and sky. Long shadows crept across the land from the wide-spreading branches of the cedars, while those of the tall larches, their tops pushing up into the heavens, plunged into the middle of the pond and, stirred by the wind, created the impression that they were trying to dispel the reflections of the white clouds as they floated lazily across the sky.

Trofim dragged a cage net from the mouth of the small spring that flowed into the pond, emptied a writhing trout from it and took up his axe. Seeing that the old man was planning to cook fish, Kazhimurat cut a branch of meadowsweet and set about whittling some twigs to cook the fish on.

The distant mountains lined up in a row, their peaks disappearing into the sky with the grey-headed Mount Saryalka in the very centre — another grey-haired old man, only this one had a broad belt of mountain aspens girding his wide waist. In the crimson rays of the evening sun, the aspen groves resembled a woman's copper-plated decorative girdle. The mountains lower down were concealed by the green-needled outline of the forest that softened into the rounded, shaggy tops of the hills at their foot. Away in the distance, purposefully crawling over the slopes of one of these hills, several tractors were busy with the autumn ploughing while, even lower down in the valleys and hollows, the evening cool was almost visibly spreading over the dark tangled undergrowth like the thick mane of a dark-brown stallion, galloping against the wind.

The old man lit the fire in silence and then, just as silently, set about scaling the fish. Only a few minutes earlier, he had been indolently moping around, not knowing what to do with himself, dragging his feet as he walked, his arms hanging awkwardly next to his knees. Now, he had transformed into the same irrepressible Trofim Kazhimurat had always known, who could always make something out of nothing, and a very useful something at that, and thus engage the attention of everyone around him.

The resinous branches of the larches burned brightly and, as soon as the flames had begun to flicker, the darkness set in, enclosing the fire in a rippling circle. The

41

nearby trees also moved and, as if they had become detached from the mass of the dark forest, headed off in the direction of the aul. The nearer they got to the houses, the sparser they became, dispersing like sheep on their way down from the pasture to their familiar enclosures. The tractors continued to crawl over the hill slopes, only now with their headlights piercing the twilight like the eyes of wolves, savagely tearing at the flesh of their freshly slaughtered prey. The highest mountains had removed the crimson shawls they had donned for the evening and were now arrayed in their customary cold, icy-grey hue. The reddish-yellow tones of the forest fringing the mountains had faded and the mountain meadows, usually a striking emerald-green, were now an ash-grey.

The larches creaked plaintively from the evening breeze and the early autumn twilight, dark and soft as velvet, seemed to carry with it a quiet melancholy that made the heart ache. Distant memories touched the soul, like the faint piping of a shepherd's flute...

The winter of nineteen forty-two had been the harshest in living memory, but the suffering that the war brought with it was far worse.

A motorcycle came hurtling down from the hill, its headlight blinding everything in its path. An unexpected light that catches a person unawares and alone is never a pleasant thing but, on this occasion, it seemed to pluck Kazhimurat from out of the darkness as he sat by the pond and fixed him in its blinding beam. A cold shiver ran right through him, as if someone had shoved an icicle down his back. The sheaf of white light passed over the bushes and brushwood, before hitting the mill and, finally, snatching up Trofim, who responded by defiantly spitting out a mouthful of fish bones.

'He rides that thing like a madman! But what's the point? The first cock crowed long ago...'

Almurat's motorbike and sidecar circled the fire and came to a stop. The figure of a man could be seen almost doubled over in the sidecar.

'Get up, you scumbag! Look at you, just lying there! I'll be damned if I don't get you sent down for this! Then you can lie around for as long as you want.'

It was clear from Almurat's tone that something quite out of the ordinary had happened. He kicked a lanky young man out of the sidecar who, with some difficulty, managed to straighten up his body, having gone quite numb from having to sit in such a cramped and uncomfortable position. He really was very tall, which became even more evident as he approached the fire.

Hey, get that stinking machine downwind!' Trofim barked in irritation — he couldn't stand the smell of petrol.

The ride down from the hill had clearly frozen the two new arrivals right through because they headed straight for the fire, paying no attention to the fish that was smoking over the coals. They both stank of engine oil. The lanky adolescent, with a barely noticeable growth of fluff on his upper lip, swayed about violently and was barely able to reach the fire before sinking to the ground, as if he had broken into several pieces. His mouth was half open or, rather, he was so drunk that his jaw now drooped.

'Looks like he filled his tank good and proper,' Trofim pronounced, looking the lad over. 'You need to line your stomach, lad. Here, have some fish.'

The young man wiped a pair of fists the size of hams on his oil-smeared overalls and took the fish that Trofim offered him, swaying from side to side and, despite his overwhelming desire to fall asleep, just about managed to bring it to his mouth.

'The scumbag should be eating prison gruel and not freshly smoked trout!' Almurat shouted furiously.

'Go on then, tell us what he's done now?'

'This son-of-a-bitch decided to take on a bull with the mounted crane that I'd wangled for you and it ended up smashing the machine to pieces.'

'Well, it all seems a simple enough matter to me. There's just one thing I don't understand. He seems a mild-mannered lad, so how did he end up taking on a bull with our crane?'

'First impressions are deceptive, Uncle Trofim, he just looks the mild-mannered type. He's actually just the sort of evil bastard who'd happily boil up a rotten sheep's skull and tell you it was a nourishing soup.' With that, he launched into the lad once more, 'You'll rot in jail for this, you bastard!'

'Well, I feel sorry for the lad, and the prison is a good hundred or so miles from here. So, you'd be better off sticking with tradition and thrashing his backside with a rope until it breaks out in boils! After all, it doesn't matter where or how you thrash an idiot.'

'A rope, you say? The bull ran away with it tangled in its horns! The son-of-a-bitch has smashed up the crane for nothing! You're as useless as your good-for-nothing father Zakhair. He only used to have to hear a dog bark and he'd run five miles to gawp at a pair of them fighting.

Ugh! I didn't want to remember what an idiot he was...
But you've forced me now.'

Kazhimurat had been watching the young man with
curiosity, for his face seemed familiar, and he smiled
when he heard the name Zakhair mentioned. Zakhair
was known throughout the aul as crook-backed Zakhair,
and he was famous for never missing a dog fight in the
entire district. The story went that he had been sitting
with some other young men out in the pasture one day,
enjoying the kumis and banter when one of them jokingly
reproached him for not being back in the aul where two
dogs were fighting to the death. Hearing the news,
Zakhair leapt onto his horse, forgetting in his haste that it
was tethered to a stake. He whipped the horse into a
gallop but after a few steps came crashing to the ground
with the horse on top of him. Zakhair's ridiculous
obsession cost him dear because he ended up breaking
his pelvis. When his friends came to see how he was
doing, he brushed away their questions in annoyance and
asked impatiently which dog had come out on top in the
fight. Zakhair had spent the entire summer in bed but the
bone never healed properly, which was how he had
acquired the nickname crook-backed Zakhair.

It seemed the old man hadn't got any wiser in his old
age. Only the previous autumn, he had volunteered to
slaughter the livestock that had been set aside for the
winter cull and had collected all the offal and blood and
taken it home with him. Adding red wine to the mix he
then fed it piece by piece to the dogs which, by this time,
had gathered next to his house from all over the aul and
a massive dogfight would then kick off. Crook-backed
Zakhair would organise every imaginable type of dog

fight: between two equally matched dogs or pitting one powerful wolfhound against an entire pack or even all the dogs of one aul against another. The latter contest would last for up to a month and became known as the 'dog festival'. A large number of enthusiasts would gather from all over. The proceedings would officially come to an end when Zakhair and his friends would tie a small silver plaque around the neck of the dog that had beaten all the rest. They would then force its owner to celebrate his victory by slaughtering a sheep for the table and providing the booze as well.

People from the aul would come up with all manner of ideas, but this was the first time that Kazhimurat had heard of a man taking on a bull. He didn't know what to believe and looked closely at the others to check they weren't winding him up. However, Almurat and Zakhair's son didn't look like they were playing a practical joke. Almurat's face, covered in a thin layer of grey dust, looked tired, while Zakhair's son was already asleep.

'Get out of my sight!' Almurat shouted at him. 'Why are you swaying as if you're about to recite the Qur'an? Get on your tractor in the morning and get that crane fixed. And get out of my sight! God help you if the authorities find out what happened! Your sorry excuse for a father doesn't even have a dock-tailed mare to make up for the damage you've caused the farm! You stupid little idiot!'

And that was that. After all, no one was going to take anyone from their own aul to court no matter how guilty they were and no matter how eye-watering the damages.

'Son of a bitch!' Almurat shouted after the lanky lad as he lurched off into the darkness. Then, he suddenly burst out laughing. 'Well, the whole aul came out to see what was going on! You know what they're like, they only have to hear a noise and they'll be craning their necks to get a look at what's going on! I'd sent the idiot to fix the cowshed, but he and a couple of his friends decided to untether our two thoroughbred bulls and set them against one another. But I swear they were a lot smarter than this imbecile! Instead of fighting each other, they charged the truck-mounted crane standing nearby. Then the good-for-nothings decided to see who was stronger, the grey bull or the crane. They secured the cable to the bull's horns and tried to pull it but the animal ended up overturning the truck and headed for home. I arrived back at the farm to find all three of these wasters off their faces, celebrating the grey bull's victory. The crane was lying on its side and there was no trace of the bull. The crane I can live with, but the bulls are another matter. We were just about to let them out into the farm's herd but now they're not going to be much use for anything.'

The aul had had its fair share of oddballs in its time. No one would have been greatly surprised to see someone riding around on a dog waving a club over their head. One man's idea of entertainment might appear odd to one person but to another, it might just seem like a bit of a joke. Here in this aul, where a broken matchstick would be classed by most as an irreparable loss, the fact that the bulls would now be of no use to the herd would, of course, be seen as a great misfortune. However, it wouldn't occur to a single person in the aul to ever wonder why Zakhair's son had become so obsessed with the weird hobby that had caused him so much grief. Why do people fail to see when people who they've been raised and lived with all their lives go off the rails? How many people have been lost as a result of the indifference that neighbours and kin show towards one other?

Trofim put out the fire. A crescent-shaped moon emerged from behind the branches of a dead tree that had been snapped by the wind and was now sticking out of the marshy hollow. An eagle owl hooted at measured intervals from the depths of the forest and the reeds rustled. The damp air was filled with the smell of rotting pond scum and the roof of Trofim's hut, thatched with reeds, stood black against the sandy promontory, like a shaggy Cossack hat.

'Well then, shall we head for home or are you going to come to mine?'

'No, we'll have dinner at my mother's.' Almurat rose to his feet.

They dined in silence and after they'd had their tea as always, they quietly tidied everything away.

After dinner, Almurat was about to head for home when Batikha calmly remarked to her son,

'There's no rush. Your wife brought your clothes and blankets over. They're over there in the corner. Nobody's expecting you at home.'

'Well, thank Allah for that!' Almurat said, perking up, his cheeks turning pink with the pleasure. 'You don't have a bottle of something going spare, do you? I think we should mark the occasion.'

'I don't know which of us has been blessed by Allah.' She said that tomorrow she was going to court and that you may as well get ready to say goodbye to your job.'

'Even better! I had no idea how I was going to get rid of her!'

'You tell a rotten egg that he's a rotten egg and he'll only stick his nose in the air in pride. There are people in the world who are both better and worse than you, but they live respectable lives. But what will you have achieved as a result of all this, except dragging your entire family and ancestors' name through the mud for the sake of that trollop?'

'Oh, all I ask is to be rid of her!' In an attempt to conceal the awkwardness, Almurat laughed loudly. 'I wouldn't worry about our ancestors! They're more than a match for anyone.'

He sorted through the things that his wife had thrown into the corner, pulled out a couple of blankets and then climbed up to the roof of the forge behind Kazhimurat. He laid out one and covered himself with the other, his head included. However, a minute later, he threw off the blanket and started tossing about from side to side.

Good grief... He'd be better off grabbing himself an armful of hay, the great numbskull. The floor's quite hard here, it looks like he's got used to lying in a soft bed with his warm wife by his side, Kazhimurat thought to himself.

Almurat had decided to sleep next to his cousin to get his advice, but now, lying on this hard floor, he was already looking for an excuse to return home to his nagging wife who was tireless in her caresses but who could pick a fight at the drop of a hat simply because she thought he hadn't been paying her enough attention.

Mind you, Kazhimurat thought to himself, observing his brother's discomfort, *what's the point of a life lived without a corner and a wife to call your own?*

'I'm thinking about getting the wife to pack her bags. What do you think?'

Kazhimurat couldn't stop himself from bursting out laughing. How could he possibly have an opinion about it? Only a few minutes earlier, Almurat had said he was going to do one thing and now he was about to do the opposite. 'I'm thinking about getting the wife to pack her bags...' Judging by his words, the best he'd manage would be a couple of days away from his wife before crawling back to her like a fly to the honey pot.

Almurat wasn't so sure about his decision himself. For now, he was happy to simply have a few days' break from the rows and endless abuse from his wife. And, although he was incapable of leaving her, the only relief he could get from the hurt he felt after every stupid argument was when he was at work, even with all its long hours and bothers. He was becoming more and more convinced that his relationship with his wife was beyond repair, it had completely exhausted him and even their quarrels and disagreements couldn't breathe any life into it. It really did seem that the fire in their family hearth had gone out for good.

Ever since his childhood, Almurat had been obedient and helpful, and he wasn't used to defying and contradicting anyone. After marrying Fatima, he had done everything to please her, anticipating her every desire and patiently putting up with all her reproaches, regardless of their injustice. It had been as if his wife had made it her goal to turn him into some sort of docile, obedient caged pet, on whom she could vent her bad moods and frustrations. But Fatima's moods had been becoming increasingly unreasonable and unbearable with each passing day. However, Almurat had clearly got used to her cantankerous nature and never-ending complaints and, even now, after she had dumped all his things at his mother's, even after this demeaning attack, he was still thinking of returning home. It struck him as strange that he could get on with other people, but he couldn't get along with his wife, whom he himself had chosen as his life partner. As they used to say in the aul, *If you want to guarantee yourself an early death, get yourself a motorbike or marry a woman from the city.* Well, he'd bought a motorbike and he'd married a girl from the city... So, he had no one to blame but himself.

His family troubles had put paid to all his human aspirations, however noble they might have been. It had been several years since Almurat and his young wife had come back to live in his native aul, after his graduation from the veterinary institute in the capital. He'd turned down a better job with better accommodation in a larger village where the central state farm was based but instead preferred to go straight to his native aul. He was worried that he'd have other people telling him what to do anywhere else, whereas here, at least, he'd be his own boss. However, things had turned out differently. Yes, he was his own boss and he was an incredibly hard worker, and yet he had achieved so little. He had gone through life like some jaded gelding, running out of steam when he was only halfway through the race. In his youth, he had foolishly taken on all the most difficult jobs around the farm. But he felt as if he was fighting all on his own, never knowing when he might see the light at the end of the tunnel.

His usual working day would begin from the early morning and each day and would stretch out into the next. He had become so used to this grey, monotonous existence now that the only thing he felt grateful for these days was his fellow villagers who, thank goodness at least, didn't add too much more to his plate. He recalled how, during the first days in the job, he had tried to change the pace of the unenviable, grey life of the little aul in its remote taiga hollow, by introducing a number of innovations. However, he was soon forced to surrender, reconciled himself with the inevitable and everything carried on just as it always had. Everything had turned out just like the popular, old song had said it would, *When the burning in your soul subsides and yearning of your heart begins to fade, when the steel yields without a fight and the fire inside has cooled...* There were moments when he felt restless and tormented in his bitter and lonely solitude and his mind would become filled with various dreams. Sometimes, he would be at home with his wife at his side, but his thoughts would be far away and he would feel as if he was once more at the start of his life's journey. When he was in this sort of mood, all he had to do was recall his distant, carefree, student days when he was unmarried and free to do what he wanted, and he would once again be filled with a melancholy yearning, and he would catch himself thinking about running for the hills.

Over time, the once modest and affectionate Fatima he had originally married seemed to have been supplanted by a complete stranger whom he had happened to chance upon on his road through life. Fatima would nag and scold him from first light, even before making the bed and in the evening, he would be greeted with screams and the crash of smashed crockery as if it was a complete stranger and not her husband who had come back to the house. Of all the bitter words that dropped from her lips, one thing and one thing alone was clear: she was leaving...

They say that it's only when you're completely frozen that you truly appreciate the blessings of the fire. And it was clear that he was only putting up with this unbearable heat now to rid himself of his numbing pain. In the same way, if you want to find out just how foolish you are, then marry a headstrong woman and she'll soon tell you what your faults are... She will judge your every move, and follow your every step, noting down all your good points and bad. A woman like that is in no hurry to praise her husband, but quick to put him down. Later, when you find yourself at the gates of hell, at least you won't have the torment of having to weigh up all your faults and sins because your wife will have already done it for you long ago.

And who knows, how many more you'll have taken upon yourself by then. Almurat imagined how much longer he would have to traipse between his home and office and then from his office around the farm, a route as random as an ant trail, constantly on the move from morning to night. Perhaps there was another road he might set out on... But now he was lying atop the roof of the abandoned forge whose furnace had long since gone out and whose bellows no longer blowed.

'Why don't you take me on at one of your logging companies? Even if it was just as a lumberjack.'

Kazhimurat didn't stir. He lay there as still and silent as the grave, his eyes never leaving the sky, over which a pale, matte sheen had spread. Whenever he was preoccupied with something, his features would take on a look of complete and hopeless grief, triggering an inexplicable fear in anyone looking at him. What was he thinking about? If human beings could die from anguish and yearning, then Kazhimurat would have left this life long ago. No sooner had Almurat thought of his elder cousin's boundless, persistent sadness than his own ordeals suddenly seemed no more than some childish affront.

They say that a person who has lost the gift of speech can regain it in an instant, prompted by a moment of extreme joy or incredible fear. Almurat recalled how in his childhood he had done everything he could think of to help his cousin. He had tried thrusting a dead snake into his shirt while he was sleeping and poured icy water over him, but Kazhimurat had never reacted in the slightest to all these pranks — in much the same way that he ignored the malicious tricks that the other villagers would play at his expense. More than anything else in life, Almurat had wanted to bring his brother joy, however small, but he hadn't succeeded in that endeavour either.

3

The winter of forty-two had been unusually harsh. But the hardships that the war brought with it were even harder for the people to bear. That year, Almurat had turned seven and, one night, during a particularly heavy frost, he recalled suddenly being woken up by a loud knocking at the door.

The room where he slept was not particularly dark, for the moon would peek in through the window, lighting up a patch on the floor the size of a saddle blanket. Stretching and raising its fur in displeasure, the family's black cat made its way across that same illuminated patch of floor. It appeared that the creature, too, had been woken by the loud banging. The shuffling of clog slippers could be heard coming from the back room where his parents slept. His mother had got up. She fumbled about on the table for the matches and lit the lamp. Then came another loud, impatient knock at the door.

'Oh, Allah!' There's nothing worse than visitors in the dead of night!' Grumbling with displeasure, Batikha threw back the hook on the door.

A man of enormous height silently tumbled into the house, filling the entire doorway. The door slammed shut behind him, the wind blowing out the lamp. Almurat sensed a sudden chill creep over him. Batikha rushed to the table to light the wick once more. Huge black shadows moved over the walls and to Almurat the stranger seemed to loom threateningly over his mother. Batikha gasped in fright and rushed into the back room.

55

'Who's out there?' His father called out loudly as if to frighten the stranger away.

The visitor stopped hesitantly upon hearing a man's voice. At least that's how it appeared to Almurat. The boy shuddered at the man's cold gaze. Almurat felt an unexpected ache in his temples. The stranger sat down on a chair in silence. He was wearing a short white fur coat with patches on its patches and a hat with the ears torn off, from which clumps of cotton wool protruded. With some difficulty, he removed his canvas boots with their turned-up, hardened toes.

'Who are you?'

The father emerged from the back room, approaching the nocturnal visitor. The latter rose to meet him and looking into his eyes, Almurat's father fell silent for several minutes, as if he had lost the gift of speech.

'Oh, Allah! Is it really you?!' he exclaimed and then embraced the stranger, held him close and burst into tears. 'Wife, look who's come...'

'Kazhimurat! Is it really you?' His mother didn't appear to be so happy to see him.

From that memorable night, Almurat gave up his bed over the warm stove to his cousin. He now slept next to his father and mother and therefore accidentally discovered a lot about Kazhimurat by listening in to his parents' long and anxious conversations.

'They said he was given a long stretch for murder!' His mother recalled, tossing restlessly in the bed.

'You can stop that talk! *They* have very vivid imaginations.'

'Do you think so? I worry about you sometimes...'

'I don't care if he's even on the run! He and I share the same ancestors and when times are hard, your relatives should always be there for you.'

'Should always be there for you!' Batikha exclaimed. 'He's going to be an extra mouth to feed! People around here are always looking over their shoulder when their plate's in front of them and rarely go out to relieve themselves while they're eating...'

'Enough!' Tazhimurat said angrily. 'Have you forgotten that there was a time when you didn't even have a single cowhide to call your own? Everything we now have in this house was given to us by his father!'

'Are you trying to tell me we're in his debt? And have you forgotten what it's been like being labelled a *family of thieves*? I think you should report him to the local police before we get into trouble.'

At that moment the dull thud of a fist banging down on the table could be heard and Batikha jumped out of the bed.

Almurat was getting more and more anxious in his sleep. He hadn't noticed how he'd dropped off and was dreaming of an unknown person pressing down on him from above and suffocating him. He began to choke and wanted to cry out for help, but could not find his voice. With the last of his strength, the boy tried to tear the thick, tenacious fingers from his throat. He flailed his arms and they hit something soft and unpleasant. He raised his head with a jerk and, covered in sweat, looked around. He realised he had been delirious in his sleep. Curled up in a ball and sleeping right on his chest was the black cat. Almurat grabbed it by the tail and sent it with a thud over the floor towards the door.

The moon had already risen and black shadows reared up eerily in the corners of the room like fairytale monsters. The cat returned and tried to settle down on his chest again. Almurat grabbed it by the back and launched it into one of the monsters. It turned out to be the samovar. His aim had been true and the cat knocked its lid off. It had been placed upside down to dry and clattered loudly onto the floor.

'Damn that creature! We should never have let him in for the night. An animal's place is outside the house!' his mother began to curse. It was clear to anyone listening that it wasn't the black cat she was berating but their nocturnal visitor. 'He wouldn't have died if he'd been left outside!'

And indeed, she very nearly did send Kazhimurat packing. He evidently realised that his unexpected arrival was a problem for Batikha, so he only ended up sleeping one night over the stove and never stayed overnight at the house ever again. From that day, he slept on the roof of the forge, on a bed of hay. In the evening twilight, Kazhimurat drove away the red-haired dog that had furiously hurled itself at him and climbed into the nest he'd made for himself in the hay. Early the next morning, he crawled out and descended the ladder to be greeted by the same savage barking. Taimas, the family's dog, only had to see Kazhimurat and he would bare his teeth, snarl and nearly choke from hysterical barking until the stranger had disappeared from his sight. You'd be forgiven for thinking that the faithful dog could read his mistress's mind — although the two of them actually had very similar temperaments. At first, Tazhimurat had given his wife a stern look or two but when he realised that his nephew really wasn't bothered about not being allowed into the house, he resigned himself to the situation. The young man did not express his feelings in any way and that included his attitude to him, Batikha and her vile dog, so he made no attempt to change the arrangement — it would have been a waste of time and a fool's errand anyway. Almurat saw his cousin as a secretive and mysterious figure and he was both drawn to and feared him in equal measure. However, folk in the aul were unanimous in their fear of Kazhimurat and they all shunned him, believing that he was a man capable of doing anything. The rumours that Kazhimurat had murdered someone and done time in prison created an aura around him as a man capable of cruel and heartless deeds. This was probably why no one in the house uttered a word of reproach when one day Kazhimurat killed Taimas the family dog with a shovel blow to the head after it had harried him one time too many. Batikha also piped down for a bit when she found out.

The winter mornings in these parts are seldom clear and, by midday, the sky would again be packed with low cloud. The gorges and hollows would be blanketed in fresh snow and the aul's inhabitants would continually dig each other's houses out, which would sometimes be buried to the rafters. Meandering like a snake's trail from the gates of Tazhimurat's house to the collective farm office, a path disappeared among the snowdrifts and then reappeared, weaving its way between the houses, barely visible beneath the tall snow. It had been dug by Kazhimurat as he tirelessly trudged from yard to yard, as if tethering a lifeline around a large herd of horses in a snowstorm. He also harnessed the farm's grey ox to the sled and delivered hay, firewood and water from the nearby ice hole to the homes of the elderly and infirm, and to the families of those whose men were away at the front.

Little Almurat had not paid much attention to his brother's endless errands and labours. It hadn't occurred to him to ask himself why Kazhimurat was breaking his back to help his fellow villagers of his own free will. Was it simply because he was just used to being constantly busy and incapable of sitting idle, or was he doing it for the cup of mealy gruel that some of the households he helped would occasionally offer him?

The reason wasn't clear but he carried on doing so until the middle of winter when the district police officer officer turned up at the aul.

It was so cold that the air took your breath away. The pale disk of the sun hung in the sky as if it had been snagged on the top of a tall larch, its hazy glow a portent of bad weather. A reddish gleam lay on the darkened ridges of the high snowdrifts, while light lilac shadows gathered on their slopes.

Kazhimurat was digging a path on that day too and he was slowly progressing towards Zakhair's house, chopping out dense blocks of snow with his shovel in sharp, powerful motions and casting the snow to either side as he went. His quilted hat with its clumps of cotton wool sticking out had now been pushed to the back of his head and steam poured from the unbuttoned collar of his coat. Taimas, who stalked him everywhere, was sitting a distance away, his eyes never leaving his sworn enemy. It was so deep that it was more like a trench than a path and only Kazhimurat had the strength to dig it. Here and there, the heads of housewives could be seen bobbing over the top as they ran to their neighbours for embers for the hearth — their supplies of matches having long since run out. The children had returned from school, throwing the oatmeal sacks they used as school bags onto the snow and divided into their customary two teams for a loud and unruly game of war. Fortunately for them, the long, deep and winding trench was almost ready. On this occasion, one group of boys had captured Zakhair's woodshed by storm, where the other team, the *fascists*, had dug in. The shed stood to one side of the house.

'The policeman! The policeman's coming!' The boys on the street cried out. 'Look, he's turning towards Zakhair's house. Hey, Almurat, the police have come to take your cousin back to prison!' Then, vying to outdo each other, they started to tease Kazhimurat, 'Here's half a ladle of thin stew! You won't find a drop of fat in it! But you'll pop your socks if you don't work for it! So, go on, clear the snow and open your mouth wide!'

The district police officer really was heading for Zakhair's house. Alongside him trotted Zlikha, the chairwoman of the collective farm. After Zakhair had been enlisted into the Labour Army, few people bothered looking in on his house. For a moment, Almurat thought that the policeman really had come for Kazhimurat. He remembered his mother angrily telling his father to call the authorities and his heart was filled with foreboding. Almurat ran after the other boys towards Zakhair's house, near where Kazhimurat was working.

He had already cleared the yard and was now clearing the way to the cattle barn. The policeman lowered the collar on his well-fitting, half-length coat, thrust his

61

mittens under the belt with his holster on it and stopped, his legs thrust apart and his hands on his hips.

'Who is this woman?'

Kazhimurat thrust his shovel into the snowdrift and turned towards the voice addressing him. An expression of surprise flashed in the official's eyes.

'Ah, I thought you were a woman...' The policeman drawled, seeing that he'd made a mistake.

He had barely finished his sentence when Zakhair's wife came running out of the house.

'If it's a woman you're after, there's only one woman in this house and that's me! Although I don't know why you need one, you've got a fine specimen standing right next to you?!'

Rapiya was well known throughout the region for her sharp wit and had been known to enter the wrestling ring, even against men. She was a woman with a mouth on her and she wasn't going to miss the chance to give Zlikha an earful. The two had never seen eye to eye. Rapiya had already guessed that the chairwoman and policeman had come to see her for a reason.

'Are you working as the watchman in the cattle barn?' The policeman asked Rapiya.

'That's right.'

'So, why did you let the wolves take the farm's ox?'

'If your days are numbered, the wolves are going to get you, regardless of whether it's you or the farm's ox.'

'Well, I am not the farm's ox, I represent the local authorities and I am responsible for order in this aul.'

'In the aul, not the collective farm,' Rapiya countered.

'In the collective farm too. So, stop your wisecracks and answer my question.'

'And I'm telling you. If I'm to blame, then I'll work extra to cover the value of the ox. My worthless hide is probably about as valuable as an ox, right now, wouldn't you say?'

'Work extra — that's just a lot of empty talk. That ox should be at the collective farm, do you understand?'

'And not in some wolf's belly! Oh, what a shame! If only I'd known, I'd have asked the wolf to bring the beast back up again for you.'

'For goodness sake, woman... There are people at the front, sacrificing their lives to defend you against the fascists and here you are mindlessly squandering public property.'

'So, why don't you go out and fight at the front then?! I don't think we sent our men out there for the fun of it.'

'For goodness sake, woman... I've already told you to leave me out of this! I am here on public service. And, what's more, I'm exempt from active duty.'

At that moment, Zakhair's only cow, a red one with a white patch, mooed in the shed. The policeman's smartly waxed moustaches twitched victoriously.

'All right,' he said, 'sign the documents. You first, as chairwoman.'

He pulled a sheet of paper from his dispatch bag, spat on the stub of an indelible pencil and passed the piece of paper to Zlikha. However, she stepped back in confusion.

'Hey you over there, what are you just standing there for? Lead the cow out!' The policeman brusquely addressed Kazhimurat, trying to put him in his place, but the young man was in no hurry to carry out his orders.

To make matters worse, the cow in the shed began mooing incessantly. Zlikha tried to explain to the policeman that everyone would try to work together to somehow make up for the damage that had been incurred, but he paid her no heed, signing the deed himself and then handing it to Zlikha. At that moment, Kazhimurat wrestled the policeman to the floor, seized the paper from his hands and tore it into tiny little pieces.

'For fuck's sake! Do you want me to send me back to where you've just come from? You think you're the big man now, do you?'

Fearing how this face-off would end, Zlikha scuttled off to her office. Rapiya was seriously worried too, and led her red cow with its white patch out of the shed and, with tears in her eyes, removed the tether from its horns. The policeman, however, confounded by Kazhimurat's intervention, didn't even look at her. He picked up his hat that had fallen into the snow, shook it off and slammed it back on his head. Then, with the look of a man who has accomplished something important, he spat through his teeth onto the snow and walked away. Kazhimurat stood there quite pale, as if he'd just emerged from a fire, while Rapiya, sobbing loudly, suddenly vented all her spleen on him.

'Instead of messing about by the hearths and hanging around the women, you could have kept an eye on the cattle... At least they'd have been saved from the wolves!'

Then she charged off after the policeman, sniffling as she drove the cow in front of her. The sorry woman had completely lost her head and was thrashing the poor creature on the side as if she were beating the dust from an old hide. The children had dispersed. Quite taken aback by Rapiya's sudden attack on him, Kazhimurat had only just picked up his shovel, when the red-haired dog pounced on him. Taimas had evidently decided that his chance had finally come. However, the cur had overestimated his strength. With a short but terrible blow, Kazhimurat felled the dog, then buried it with snow while its paws were still convulsing, and stamped down on it for good measure, before walking away.

Batikha had got into the custom of getting dinner ready late when the entire aul had gone quiet and no one was likely to come visiting. The house was dark, they were saving on kerosene and would only light the lamp come nightfall. Two rays of flickering light like the myopic gaze of a giant's bloodshot eyes peered out from behind the badly-fitting door of the stove, made out of an old iron barrel. They snaked across the colourful patterns on the decorative *syrmak* felt rug covering the floor. The ram's bladder that had been stretched over the window had cracked in places and now resembled wrinkled skin. Batikha was sitting right next to the red-hot side of the stove, noisily sipping her tea. Her brow glistened with perspiration. Almurat was convinced that this cast-iron potbelly stove was his mother's closest confidante. Her relationship with the stove, which churned out the heat, reminded him of the meetings of the aul women who would pop round to one another's houses for embers to start their fires and then greedily share all manner of gossip. And right now, Batikha's confidante seemed to be saying to his mother, 'How can I fill you to your heart's content with piping hot tea,' and Batikha knew only too well that the answer was to fill the stove's insatiable mouth with more fuel. The stove was already red-hot, but Batikha still frowned in displeasure.

By the time Tazhimurat came back home, Batikha was limp with sweat and already onto her thirteenth cup of tea.

'Are we playing *blind man's bluff* again? Light the lamp, woman! You'd think kerosene was as rare as the blood of a sandpiper...'

Tazhimurat had never joined the collective farm. He liked living alongside other people but did so on his own terms, looking down on the workers, busy with their endless duties and responsibilities on the collective farm. At first, he earned a living out of his carpentry, then by running the mill, but later on, he turned his hand to blacksmithing — realising that there was more money to be made patching up cauldrons, soldering broken legs onto samovars and attaching handles to enamel cups. It was his strict rule only to take payment for his work immediately upon completion. Tazhimurat's household never lacked for anything, there was always enough food and decent clothes for everyone. His skilled hands had helped him avoid being called up into the Labour Army.

Today, he had evidently not been paid in full for the work he'd done, because instead of handing the money he normally kept tied up in a handkerchief with a satisfied look on his face, on this occasion, he carelessly tossed it down on the table in front of her.

Batikha lit the lamp and took a pot of meat stew from the stove. Tazhimurat's swollen red eyes stared fixedly at a single point in the room.

'Did you feed the dog?' He asked suddenly. 'For some reason, I didn't see him out in the yard.'

'Don't worry, the scraps won't go to waste. If the dog doesn't get them, someone else will. There's never been a problem in this house finding mouths to feed.'

The moment the conversation turned to the dog, Almurat remembered Kazhimurat and defiantly left his food untouched. His mother's words jarred and, for the first time, he was overcome with a feeling of disgust for her. Disgust at her thin, pursed, dissatisfied lips, which were always stingy with praise for others but always ready to sting with a calculated barb or two, and disgust at her round face with its smooth skin, steamed red from the heat and the tea she had consumed. Previously, he had always thought his parents were better than everyone else's in the aul — they never argued or swore like other people and their neighbours never made jokes at their expense. But it was precisely today that Almurat realised the true value of their life that, at first glance, appeared so tranquil and pleasant. The life that they had won at the expense of other people, was detached and jealously guarded. All it had taken was for one person, their closest living relative to enter into his parents' isolated and carefully concealed world for them to feel as if they'd been visited by a plague. They portrayed themselves as the poor victims of circumstance, who had been deprived of their last crust of bread.

A funereal silence hung over the immaculately clean and spacious house with its rows of neatly folded blankets and pillows, which towered over the felt sack packed full of clothes and fabric.

'Why aren't you eating?' His mother asked. 'Are you full? Or is it heartburn?'

Previously, she would only have had to give her son a single look for him to start eating or go to bed. Almurat lowered his eyes. He imagined his mother had guessed what he was thinking about. His father had already finished eating and was getting ready for bed. That day, he had not uttered a word to Kazhimurat, as if he wasn't living with them at all. However, that was probably understandable...

A week earlier, Zlikha, the chairwoman of the collective farm, had dragged a full sack of wheat all the way up to their house. 'I've had no choice but to bring this to you from the collective farm,' she confessed in a weary voice. 'Let's agree that you've taken nothing and I've given you nothing on the condition that you please fix the farm's carts and sledges. The tractor has broken and all work has come to a halt.' She had pleaded with him at length to help the collective farm. However, despite citing his health, his lack of the right tools and how busy he was in order to get a better price, Tazhimurat managed to lose out on the deal altogether. Kazhimurat, who had been listening to their conversation in silence, simply stood up, loaded the sack of grain onto his back, took it back to the collective farm barn and, over the space of two days and two nights, repaired all the carts and sleds. By the time he had finished, they almost looked as good as new. No one in the house mentioned a word about the incident, except on one occasion, over dinner, when Tazhimurat quietly remarked to Kazhimurat,

'They say that when dog shit becomes a valuable medicine, they'll start selling it across the ocean for export. Seeing as you're one of those types who like to earn a living through honest work, if you ever find you get too much of it, don't forget about us, eh?'

It was clear that Tazhimurat was still unable to forgive Kazhimurat for the incident with the sack of grain, seeing as he hadn't even enquired after him.

Almurat defiantly left his food untouched. He found his coat, plonked his fur hat onto his head, shoved a flatbread into his breast pocket and headed for the door. His mother had wanted to say something, but his father stopped her.

'Leave him be. It looks like he is growing up to be just as stubborn as his grandfathers were before him.'

Almurat searched the entire aul for Kazhimurat, looking in almost every yard and every barn, but his cousin seemed to have disappeared without a trace. And various terrifying ideas entered his head. He remembered how the local policeman had threatened to put him back in prison and he became almost completely inconsolable. He imagined that he'd never see Kazhimurat again.

He climbed up onto the forge. The nest in the pile of hay was empty. He figured that Kazhimurat would eventually return here to sleep and so he curled up into a ball, packing himself in with bundles of hay. *I won't go home, even if I have to freeze to death here,* he decided.

The frost got worse, creeping into every bone. By midnight, the wind was howling as well. The aul had fallen completely silent as if it were reconciled to submit itself to the winter's authority. Faint lights could be seen making their way along the aul's paths reflected against the snowdrifts — the only ghostlike signs of human life that could be discerned from where the boy lay. An incessant creaking sound and the occasional clatter of hooves could be heard coming from the barn, which sheltered the dark-bay mare and the yearling with the white patch. The heifer sighed, listening to the horses feed. *I wonder if they'll really take Rapiya's cow away?* Almurat wondered as he tried and failed to work out which of the lights marked Zakhair's house. Clearly, after losing the last of her cattle, there were fewer chores to be done around the yard and the members of Zakhair's household had turned in early. Had the wolves not taken the grey ox, everything would have been fine. Rapiya had clearly been unlucky for the wolves could have attacked a cow in one of the homes where plenty of cattle were kept. The door creaked and Almurat could hear his mother's voice, calling the red-haired dog.

'Taimas! Taimas! For goodness sake! Even the dog in this house is misbehaving! Taimas! Taimas!'

No one in the house other than Almurat knew that Taimas had been sent to meet his forefathers even before the evening prayers had been said. At first, what Kazhimurat had done had repulsed Almurat with its cruelty, but now the dog's demise did not evoke the feelings he had experienced when he saw it being killed. After all, how could he mourn for a dog when an unfortunate family had had its only cow confiscated, dooming it to an existence close to starvation?

'Taimas! Taimas! Well, you can drop dead as well!'

Almurat's mother noisily threw the scraps into the dog's wooden trough and went back inside, slamming the door with a bang. Almurat choked back his tears — they were looking for the dog, but the dog was no more. *I'm not going back inside, even if I freeze to death by morning...*

70

He felt hungry, so he broke off a piece of the flatbread and began to chew, still looking out at the lights in the aul. There were fewer of them now and the wind was blowing stronger. The dark-bay mare was crunching on the dry packed hay, while the yearling was evidently dozing. Almurat shoved his cold hands into his breast pockets.

A few rare stars shone in the cold, black sky. All he could make out were the Seven Sisters and the Great Bear. Now that the wind had picked up, he could clearly hear the whistle of the telegraph poles and the mournful buzzing over the wires in the darkness. From time to time, a bough or branch of a frozen larch would crack and fall to the ground with a dull thud. The plaintive howl of a wolf resonated out from the nearest patch of forest. The wind whistled in the cracks in the hay. The many and varied voices of the night began to ring in Almurat's ears and he felt his head spinning.

The blizzard howled like a lone dog that has been abandoned and forgotten at a way camp by its owners. Drifting plumes of white cloud first hid and then revealed the last few visible stars. It seemed as if they were shaking them up and then scattering them afresh across the night sky. Almurat suddenly imagined Kazhimurat all alone on this pitch-black night, in the centre of the storm, surrounded by a deadly ring of wolves, closing in. His mouth was dry and he licked his lips, now salty from his tears. Only then did he realise that he had eaten almost all the flatbread he had taken from the table for Kazhimurat and felt utterly dejected.

The blizzard raged on and the phantom lights of the aul's houses continued to blink through it, betraying the whereabouts of their inhabitants who were long oblivious to it.

All that remained of the collective farm's cattle shed was a ribbed shell; the starving cattle had nibbled away at it right up to the very rafters of the poorly thatched roof, covered with rotten straw. Even the last stack of hay, piled up behind the barn was now melting away. It had been carefully kept in reserve since the autumn just as a thrifty housewife saves the last piece of butter in her larder. It had decreased in circumference and sunk lower with each passing day as if incapable of holding up the fat cap of snow on top of it that now resembled a heavy, oversized turban. Having dispatched all its menfolk to the front, the aul was not even able to mow enough hay for itself. The previous year, the harvest had been poor, having been brought in late, just before the snow had arrived. The wheat had been gathered into a single, small pile, but the aul had failed to mill it in time, which was why the old thresher at the collective farm was rattling away even now. It would often break down and come to a stop and, after a silence of two or three days, it would stutter back into life again, rhythmically and quietly. The grain came out light, but they still gathered up every last bit into a sack and sent it off to the front. It was no wonder that many in the aul had long been living off nothing but watery gruel.

Kazhimurat had known neither sleep nor rest. From early morning he would drag sacks onto the threshing floor while at night he would watch over the cattle. The rest of the day would be spent clearing the path between the houses and taking water and firewood to the villagers. The grey ox had been taken by the wolves and now Kazhimurat had to deliver the firewood and water on his own back. Just like that, he had become the aul's *de facto* foreman, which meant that he had to perform any job that might arise at the collective farm. It was not in Kazhimurat's nature to allow the women or the old to do heavy man's work, so he took on everything he was asked to and a lot else besides. However, Kazhimurat's new position gave him no sense of pride or self-importance. He knew that if he had not been there to do it, then someone else would have done it in his place. The fact of the matter was that there was simply no one else. And so, life flowed on in the aul, hidden in the hollow of the taiga, blanketed to the rafters in deep drifts of snow.

Kazhimurat was completely exhausted, he had just been trying to lift an emaciated cow to its feet in the barn to lead it to the watering hole.

All the farm's livestock — a dozen cows and several horses — were kept in a single barn. The women would come to the morning milking in the hope of collecting at least half a bucket but they soon realised that there was nothing to be squeezed from the empty udders and so, they had returned to their homes. The farm was empty and there was no one to help Kazhimurat. Finally, realising that he could not manage to lift the cow on his own, he gave up on the idea, took up his shovel and started plugging the holes in the barn wall with cow manure to stop the wind howling through them and letting in the snow.

Kazhimurat heard footsteps outside and thought for a moment that maybe the cattle had returned early from the watering hole. He headed towards the exit and decided to scatter the remains of the hay around the pen, but the footsteps turned out to be Zlikha's. She had come over to the farm to see how he was getting on. As usual, she was dressed like a man, in a short coat, trousers and a worn-out man's hat with ear flaps. Zlikha, who had barely reached thirty, likewise moved and had the mannerisms of a man. In any event, female coyness was not in her nature and she had none of the inherent timidity that is a common feature of Kazakh women. Zlikha was not ashamed of and made no attempt to conceal her large, heavy cast frame and her gestures were expansive and judgements, decisive.

Zlikha's bright face was flushed from the frost, the collar of her coat was unbuttoned, and it seemed to Kazhimurat that he could almost smell her powerful, clean body. She approached with long, energetic steps, then stopped, taking in the shabby barn, the remains of the haystack, the emaciated cows and horses, returning slowly from the watering hole next to the mill pond, and Kazhimurat, towering in the middle of the pen, exhausted and dressed in rags. A mixture of concern and dismay flashed in her eyes.

'So, Kazhimurat, what are we going to do with these poor puny beasts? We've managed to keep them from the wolves but what's the point? They're going to die of starvation and all our work will have been for nothing. So, you've nothing to say again, eh? All we'll have to show for all this will be the crust of salty sweat on our backs.' Zlikha sighed. 'If only you'd popped over to the office and consulted on the matter...'

What's your office to me? Kazhimurat thought. *Words are not hay, you can't feed them to the animals.*

Using a pitchfork, he scattered the chaff gathered on the threshing floor and a little straw from the stack. He happened to glance over at the shed and immediately rushed over to the enclosure, where two oxen were contentedly chewing his old homespun coat that he had left hanging on the fence. He just about succeeded in retrieving his coat with his pitchfork but two big holes had been chewed out of it and it was now a pitiful sight. It now hung in tatters, as if it had been torn apart by a pack of wild dogs. The oxen remained standing a few paces away from him, their horned heads lowered, eyeing the coat hungrily in the hope of getting another chew. Zlikha turned away, simultaneously choking back her laughter and tears.

The emaciated horses returned from the watering hole, their joints creaking and with great lumps of frozen mud on their hooves. Before the war, hoarfrost wouldn't have stuck to these beasts' silky flanks, but now, bereft of their caring owners, they had become shadows of their former proud and mighty selves. It was too much for the womenfolk, so weighed down by overwork and grief to keep watch over these steppe herd horses.

'Kazhimurat, I'd like you to make a list of the households that still have some hay left,' Zlikha requested. 'We have no alternative — we're going to have to give half of the livestock to the villagers. They're not likely to let them starve to death. At worst, they'll feed them chopped birch bark. What do you think of my decision?'

Kazhimurat was in no hurry to answer. He stood there at length, his chewed and tattered coat draped over his shoulders. He wasn't so much mulling over Zlikha's proposal as worrying about their frankly hopeless situation. Zlikha had practically lost all patience and was about to leave when Kazhimurat finally handed her his notebook, in which he had written down his opinion: *I am afraid that you will end up drowning in these unfortunate women's inconsolable tears.* Zlikha read the note and was surprised at how accurately Kazhimurat had expressed what would inevitably come to pass. After all, until only recently, he could express himself much better in Russian and had been barely able to string a sentence together in Kazakh.

'Then let's go to the threshing floor,' She suggested to Kazhimurat. 'We'll talk with the women and hear what they have to say on the matter.'

The little *Universal* motor, which the Kazakhs called the *Ondirsal*, had finally got the threshing machine into motion. It shook violently, creating the impression that it might fall to pieces at any moment. A dense cloud of dust hung over the mouth of the drum, into which, choking and coughing, the women would throw the sheaves of wheat.

'Look sharp, girls, here comes thunder-thighs!' For a moment, Rapiya let go of the winnower handle and brushed the dust from the neckerchief that had been tied round her mouth.

'Look, our Kazhimurat is stepping along like the trace horse to the leader!' said the young, attractive and sharp-tongued Shamshinur, who was sewing up the tops of the sacks, now lined up in a row. She looked at Kazhimurat much as a hawk eyes its prey and then burst out laughing. 'Watch me, I'll soon have him bent over double with his nose to the ground. Hey, Kazhimurat, take these sacks into the barn for me, would you?'

'You're positively radiant today, Shamshinur!' Zlikha remarked with a smile. 'Did you get a letter from your husband?'

'Yeah, right!' Shamshinur replied with a dismissive wave of the hand. 'They say that a man who hasn't seen a woman for a whole year will have his head turned by a granny gathering dried cow dung for the fire. And we girls are no better, getting flustered at the sight of the first crook-backed or lame man we see.'

Kazhimurat heard enough to realise that the last comment was addressed at him and prudently resolved not to hang about more than necessary. He needed to be careful not to fall into a trap that would only land him in disgrace and make him a laughing stock. Not only that but when he and Zlikha had entered the room, the threshing machine had been turned off and he was only too aware of the two dozen curious female eyes filled with hidden yearning that had been fixed on him. However, it was Shamshinur who helped him out of this awkward situation, by loading a sack of wheat onto his back. Crouched like a spring under its heavy weight, he escaped at a swift trot in the direction of the barn.

'Well, you got lucky getting your claws into a bachelor, rather than some widower who's completely stuck in his ways!' Shamshinur merrily remarked to Zlikha.

'Why don't you keep your forked tongue quiet!' Zlikha said, flaring up and bringing her down a peg.

'What, you've decided to live without a man until your last tooth falls out?'

'Listen, did I ask you to find me a husband?' Zlikha was clearly out of sorts. 'Or perhaps you're afraid I'll deprive you of your bit on the side?'

'Well, there's no pleasing you, is there?'

'If you really are so kind and caring, why not take one of the farm cows for a time.' Zlikha replied, striking while the iron was hot to solve the problem that had been bothering her for some time. 'Then you'd be doing something to please me.'

'What are you up to now?' Shamshinur asked warily.

'If you bring it back to the collective farm in the spring, I'll wipe off all your debts to the farm.'

'And what if it drops dead on me? Will you then order me to bring my own healthy cow in its place, is that the idea?'

'Just make sure it doesn't die then! You can do that! Just look at you — so much power and drive that you could melt iron.'

'How do you know what power and drive I have? Perhaps you've been peeping into my bedroom at night, is that it?!'

'That's enough, Shamshinur!' Rapiya cut her off. 'You started off with a joke and now you're getting out of hand! Listen, Zlikha, were you joking about the cows, just now? Or have you really decided to distribute the farm's cattle around the houses?'

'I'm not making the offer because everything is going well,' Zlikha replied with a sigh. 'Look, I'll leave it for you all to decide.'

The sacks of grain had first to be placed on the scales and then taken to the barn and it was no easy task rushing up and down the narrow, rickety plank of wood. By the time he had dragged the last sack to the barn, Kazhimurat's legs had turned to jelly and when he come down the steps, he collapsed onto a pile of frozen grain. His head was buzzing and sparks flashed before his eyes. He felt nauseous with hunger. He could vaguely make out the silhouettes of the women standing in front of him. They had not uttered a word in response to Zlikha and it seemed that the chairwoman's proposal had not been to their liking. But they couldn't be blamed for that. And, if truth be told, there had never been an occasion when these women had ever spared themselves and refused to take on any job asked of them. They had been hard at it for days on end, bent double in the field, on the threshing floor or at the farm. At night they would busy themselves around the house with the children, keeping watch over their empty houses, making sure the fire in the hearth never went out.

'Sleep on it and we'll talk about it again in the morning,' Zlikha said, ending the conversation as gently as she could. 'And Rapiya, take back your cow. Let the children have their milk.'

Rapiya, her waist tightly bound as always in her grey belt, cast a sidelong glance at the chairwoman as if trying to work out how sincere she was being.

Deciding not to try her luck any further, Zlikha got up and headed off to the farm office. There was no point in screaming, shouting and losing her temper just to show them who was boss. All she needed to do was persuade one of them that she was right and then human nature would take its course and the others would follow too. Kazhimurat understood what the chairwoman was up to. *When you've been taken by cunning, you know you've been had by a woman*, he chuckled to himself as he watched Zlikha departing towards the aul with her distinctive and decisive gait.

Meanwhile, dark clouds had filled the sky. The wind had died down and the frost had subsided. The peaks of the Altai, as sharp as spears, pierced the cloudy sky, rising up proudly. Far down below, white wispy puffs of fog rolled out of the endless black forest. There was an aroma of fresh snow in the air. Everything was still but the tops of the cedars and the pines groaned as if they were straining under a storm. As usual at this hour, magpies and crows had flown in from somewhere, filling the air with their restless, loud cries. The pale sun disappeared behind the hill looking like a reflection of the moon, floating in muddy water. Several stars twinkled far away in the east as if to spite the oncoming fading winter's day. Night falls the moment the sun sets in the taiga.

The freshly dug paths led the women from the farm office and the barn back to their homes. A magpie on the fence seemed to be intent on driving Kazhimurat out of the threshing room with its incessant and harsh cries. But where was he to go? He recalled his loneliness and lowered his head dejectedly. Then he thrust a handful of raw wheat into his mouth and chewed it for want of anything better to do. His mouth was filled with a gooey soapy mash. He felt sick to the pit of his stomach... *Oh, for some strong tea right now!* He had already forgotten when he'd last drunk any. How marvellous it would have been to drink his fill of hot, strong tea until the beads of sweat appeared on his brow! For days now, Kazhimurat had got by on a couple of spoons of millet meal or a piece of flatbread that Almurat would secretly bring him without his mother finding out. Kazhimurat couldn't help casting an envious glance at the chimney stacks smoking invitingly on the roofs of the village houses.

'What are you doing sitting here?'

Kazhimurat started up in surprise. Old Zhusup, who kept watch over the collective farm threshing room walked over. 'No need to get up! There's no fire to put out. And you don't look the type who feels the cold either, Kazhimurat!' Throwing down an enormous sheepskin coat, Zhusup settled down on the grain and then, lifting the hanging flap of his fox fur hat, stared up at the sky. 'Look how quiet it is! And yet a storm is coming. In the old days, they used to say: *You can expect your sister to play tricks on you in early spring and your wife, in late autumn.* Hee-hee-hee! That old aunt and uncle of yours don't do anything for the collective, so there's not enough firewood. But we don't want to end up having to stoke the fire with our footwraps, now do we? Has Kiyakmurt the policeman shown up again? What a swine he is! There's one like him in every generation... But the times we live in are particularly cruel!'

The old man looked up at the sky again.

'A perfect night for the thief. I remember when your old man used to take me on his raids. Oh, how the time flies! There aren't many like him these days, although there are plenty of *heroes* around who'd happily skulk in the shadows and grab any passer-by like a stray dog if given half the chance. No respect for anything! Ugh! You know what? Let's go to the office, we'll be better off in there. It's still early evening and no one is likely to dare poke their nose in here. Have you heard the news? They say those bastard fascists have been thrown back from Moscow!'

Shaking down the flaps of his coat, the old man got to his feet. When he was on duty, Zhusup would go to the office from time to time to stoke up the stove and warm himself with some hot tea. Kazhimurat, who had long dreamed of such a treat, didn't wait to be asked a second time. The evening would pass much more pleasantly over a hot glass of tea.

'Oh, how the time flies!' The old man sighed. 'Of course, we'll beat the fascists, but when will we be free of that local policeman with his fancy moustache? That devil just won't leave us in peace!'

Kazhimurat laughed to himself at the unexpected comparison.

'So you think it's funny, do you?' The old man asked, looking right at him. 'Well, go ahead, laugh all you like... What else is there left for you to do, you poor soul?'

Without taking his coat from his shoulders, Zhusup opened the door of the stove, stoked the fading embers with a twig and then, putting it out in a bucket of water, threw it out of the door. He placed the blackened kettle onto the stove. The pine logs crackled to life and the room was filled with a pleasant warmth. The old man took a broom and swept the scraps of paper and kindling towards the stove.

'No matter where you go, you can always tell when a woman's been around recently!' He remarked caustically, noting the untidy state of the room after the working day. 'Oh, those women!'

He was over seventy and it was perhaps a little strange that he'd chosen to talk about women. However, perhaps by doing so, the old man was merely expressing his hope that his four sons, who had departed for the front, would return unharmed, and that he might still be able to sit in the seat of honour and hold forth with them as befitted a man of his age. Or perhaps he had already resigned himself to his solitude and was now preparing to meet his fate just as stoically as he had once met the joys in his life. Who knew what was on his mind?

Zhusup threw off his coat and it was then evident that he had lost weight and become frailer. His bald shaved head protruded from his thin, wiry neck like a vulture's. His skin was red and dry, with the occasional white hair sticking out and it looked as if a dry colt hide had been stretched over his skull. From behind the stove, the old man took a small porcelain kettle with a chipped spout, two small drinking bowls, all cracked and bound with wire mesh, two or three slices of dried flatbread and a bag of oatmeal, and placed it all on the shabby table. Kazhimurat felt sorry for the old man — his diligent efforts to keep himself fed appeared so trivial. However, his eyes remained completely focussed on the blackened kettle that Zhusup had placed on the stove top. Kazhimurat chuckled. There was evidently a lot of truth in the saying that a man with no conscience never lacks for food...

'Kazhimurat, how old are you?'

Kazhimurat really wasn't interested in how old he was right then. With all the tribulations that had befallen him during his life, a man might easily forget his age and, in all likelihood, even more important things too.

The kettle came to the boil and water hissed from the spout onto the coals. Muttering to himself, the old man placed the kettle on the table.

'I don't remember whether it was March or April... And which Murat was it? I think it was when Curly Murat's wife almost got mauled by a wolf! That was the year you were born.' Zhusup grinned, happy that he had remembered. 'You see, I haven't forgotten! That means you must already be twenty-five. Time to get yourself married, Kazhimurat.'

He pulled a handkerchief from the chest pocket of his jacket, which contained tea in a knotted corner. He untied it and threw a pinch into the teapot with the chipped spout. Then he poured on the boiling water and placed his fox-fur hat on top to keep it warm.

The telephone on the wall began to ring. The old man picked up the receiver and, first of all, he blew into it several times.

'Eh? What... Which Murat is it you want? Eh...?! The collective farm, you say? Yes, yes, Murat. The collective farm... That's what I said – Murat. The collective farm! Eh...?! The women have already left. They've gone home, I tell you. From the district? Well, if you're from the district, assalamualaikum! Eh? You need the person in charge? Curly? If you are talking about our boss, you won't find a hair on his head. He has a moustache though. What? A moustache, I tell you! So what if you need the boss urgently?! How do I know which woman he's with tonight? He's to go and see Curly urgently, you say? Okay, I'll pass it on if I find him.'

The old man replaced the receiver back on the hook and turned the handle to end the call. He appeared to know what he was doing using the telephone.

'That was the main district management,' he explained to Kazhimurat with a satisfied air. 'Oh, damn it! I forgot to ask about my boys! The enlistment office is right next door.'

It was eight o'clock and a low, melancholy ringing sound floated across the room as if the wall clock was reluctant to measure the time. The old watchman, his forehead sweating, sipped his hot tea with pleasure. And having got his hands on a cup — Kazhimurat no less so.

The brew had already cooled and the steam had stopped twisting and curling from the chipped spout. The front door slammed suddenly and someone could be heard stamping about, shaking the snow from their boots. In a fluster, Zhusup quickly grabbed his coat.

It was Almurat.

'Ah, so it's you?' The old man's voice betrayed his annoyance. 'I thought that devil with his fancy moustaches was doing his rounds. What are you doing out at midnight? Just like your father, you poor thing!'

Almurat looked out of sorts. He had put all his clothes on as if he was planning to set off on a pilgrimage to the holy sites. And he was holding his bag full of schoolbooks. Kazhimurat felt uneasy when he saw that the boy was completely covered in sparkling flakes of snow. He suddenly remembered the hungry farm cattle that had been driven into the cold barn and it seemed to him that his own body was shrivelling from the unbearable cold.

'Come on in and have some tea!' the old man invited Almurat good-naturedly.

There was almost nothing left in the pot but Zhusup tried to be as welcoming as he could.

The boy looked impatiently at Kazhimurat. It was evident that he had something serious to say, but Kazhimurat paid him no heed. He stared intently out of the window, where the thick snow was now falling. A whitish sky could just about be made out beyond the blanket of snow. Kazhimurat recalled the old man's words: *A perfect night for the thief* and he sensed a growing sweet yet anxious feeling coming over him. *And then, you'll see, a storm will strike,* He said to himself. *In weather like this, there'll be no tracks out there! Everything will be blown over. No, we have to try and bring the hay in today. I'll take Almurat and get going...*

Zhusup had already managed to dress and was dragging an ancient *Berdan* rifle from behind the stove. It only vaguely resembled a firearm now.

'Kazhimurat, when you get a spare moment, could you fill a couple of cartridges with salt for me? And what does an old man like me need them for, I hear you ask? If I spot him, I'll pepper his arse with salt for him. That Kiyakmurt has been asking for a good salting for some time now. Hee-hee-hee!' He turned off the lamp. The women would kick up a fuss the next day, saying he'd used up all the kerosene.

There was a deathly silence outside. Even the dogs had fallen silent and they never usually ever let up. The rustling of the falling snow resembled the muffled tinkling of the *sholpy*[10] metal bells and trinkets that girls weave into their hair braids. The air was still and clear. The soft, cold snow tickled Kazhimurat's open neck pleasantly. He felt as if the ground under his feet had been scattered with an invisible, soft down. It was as if Kazhimurat had once more encountered the world of his childhood, which he had managed to quite forget being so far from home.

The horse is a sensitive creature and the traveller's support and rock. Kazhimurat remembered this saying as he harnessed Zlikha's chestnut horse. Of all the animals in the aul, none could beat him for cutting a path through the deep snow. He paired the horse with Kiyakmurt's bay gelding that had been well-fed on oats and sagged a little in the belly. Kazhimurat harnessed a pair of oxen to each of the other four sleds and linked them in a chain behind the horses' harnesses. At first, the well-fed bay was reluctant to advance, glancing back at every house it passed. It was clearly accustomed to its owner stopping at the very first house it came to. However, after Kazhimurat gave it a tap with his weighty pine club, it trotted on at a decent pace, taking the chestnut horse with it.

The night was so warm that butter wouldn't have frozen if left outside. A waning moon wafted behind grey downy clouds. The scraping of the sled rails and the creaking of the horseshoes that crunched on the clean, untouched snow, echoed in the dense forest that stretched along the lake, frozen in its nocturnal slumber. Almurat sat in the last sled, driving the oxen, but as soon

---

[10] *Sholpy* – A gold or silver ornament worn in a young woman's hair.

as the string of sledges entered the forest, he went to sit with Kazhimurat — clearly, the trees that loomed over the road from both sides had spooked him. Although anyone, regardless of their age, might have been spooked by the cedars and firs that bowed over the road under the weight of their heavy caps of snow, the long and the shaggy branches, frozen in their icy armour, which whipped the face at every turn, as well as the dark, centuries-old trunks, the unsightly sunken logs and the unexpected gaps in the thick forest that opened up like the black mouths of caves.

Even sitting next to his cousin, Almurat looked around in fear. Kazhimurat made him a cosy nest in the straw, got down from the sled and walked alongside. Gradually it began to get colder and, to warm himself, Kazhimurat occasionally ran along the line of sleds, prodding the dawdling oxen into action. Now, the creaking of his rough canvas boots on the snow added to the crunch of the hooves and the scraping of the rails.

The chestnut horse suddenly snorted and, shuddering, veered away from a small heap on the ground. The snow had not yet managed to cover the bright-red bloodstains on the ground, and the torn hide, mangled head and hooves of a deer which lay on the broken branches. The unfortunate creature must have sought refuge from its hunters on the road that led to human habitation. Wolf tracks trailed off into the forest through the snow that stood as deep as a man. Kazhimurat felt a chill run down his spine, but then remembered that wolves were unlikely to attack the sleds. It would have been another thing if he had been riding in a single cart, for the wolves wouldn't have given him a second glance, even if he'd been armed with a rifle. *When famine hits, it invites all its relatives along with it,* they say and, as if to prove the truth of this proverb, there were far more wolves on the prowl than usual that year. Not only did they lay waste to the wild animals in the forest, but they would now fearlessly enter the livestock pens, even attacking the dogs that had been pressed right back to the thresholds of their masters' houses. And all this was happening in broad daylight. Different people in the aul had different opinions. The old men were convinced that the wolves from the local forest would never attack human homes, even in large packs and that that winter must have seen the arrival of wolves from elsewhere, whose habits differed from ours. Perhaps they were right. After all, what was stopping the wolves from wandering where they liked if the war had scattered the people every which way?

Kazhimurat's back was now wet from all the running he'd been doing. He jumped back up onto the first sled once he felt his toes begin to warm up. Kazhimurat had worried he might miss the turning to the lake but, after a closer look, he realised he had no cause for concern. Back at the start of the winter, he had come to the forest for hay and firewood and had spotted a number of stacks in a secluded spot and was counting on loading these onto the sleds today, to feed the cattle back in the aul. If he happened to encounter the hay's owner, it would most likely be one of his relatives, albeit probably a distant one, and he would probably get away with an explanation and an apology. But if it was taken any further, then he would probably find himself back in prison again. Well, he had already confronted his fears there and he laughed at his thoughts. Almurat was lying in the sled and chewing on a stalk of hay. He heard Kazhimurat's laugh and looked around at him, before asking him something he originally had had no intention of asking.

'Aga[11]... Are we a long way from Koktas?'

Kazhimurat didn't answer and, after a while, the boy hesitantly asked,

'Aga, could you take me to the orphanage?'

Kazhimurat had realised the boy was very upset about something the moment he had entered the farm office, but he had not shown it, for any offence at his mother, however strong, would pass in a day or two (and Kazhimurat didn't understand the reason for his younger cousin's distress). He realised it would only make things worse if Almurat were to run away from his parents because the grievance he was now feeling would only later turn into a general bitterness against his wider family, and he would become an outsider altogether. This was precisely what Kazhimurat, who had been through plenty of hardships himself and forced to roam foreign parts as a result, did not want. However, it seemed like Almurat had worked out for himself that asking to be taken to an orphanage was nothing but a pipe dream.

'It's a shame I'm still too young, otherwise, I'd have signed up and gone off to fight,' he sighed, gazing up at the cloudy sky.

They won't take me into the army because I am mute, Kazhimurat chuckled bitterly to himself. *But what use would you be on the front, Almurat? Although, unlike me,*

---

[11] A respectful form of address to an older relative, literally meaning 'uncle'.

you'd at least have the advantage of having been led by your dreams. I don't have an ounce of anything like that left in me...

Indeed, when a man has abandoned his dreams and is no longer driven by his desires or passions, his life loses its beauty and becomes devoid of meaning. And yet... When he thought about it, even though Kazhimurat saw himself as little more than an empty worn-out old sheepskin coat that has been stuffed with straw and left out in the field to scare the crows, he did at least harbour the hope that, like a scarecrow, he might still serve some purpose to his fellow man. And why not?

'Aga, I'm never going back home. Let them beat me, let them even kill me, but I'm never going back.' There were tears in Almurat's eyes. 'I'd rather carry firewood and hay with you, clear up after the cattle and keep watch over the farmyard. Only promise you won't drive me away. We won't go hungry. Yesterday, I hid a ram's bladder of oil and a haunch of dried lamb in the hut, and I also dragged three bags of bricks there, so we could easily build ourselves a stove.'

This was the first time Kazhimurat had ever heard himself addressed as *aga*. He was unaccustomed to it, but it was nice nonetheless. He felt warm inside at the boy's words, still untainted, never having tasted either total joy or hopeless grief. Kazhimurat had never thought anyone would call him *aga*. His heart skipped a beat.

He remembered how Tazhimurat had led him through this very same forest on a sled in winter and a heavy snowfall as severe as this one. The people had really suffered that winter. Kazhimurat could still see the starving aul, the people going off in search of work and food, the watery stew with the husks floating on top, the faces swollen from malnutrition and the puffed lips.

Tazhimurat would fell wood at remote sawmills and come home only occasionally when he had saved up enough food to make the journey worth it. There was enough flour in the house, which he had saved secretly away from the prying eyes of others and the family didn't have that many hungry mouths to feed. However, Tazhimurat was not the sort of man who could simply sit through such troubled times just getting by with what he had without making sure that he had that little bit of extra that others didn't. And, like Batikha he saw Kazhimurat as one extra mouth too many to feed, so he ended up deciding to leave him with the orphanage. 'You'll be well fed and warmly clothed there,' He had said to his nephew. 'The Soviet authorities have decent doctors and they'll teach you how to speak again.' He had said a great deal about the orphanage back then, but Kazhimurat had a bad feeling about the place the first time his uncle mentioned it. The boy had a foreboding he would be lost forever the moment he left the warm familiar embrace of the aul.

He remembered that it had been on this very road that he had jumped from the sled and run back towards the aul, barefoot and with nothing on his head. Thick snow was falling from the grey sky. Tazhimurat had unhitched the horses, caught up with him on horseback and, like a pup, had driven him back to the sled, thrashing him with his whip. Then he had brought him to the district centre or, to be more precise, he had finally rid himself of him. However, things had worked out for the best. Kazhimurat had lived in the district centre, then in the town and he had no complaint against the orphanage. He had tasted freedom: he had learned how to take a train, ride about on it to his heart's content and you could say he had seen the world. The orphanage fed him, dressed him and taught him. He completed seven years at a special school for the deaf and mute. The one thing where he had not been so lucky was regaining his speech. The orphanage had lacked the specialist doctors who might have helped Kazhimurat overcome his unfortunate condition. Perhaps he had wanted too much from his new life. A bit like the dream of the hungry deer that wanted to be looked after and fed and yet live in the wild with its herd.

'Uncle Kazhimurat, is it true that you killed a man?'

The question caught Kazhimurat unawares. The child's question shook him as if he'd just had mercury poured down his throat. They had finally reached the clearing indicating that the forest had ended, and Kazhimurat pulled on the reins. The ricks of hay he'd been planning to take back to the collective farm should have been around here somewhere.

The pristine white snow blinded his eyes. The sky was clear. The forest stood dead still in its frozen white finery. The chestnut horse pawed the ground with its hooves next to a chee bush, searching for grass. The icy crust crunched under the fresh covering of snow. Kazhimurat, who had gone to search for the hay, was nowhere to be seen and Almurat began to get worried. He called out to him but his voice sounded strangely subdued. His head spun at the sight of the snowflakes flying chaotically above him in the air. The enormous trees, frozen under their thick snowy caps, the unsightly thick roots and semi-submerged logs looked like monsters about to pounce on their prey.

Several times in the aul he had heard that the forest was crawling with thieves and murderers. They said that they had knocked one rider from his horse, stripped him of everything and left him to walk back home naked. The sound of the chestnut horse munching the hay in the sled and the lowing of the oxen as they became more restless only stoked the boy's imagination further. He was already regretting leaving home and hitching up with Kazhimurat. He might now have been happily sleeping in his warm bed above the stove. He only had to conjure up the image of his warm house to imagine his parents standing right before him. They must have scoured the entire aul looking for him by now... But could he be so sure they'd started looking for him? Only two days ago, they had been so angry with each other about the disappearance of a ram's bladder containing some leftover oil and a dried-up haunch of lamb that you'd have thought they'd lost a camel and her calf. All night they had blamed one another for the loss and finally ended up running themselves ragged with their quarrelling. They had then shut the curtains tightly so that no one might see his mother hiding all the provisions and things they had acquired from others in the house's enormous chests, while his father had opened up the secret hiding place under the stable floor and poured all the house's remaining grain into it. By the next morning, they were both dead on their feet. Almurat's father had glanced over to where he was sleeping on the stove. 'This is all that wretched boy's fault,' he muttered to his wife. 'He just can't keep his mouth shut.'

After that, the aul's mullah had turned up at the house and, fiddling with his prayer beads, proceeded to talk rot all evening. 'They say that the Soviet authorities are living out their last days,' he had muttered under his breath. 'They might defeat the Germans, but those Turks are standing at the ready with their victorious green banner. There'll be dark days ahead and soon they'll start taking everything we have right down to the last grain. So, make sure you don't do anything foolish, Tazhimurat!' Almurat's father had listened to the holy man's drivel so attentively it was as if he was spraying gold and not spittle everywhere. Then, he asked the mullah to read his fortune so that he might learn what lay in store for the family. The guest modestly began to make excuses, obviously trying to get more money out of his father. Eventually, he yielded to Tazhimurat's request. Mumbling something incomprehensible, he scattered the stones, organised them into piles and then pronounced that Tazhimurat had already suffered losses and that, if he didn't want things to get worse, he should make an offering to himself as Allah's humble servant. Almurat's parents' eyes nearly popped out of their heads, because, only just before the mullah's arrival, they had discovered that the last of the oil and the dried haunch of lamb had gone missing.

Almurat's home had been an unhappy place for him for some time now. He would leave on any pretext and only return from school long after his lessons were over. *It's such a good thing that I left with Kazhimurat*, the boy thought. *It would be better to spend the night in the forest than have to return home.*

In the meantime, Kazhimurat had returned. He took the chestnut horse by the harness and, without hesitating, led it deep into the forest. The boy jumped straight down from the sled and ran in front of his cousin and took hold of the harness. He didn't want Kazhimurat to guess how afraid he was. It was not easy walking through the deep, loose snow in his heavy, uncomfortable clothes. However, they didn't have to walk far and soon they had stopped by some heaps of hay, that had been placed so tightly together that they had formed a single, reasonably sized stack.

The place was secluded, right under the branches of some densely packed pines. The reason why Kazhimurat hadn't returned sooner was because he had already climbed up onto the stack and cleared the snow on top. Almurat recognised the stack. That summer, when his father had avoided his call-up into the Labour Army, he had been hired to make hay for some district manager. For a whole month, Almurat had helped his father cut and stack the hay. Naturally, his father had been paid in full for his work, but the hay was never taken away and remained in this secluded spot covered with snow.

'But, Aga, this hay doesn't belong to the collective farm!' He exclaimed.

Well, so what if it doesn't? It must belong to some official or other and it doesn't look like his cattle is starving, seeing as he's left this hay out in the forest under the snow, Kazhimurat replied to himself. In fact, there would have been no one to bring it in until the snow melted, which meant it would remain here all winter, unused. Kazhimurat unharnessed the animals. He gathered some dry brushwood, made a fire with the kindling and lit it on the windward side of the haystack. He then fetched a heap of dry pine twigs and threw them down near the fire. He pulled all the sleds nearer to the haystack, to fence in the feeding animals, threw his old half-coat over Almurat's shoulders and took up his pitchfork.

White snowflakes fell into the fire and instantly disappeared in the flames. It felt as if the heavens were intent on smothering the only fire in the entire forest kingdom come what may. It was warm by the haystack and the grass, which had been cut at harvest time, gave off a rich aroma. How delightful it was to find himself in the wintry forest and see the sparks flying from the burning dry twigs, at first blazing red and then disappearing in the frosty blue. Almurat's coat and mittens, stretched out like damp sheep gut, smoked with moist steam.

Suddenly the report of a gunshot rang out. By the sound of it, someone had just wasted a cartridge they'd been saving up all winter, firing it into the unknown at the sign of a wolf. The sound raised Almurat's spirits, dispelling the overwhelming feeling of loneliness that the winter forest had cast on him. Now, he just wanted to be of some use to Kazhimurat but there was nothing for him to do. Kazhimurat had even knocked the thick layer of soot off the bottom of the cooking pot with a single deft blow of the heavy staff that had probably been brought for a more serious job such as seeing off the wolves rather than stoking the fire.

The oxen had gone halfway into the haystack and all that could be seen of them were their protruding behinds. The poor beasts were probably getting their first proper feed of the winter. They were barely afforded any care anymore, although they were utilised to their full potential; they were ridden, harnessed to mowers, used to carry hay and firewood and even to thresh the grain when the farm's only threshing machine had stopped working. Blood blisters had appeared on their necks, the skin was peeling from their backs and the edges of their hooves had cracked and broken off, but these patient creatures had still kept the entire aul fed.

The oxen were never scolded for being slow and it was never considered a disgrace to be seen riding one. Each of them had their own pet name, Swift Whitehoof, Restless Pied Shaitan, Punchy Chestnut, Black-faced Whiner and everyone's favourite — Grey Singer. The names not only reflected the animal's colour and temperament but also, more accurately, the great suffering that the aul was going through. For the people working on the collective farm from morning to evening, these amusing names offered a brief respite, bringing a redemptive smile to their faces.

Unlike his peers, Almurat had never made hay or walked with the plough. There was no way his father, who would ever have let even his lousiest goat out to pasture with the common herd, was ever going to allow his son to even bind a single sheaf of wheat for the collective farm. Almurat would be left behind in the aul while the other boys would join the adults out in the fields to get the grain or hay in. The stronger ones would bag the horses for themselves, leaving the weaker ones to climb onto the oxen and beaver away alongside the adults. Only Almurat was always left out of this duty of communal labour. He had had to collect the hens' eggs, and his mother and father had a whole hen house full of them, and he had to guard the ducklings and God help him if the fox even took one of them. He also had to keep his eyes on the lambs and kids to make sure that they didn't get mixed up with the communal herd when the sheep and goats were milked and to stop anyone else's lambs from feeding from their ewes' udders.

Almurat felt lonely left all by himself in the aul. He yearned to be with his friends, who would spend the spring sowing the fields, the summer mowing and the autumn harvesting. No matter how hard the work was it was always like a holiday for them, but he lived a lonely life around the house, which could barely even be seen by anyone else behind its numerous stables, chicken coops, forges, bathhouses and barns. He was convinced that the other aul boys were living much happier lives. After the tiring and unbearably long school year, cooped up within four walls and after their daily chores around the house, they would leave for the fields, the meadows and farmyards with the other collective farm workers' children and they were pretty much their own masters. They might have only been given the thin communal stew that stank of rennet to eat at the end of the day, but at least it had been hard-earned.

There were times when Almurat regretted the fact that his father had not been drafted into the army like the other men. He was a strange man — he was so lean that it seemed if you were to cut a strip of flesh from his body, he wouldn't shed a drop of blood. Tazhimurat was like a man who had taken mortal offence at himself, for he was always cursing himself for things no one knew anything about or would ever learn. His black face wore a cold expression and he was both unsociable and sullen, like the morose Bactrian camel at the collective farm that had failed to sow its oats over the winter and was now lying in the garbage heap in the summer.

Almurat had lived a withdrawn life, much like that of his own father. He had not experienced the warmth and parental affection that others had and he kept his distance from the other members of the aul, reading regret and silent reproach in their eyes. Only with the arrival of Kazhimurat had a glimmer of joy appeared in his life. It was as if an unknown and fascinating world had come to visit him and he was drawn to Kazhimurat who he was convinced must have seen the entire world. In a short time, he had become very attached and an innate sense of their blood ties grew that had hitherto lain dormant along with a boyish desire to please, which arose from his admiration for a man who was so strikingly different from everyone he had ever known before. Something seemed to light up in the boy's frozen soul whose parents had denied him the joys of childhood. He now lived for a single dream and that was to become an adult as soon as possible and to become Kazhimurat's equal. However, as they say, everything comes in its own good time. Some can reach maturity early by dint of their wisdom, but the fact of the matter remains — until you reach a certain age, you are still just a boy. There's no point biting off more than you can chew...

Almurat looked at the fire and felt bad that he was only able to sit on the sled and warm himself by the fire, but wasn't old or strong enough to take the pitchfork from Kazhimurat and help him load the hay.

The dry brushwood had run out, the fire was burning out and the coals were now hissing under the continuing heavy snowfall. The flakes scurried about like ants flocking to their prey, before disappearing in the hot ashes.

The cloud-filled sky had darkened and the moon could no longer be seen. The forest had lost its recent imposing outline and was now crumbling and dispersing into the air like the white breadcrumbs scattered over a large tablecloth. The wind blew in from the north and the snowflakes flew up and swirled about, stinging the face like hungry mosquitoes. A sad moan came from somewhere deep in the forest.

The belly might be full but the eyes are insatiable, the people say. Kazhimurat had loaded so much hay onto the sleds that the horses were barely able to set off. Flattening the now chest-high snow with his legs and feet, Kazhimurat drove the front sled onto the road and then returned. Hot and breathless, he scooped up mouthfuls of snow as he came and shoved them into his mouth to quench his thirst. Then he rubbed the palm of his hand vigorously across Almurat's cheeks, and the boy felt his face flare up as if they'd been rubbed with sandpaper.

The night was getting even colder. The snow, which had until recently been lying like soft down, had now begun to coil and curl like lambswool. Kazhimurat pulled his half-length, half-eaten coat under the arms, over his shoulders. It served little purpose, for it was too small for Kazhimurat and it sat on him just like a shaggy fleece blanket on a five-year-old horse. He went over to Almurat, lifted him up and sat him on top of the hay on the sled that ran behind the others.

What could be better than a winter road when you're setting off in good spirits on a decent sled? Even the sound of the sled runners was like a melody that you could listen to forever and which lifted the soul. You could cast your mind's eye to many things you never thought were possible. You lie there, wrapped in your warm coat, your weary soul luxuriating in a rare sense of peace, your heart tight with unknown anticipation. Then you fall into a sweet, deep sleep, the likes of which you have not known for a very long time.

Almurat had sunk waist-deep in the fragrant, soft hay and, rocking as if in a cradle, he listened to the sounds of the night. He sensed the crunching of the hay much less now and he realised that it had grown thick with frost. The hum of the forest, however, seemed to have sneaked up to the sled and hung right over his head. Zhusup had been right about the harmless snowfall becoming a heavy blizzard, the boy thought. The wind was now blowing in gusts and the thin, pitiful whistling of the hay merged with the incessant scraping of the sled's runners. The aul folk used to say that musicians would tune their reed pipes on a windy night to the whistling of a dry bulrush, which was probably why the pan-pipes always have such a mournful sound.

The sled swerved, hit a bump, tilted over and Almurat flew into a deep drift. His mouth and nose were filled with snow and he almost suffocated while struggling to clamber out. He might not have made it, had Kazhimurat not come to his rescue. Almurat felt as if he had been pulled from icy water and all the memory of the blissful warmth he had felt only a few moments previously deserted him in an instant. By the time he had settled back down in the sled, his teeth were chattering from the cold. But this time, the sound of the sled runners grated on the ear, while the oxen, as if to spite him, were barely placing one leg in front of the other. It really doesn't take much for the world to lose its wonder and appear in a dismal light to man!

Kazhimurat was calmly walking behind the five sleds that progressed at an unhurried pace. He too looked as if nothing would force him to pick up his pace even if the sky were to fall to the earth. They were now on the familiar road with the deep ditches on either side that would lead them straight to the aul. No one was rushing Kazhimurat along and no one was waiting for him at the end of his journey. He had plenty of hay, the animals had been fed and the sleds were in good working order. And anyway, he didn't have anywhere to rush to, so what was the hurry? Better to wander the endless snowy expanses of the night with your thoughts for company than to sit in some unheated shack, mulling over the joys of your unfulfilled bachelor existence.

The wind was whistling softly yet poisonously right into Almurat's ear, like an angry mosquito. The telegraph poles stretched along the road added their own dreary howling to the endless screeching of the sled runners. It seemed that the dark of the night was full of menacing predatory creatures. There was evidently a great deal of truth in the saying that fear makes the senses keener because now Almurat could see wolves lurking on all sides waiting to spring from every roadside tree. At times, the boy would look up to see his cousin walking serenely behind the sleds. Let the wolves have the oxen, the boy thought, just so long as Kazhimurat might make it onto the hay cart in time to avoid their snarling fangs. But Kazhimurat, showed no sign of fatigue even though he had done the work of five men and continued to walk along the snow-covered road oblivious to everything. The snow creaked under his canvas boots. His clothes were streaked with snow as if he had been covered head to toe in white flour and, to any onlooker, it looked as if the sleds were being followed by a ghost rather than a living breathing human being.

If Almurat had had the strength of five men, he too would have felt no fear. Ever since that day when Kazhimurat had playfully hurled Kiyakmurt like a finely moustachioed rag doll into the snow, to Almurat there seemed no man who was stronger and more fearless than his cousin. And now, on this frosty night, filled with the most terrifying dangers, the boy saw Kazhimurat as his only protector and saviour. It was just a pity that God had deprived his cousin — as usually happens with kind and considerate people — of one of the blessings in life that he never seemed to begrudge the heartless, the indifferent and the unkind. If it had been down to Almurat, he would have shown Kazhimurat this favour first and ensured that he was among the first to be happily married. In his mind's eye, he went round the homes in the aul, contemplating all the women he could recall, and he realised that there was not a single girl left to be married off. All the women were either widows or soldiers' wives. But was Zlikha any worse than any of the other women available? She was young and held a position of authority. How wonderful it would be to just once be allowed to ride the chairwoman's chestnut horse! And Kazhimurat would be riding it all the time if he were to marry Zlikha.

Almurat imagined what else would his brother be allowed to do if he took Zlikha for his wife and it seemed an awful lot. *Although that's not the life for Kazhimurat,* the boy mused calmly. *And would it work, anyway? No, it would be better to think now about how to defeat the fascists faster! Now, if only it were his bullet striking the enemy, or his sabre taking them down.*

He imagined himself fighting a huge enemy horde, not in battle, but rather a total bloodbath. The enemy fell from his mighty blows, like the green reeds under the sharp scythe. There were hundreds of rifles all pointing at him and a hail of bullets heading his way. However, he brutally put paid to the enemy and ended up the last man standing amidst the smoke, fire and destruction. For a moment, the boy thought it was not bullets whistling about him, but a fierce storm. He wandered the blizzard-swept steppe, the horizon disappearing behind a white wall of snow. It was impossible to find his bearings in that vortex of white that whirled around him. Wolves suddenly appeared in the breaks in the swirling snow, encircling him just as the countless hordes of fascists had done a minute before. He had to shoot! He discovered that he was now holding Zhusup's old Berdan rifle, loaded with blanks.

Then it seemed that what he could hear was not the whistle of bullets or the howl of the storm, but the piercing scraping sound of the sled runners. And it was not wolves that were rushing towards him in the nocturnal blizzard, but rather the hungry farm cows running after the sled once they had got the scent of the fragrant hay lying on it. He tried to shoo them off, but he realised that all he was holding were the tongs for the stove. The animals, however, had now clumped tightly together and were running after him along the road, mad with hunger, their eyes focussed on the hay and nothing else. He wanted to chase them off but could not. Another moment and the boy would be trampled...

Almurat tossed and turned, screamed in desperation and then woke up. He looked around and was surprised to see they had already reached the yard at the collective farm. They had indeed returned to their native aul. Hearing the creaking of the sleds and sensing there was hay, the farm's animals had begun to roar in the shed and a deafening commotion had kicked off in the aul.

* * *

No matter how determined Almurat was to leave his home, it was to no avail. Both the orphanage and the front remained but an unattainable dream for him. The day after returning to the aul, on Kazhimurat's advice, he had returned to his parents the ram's bladder with the leftover oil and the haunch of lamb that he had stolen for the journey. Of course, doing this did not earn Almurat a kind word from his parents. He returned to his home in silence, his heart now harder than ever. The boy did not bow his head, although he had no choice but to accept his situation. He rebuked himself for his weakness and meekness, which had prevented him from achieving his goal. However, now he felt more attached to Kazhimurat than ever, almost worshipping the ground under his feet. This was all in spite of the fact that the boy had returned home, heeding his advice.

However, the most important thing that Almurat achieved upon returning home was his freedom. He now no longer had to drag the firewood and the water into the house, he no longer had to watch over the cattle from morning to night, he no longer fed, watered or cleaned up after them and he spent all his free time after school with Kazhimurat. Perhaps the significant fact that he was an only child had weighed in his favour, or perhaps his parents had decided to leave him in peace and let him have his way, surprised at his boyish bitterness and anger instead of the filial love they had anticipated and expected. No one knew for certain. But whatever the reason, neither his father nor his mother now asked Almurat where he had been or what he had been doing. Moreover, from that moment on, they no longer allowed themselves to carp on about the aul folk or curse Kazhimurat behind his back when the boy was around. Almurat sincerely rejoiced at this small victory.

That was the moment many years ago when Almurat finally freed himself from his parental shackles and tasted freedom. He had become disappointed in his parents from an early age and he no longer had any room left in his heart for them.

4

After that memorable journey, Kazhimurat made several more night-time trips for hay. Put simply, he would steal it. Almurat would accompany him on every occasion even though the only practical thing he could do was hold the reins. The aul was split into two camps. Some would praise Kazhimurat, saying, 'Without him, the cattle would never have made it to spring. The only thing we'd have been taking out of the collective farm's barns would have been their skin and bones. Say what you like about him, but a man should act like a man, and without this one, the hearths in our homes would have long gone out.' Others, on the contrary, spoke ill of him: 'It's no wonder they say that his family is nothing but a band of brigands and he's evidently inherited their talent for thievery. They say they never judge mute people properly, but Kiyakmurt has drawn a case up against him and has sent it to the town.'

Sitting at the desk by the school window is not a privilege everyone attains and that's because the window seat is only ever reserved for the strongest pupil in the class. You only have to occupy this seat and even your desk partner becomes your obedient servant. He will do your lessons and homework for you and even carry your bag to school. This is because the pupil who sits by the window gets to see everything that goes on in the aul and he is the person who connects the rest of the students with the outside world.

Beyond the window, the houses appear black against the snow-covered forest that looms beyond them and towering over them all are the snow-white peaks of the

Altai. That's quite a lot to take in when your head is spinning in anticipation of the bell. You might imagine that you're wandering through the thick forest — preferably one populated with cedars or firs, as they are prettier — or climbing the tall mountain peaks, before slowly ambling down and strolling through the *tugai* wetland forest. This way, you could easily climb the same peak several times during the course of a single lesson.

It was warm outside and it was impossible to look at the snowdrifts, built up on the downwind side of the low wall, as the snow appeared to have been strewn with finely broken glass. Black and white magpies hopped about over the shiny shards, finding things to eat between them. The thud of a crowbar could be heard. Since the previous day, Kazhimurat had been breaking the ice on the frozen pond that had covered the mill wheel with thick sheets of ice. People would travel several kilometres to Trofim the miller, to get a sack of grain milled, which was a strange arrangement these people had, Almurat thought. They had their own mill right under their noses, but the aul was simply too lazy to spend a couple of days repairing it to get it to work again. Instead, they continued to drag their grain across seven hills for the privilege of kowtowing to Trofim. All this time, Kazhimurat had been chopping away at the ice with an axe, smashing it with a crowbar and clearing the ice cover from the pond, but it never occurred to a single person from the aul to give him a hand. After all, he wasn't doing this for his own benefit but for theirs.

'Almurat! Stop gazing out of the window and get back to your grammar!'

He shuddered as if someone had poked him in the side, and he grabbed his textbook, before mumbling the cases to himself, *atau, ilik, barys, tabys, zhatye, shygys, komektes.*

'Miss, why does Kazakh have seven cases but Russian, only six?'

'The Kazakhs clearly need an extra one for all the gossiping they do.'

The class buzzed like a hive, some reading a story, others learning their grammar. A lot of the class would rather have been outside and they only took up their textbooks when directly scolded by their angry teacher. The teacher was knitting that day, and so fast that her fingers were little more than a blur. Such was a teacher's life in those days – each day she would sit the pupils down with a task and pick up her needles. Over the winter, the teacher had managed to knit herself a complete outfit: a down shawl, a knitted dress, a sleeveless jacket, and now she would take a finished mitten home with her every day. But it was unclear for whom she was knitting all these woollen mittens. To some of her pupils, it seemed that she was just doing it to show off her skilful and diligent yet long and attractive fingers. These attractive fingers never knew any rest. Anyone who studied poorly would receive a slap that made the head buzz while those who gave good answers during the lesson would be stroked on the head with such a gentle, tender touch that it would remain in their memories for the rest of their lives. *Atau, ilik, barys...* Several months had gone by and the class could still not master their accursedly tricky cases.

'Miss, may I go to the toilet?'

'Is it very urgent?'

'Very much so, miss!'

'Well, off you go then! Only don't even think about tearing off a piece of the wall newspaper for your business! If you do, I'll be tearing strips off you...'

'I won't touch it, miss. No one's written anything nasty about me on it?'

His desk partner looked at him with undisguised envy. He had only just come up with an excuse to get out of the lesson but Almurat, for the umpteenth time, had beaten him to it.

'Bring me back a flatbread, or I won't carry your books for you!' he warned the fortunate boy.

'Like hell I will!' Almurat whispered into his ear.

A large crowd had gathered around the mill, the air blue with agitated and angry female voices. It did not bode well. Five men on horseback, wearing black half-length fur coats, were hurriedly riding out of the aul and heading for the road.

Zakhair's pug-nosed son leapt out of the crowd and rushed over to meet Almurat.

'Hey, your cousin's been killed!'

Almurat ran to the mill and stopped in his tracks, completely stunned.

Kazhimurat was lying unconscious in the snow, blood coming from his throat.

The women, who would kick up the most unimaginable fuss for the smallest reason, were in an uproar. Some were crying, others were cursing, others were threatening goodness knows knew who.

'Cut it out!' Zlikha cried out to the women as she cradled Kazhimurat's head. 'Don't lose your heads!

You'd think none of you has ever been struck by misfortune! Go and fetch the sleds!'

Zlikha removed her down shawl and then her white silk handkerchief, which she used to bandage Kazhimurat's bloody head.

For a moment, Kazhimurat came round and looked straight at Almurat, although it seemed he didn't recognise him. His eyes rolled back and his swarthy face became as pale and lifeless as glass. Rapiya and Shamshinur brought the dirty sled that they would use to bring the manure out from the cattle yard. The women picked up Kazhimurat's enormous, motionless body with great difficulty and carried it to the sled. Rapiya grasped the shafts of the sled and turned to Zlikha,

'So, where are we taking Kazhimurat.'

As one, the women all fell silent and looked at one another, in anticipation that one of them would offer their services first. But no one spoke up. It was hard to tell what was holding them back, but at least their faces showed genuine compassion. Perhaps it was because they were afraid of the scandal of bringing Kazhimurat into their homes while their husbands were at the front. Or perhaps it was something else holding them back. Everyone lived in poverty and there were no extra scraps, meaning they would have to take food from their children to feed Kazhimurat.

'Take him to my house!' Zlikha ordered. Straining as hard as they could, two of the women dragged the sled along the street, with Kazhimurat's huge, long legs dangling over the side. Almurat wanted to follow after them but the horror of what he had seen seemed to have riveted him to the ground. His eyes were hot with tears.

Kazhimurat had been taken to someone else's house and he thought he would never see him come out from it alive.

The sled was already near the pressed path when old Zhusup appeared and pounced on the women like a hawk.

'What's all this fuss about? Go on, get out of here! You're making more racket than a mob of crows! Get lost, I tell you!'

Even though the old man was weak and liked to shout, he did enjoy the respect of his fellow aul folk. He was a respected elder with a sharp tongue to boot, after all. Little by little, the women began to go their separate ways. One of them, however, could not help herself and turned on the old man,

'It's a feeble bush that shows its thorns once the enemy has gone!'

At that moment, a half-witted girl called Bakhyt appeared as if from nowhere and, formidably cursing the fascists in a sonorous voice, she launched herself at Zhusup.

The old man, who, only a minute before, had been all hot under the collar, was taken by surprise. He whirled round, tearing himself from the girl's arms and then shouted for all the street to hear,

'Save me from this mad woman!'

Some people laughed at such an unexpected turn of events, while others, on the contrary, grew more sombre as they recalled the war. No one intervened! It was as if the people decided to let them scream and shout and lift the weight from their souls.

In the meantime, Bakhyt had grasped the old man by the collar of his half-coat, dragged him to the mill and locked him in. Having dealt with the old man, the girl went over to the women, who were up to their knees in the loose snow. Bakhyt, however, was barefoot and without a hat. It seemed she could not feel the breath of that frosty day. Bakhyt's face was clear, her eyes radiating anger. Her thick, pitch-black hair was neatly combed into a straight parting, while two tight, thick braids rested on her high chest. She was dressed any which way. Some of her clothes were too big, some were too short and they had all belonged to someone else. Had it not been for her condition, Bakhyt would have been the prettiest girl in the aul. Few would view her clean, white face, as if carved from marble, without emotion.

When Bakhyt was calm, her face betrayed no feelings, but sometimes she would become withdrawn and sit for hours, staring at one point without blinking. It was then that people could see an incredible radiance in her bright, bottomless eyes, displaying a courage that not all men possess, alongside a sad light, by which people capable of deep, subtle feelings are recognised. Strangely enough, people in the aul believed that Bakhyt had a terrifying gaze. She looked at kind people with a certain reproach that made them feel guilty, while she looked at the unkind as if she were accusing them of all the mortal sins known to man.

Bakhyt's state of mind was inconstant: she would become violent at the dawn of a new moon and then be calm when the moon was full. At times, she was so calm that people would say she entered the house with fire and emerged with the ashes. From early morning until late into the evening, Bakhyt would help the women wash the linen, do the dishes, tend to the livestock and then fall asleep whenever she became overcome by fatigue. In summer, she lived in a remote hut in a little place called Batpaksai. People avoided Batpaksai, believing it to be the home of an evil spirit, the same spirit that put a curse on poor Bakhyt.

Zhusup's elderly wife came over, embraced the girl and took her inside. Either she had come to help her old man or she had felt sorry for the girl. The girl's bare footprints remained on the porcelain-white snow and the old mill stood black and silent among the deep drifts. Old Zhusup looked out of a broken window at the mill, waiting for the people to disperse. He had now come to realise, it seemed, that he had made a fuss over nothing. If he hadn't shouted at the women, then half-witted Bakhyt wouldn't have got upset and reacted as she did. He quietly opened the door, climbed out and sat down on the wooden edge of the pond. He pulled out his ivory snuffbox from his high boots. It was only then that he noticed Almurat, leaning against the corner of the mill, softly sobbing. For a while, Zhusup stood and stared at him through narrowed eyes, as if wondering whether the boy had had anything to do with the incident.

'Hey, sonny! What's with the sniffling? There are plenty of others shedding tears without you as well, believe you me!' The old man rose to his feet, walked over, put an arm around Almurat and sat him down next to him. 'Is your father still alive? Why doesn't he show his face outside his house, like a bear hiding in his den? Or perhaps he's reading Kazhimurat his last rites. Eh?'

Zhusup tapped his snuffbox on the heel of a boot and tapped some snuff onto his hand.

Although he was completely grey, there was not a wrinkle on his ruddy face. The old man had reached a ripe old age but, at first glance, it appeared he had not aged at all. He always held his back straight, he had an attractive, straight nose and a keen, hawkish gaze. Zhusup was a descendant of the *biys*, the wise men of the steppe who ordinary folk would go to for advice and adjudication, and he had inherited many qualities that set him favourably apart from others. On that day he was, as ever, dressed in his best clothes, as if he were going to Mecca on a pilgrimage. He sniffed the tobacco with his customary air, throwing his elbow back and holding it aloft.

'They say that he who has a big appetite has an arse like a bucket. Can't your father find the right plug to curb his appetite and prevent his belly from constantly emptying?'

The old man Zhusup was in the habit of never leaving a man in peace if he had ever committed the slightest fault. Once he started plucking away, there would be no getting rid of him until he had picked the man's character bare. Like a magpie sitting on the wounded back of a cow, he could find the most painful spots on his victim, mercilessly open them up and then sting them with such poisonous words that no one could bear it. The aul folk tried to avoid him as much as possible and old and young alike would conceal any gossip from him, however small, for Zhusup was likely to make a mountain out of a molehill. That was the kind of man Zhusup was. He would make the most miserly of misers pay up and find fault in even the most wonderful person.

Almurat felt ill at ease after hearing Zhusup's words, addressed at his father. However, there was nothing he could do. He could not raise objections to the old man for he himself knew the true nature of the deeds of his father, a man disliked by everyone in the aul. And it was awkward to walk away because the old man had led him over and sat him down bedside him with such a kind look on his face.

It turned out that Kazhimurat had chipped a considerable amount of ice from the mill wheel and there were large white piles of it here and there. A shovel and a pick lay at the other end of the pond where they had been discarded, while the weighty crowbar, weighing at least two stones, was still stuck in the ice, a solitary reminder that work had been in full swing here only recently but had come to an abrupt halt. Almurat's heart felt heavy. He looked round and saw black smoke billowing from the chimney atop Zlikha's peak-roofed cottage. Her cottage stood out from the others because it had no fence and there were none of the customary outbuildings. No one apart from the recently widowed Zlikha lived in this house. Its lack of accoutrements seemed to emphasise that the life lived in it was nothing like that of all the other houses. To be more precise, it bore little resemblance to a human dwelling at all. It seemed to Almurat that even now having swallowed up Kazhimurat the giant, nothing in its appearance had actually changed. Suddenly, the boy felt anxious for his cousin. He was sure that Kazhimurat's arrival at Zlikha's house would not be without consequences.

Rapiya and Shamshinur, bent double, dragged the empty sled back to the barn. The winter day was short. In the evening light, each snowflake underfoot could clearly be made out. The ground seemed to have been strewn with a myriad of shiny, brittle needles. The blue sky, upended above them, appeared incredibly deep and that meant the night would be frosty. The sound of an engine rumbled from the barn and then the threshing machine began to clatter, churning out clouds of dust. Having had a little rest, the women got down to their second shift of work. Now, they would work flat out until the morning. Almurat didn't know what to do with himself. Previously, he would work away until well into the night alongside Kazhimurat, tying sacks full of grain.

Old Zhusup, who had been dozing on a log with his ramrod back as straight as ever, suddenly said to the boy,

'Get up!'

Almurat stood up.

'You know there's an old saying, *If you are to live until morning, prepare yourself provisions to last until midday.* Have you ever heard of it?' The old man asked Almurat and then went on, not waiting for a reply, 'Pick up the shovel, pick and crowbar and put them back where they came from. Then saddle up Zlikha's chestnut horse and bring her here to me, you got that? Tell her that Grandfather Zhusup is planning to go to the enlistment office to find out what's happened here. He who stays silent when a man is mocked will remain unmoved when a woman is shamed.'

In the old man's eyes, the enlistment office was the symbol of order during those difficult war years. It was the enlistment office that issued the call-up papers to all men — young and old. And it was the enlistment office that provided news of who was still bashing the enemy, who was still alive and who had died a hero's death. Therefore, Zhusup was convinced that the enlistment office would also stand up for and protect those who had been left behind in the aul. There was no telling what he would be able to achieve at the remote district centre, but Zhusup mounted the chestnut horse with the air of a man intent on turning the world on its head. However, once he had started to ride around the aul, collecting a few roubles or even a little food from every house, some of the householders began to suspect that old Zhusup was perhaps more concerned with his own interests rather than Kazhimurat's misfortune. However, once Zhusup found himself atop the collective farm's only decent horse, he was filled with his own sense of self-importance and would listen to nothing his neighbours had to say. Before departing, he took his old woman to one side and ordered her in no uncertain terms to keep a close eye on their only cow and the brown bull that was lying in the barn, half-starved and unable to get to its feet. Then he listed aloud all the relatives he had not seen for decades. Some, it turned out, had not visited for a long time, while others had passed away. They were all due something, so the old man took the last piece of butter that the old woman had been saving and the remains of the meat saved for winter — a very lean and meagre haunch of mutton. There was little doubt that Zhusup had decided to use the occasion as an excuse to visit all his relatives, and that the undertaking might take him at least a year. The preparations were laborious and long. His neighbours at least comforted themselves that perhaps the old man might be able to look in on their kinsfolk on the way back. However, once Zhusup had pulled his festive quilted gown from the bottom of the chest and put it on under his half-length sheepskin and tightened it round his waist with a sash, tearing off a piece of cloth almost 15 inches wide for this purpose, no one was remotely convinced that the old man was really setting out to bring those who had so cruelly attacked Kazhimurat to book.

Evening closed in.

'It's already getting dark. They say there are a lot of bad folk wandering the roads these days...' the old woman had begun, but the old man interrupted her,

'If God permits, I will spend the night at Algabas,' he answered his wife with an important air.

Even Almurat was surprised at these words. The Algabas collective farm was only six kilometres from the aul and if the old man was going to stop for the night every six kilometres, how long would it take him to cover the sixty kilometres that separated them from the district centre?

After seeing off the old man, the boy aimlessly wandered around the aul for some time. He looked into the cattle yard, walked around the barn and then returned to the mill. Without Kazhimurat, life seemed to have drained from the aul. He entered the mill. Dark and empty, it looked rather like a *mazar*, a gravestone, and he stopped on the threshold. Suddenly, he thought he saw someone lying in the corner. He stopped in his tracks. Could it be that Kazhimurat had returned and was lying in his usual place? Then why wasn't he moving? Had he already died? The boy's heart sank. There were only a couple more steps to the door, but his legs suddenly felt weak and he couldn't even move them. His ears began to ring. He thought he heard someone kicking the wall but a moment later he realised that that was his own heart beating.

Suddenly, the iron stove by the door began to drone and the dark belly of the mill responded with a long, sad groan. The hairs on Almurat's head bristled in terror and he slowly turned towards the door, taking one step, then another. He imagined that an invisible monster was creeping up on him. He stopped by the stove and froze, listening in to the silence. He could feel the invisible monster's warm breath on his neck. The moment seemed to last for an age. The monster too had frozen expectantly behind his back.

Almurat was now quite beside himself. He leapt up, kicked the door open and rushed outside in an instant. No one jumped out after him. The wind was simply rustling the straw thatch on the mill roof. The moon was emitting broad streaks of light which stretched in all directions — a serious frost was on its way... A few stars flickered in the dark-grey sky. The hum of an engine and the clattering of the threshing machine, reminiscent of the clattering hooves of a trotting horse, could be heard. The only light in the entire aul shone from a window in Zlikha's house. Almurat gradually calmed down a little and looked back inside the mill. This time he could make out Kazhimurat's coat on the bench in the corner and he could see the door of the potbelly stove was still open. It was this that had produced the humming sound in the metal chimney. It must have been a long time since it had been stoked. A pile of wood chips and thick pine logs, stacked near the stove, remained untouched.

Almurat tore a piece of wool from Kazhimurat's old coat, brushed it off and lit the fire with steel and flint. He placed some wood chips on top and then firewood. Soon there was a roar and rattle in the iron stove as if imps had gathered there to play their devilish games. The stove burner swallowed thick, stout, new logs and belched red flames like a fire-breathing monster out of some fairy tale. Almurat closed the doors more tightly, pushed a large birchwood stump closer to the stove and settled down on it. The small stove was not big enough to warm the spacious, high-roofed mill. The fire burned hot on his face, but the cold still insinuated its way up his sleeves and under the flap of his coat. His back was stiff. Shadows danced in the dark corners of the mill, like yellow leaves whirling in the autumn air. Almurat threw his cousin's old half-coat over his shoulders and felt a lot more comfortable. They say that he who lives with a cripple learns how to limp. Recently, Almurat had grown accustomed to his solitude and he'd learned how to sit motionless for hours in silence, much like his mute brother. Now, all he was missing was Kazhimurat, his only, silent friend and confidante. How was he doing now, Almurat thought. Perhaps he should go over to Zlikha's? But what would his expression be if he were to appear there?

Almurat ached inside at the thought that his father Tazhimurat had not defended his only nephew, when he had been attacked and so badly beaten, that he had done nothing to help him, leaving him battered and bruised and lying in the snow. What would he actually do if he went to Zlikha's house? Everyone in his house had avoided him like some stranger when he had lived with them. So, how was he going to reassure him now? Just tritely say: 'Don't cry and wipe away your tears, everything will be all right?' No, Almurat would not go to Zlikha's but he wouldn't go home either. He had long since expressed his feelings at home and would no longer sit at the table with his parents, that was beyond him. Therefore, he would hurry to eat earlier than them and, if he came back later than usual, he would stuff his food into his school bag or his pockets and run out. Partly because of this, he always had food with him. On this occasion, too, he sat before the fire and nibbled at some pine nuts that he'd stuffed into his pockets.

Almurat threw several thick logs into the stove, which was now red hot. It was no longer as cold as before. The heat had made the place smell of uncooked dough, evidently emanating from the flour dust that had clogged all the cracks and corners in the mill. Almurat swept the floor and threw the rubbish into the stove. *Let it smell of human habitation,* he thought. Feeling the invigorating warmth, mice began to scuttle about in the cracks of the walls, feasting on the free wheat they could find there. *The mice, too are happier when people are nearby,* Almurat thought. The scrabbling of the mice intensified, something Almurat did not like. He lit the lamp, but the dilapidated room, once dimly illuminated, was such a depressing sight that he instantly put it out. Someone carefully knocked at the door.

'Almurat, open the door!' Came the quiet voice of Zakhair's son. 'Don't be afraid, it's me, Bekmurat!'

'Come in! It's not locked.'

The ginger, pug-nosed kid came in and closed the door on the latch, then walked over to the stove and stuck his bare feet closer to the fire. All he was wearing was a light sleeveless jacket. Almurat had been irked by Bekmurat's 'Don't be afraid' comment. At first, he hadn't wanted to let him anywhere near the stove, but then he took pity on him and moved another birchwood stump towards the boy, albeit reluctantly. The ginger lad, shivering and thoroughly chilled by the cold, sat down.

'Is someone after you? Why are you dressed like that?'

'I'm running from home.'

'And why are you only half dressed?'

'Well, if I had put my coat on, my mother would have realised I was going out for a long time. I told her I was just popping outside and then I rushed straight here. Red-eyed Murat is looking for you.' He broke off, looked at Almurat and then continued, speaking quickly, 'Your father is looking for you and it looks like you're in a lot of trouble. He asked me where you were but I didn't let on.' The ginger lad passed Almurat something the size of his fist. 'Here, I've brought you some first milk.' I put it in a bag, it's probably gone cold by now. Yesterday Lysukha was calving, you see. You know, her calf is the spit of the grey bull, you couldn't tell them apart!'

Almurat softened slightly — not every friend would have gone looking for him in that weather, half-dressed and with a gift. He took off his coat, placed it round Bekmurat's shoulders and tucked in the edges to ensure he'd be warmer. He pulled out a handful of pine nuts from his pocket and poured them into his companion's hand.

'Where did you see my father?'

'He came to see us.'

'So why is he looking for me?'

'He didn't say. I thought he'd come over for a taste of our first milk,' Bekmurat surmised.

He was missing several front teeth and when he spoke, his pink tongue would keep sticking out. However, despite the lack of front incisors, he managed to crack the nuts probably faster than any taiga squirrel. Bekmurat never thought about removing his blistered feet from the hot fire. His feet had never known shoes, be it in the sultry summer or the frosty winter. Quickly finishing off the nuts, he shook the hem of his sleeveless jacket and several potatoes tumbled out in front of the stove door.

'Well, how's that first milk?' Bekmurat threw the potatoes one after the other into the stove and covered them with the hot ashes. 'We have nuts at home, too.'

A hint that he wouldn't say no to another handful.

Almurat pulled a glass bottle from his pocket, full of pine nuts and placed them at his feet.

Pug-nosed Bekmurat snuffled and hawked appreciatively. Bekmurat was the youngest of Zakhair's six sons and the boys in the aul would sometimes call him Ginger Housewife. He would be forever doing the chores about the house, stoking the hearth three times a day and setting up the black cauldron in which the entire family's meals were cooked. He would grind grain with the large pestle and mortar, sweep the house and help his mother milk the red cow with the white bald patch that had calved only the day before. Bekmurat would spend the rest of his time collecting the latest aul gossip. He should have started school last year but because he had no shoes he had been unable to attend until the first snow had fallen and that was why he had been held back a year. The boy had sat at home the entire, long winter except for the times when, bored out of his mind, he would run outside, dressed as he was now, to learn the aul's latest news. At the first sign of an argument or commotion, there'd be no keeping him at home, even if he'd been tied and bound. He would always be the first on the scene and the first to learn what had happened. He kept tabs on everyone who came to the aul, learning where they'd come from and what their reasons were. If there was any news in the aul, he would know about it. The women, with their houses full of growing children, would shake their heads enviously, 'Just take a look at Rapiya's youngest! He's quick-witted and smart and he knows everything that's going on above the ground and under it too!'

'Listen, Ginger Wifey, didn't I give you my felt boots?!' Almurat recalled.

'I gave them to Telmurat,' Zakhair's son replied with a sniff. 'He's my elder brother, after all, so let him study. I'll get by without studying. What's wrong with herding sheep, I say?' These were obviously the words his mother had used to comfort her son.

Bekmurat picked up the tongs and turned the potatoes over.

'Yeah, your half-witted uncle...'

'If you call him that again, I'll shove that red coal there under your tongue, you got that?'

'Got it. Only don't go calling me Ginger Housewife, all right?' Bekmurat said, to save losing face. 'Zlikha bathed your half... Your uncle Kazhimurat, gave him clean linen and put him in her bed!'

'Horseshit!'

'I swear to Allah! May I be struck down if I am wrong! Why don't you believe me?' He rolled the potatoes out of the embers to stop them burning. 'How are you going to know what's going on in the aul while you're here keeping watch over the mice at the mill.'

Bekmurat divided the potatoes into two equal heaps but then, thinking that his words might have been a bit too harsh, he rolled one potato from his heap over to Almurat's as a peace offering. Bekmurat's words burned Almurat more painfully than the hot potato he'd just been passed. Something seemed to break inside him. At that moment, the outer door suddenly tore open and Tazhimurat entered the room.

'Damn it!' he said, glaring angrily at his son. 'Just you wait... I'll burn this ramshackle building to the ground!'

Bekmurat darted towards him, ducked between his legs and was off.

That night, something appeared to have come over the miserly Tazhimurat. He slaughtered a well-fed ram, dressed the carcass, placed all the meat, right down to the last morsel, into the hide and then sent it with Almurat to Zlikha's house.

* * *

Kazhimurat sat up in bed, gasping for air, convinced he was being sucked into a whirlpool. He opened his eyes and instantly everything before him began to spin and the room began to fall headlong into a dark void. His ears felt

127

like they were going to burst with the sharp, unpleasant ringing that assailed them and he felt as if a thousand needles were stabbing his temples. He thought he was getting another of the awful headaches that occasionally plagued him and was about to reach out for the headboard of his bed, only his hand hung limply in the air and he collapsed heavily to the floor. The ringing in his ears stopped and the black ceiling stopped spinning. Kazhimurat could make out a weak flame and then, in the pale, diffused light of the lamp, he caught sight of Zlikha, undressed, her frightened eyes staring at him, her hair dishevelled.

After a while, the flame split into two, then there were many lights. Hundreds of faces were now staring at him, all like Zlikha. There was a multitude of faces, all holding lamps and all spinning around him. His eyes began to ache unbearably and his surroundings slowly swam together in a yellow haze.

From the minute Kazhimurat had been brought into her house, Zlikha had not once turned out the light in the back room. She was accustomed to tending the sick, so Kazhimurat had not been much trouble for her. Every day, Zlikha would change his bedclothes and feed him with a spoon. She did not even consider it shameful to help him relieve himself. There were no wounds on Kazhimurat's body, except for the ring-sized mark left on his forehead from a blow from a heel, but he felt his body was not his own and would not do his bidding. He would lose consciousness almost every other day. Zlikha had thrust pencil and paper in his hands and pleaded with him to write down where he was feeling pain, but Kazhimurat would not open up to her. Zlikha assumed he had suffered a serious concussion and, therefore, wouldn't allow him to move. During the day she would leave the ginger lad Bekmurat by his bed, while she spent the night by the patient's bedside herself.

That day, Zlikha had returned from work tired and she had been about to drop off in her room when she heard the thud of a body falling. It turned out that Kazhimurat had tried to get out of the bed and had fallen.

'What's the matter? What's the matter?' she asked, holding the lamp. She was shaken and scared.

Kazhimurat was lying on the syrmak[12] floor covering and his swarthy face had acquired a deathlike paleness. She rushed over to check his pulse, then moistened his lips and placed a damp towel on his forehead. It was clear that Zlikha's efforts had only added to his torment because Kazhimurat shook his head weakly twice, as if asking her to leave him be and, quite agitated, she dropped her arms. Some time went by before beads of sweat appeared on Kazhimurat's brow. His breathing became more even and he closed his eyes.

She was unable to move Kazhimurat back into bed on her own and there was no one to send for the neighbours. As luck would have it, Bekmurat had come up with some excuse — she couldn't remember what it was — and he had rushed back home that evening. Naturally, the boy had been itching to tell the aul what was going on at Zlikha's house. The women who had dropped in on her in the early days to enquire about Kazhimurat's health were now visiting less frequently. Not only that, but some had even begun to spread rumours that Zlikha was

---

[12] A felt floor covering with an overlaid pattern

keeping Kazhimurat in her bed on purpose, even though he was almost completely recovered. No, she had no one to help her.

Zlikha laid a large *tekemet* rug on the floor and folded it in three. On that, she placed a blanket and a pillow and carefully rolled Kazhimurat onto this makeshift bed. He groaned in pain, straightened his enormous body and the room suddenly became cramped; his head lay on the seat of honour, while his feet reached the threshold. *How on earth did he fit on the bed?* Zlikha wondered, looking at Kazhimurat, now sprawled across the floor. She folded in the edges of the blanket to stop him from catching a chill and remained sitting at his side. Zlikha's eyes were drooping with fatigue, but she couldn't leave Kazhimurat on his own.

She got up, turned down the lamp and then lay down on the bed, but the smell of the man's body, which had soaked through over the last few days, put paid to any thought of sleep. Zlikha looked around the room. She had lived here all alone, all winter and all through the long summer, but now she had a distinct feeling that she was in someone else's home. She realised that this feeling had arisen from this unfamiliar aroma, the smell of a man's body, something her house had become estranged to, and yet she could not get herself to settle down. A strange rustling could be heard coming from the corners of the room and the front doors banged and creaked in the stiff wind.

Zlikha got up, closed the doors more securely and threw the latch once more, but a minute later she heard steps under the windows. It was as if someone were wandering about near the house. Zlikha guessed it was a hungry cow in search of something to eat but there wouldn't be a single shrivelled stalk to find anywhere near her place. If only the wolves didn't attack the poor creature. With that thought, Zlikha instantly remembered the animals in the collective farm barn, a structure the wind would have blown right through. There were still two months until March but, although that was seen to be the start of spring, it did not bode well for them. The frost still had such a hold that it felt as if the lifesaving spring would never come.

The only thing keeping the collective farm together, and the entire aul, for that matter, had been Kazhimurat, and here he was lying in front of her, beaten half to death by unknown assailants.

As soon as Zlikha began to think about the challenges facing the collective farm, she instantly forgot her recent worries about her own unsettled fate and the gossip going around the aul.

The auls used to honour a young woman if she could properly maintain her home, calling her an exemplary *kelin*[13] daughter-in-law. But Zlikha had to think of the welfare of the collective farm and the entire aul, protecting the honour and dignity of the women who worked under her. Now, she was responsible for the well-being of every soldier's family, its hearth and its children. God alone knew how agonising and unspeakably difficult this had been. And now there was all this gossip...

---

[13] *Kelin* – refers to a young bride who enters her husband's home and lives there, performing all the household chores and tending to all other family members living in that house.

Zlikha sighed bitterly, turned towards the stove and saw that Kazhimurat had come untucked again.

She wrapped him up again, noticing with relief that he was no longer sweating and was breathing much easier than before.

You poor thing, at least you're still alive, she thought, blaming herself for what had happened to Kazhimurat.

The dull rattle of the threshing machine came through the howl of the wind and the creaking of the door. Having finished their work at the farm, the women were now labouring away on the threshing floor, where they would remain until the morning. How many days in a row had it been since they had slept the whole night through? Zlikha tried to be by the aul women's side when she could, either throwing sheaves into the threshing machine, or dragging sacks of grain, but now she had had had to remain at home an entire week to care for the sick Kazhimurat.

How she needed to be on the threshing floor on that windy, frosty night. She could have cheered someone up with a kind word or sent someone home for a few minutes to get warm. How many days had they not had anything decent to eat? Recently, Rapiya had been dragging a heavy sack when she was sick and brought up nothing but bile. Her stomach had been empty but she had also swallowed her fair share of dust during the threshing. How could she help the women? Perhaps she could organise a temporary stove, at least to ensure they had boiling water to hand. Or perhaps spare them a little milk. Let them have at least a spoonful to keep their strength up. Death certificates would come in every day, for many fine young men had fallen on the battlefields. It was unacceptable that, back in the aul, a widow should also part with life... No, she would send some of the families a little of the grain that had been set aside for sowing. That way, they would at least get something for all their hard work. It was not good that the collective farm could not even deliver half of the planned grain. Taking it to the district centre in a winter such as this one, some sixty kilometres away, and on the poor transport they had would have been no easy task for any man, let alone a woman.

Kazhimurat was sick and, apart from him, there was no one who would be able to carry out such a difficult task. In some two to three weeks, they would have to make preparations for the spring work in the fields, repairing the sleds, ploughs and harrows. But who was going to do this? There were no draft cattle left; they would probably have to select some of the younger cows to do the job. Which was all very well, but they would also need to till the land. These endless worries took their toll on Zlikha. She felt so downcast from the burden that she got to her feet and wandered through the house, pacing all four rooms from one end to the other. Bekmurat had evidently not stoked the stove the day before because it was cold in the spacious sitting room. The hands on the wall clock told her it was three o'clock. She glanced at the photograph of her husband, who had died the year before. She stood before it in the centre of the room, talking to herself, before sitting down on the large chest by the wall. It was quiet in the room where Kazhimurat was lying, the only sound was the ticking of the clock. Zlikha suddenly imagined that the sound was not the clock but rather the disapproving cluck of her husband's tongue. She involuntarily shuddered, rushed out of the living room, shut the doors and leaned with her back against them, as if afraid that Toremurat might follow her out and find Kazhimurat in the house.

Her husband had returned wounded from the war, where he had lost both legs and his death had been slow and painful. Zlikha threw herself onto the bed and covered herself with the blanket, her head included. However, a short while later, it became stuffy and she threw it back. The frosted windowpanes had cast a pale, dusky light as if they had been placed there to prevent too much light entering the room. Kazhimurat wasn't sleeping. He lay there with his hands behind his head, staring motionlessly at the ceiling. What was he thinking about? His large, masculine face had become gaunt, his cheeks sunken and stiff, his aquiline nose now particularly prominent. He had not the slightest care for Zlikha or her worries. Kazhimurat's enormous body seemed to have been carved from stone. Zlikha looked away. The paraffin in the lamp had run out, the flame had gone out and the wick was smoking, filling the room with acrid smoke. She needed to take the lamp out but Zlikha felt uncomfortable showing herself to Kazhimurat dressed only in her nightgown. Although she had grown up in the town and had never been particularly self-conscious in public, she now found it hard to make herself get up from the bed. *Oh, Allah, what is he thinking about?* Zlikha thought angrily. *He could at least turn away.* However, Kazhimurat lay still as a corpse, only with open eyes staring sadly at the ceiling.

The cockerels crowed and it became a little lighter in the room. It now struck her how untidy the place had become. Kazhimurat was lying on the floor, Zlikha, on the bed. Each of them was immersed in their own thoughts. It was time to light the stove, put the kettle on and, after some breakfast, run to the office. The district centre had been ringing the whole day yesterday, calling Kiyakmurt and her into the district committee offices. They probably wanted to give them a dressing down for not delivering the grain on time. But how were they possibly going to be able to deliver it to the government store, she wanted to ask. Zlikha wouldn't be able to swallow a single piece of bread until she'd done her morning rounds. Where was that ginger scamp — whose house would he be in this time? She needed to find Bekmurat and leave him with Kazhimurat while she ran to the threshing floor.

'You feeling any better?' Kazhimurat barely nodded, his eyes remaining fixed on the ceiling. 'You were in a bad way, so I stayed here last night... I have to go to the district centre today. You look after yourself. Don't get up and try not to move much. I'll be back soon.' Zlikha got up, covered her exposed shoulders with a blanket and, stepping awkwardly, left the room, not forgetting to snuff the wick with her fingers as she went. Zlikha went outside having put the samovar on, but not waiting for it to boil. She couldn't sit there any longer, something was troubling her. The smell of burning pine logs and the crackling of the hot stove brought the house back to life again. It was warm and cosy. Sparrows chirped outside the window, heralding the arrival of another morning.

For the first time in all the days he had spent at Zlikha's, Kazhimurat looked attentively around the room. There were red silk curtains on the windows, a red satin quilt, a red velvet tablecloth with lace edges, a rug with red decoration, a cabinet with a coat of red varnish and a stand of shelves in the corner with various women's trinkets. *A woman remains a woman even in the hardest of times*, Kazhimurat thought. The frost had melted on the windowpanes and a fragment of golden sky had appeared. The sun was now up. Kazhimurat wanted to go out into the fresh air. The bed had been unimaginably cramped for him and, those last few days, he had felt as if someone had lowered him to the bottom of a deep well. It was good that he'd spent at least a little time lying on the floor. More than anything, however, he was tormented by his powerlessness. Kazhimurat couldn't stand being pitied, no matter if it were by strangers or his own kin. Now, as fate would have it, he had found himself in a stranger's house. The situation he found himself in was simply too strange for him, a soft bed under a quilted silken blanket of fine camel hair, clean, snow-white linen, food and drink provided from the hands of a woman who cared for him in a way he could never have dreamed of. The obligation he felt weighed heavily upon him and Kazhimurat didn't know how he could possibly repay this kind and sensitive soul who had taken him in in his time of need.

He would rather have died than find himself in such an unthinkable situation for a man of his nature. Kazhimurat rose to his feet but immediately felt dizzy, his heart froze, all his joints seemed to have become weak and he involuntarily leaned against the back of the bed. Two or three minutes went by before he was able to take his first independent step. He emerged unsteadily into the front room, where the decoration reminded him of his life in the town years before. There was the high dining table, chairs with high backs, a red-leather couch by the wall and a glass-fronted cabinet packed tightly with crockery.

He was affected by these unfamiliar surroundings, for it seemed to him not so much opulent as delightful, for he appeared to sense Zlikha's presence in everything around him. He started looking for his old half-length coat and worn canvas boots but he had no luck. Aggrieved at his helplessness, he took the large sheepskin coat that was hanging on a nail, thrust his bare feet into enormous felt boots and went out of the house.

That was when he realised just how precious the free world that he had always inhabited since his early childhood was to him. The frosty morning air, like a cleansing flame, struck his nose and he breathed in a chestful. The bright rays of the sun that had barely risen over the nearby hill made him squint. Tears welled up in his eyes. Kazhimurat staggered like a drunk, struggling to reach the log pile by the porch, and sank down onto it.

The world around was clean as if it had been washed with milk. The trees, their white crowns blown away by the wind, were now covered in a radiant, silvery hoarfrost, the tall wooden roofs of the houses and the boarded fences that surrounded them shone a silver-brown colour like the slick coat of a chestnut horse after a long ride. Last night's wind that had blown so hard against the walls of the house had been a warm southerly, rippling down along the long gorges of the Altai. If the wind was blowing from the Altai, that meant that the snow would melt in a matter of days, foreshadowing the coming of spring. Smoke billowed from the chimneys straight up into the sky. The staccato clatter of the cows' hooves and the velvety snorting of the horses returning from the watering hole, the hoarse coughing and chattering voices of the old men and women who had emerged to watch the livestock were so clear and loud that you'd be forgiven for thinking it was all going on in the yard outside. Nestled in its hollow, the aul breathed peacefully, seemingly oblivious to the cruel war and the incalculable hardships that it had brought with it. Only the collective farm office, now completely covered in snow, looked out onto the street, lonely and forlorn, with its unlit, frosty windows, waiting silently for the people who had once filled its rooms with their voices.

Who needs a khan's palace when it's been abandoned by its people? Kazhimurat had not been at the office for a while and it was clear that no one had bothered to heat the stove or keep the records of the work performed by the collective farmers either. The paths between the houses were also blocked with thick snow. *It turns out the aul really does need me*, Kazhimurat thought with satisfaction. Studying the village more closely, he now saw the neglect, or rather, the failure of others to attend to the jobs that he had done before. A feeling of pride he had never experienced before rose up inside him. For a long time, he had seen himself as superfluous to everyone's needs but it had turned out he had been wrong to think such bitter thoughts. There were people who needed him. The war-ravaged collective farm needed him. And there was no point worrying about what had happened to him. God would be his judge, he had suffered for the sake of the farm, for these people who were bravely standing firm in the face of this unprecedented, bloody war. *No point throwing your coat on the fire at the first louse you find,* Kazhimurat chuckled to himself, recalling how brutally the people from the local district centre had punished him for stealing their hay.

One way or another, I'll find you and we'll have a good heart-to-heart about this.

Kazhimurat felt his former strength returning.

The severe headaches of the last few days that had clamped his head like a vice had now gone. His eyes felt warmer, his furrowed brow had smoothed and the blood now seemed to be flowing faster through his veins.

He heard the distinctive creak of a wooden cane sinking deep into the snow under the weight of the body leaning on it. Then he heard the accompanying shuffling footsteps. Old Zhusup was approaching from the collective farm barn with his careful and dignified gait. As always, he stood upright with a haughty air, and his white beard covered his entire chest. Kazhimurat got up and hurried back into the house.

* * *

Beyond the aul, the chestnut horse was trotting smoothly along and the hay sled it was pulling slid along the snow at pace. The intermittent clumps of trees on the side of the smooth straight road seemed to have given up trying to keep up with the horse and had now turned in on themselves and remained behind. The chestnut stallion had been sired by a Russian pacer that had arrived in these parts with its settler owners and a local

Kazakh long-maned *Karabair*[14] mare, a breed famous for its incredible endurance, making it especially agile and swift, both when harnessed and when saddled.

There is an old folk saying that a woman who lacks a certain gift but nevertheless appreciates this gift in others is like *A bride who has come from an aul not famed for the quantity of its sheep but whose parents had an abundance of goats.* And this expression could have been coined with Zlikha in mind. She had never kept a decent horse in her life, but she knew pretty much all there was to know about them. Zlikha was grateful to her chestnut horse, whose fast pace helped dispel her heavy thoughts. The stallion held itself erect, did not veer from the road and walked with a sweeping gait, planting its front legs well in advance of its body and pushing off vigorously with its haunches, stretching out as if flattening its body on the run. Entering into a gallop, it would jerk at the reins now and then, demanding its freedom and, in so doing, would hold its head, tilting it angrily a little to one side. Tokmurat, the former chairman of the collective farm, had acquired the horse from some Kerzhaks living in a remote taiga settlement, exchanging it for eight young, three-year-old mares. Back then, the aul had said that Tokmurat had paid too much for the chestnut stallion but later admitted that he had made a good bargain. A horse as fine as this might perhaps be worth the combined livestock wealth of eight Kazakh clans. Before leaving for the war, Tokmurat had personally handed the stallion over to Zlikha along with the bridle, saddle and riding tackle, and said to her that he wanted it all back from her

---

14 Karabair – A long established Central Asian horse breed renowned for its hardiness

in person if he were to return from the war alive. Zlikha had kept the horse on oats and good hay throughout the winter and had tried to ride it only on rare occasions. In the summer she had released the horse into the steppe pastures with a herd of non-calving mares. No one had ridden the horse apart from Zlikha herself. Except for the recent occasion when old Zhusup had used it.

The chestnut horse had caused no end of trouble for its new mistress. After Toremurat had left for the war, many of the high-ups from the district authorities had tried to get their hands on the stallion. It was a fine horse indeed, and there was none to compare with it in the entire district. Whenever they would come to the collective farm, they would size up the horse and start to flatter Zlikha as best they could. Some of them begged, others shed tears, while others even tried to frighten her with threats. It got to a point when other ill-wishers even spread dirty rumours about Zlikha, believing that she would give in, but to no avail. Toremurat would return and collect his horse, but who would heal Zlikha's emotional wounds, inflicted so undeservedly simply because of some well-known and fine-looking horse?

The rare visits she made to the district centre would normally pass without grief, but on this occasion, Zlikha found herself in trouble because of the disruption in the grain deliveries. She refused the invitation of the district managers to visit their homes and she also refused the invitations of acquaintances to sit a while for a chat. She knew that by no means all of them just wanted to get close to her to get their hands on her famous horse, many had designs on her as a single young woman. Therefore, Zlikha had decided to spend the night at a guest house.

Naturally, her room was cold and uncomfortable but, all the same, she felt more at ease there than she would have anywhere else. In the morning, she saw to some affairs left over from the previous day, hastily drank down the boiling water the cleaner had prepared at the guest house and set off on her return journey, without dallying a single minute more than necessary. She had to return home as soon as possible.

Zlikha had set off from the district centre in a bad mood, but the warm, clear sun warmed her stiff body and the fresh breeze on her face and the swift pace of her horse noticeably lifted her spirits.

The wide grey-brown valley, fringed on all sides by hills, was soon left behind. It cut its way through the ravines that gradually narrowed into a road, which curled its way like the handle of a ladle into the tight Kurdym Gorge. This road ran alongside the Bukhtarma. It is a deep gorge where even at midday the sun's rays fail to get a look in, and the pathway draws you into a seemingly bottomless ravine. Hurricane-strength winds blow here all year round, leaving the gorge free of snow throughout the long winter and without a single pebble in the hot summer. Everything has been blown and swept away from this desolate place.

Little wonder that the local people referred to it as the *Kurdym*, meaning *Black Hole*.

The hay sled had been flying as easily and weightlessly as if it were on the ocean waves, but now its runners rattled over the dry, rocky earth and noticeably slowed. Up ahead, the shrill shrieking of women could be heard,

'Heave, heave! Why aren't you moving? Oh, heave, damn it!'

Then the women themselves came into view, pulling sacks of wheat on their shoulders. Soon, Zlikha saw the long-horned oxen, lying helplessly on the smooth, stone road. The creatures seemed unable to withstand the wind. It was one of the sled trains, carrying grain to the central district store. Zlikha recognised the women from the neighbouring Algabas collective farm. She turned off to the side and climbed down from her sled. The hurricane wind had knocked over the oxen, harnessed to the heavy sleds and the people who had been carrying the sacks on their backs. No one answered Zlikha's greeting, for they had no time for that. She caught sight of the women's sombre, tired faces and turned away sadly. Okas, the chairman of the collective farm, tiredly lowered the sack from his shoulders as he came up level with Zlikha and extended his left hand in greeting.

'You coming from the district centre?' Okas pulled up his overcoat that had slid down from his right shoulder and wiped his perspiring face with his empty sleeve. 'As you can see, I never did make it to the district centre on time. What were they saying at the office?'

'They're demanding that we speed up the grain deliveries,' Zlikha replied. 'You know as well as I do how they like to shout and scream at the district office these days.'

'That's how things are now, my dear Zlikha. Don't take it to heart, we're all in the same boat here. So, they had a real go at you, did they? Let's sit awhile. It'll give me a chance to catch my breath.'

They sat down on the sack. Okas pulled his tobacco pouch from his pocket and, turning away from the wind, skilfully rolled a cigarette. His cheeks were sunken and his cheekbones protruded. He was so thin that it seemed his body might crumble under the violent assault of the wind.

Okas's wife appeared bent double under the weight of a sack of grain. Behind her came their son, who was helping the oxen pull the sled using the draught pole. The woman caught sight of Zlikha and was about to turn towards her, but Okas cried over to her,

'Don't stop! You shed that sack and you'll never be able to pick it up and put it onto your shoulders. Keep going!'

Zlikha felt uncomfortable at the sight of the poor woman. Tears had frozen on the cheeks of Okas's son. She felt ashamed that she was sitting there while others were dragging heavy sacks on their backs using the last of their energy. Had it been the right time for her to go to the district centre? How much had been lost en route? But just try ignoring a summons to the office and you'll get it in the neck even worse.

'We're taking all the sweepings from the barns and taking them to the grain store!' Okas said with furrowed brow. 'We have nothing left for the sowing. I literally have no idea how to complete the annual report now! My conscience won't allow me to lie to them but no one's going to be happy with the truth. So, how are things with you?'

'No better, Okas. You are at least delivering all the sweepings, but I am still busy with the threshing. One consolation is that we'll somehow achieve the plan, as a dozen or so sheaves have still to be threshed. I am thinking about handing out the leftovers to the workers. We've already filled the barn with next year's seeds.'

'Oh, well done, you, Zlikha! Well done! Unfortunately, I have nothing to give my people. We are eating nothing but potatoes as it is.'

The grain train slowly made its way past them and, when the last ox-drawn sled had emerged from the ravine, with a sign of relief, Okas too got to his feet.

'Truth be told, I'd have been better off fighting at the front,' he chuckled sadly, waving farewell to Zlikha. 'But they won't let me go, saying this one-armed man has done his fighting. Say what you like, but it's easier for a man to bear the hardships of war than to see the suffering of his people. Take care, Zlikha!'

Zlikha could not allow herself to let him go in such a downcast mood. She grabbed his empty sleeve and held him back.

Don't worry about the report, Okas. If you don't have enough grain for seed, you can take some of mine. Just make sure the district centre doesn't find out. Otherwise, I'll really be in trouble, you understand? And another thing. I also need your help, Okas.'

'What is it, Zlikha? Speak up, don't be shy.'

'You have Russians in your village and when there is no bread, you get by with potatoes and cabbage. But what are we to do? The folk in our aul have never held a hoe in their hands and never worked the land in their lives. Here's what I was thinking. This spring, I would like to fence off a plot next to the settlement and plant vegetables. I think I can persuade the collective to agree to this idea. If you have any potatoes going, would you be able to spare some for us to plant? Here, let me help you get that sack on your shoulders.'

'Thank you. I'll manage by myself, don't worry, Zlikha. I won't have you around to help me out every day, you know. For a one-armed man, a sack is still no burden!' With a deft motion, Okas tossed up the sack and settled it onto his shoulder. 'Thank you for everything, dear Zlikha. And you be careful, too. There was a snow slide near Kuiga.'

Zlikha pulled on the reins and set the steaming horse off at a brisk pace, not because she was afraid of a snow slide, but rather because there was no reason to travel at breakneck speed. It was just that the short winter's day was coming to a swift close between the two overhanging cliff faces. Much like the gorge, her mood turned sombre once more with the darkness drawing in. She leaned back on the hay, piled up against the back of her seat, and looked up at the dwarf pines climbing up the mountain ledges and at the narrow strip of sky still visible above the trees. It was cold and silent. The roar of the tireless Bukhtarma could still be heard from under its icy shell. The clatter of the horse's hooves and the creaking of the sled rails echoed as they filled the gorge with their rumbling. The sled shook as it travelled over the frozen icy mounds. The chestnut horse snorted its displeasure. Zlikha's head began to ache. Now, it was the unusually early warm wind that was blowing in that worried her. There might be a landslide blocking the road and then she would have to sit and wait it out until a way through could be found. Just so long as the others managed to deliver the grain to the collection point. The chestnut stallion stopped abruptly.

An avalanche of snow lay on the road up ahead. It looked as if it had slid down the mountains after the sled train had passed through. Zlikha took the horse by the reins and led him around the obstruction, looking for a higher point where it might still be possible to reach the road although not without difficulty. Her heart shrank in terror when she caught sight of the head of a hare sticking out among the branches and rocks, its eyes bulging from its sockets. She looked up and saw the avalanche's deadly wake stretching down the mountain slope. She wanted to get out of that gorge as quickly as possible. Having inspected the huge drift, Zlikha quickly returned to the sled and, without a second look at the hazardous mounds of ice, lashed the chestnut horse forward. She only regained her composure once she had made it to the Aksuisk Valley. She stretched and straightened her back, which had gone numb from the long and jolting journey.

The twilight sun was rolling over the tops of the snow-covered hills. To her right, in the forest thicket, she could make out the shrill call of the Siberian ptarmigan followed by a wood grouse that sounded like the distant whinnying of a horse. In that desolate wilderness, the reassuring voices of the birds sounded like a chorus of salvation. However, all Zlikha could see were the staring eyes of that unfortunate hare that had met its death in the avalanche. She tried to shift her thoughts to something else, but all she could think of were her husband's dying eyes, his sad yet simultaneously demanding stare...

Zlikha had never known the true happiness of married life. During their short time together, she had not had the time to become attached to Toremurat, and she had not experienced the prolonged affection that comes with close familiarity. The hot passion of youth had not yet cooled when he had passed on and all her ardent feelings had been transformed into the bitter pangs of loss in one fell swoop.

Toremurat had been over thirty-five when Zlikha had graduated from the accounting technical college in Semipalatinsk. Her father was a canny man and thought that his daughter, by working in trade, would be well-fed and clothed and might marry a man of means. However, Zlikha never heeded her father's advice and chose for herself a modest, lonely officer who was far from wealthy. Not six months had passed after Zlikha and Toremurat had married when the war broke out with the Japanese in Mongolia. Leaving for the front, Toremurat took his young wife to the Murat collective farm, where he and his kinsfolk lived. He had believed that Zlikha would find it easier among them. Zlikha, who had grown up in a town, knowing none of life's worries, had never thought she would end up in a remote aul lost in the middle of the taiga, but the years passed and the carefree girl who used to wear a white beret over a mischievous short haircut, had now become a young woman, burdened with the onerous lot of a widow.

Toremurat's relatives were kind to her. They gave her a house, helped her get a job at the collective farm and, in time, she became the chief accountant.

Toremurat had been seriously wounded at Khalkhin Gol in Mongolia, remained in hospital for a year and returned home with his legs amputated. Zlikha had greeted Toremurat's return the way any loving wife would meet her husband, caring for him day and night. However, she could do nothing to prevent his death. The gangrene had done its work and after a year of lying bedridden at home, Toremurat had finally died. He had passed away in silence, bitter at his lot and never saying his goodbyes to Zlikha, and all she could remember of him was his long, sad and questioning gaze.

Now she was living the life of a widow. Zlikha had never thought that she would ever become the chairwoman of the collective farm, thinking that this was the domain of men alone. However, the war came and the aul's men left for the front and the collective farmers elected her as their new chairperson. She had tried to justify the faith the aul folk had placed in her and spared no effort in her work.

Towards evening, a strong wind blew down along the river and it grew cold. Zlikha put on her heavy overcoat lying at the front of the sled. She decided not to drive the horse for there was no point; the chestnut stallion would find the way home in even the coldest and darkest of nights. In any event, it was not far to the aul. Zlikha wrapped herself in the enormous overcoat, her arms and legs completely hidden from view and her nose buried in the large, warm collar, and she leaned against the back of the sled. She wanted to recall fond memories and soothe her nerves, but, alas, nothing pleasant came to mind.

It was silent all around, the only sound in the air was the creaking of the runners on the frozen snow that now resembled grains of salt. The twilit air glowed pale blue, which meant the moon must have risen. Through the gap in her collar, Zlikha saw the three stars of the Great Bear, shining far to the north. It always amazed her how the stars shine differently with each new season. In summer they shimmer like radiant clusters while, in winter, they burn with a cold, unearthly glow. Nothing could compare with the Altai night sky and its invigorating air. Strangely, for a long time, she had missed the town life where a misty haze would hang over the streets in winter and a cloud of dust in summer. Now Zlikha tried to conjure up an image of the many crooked streets of Semipalatinsk and the old merchant's house with its familiar green gates, which had been built centuries earlier in this backwater of the empire. She tried to imagine her father and mother running out to greet her and embracing her, yet even this memory seemed shrouded in a misty haze and she could not even recall their dear faces. Although this did not unduly upset her. It was clear to her that her childhood, spent with her parents, had all been a long time ago. Zlikha's memories had been overwhelmed by the bitter yearning and solitude that accompanied her premature widowhood that had come at a time of her life when she should have been caring for her own family — loving and being loved. And yet it was thanks to her meeting her unforgettable Toremurat that had led her to the Altai, living in one of its auls and giving her all for its small collective farm. There could be nothing more precious than a life that strengthens one's faith that a happy life is just around the corner. Perhaps the strongest feeling a person can have is a dream that gives them confidence in a better future. Zlikha thought that she was blessed, for her dream was more precious than everything she had lived for up to that moment.

Zlikha awoke from the jolt of the sled that had come to a sudden halt. It turned out that she had dropped off without noticing. Probably from the cold but perhaps

150

from having lain there for so long in the same position, but she felt pins and needles in her toes, and her whole body was numb. Her head was buzzing.

The windows of the lone house were dark. There was no one to greet her after her long, arduous journey and help unharness her horse. The chestnut stallion squinted at her, snorting demandingly, and Zlikha stopped herself from going indoors, even though she was out on her feet. She did not just send the horse out to the paddock as she usually did, but untethered it, removed the harness, threw a horsecloth made from an old felt blanket over its back and put a nosebag over its head with a couple of handfuls of oats at the bottom. She had barely completed this when she heard cautious steps creeping up behind her.

There, dressed in an enormous quilted *chapan*[15] gown and felt boots, borrowed from God alone knew where, was ginger-haired Bekmurat. His eyes alone gleamed from the depths of the oversized gown. He stood there a little while like a garden scarecrow, before clearing his nose and announcing,

'Auntie Zlikha, Grandfather Zhusup wanted to invite you over to celebrate *Nauryz*[16] with us and he says to hurry up. He's worried that the broth might lose its flavour. He also asked you to bring three or four cups with you for the tea.'

'Are there going to be many people there?'

'I think he has invited all the aul's women...'

---

[15] Chapan – a long quilted coat worn over clothes, usually during the cold winter months. Usually worn by men, these coats are adorned with intricate threading and come in a variety of colours and patterns.
[16] *Nauryz* – The Muslim festival to herald the coming of spring.

Having ascertained that Zlikha would be coming, Bekmurat hurried back, dragging the tails of his chapan along the snow as he went. The times when people would invite each other over were long gone, the last remnants of their meat stores were coming to an end and for many, they were a distant memory.

Smoke billowed from old Zhusup's house. She felt awkward heading straight over, even though Zhusup had said for her to hurry. What was she to do? It was then that she remembered Kazhimurat and, reprimanding herself for having forgotten about him, she opened the door, to be greeted by the cold waft of an uninhabited house.

Old Zhusup's house, whose two rooms opened onto a small kitchen in the middle, was full of women and children, and it was as hot and stuffy as a bathhouse. Old Zhusup met Zlikha in the yard. He was wearing a chapan over his shoulders and goatskin boots on his bare feet. Fussing around Zlikha, the old man asked how her journey back from the district centre had been and how she was feeling. Having barely entered the house, he launched into his old wife,

'Oh, for the love of God, woman, I told you to take the calf and the lambs to the barn for the day! The entire house stinks of droppings!'

'I didn't want the poor things to have to stay out in the cold!' The old woman was busying herself by the hearth. 'Anyway, what's your problem with having them here? It's not as if this is the first time we've had them in the house, and it's easier to slaughter them when you've got them to hand!'

'Are you out of your mind?'

Zhusup stared at his wife in disbelief. Either the old woman had thought there were too many people in the house or it was just because of her nature, but she followed up her gruff reply by stirring the coals so vigorously with the tongs that the ashes began to pile up. Then she snatched the jug of water from her husband's hands and pushed it somewhere behind the stove.

Zlikha felt awkward and wanted to make her way through to the small room where the women were sitting, but Zhusup pointed to the sitting room, from where the chatter of the old men could be heard.

'My dear, you are more like a *dzhigit*[17] to us, so you come this way.

Kazhimurat was not among the old men and she knew he wasn't in the next room either, because Kazhimurat was not in the habit of spending time in female company. The guests were engaged in a leisurely conversation about everyday life, letters from the front and fond recollections of their lives before the war. Zlikha replied to the aul folk's questions and then sat in silence, gripped by her thoughts.

Those same collective farm problems, which she had been unable to resolve since the previous autumn, were still bothering her, day and night. Before she knew it, the dinner was over, even though goat had been the meat of the day. As was the custom, Old Zhusup, who had done the carving himself, sent the tastiest morsels to the women and children in the next room, among whom

---

[17] *Dzhigit* – A word of Turkic origin which is used in the Caucasus and Central Asia to describe a skilful and brave equestrian, or a brave person in general. In certain other contexts it is used to describe young menfolk in general.

were his daughter-in-law and nephew. In the end, the old men were left with little more than the bare bones. Dinner had been devoured in the blink of an eye. One of the old men blessed Zhusup's hospitable home and all his guests, after which Zlikha made her excuses and went out into the kitchen. She was not tempted to sit with the women who had become flushed by the mead and whose shrill songs, which contained more of a sad submission to their fate than a desire to resist its impact, she found unpleasant and irritating.

However, once she had gone outside and stood alone under the cold, clear sky, she instantly regretted not having accepted their invitation to join them. Once again, she caught sight of the knotted, kind hands of old Zhusup, who was carefully chopping meat, the trembling, work-worn hands of his old wife, offering the guests the *kozhe* — a drink made of sour-milk and oat broth, and the sad women, punctuating their sorrows with liquid mead and melancholy songs. She was alone. The Seven Sisters were shining directly overhead — dawn was still a long way off and there was a long winter's night ahead.

For a lonely person, a night such as this seems longer than it is in reality.

She approached her house and cast her eyes around, looking for the chestnut stallion. Then, rather perplexed, she stared at the gate and understood she had not come home but to the old mill. Realising this, Zlikha abruptly and screwing up every ounce of her strength threw open the door and said to Kazhimurat, who was sitting there, hunched over the stove,

'Let's go home!'

154

5

'This foreign species takes root fast and grows quickly,' Zakhair said as he pointed with his whip handle to the nearby hill, its southern slope covered in thick birch saplings. 'There were just dry twigs, the size of your little finger at first but in five years they have taken off and have completely changed the landscape. It's a shame we planted so few of them. We had no idea that these larches would make the land so beautiful. Now, though, you can't get your hands on these saplings anywhere.'

The old man strapped five or six ptarmigans and a couple of partridges he had shot that day to the saddle. With a short flick of the thumb, he inserted the bit into the teeth of his sag-bellied, bay horse.

'You good-for-nothing cross-breed! You're more pig than horse. It's high time we plugged up that belly of yours!'

The dense woodland thicket steamed, the air heavy with the smell of resin. Spiders were tumbling from the tops of tall larches, portending rain. Given the way the low-bellied bay was keeping its head in the grass, it was clear the shower would soon pass.

Zakhair still had his strength, for he would leap into the saddle like a young lad and sit upright in the saddle. Only recently his thin, protruding beard had begun to reveal the odd grey hair. The sun would shine through his large red ears the size of burdocks and the skin on his face had a greasy sheen. His forehead was still smooth and his neck as strong as ever, without the sinews and hanging skin you'd usually expect to see on an old man. He still rode with his right shoulder forward, as if cutting through the air, and his whip rocked in his right hand in time with the horse's motion. You could spot Zakhair the hell-raiser and livewire from a mile off. Kazhimurat had rarely seen someone who, at the age of seventy, remained so immune to the ravages of time.

The old man yanked on the girth strap after he had climbed into the saddle. The bay horse jerked forward, its hooves angrily striking its belly. The creature's eyes almost leapt from their sockets and one might have thought the poor creature had been stabbed with a knife.

'They say it's best when the animal's character is aligned with the master's,' Zakhair muttered. 'But this, my one and only horse, behaves like it sprang from a cow and kicks out as if that's what it's one purpose in life is for! For God's sake! Drop dead, already!'

Kazhimurat was tired, he was unaccustomed to being on horseback. His legs were cramped from the tension and his backside was numb from his awkward and uncomfortable position. Almurat's much-vaunted steed, which he had boasted was powerful and quick, had turned out to be a timid beast. It quailed at every shadow along the way, shook its head restlessly and incessantly tugged at the reins so that after an hour in, Kazhimurat's arms had become quite sore.

'Let's quit while we're ahead and turn for home,' the old man said. 'My old woman is probably whinnying away at home like an impatient foal for its mother. Hee-hee-hee! What a wife she is! There are times she might rush at me with fists flailing and there's no place to hide. Oh, there is nothing worse at this age than being on the receiving end of a beating from your own wife. Have you seen her eyes? They're like a butting billy goat's, they are!'

Even when joking awkwardly like this, Zakhair would remain true to form. He had been one of the first in the aul to return from the war in the summer of nineteen forty-five. True, he hobbled rather than walked but that was because he was wearing a felt boot on one foot and an army one on the other, and he sported a single medal on his chest. For several days his compatriots never left his side, asking him what the medal was for and Zakhair made some awkward joke that it had been 'For drinking vodka by the glassful. In our parts, we judge a man's ability to take the drink by the ladleful but there they measure a man's strength by the glass.' Kiyakmurt had scolded him terribly, saying that it was most unbecoming for a frontline soldier to say such things. Zakhair had allowed him his angry dressing-down and simply grinned to himself.

The bay horse was trotting obediently along the banks of the Bukhtarma. A malignant northerly wind had blown away the spider webs between the trees and was now burrowing into the travellers' bare necks like a wasp's sting. Down below, at the very bottom of the ravine, small houses could be seen along the river banks, the run-down cottages of a livestock farm. Smoke billowed from the chimneys.

'Those old Altai auls used to be full of life!' the old man remarked, pointing down with the handle of his whip. 'The forest has thinned like my beard. You can't keep the livestock out on the summer pasture where the grass has all been trampled, while the taiga is nothing like what it used to be and has very few birds and wild animals now.'

The old man was right. On the hills, once covered with forest, sparse, bare trees stood like gravestones. The mountain tops were now bald, their slopes like bristly, unshaven cheekbones. Instead of dense green forest, it was now bare with the occasional stand of scanty bushes. Even on the bends of the Bukhtarma, the larches stood black and orphaned, one crooked, the other with its top split. They looked like the lumber and other detritus that had been left unwanted and abandoned at the site of the old aul. There was nothing here now to remind Kazhimurat of the magnificent landscape that he had witnessed in his childhood long ago.

'Ugh, you pig!'

The old man whipped the bay horse in the groin for stumbling on even ground. The whip bounced off the horse's hide as if from a dried canvas sack. The horse didn't flinch. Not even an ear flickered. All it did was tear at the reed heads with its lips and continue to plod down the slope. The wind blew, twisting the dry, black blades of grass by the sharp-peaked haystacks in the small hollows. Hawks perched motionless on top of the haystacks, on the look out for field mice. One might be forgiven for mistaking them for rocks placed there to keep the hay in place. And that was about all that was going on in the taiga at this time. In place of a rich, verdant forest, with plenty of hay and wheat sown out in the meadows, all that grew now were gaunt birches with unhealthy brown.stripes on their trunks. The further they descended, the broader the path became and soon Kazhimurat was riding alongside Zakhair. The bay horse, accustomed to having the tufts of grass to itself, immediately flattened its ears to its head, bared its teeth and bit the gelding carrying Kazhimurat.

'Oh, for the love of God,' The old man snapped once more.

Large drops of rain from a thin shower pattered onto the old man's raincoat and the horses' flanks. As soon as the path reached the mountain stream, the bay horse, ignoring the urging of its rider, rushed down and only came to a stop once it had entered the bubbling water. You might have thought the creature had just trekked through a desert and not the taiga, where the water was plentiful at every turn. The old man stared at length at the horse's pointed ears, which twitched with every gulp of water it took. The bay's belly became even more distended. Finally, it tore its head from the water and cast a glance back, as if making sure there really was no space left. Then, with a shake of its lips, it trotted decisively on, its hooves crunching on the pebbles below. Inflated like a balloon, the bay horse clambered onto the opposite bank and Zakhair, seemingly waking from a torpor, spoke again:

'These places were taken away from the farm and given to the logging enterprise the same year I returned from the Labour Army. Since that time, the logging enterprise was put *in charge* of these parts. It was as if a fire was deliberately set and spread through the hills. After that, they just abandoned these places to the mercy of fate and simply left. There's a *sovkhoz*[18] farm here now

---

[18] Sovkhoz – A large, state–owned farm in the Soviet Union. The average size of a sovkhoz was 15,300 hectares (153 km²), nearly three times the average kolkhoz (5,900 hectares or 59 km²)

but the land is no good for anything anymore. About five years ago, the logging enterprise planted five thousand fir saplings here. Not a tree has been planted since then. The farm has no time for that kind of thing, you know how it is. And that is how we lose the riches of our region. Oh, for the love of God!'

The old man yanked hard on the reins as the horse lowered its head to drink again, as they passed through a ditch along the way. Then he smacked his booted heels against the creature's ribs, but the horse simply switched its tail, curled like a twig, and came to a halt. The horse had won that little battle and the old man returned to his conversation.

'You know Russian, right? Can you help me write a letter to the authorities?' He asked Kazhimurat. 'What will be will be... We Kazakhs have a reputation for writing proposals and letters of all sorts, so let mine, an old forester's, be added to their pile. If it results in a few more trees in the world that would be a good thing. Although I don't know what good it'd do...'

A brief shower of rain pattered down, the horses' sides grew darker and the clatter of their hooves became softer. The rain began to recede along the Bukhtarma, and soon a bright rainbow glowed in the distance, hanging like a technicolour tabernacle over the dark gulley below. The rays of the setting sun lay over the aspens and birches like a golden-yellow blanket. The evening breeze dispelled the heavy dampness that had been reposing in the forest glade. In the meantime, the old man's complaints poured forth like a torrent. If it were up to him, he would forbid anyone from taking an axe to even the rottenest tree. After all, even a tree like that has its purpose in nature. However, now every regional and district authority and every household and individual seemed to see the taiga as some implacable evil enemy that needed to be exterminated at all costs. Everyone had taken something from the bountiful taiga's parlour, only they never bothered replenishing it. The old man was still listing the sins of the region's local residents when they finally reached a small village, nestled on the banks of the Bukhtarma.

A small gable-roofed log house was surrounded by outbuildings. About twenty sheep and goats were crowded in an open pen and five or six cows and their calves lay tethered nearby. Old man Zakhair had done rather well for himself.

'As you know, we Kazakhs like to count our wealth in livestock rather than money,' Zakhair remarked, catching Kazhimurat's look. 'It was thanks to these few head of livestock that I was able to get a job as a forester. During the summer there's plenty of grass while, in winter, they give you a combination of mixed feed and fodder. I didn't build the house just anywhere but on the land of the *sovkhoz* collective farm. And with good reason. You see, it is easier to live with people close by and the farm gets something from it too.'

The old man kept looking round at Kazhimurat who was now lying on a felt rug on the wooden floor of the covered gazebo. He wanted Kazhimurat to pay full attention to everything he was saying.

'My children are of little use, they've all remarried and gone away now. As they say, your own calf is dearer to you than the ox that is held in common. They come to see us if there's something worth having. You know our

Bekmurat, don't you?! Well, he's hanging about in Alma-Ata these days. He got it into his head that he wants to become a journalist. Occasionally they print certain things of his in the papers. The only thing is that he doesn't have the... I don't know... the nous... the gift. Where could he possibly get such a thing when there was not a single person of worth on his mother's side?' Zakhair gestured with his chin towards the awning, under which the old five-seater GAZ jeep was standing. 'He bought this car but now it's just sitting here rusting without an owner.'

'Oh, Allah, who would have thought that Kazhimurat would come visiting?' Old Rapiya could not conceal her surprise at the arrival of the unexpected guest. 'It's been so many years! We have often thought of you here. You've been missed, you have. Oh, so missed!'

Rapiya found time to milk the cow and drive the creature back into the barn. Once she had been large, broad in the bone, so to speak. Now, not quite at sixty years old, she had grown so big that her doughy body protruded from her fully buttoned doublet, and her plump face glistened beneath her *kimeshek* headdress. 'What's with the waddling about like a duck before feeding time?' The old man shouted at her. 'Off to the stove with you! Have you browned that leg of mutton?'

'The kitchen is my business! Quit poking your nose where it doesn't belong!' Rapiya snapped back, her enormous frame swaying.

Zakhair raked the glowing embers from the hearth and crouched down, holding the ptarmigans, strung on a three-pronged birch branch over them. Their drooping necks jerked the moment they touched the flames as if

163

they had come back to life. The old man ran his fingers over the charred remains of the birds' feathers and, waiting for the grease to drip onto the fire, he raked the embers some more and raised the branch higher.

'Hey, wife, bring me some flour would you?! Or else all the fat will go to waste in the ash!'

Rapiya silently moved in the direction of the house.

'You see how your auntie's let herself go?' The old man said, his eyes following his wife. 'Not like before, you remember? More like a mare than a woman these days! Nothing like what she used to be... She spends all day moaning, complaining about her heart or some other condition. Takes a few steps and gets quite breathless. I reckon all her ailments are the result of her idleness. Even the *Karabair* gets fat when it hasn't been touched by the whip for a long time.

Rapiya approached, shuffling along in her boots.

'Have you gone mad?' The old man exclaimed, seeing that she had brought a full bowl of flour. 'It's not as if I'm smoking a yearling here!'

'I have my own things to attend to. I still have to bake the baursak buns. And here you are sitting there, taking up the entire hearth and keeping me from getting on with the cooking.'

'Ah, what's the hurry? Ptarmigan loses its flavour if you don't take your time roasting it. It's been such a long time since we last had game. Run along to the garden, eh? Bring me plenty of onions.'

Zakhair rolled the fat carcasses of the birds in some flour and then, holding them over the fire, he took a handful of flour and carefully sprinkled it over the places where it had yet to stick. Soon, the ptarmigan had swollen up to become the size of two fists. Rapiya's shuffling boots could once more be heard coming from behind the old man's back and a bunch of spring onions dropped to the floor beside him. The shuffling sound then began to recede.

'Hey, wife, why don't you get some help from those mares, idling away down on the farm?! They're going to burst one day from all the food they scoff at our expense!'

'They'll be round any minute now as it is!' Rapiya's voice replied from the kitchen. 'You watch, the first to arrive will be that Kiyakmurt and his Zlikha!' Kazhimurat shuddered on hearing the familiar name. Rapiya put a bottle of vodka and some glasses on the table. Noticing the change in Kazhimurat's face, she began to cautiously tell him about the changes that had taken place in the village while he had been away.

'My dear, our Zlikha now works as the head of the farm. After you left, she married that Kiyakmurt. He's working with the cows now. Poor woman, she was never destined to have her own child. She adopted a little girl from the orphanage and is raising her.'

Kazhimurat's heart skipped a beat, but he gave the old woman no indication of his agitated state. Rapiya took a bag of kurt and irimshik that was hanging on a nail and emptied the contents onto the table. Walking out, she nudged the old man in the side, who was still tinkering by the hearth.

'What are you doing still loafing about here for nothing? Give me back my hearth, you hear? Go on, off with you!'

Zakhair didn't even grace her with a look. He took the ptarmigans from the branch, removed their feet and wings with his knife and placed the birds onto a flat bowl. Then he rinsed the onions in a bucket of water, put them on top of the birds and placed the dish before Kazhimurat.

'I see that my old mare of a wife has spoiled your mood.' The old man filled two glasses to the brim with vodka. 'That's all those women are good for, chattering their heads off whenever they get the chance... It must be twenty whole years since we last saw you. So, let's drink to meeting up again!'

However, the old man didn't drink much and he ate even less. He turned the birds over from one side to the other, pushed them closer to Kazhimurat and began pouring out his heart again.

The old woman, now busy cooking the baursak buns in spitting oil, was also more relaxed. The dusk was descending, the damp chill of the river was beginning to fall, and the murmur of the Bukhtarma was getting deeper as if its waters were flowing beneath a crust of ice. The fire in the hearth had gone out and the smoke was beginning to disperse when the women appeared, the idle 'mares' from the farm that Zakhair had been referring to. A diesel engine rumbled in the distance and Zakhair's house filled with light. Bulbs burned in the rooms, out in the yard and in the barns.

'Hey, old man, why don't you come inside and show off the rich dowry your wife has brought you?' Rapiya's voice resonated from the kitchen, where she was still fussing over the food. 'You'll be eaten alive by the midges out there!'

'Nah. It's better sitting out here in the open air than suffocating inside.'

Zakhair pulled a long, yellow-handled knife from the pouch attached to his belt, turned over the edge of the blanket and took a whetstone. If the old woman had called them in that must have meant the meat was ready.

Kazhimurat initially found Zakhair and Rapiya's exchanges puzzling, which were at best barbed and often downright rude. They didn't strike him as having lived a long and difficult life together. Later, however, he realised that Rapiya, once a mighty, tireless ox of a woman, and Zakhair, who had never turned down any job or shown fatigue were now showing their age and these clumsy jokes of theirs were simply their way of cheering each other up. Their old life had passed and they were trying as best they could to fill the void. Further evidence of this was the fact that Zakhair had immediately gone to slaughter a ram and Rapiya, to prepare the baursak buns — a sign of their eagerness to alleviate their loneliness and see their neighbours in their home.

As soon as the guests would arrive, they would both come to life, happily bustling about, seating the newcomers in their seats and doing their best to keep them entertained. It was clear that the aul's small community had long grown used to Zakhair and Rapiya's hospitality because the place was soon overflowing with people, old and young.

Kazhimurat was surprised to see how many members of the aul he didn't know. The young people, of course, had grown up in the long period of his absence but it struck him as strange that there were so many unfamiliar faces among the older guests. The aul wasn't the sort of place that strangers would choose to settle in.

The women, as Zakhair had remarked that day, and not without a certain irony, really were quite plump and healthy and it seemed that their dresses might burst at any moment. Shamshinur came in, her tongue as sharp as ever and she immediately got her teeth stuck into Kazhimurat:

'You must be about the only Kazakh I know who prefers to hang around with the Kerzhaks. Why haven't we heard any news of you for so many years?'

'Well, he's here now, so you can share all the news you've been saving up right now, can't you?' Rapiya said, in an attempt to bring her to reason. 'There you go, chattering away at him like a magpie. You could at least have said *hello* first, you rascal!'

However, stopping Shamshinur was never going to be that easy.

'Whatever news I might have been saving for him has long since gone to others. How was I to find him?'

'Stop ruffling your feathers like a cock at the hen house! You'd be better off helping me with the meat instead!' Rapiya invited Shamshinur to get up from the bench and join her at the hearth.

'Hasn't Zlikha arrived yet then?' Shamshinur cast a final barb to rub salt into Kazhimurat's wound. 'Is she dealing with the calving or something? Her mild-mannered moustachioed husband appears to have become a mouse among men, just like our Uncle Zakhair here.'

'Go on, don't pull any punches?' Zakhair replied, upset. 'Be sure to hang all my dirty laundry for everyone to see, be sure not to forget anything!'

'Well, in seventy years your laundry has become so soiled, Uncle Zakhair, we can barely see the dirt for the linen.'

'Go on, get away with you! What a gob, you've got on you!' Zakhair laughed as he followed her with his eyes.

Kazhimurat prayed that Zlikha wouldn't come. He hadn't known that she had married the former local policeman Kiyakmurt and every time it was mentioned it made his heart ache. He was angry at his brother Almurat for not letting him go home after repairing the old mill and for persuading him to stay in his native aul, insisting that he visit this remote farm as well. There was evidently much truth in the saying that joy is never far from its sister, woe. That whole day Kazhimurat had listened to the old man with a quiet joy, laughed at his jokes, let off steam on the long journey through the taiga and had even enjoyed a decent bit of hunting. Now, however, as if by way of pay-back for all the good he had enjoyed that day, he had now been informed about Zlikha and the past clouded his eyes once more. His heart ached with the pain, reminding him of the incredible loss that he had once had to suffer.

Rapiya decided to feed the hungry children first. She was worried that they might fall asleep where they sat while the adults were eating, so she chased them into the house, fed them and only then served the food to the adults. She brought in a mutton head on a platter which, in a Kazakh home, would be served to the most honoured guest. The skin on the head hung in juicy flaps. It appeared that Rapiya had been fussing over the children and had failed to keep an eye on the meat, causing it to become a little overcooked. The light bulb hanging from the wall flashed as if it had been waiting for the hostess finally to join her guests.

'Oh, Allah, is it twelve o'clock already?' Rapiya said, agitated. Someone run to the mechanic and get him to keep the lights on until the morning.'

'Don't worry about it, Auntie Rapiya!' Shamshinur interrupted. 'He does this every night. As soon as anyone gathers together for dinner, he starts playing his tricks again. As they say, every village has its idiot. We should send him a glass of vodka and then he'll fall asleep at his post until morning.'

Everybody laughed in unison. At that moment, two figures appeared in the evening twilight.

'I should have known, wherever there's a commotion Shamshinur will, sure enough, be at the centre of it!' Zlikha's voice rang out. 'There's never a house with smoke wafting from its hearth where she isn't a guest.'

'Are you worried there's not going to be anything left for you?' Shamshinur responded in kind. 'You shouldn't have spent the entire evening plastering on all that make-up, it's not as if anyone's going to be looking your way in any event.'

Kiyakmurt greeted Kazhimurat stiffly and Zlikha, seeing him, stopped what she was saying mid-sentence and went unusually quiet. There was no mistaking her silence for the usual restraint of a Kazakh woman who refrains from joining in the conversation when there are men seated around the table. As bloated and huge as a *saba* leather bottle made from the hides of five mares, Zlikha was barely able to squeeze into the vacant seat. She was so overweight that it was hard to recognise the young, energetic woman bursting with life that she had

170

once been. Kiyakmurt, who had never been particularly large, now looked like a gnarled, dried-out old tree stump.

'I thought that Almurat had come to see the livestock...'

Zlikha had barely completed her sentence when the sound of a motorcycle came rattling through the night. The bright headlight cut through the darkness and soon the motorbike came to a stop in the yard, blinding everyone sitting on the wooden benches inside.

'Oh, speak of the devil!' Shamshinur said. 'The management simply couldn't possibly allow any meal served on their premises to be eaten without them. He might have been a day's ride away, but he'd have made it to the table in a flash.'

'Oh, my dear auntie, I see you are as generous with your kind words as ever!' Almurat removed his helmet and tossed it into a nearby empty cradle. 'What is it they say — the poor man has the well-being of the rich man at heart? So, why don't you help me wash some of the road off me after my journey.'

Shamshinur rushed over with the long-necked water jug and carried on where she'd left off, as she poured the water over his hands.

'In your childhood, I would have given your ears a good boxing for that but now, unfortunately, my arms aren't long enough. You're not such a big shot, really, but to us, you are still the management. That said, you do have your shrewish wife who has you wrapped around her little finger to give you a hard time. Poor Almurat! Yours is not such an easy lot, is it?'

'I've just sent her back to her family!'

'Well... Today you sent her back, tomorrow you'll be running after her again. I know you only too well. It's just another argument that's going to cost you your entire month's wage packet.'

'I don't think so this time, Aunt Shamshinur.'

'My dear boy! Don't go throwing bad money after good! It's much easier these days to lose your motorbike and have to get around on foot than it is to get rid of a shrewish wife.'

'Stop wagging your tongues, the pair of you!' Old Rapiya interrupted them angrily. 'Now sit down at the dastarkhan or the meat will get cold!'

'Quite right! The meat won't taste so good if it gets cold,' Zakhair backed her up. 'I don't know what's wrong with the sheep these days. Before you finish carving it up, it becomes as hard as a goat and all the fat ends up on your fingers instead of the plate.' Zakhair sighed.

There was a lot of truth in what the old man said: the mountain auls no longer kept the breeds of sheep that they used to have on the steppe. But it wasn't the sheep's fault that the guests did not immediately sit down and set to. A certain chill and awkwardness had fallen on the company after Kiyakmurt and Zlikha's arrival and the old man, in his own way was trying smooth things over. Even Shamshinur's efforts at injecting a bit of jollity into the proceedings couldn't dispel it.

After Almurat's arrival, the young people moved a bit closer to the door, making room for him at the place of honour. Rapiya poured the rich broth over the meat, and Zakhair opened a bottle of vodka with the tip of a knife.

'I reckon life will be a bit dull without her, my dear boy!' The old man grunted. 'What do you say Almurat, do you think it's time for a warmer?'

'I'm driving!'

'But there are loads of others here who came on foot,' the old man objected.

'Where are you going to ride off to at this time of night?' Rapiya turned to Almurat. 'You were only just boasting that you're as free as the wind, there's no one you need to rush back to tonight. Why not stay over the night with us? Your old Auntie Shamshinur has a spare *syrmak* under her bed.'

'Oh, don't leave him here, Auntie Rapiya!' Shamshinur carried on winding Almurat up and looking pointedly at the young girls and women. 'You won't get an ounce of goodness out of him but you will get a whole hundred weight of grief. There'd be no end to the gossip... Ow!'

Rapiya had just given Shamshinur a painful pinch. Everyone around laughed merrily.

Quite aware that Shamshinur would stop at nothing until she had hung everyone's last bit of dirty laundry up for inspection, Almurat distracted her with a large glass of vodka.

'I stopped by the central office,' he said, filling a dozen empty glasses clustered on the dastarkhan. 'They say there's going to be a regional gathering of livestock breeders. I don't know how our top workers are going to be feted, but one thing's for sure: Uncle Zakhair will return from it with a new *chapan* on his shoulders, and Auntie Rapiya with a carpet in her hands. Although I have to say, we're a long way behind the women at the

Aksu farm. They know a thing or two about their thoroughbred cows!'

Shamshinur immediately rose to the bait. 'If you can get me ten more milking cows then you'll be walking around like the cock of the walk!'

'Why don't you ask Zlikha for them? She's in charge of that department.'

'What'd be the point, she'd never give them to me! All her cows are infertile these days...'

And realising too late that she'd inadvertently put her foot in it, Shamshinur abruptly changed the subject of the conversation.

'Prizes aren't the most important thing, they get given to those who've worked hard,' she said. 'Summer is coming to an end, Almurat. You've driven us out into this wilderness, and none of us has seen our families all summer. And what about the young folk? People need to see each other — it's no joke, our most esteemed chairman. People need to get out, you know...'

Shamshinur threw the sheep's shin bone in front of Almurat. It was a custom in the aul for a man to be given the shin bone and for him to break it with a blow of the fist and offer the marrow to the elders. But Almurat did not manage with his first blow and it went spinning round in a circle. Kiyakmurt also failed to prove his strength. Finally, the thick five-year-old ram's thick shin bone was placed in front of Kazhimurat. With one blow of his huge fist, it cracked, and a section of it rebounded off the wall and hit Kiyakmurt on the cheekbone. Kazhimurat pulled up short and cursed to himself. As if things weren't bad enough! Kiyakmurt had clearly taken this freak accident as a personal affront because he sat where he was for a minute and then got up.

'I've sat around longer than I meant to, it's probably time to drive the cattle to pasture. Otherwise, you'll give me a hard time if the cows start producing less milk.' He turned to his wife. 'Are you going to stay on here?'

Zlikha felt it would be awkward to immediately jump up and run after her husband. And it was unfair of her husband to turn this accident into a deliberate slight on Kazhimurat's part.

'I'll sit with everyone else for a while if it's all the same to you,' she answered with a menacing, heavy challenge in her voice. 'I'll leave it to you to drive the herd to pasture on your own if that's okay?'

Kiyakmurt left, and Zlikha was able to settle down more comfortably, literally, now that her husband's place had been freed up next to her. Her plump warm knee touched Kazhimurat's leg.

The cockerel gave a stifled crow. With a resigned sigh, the cows lying tied to their tethers began to get up. Zakhair did not want the guests to go so early and he began to fuss around them again.

'What's the rush, the morning is still far over the horizon,' he began to persuade them. 'The nights are now long and you'll have plenty of time to sleep.'

'Hey, old ladies, are we just going to sit here and squawk like chickens?' Shamshinur exclaimed. 'Let's sing a song.'

The women nudged each other but none of them dared to get things going. Then, one of the younger girls asked Shamshinur to sing, but this proposal did not arouse Almurat's enthusiasm.

'Whatever you do, don't ask her!' He exclaimed in mock horror. 'If Auntie Shamshinur starts singing, the melancholy and anguish will kill us all.'

But Shamshinur had already started:

> '*How many years have gone by since?*
> *My hand was given in marriage*
> *And cursing my woman's lot,*
> *I now live and reproach my fate.*
>
> *More and more often I dream at night,*
> *Of the time of my carefree youth,*
> *When the burden of my bitter years had not yet stooped my shoulders,*
> *Old age is a cruel and heavy mountain!'*

Her weak, quavering voice was barely audible at first, but then it got stronger, and when Zlikha sang along with her, the melody gained strength and floated over the night-time aul. It was as if the darkness had been chased away and everything all around felt more spacious. The melody splashed over the small village of livestock breeders and Kazhimurat's heart ached, not having heard his aul's native songs for so long. It was as if burning embers had been thrown into his soul, and his memory of the old days had been rekindled with its everyday, semi-starved, hard, collective farm life and thin girlish faces with heavy braids on their shoulders... He remembered what Zlikha had been like, recalling her statuesque, almost sculpted, young body, her high breasts, peeking out from under her unbuttoned sheepskin coat, the intoxicating warmth that she exuded, and it seemed to him, he could once again feel her heat, desire and longing being transmitted through her knee that was now tightly pressed against his. Kazhimurat's body instantly froze, his heart pounded loudly, invitingly. He wished that this feeling would never leave him again, so that that dear and distant world might not sink back into the past and oblivion, but the song ended as suddenly as it had begun. Zlikha rested her elbow on Kazhimurat's knee seemingly without even noticing it.

'Of all the songs they could have come up with!' Aunt Rapiya sighed. There were tears in her eyes. There was silence for a while, everyone contemplating their own lives full of their own share of joy and pain.

'Right, that's enough, I'm emotionally exhausted,' Zlikha exclaimed and nudged Shamshinur, 'Let's go home! Otherwise, your old man will take a stick to your back, Rapiya, for keeping him up so late!'

'Oh don't worry. He'll just grumble and then calm down,' Rapiya replied trying to lighten the mood. 'And we all ought to be used to the stick by now, we've put up with it one way or another for long enough.'

'Well, I'd better be on my way!' Zlikha said. 'Kazhimurat, could you walk me back? As you know only too well, at night here it's dead easy here to slip and break a leg.'

The road was covered with a silvery frost and it was indeed slippery. The hills piled up like waves and the watery mist that shrouded the river obscured the horizon. It was quiet in the village, only a few of the houses still had their lights on. The muffled hum of the separators issued from the oil station like the rumble of a receding aircraft. Zlikha's house greeted them with silence and dark windows. She hesitated at the door and suddenly suggested to Kazhimurat,

'I still can't sleep tonight. Let's go up to the next hill.'

Kazhimurat shifted uneasily from one foot to the other. The recent scene in Zakhair's house was still fresh in his memory: a husband is still a husband, and Kiyakmurt had left unhappy.

Zlikha dispelled Kazhimurat's doubts.

'I'm not of an age when a husband gets jealous,' she sighed, smiling sadly. 'What's there to say? It's clear we are just two halves of a single whole. Each of us has their own half, and that's how it's remained...'

In Zakhair's yard, a motor rumbled and a headlight flashed, as if it was searching for something in the night, and a motorcycle emerged onto the road and sped off towards the taiga. The aul dogs barked hoarsely but immediately fell silent and, following their lead, the motorbike, which had illuminated up to a dozen houses, did likewise. A heavy silence hung over the village.

Zlikha told Kazhimurat about her life, but her story was far from the open confession he feared it might be and he was grateful to her for that. There was a fresh breeze at the top of the hill. After wandering a little along the ridge itself, they descended down to the conical haystacks. The hay was surrounded by a ditch and, in order to get over it, Kazhimurat had to lift Zlikha in his arms. And again, the familiar smell of her body hit him, and almost the only really precious picture from his difficult and lonely life appeared in his mind's eye: the young, statuesque Zlikha in an unbuttoned sheepskin coat with her black hair poking out from under her downy scarf, her cheeks rosy from the frost... He didn't even feel her weight. He leaned towards Zlikha's face and saw the familiar, warm radiance of the eyes of a woman who had once been the only person in the entire aul who had taken his pain and suffering to her heart and warmed his soul that had frozen like a stone. He was ready to do anything to make her feel good, at peace...

They were sitting on the leeward side of a haystack smelling of summer, and Zlikha laid her head on Kazhimurat's shoulder and wept. Her plump body trembled with her sobs and in the restrained moans there was so much bitterness and resentment for a failed life that Kazhimurat groaned, squeezing her in his arms. Probably, only he could have withstood the hardships that fate had hurled at him, and only a nature as strong as Zlikha's could have endured the hardships that had fallen on her female lot and which would have crushed any other woman in her place. It is strange that what has long been experienced does not leave a person until the end of their days... Zlikha's hot breath and bitter tears transported Kazhimurat back to the forties once more...

* * *

The warm days had finally set in, and the southern slopes of the hills were covered with vegetation. It was a difficult spring that year. Somehow or other, they had managed to get through winter. God alone knew how they had managed to cling to life when suddenly a new misfortune hit: a dust storm hit the aul and encircled it for a whole week. People wandered around like shadows, and there was nothing left on the livestock but skin and bones. The aul only came to its senses when the sowing was finished and people gradually began to put themselves and their ramshackle households back in order again. Kazhimurat had now been tasked full-time with the heaviest and most difficult work: day and night it was his duty to deliver the grain to the regional collection office. The ice on the rivers became thinner and the roads were washed out completely, but he daren't ask for help from the old men who could barely shuffle around the aul or the women who already had so many cares on their plate.

Single-handedly, he was left in charge of driving a column of twenty sleigh teams. He would head out onto the road early in the morning, while the road had not yet been washed away. On the way, the sleds fell apart, the knees of the oxen and horses buckled from fatigue, some of them falling right onto the road, and Kazhimurat was forced to drag the sacks of grain on his own back to make it easier for the unfortunate animals to make it up the frequent ascents. And, indeed, he himself sometimes collapsed from exhaustion, but he would get up again and, gritting his teeth, he would plod onwards. His journeys through the hills and taiga were as arduous as a furious assault. But even in those incredibly difficult days, no one heard a single complaint from him. Ragged, emaciated and wearing a sheepskin coat that hung in tatters from his shoulders, he looked like an old wolf, slowly and surely making his way despite his continuous battles with enemies. The steppe wolf, it is well known, never shows any sign of weakness even in the dying moments of his life.

On one occasion, Kazhimurat left the village at noon, changing his usual rule of trying to drive the teams most of the way at night, when it was still cold, or early in the morning, when the ground was still hard. On that day, he had been held up for several hours trying to put the draft animals in order. But when Zlikha asked him, he could not refuse her persistent requests. Kazhimurat understood Zlikha's anxiety and her desire, albeit belatedly, to deliver the last sacks of grain to the district centre. Of course, there was also the matter of Kiyakmurt writing a report accusing the collective of sabotage, so there was nothing for it but to hitch up this last consignment at this inconvenient hour. Kazhimurat did not wait for night to set in and he left at noon, hoping that perhaps he would be able to make the sixty-kilometre journey to the district centre without incident.

The wind was blowing hard on the mountain peak and the northern slopes, still completely covered with snow, had avalanche trails stretching all the way down them. It was warm in the taiga — the damp snow, the consistency of wet salt, stuck to the runners and the sled's progress became more and more difficult. The column train stretched for a whole kilometre and Kazhimurat only managed to collect all the sleds together at the drifts that had heaped up next to the Bukhtarma. Then he took a deep breath and ordered Almurat, who had followed him thus far, to return home. Further on, he would have to pass over thin ice, and he did not want to put the boy in any unnecessary danger.

Almurat had got into the habit of escorting him to the *Black Hole* every day. He didn't want to leave Kazhimurat on his own. The boy felt sorry for him and it seemed to him that the hardest work was always being foisted onto his cousin's shoulders because he was all alone in the world. No one would look for Kazhimurat if he were to get lost in the taiga and no one would mourn him if he died... But Kazhimurat had no time to be worried about his young cousin's feelings. So, this time, like all the others, having reached the *Black Hole*, Kazhimurat waved his hand to him, which was the sign that he should now return back to the aul.

Almurat, constantly digging his heels into his two-year-old bay stallion with its muddy matted coat, climbed the hill and looked back. The ice-bound river gleamed in the sun like the back of a dark brown snake, and the caravan crawled along it slowly, stopping first in one place and then another, separating and reuniting again, and behind it walked Kazhimurat, his tiny figure moving like a tiny dot against the immense landscape. The thought entered Almurat's head that his cousin was leaving for good, reproaching everyone for leaving him all alone on this deserted winter road. He wanted to whip his bay stallion, gallop after the caravan and catch him up. After all, Kazhimurat was the only person in the whole wide world who he held close to his heart. And now, as he diminished further and further in the distance, finally disappearing beyond the thick foliage of the taiga, it suddenly seemed to the boy that just a little further and he would lose his cousin forever. But stronger than his initial boyish impulse to follow him was the realisation that in this boundless expanse only someone as immensely strong and dogged as Kazhimurat could fight and survive... For the first time, Almurat imagined how powerless and tiny his own heart was and how weak and pitiful he was. He wiped away his tears with his sleeve, whipped the two-year-old and galloped towards the village, not waiting to see Kazhimurat turn towards the *Black Hole.*

The most difficult thing for a lone traveller is to find something to do that might at least distract him for a few minutes from the obsessive thoughts associated with the dangerous road ahead. Kazhimurat no longer remembered how many times he had walked back and forth along the column, checking the teams' harnesses. But even this did not help — his heart still felt a certain restlessness. He tried to banish all thoughts from his head and look down at his feet, but soon his head began to spin. Then he decided to take a break: he caught up with the last sled, fell on it and immediately felt very tired — his legs ached and his body felt as if it had been filled with a lead weight.

The fathomless sky circled slowly overhead, the trees scattered to the sides, the jutting horns of the oxen swayed through the clear air in a measured fashion, and the sled moved in smooth jerks. He found himself dropping off. It occurred to Kazhimurat that it would take a lot of effort to drag himself up off the sled again. But then he remembered that the main trials lay ahead when he would still have to lift and carry sacks on his back, unharness and harness the oxen back to the sleds and untangle and repair the traces. He wanted to lift himself up and at least sit, but he did not even have the strength to do this. His forehead was burning and his eyeballs pressed back into their sockets. At moments like these, the best thing you can do is to fall asleep for a minute or two, but even this was not possible and so, he rode on in some kind of hellish half-sleep, a sort of incomprehensible limbo between dream and reality.

Vague pictures and a few fragments of phrases came to mind; something bothered him, not letting him forget... An image of iron bedsteads, standing in a row in the cold dormitory of his orphanage, and then the prison cell with its small barred window floated into his mind...

In his brief twenty years of life, he had drunk as deeply from the cup of suffering as many others do over an entire lifetime. Like many other people looking for an easy life, as a young boy, he left the orphanage. He boarded the first train he came across, as if it were a steed his own father had given him, and then rode it aimlessly far and wide throughout Siberia, spending his nights on the station platforms, as if his own mother had made a soft bed for him there. He must have met every kind of person on his travels! All of them claimed that they wanted to help him, promising him all sorts of wonders. But in reality, none of them wished him any real good, and his wanderings ended up teaching him little more than how to be a vagrant.

The years spent away from his native parts increasingly began to seem like a fruitless ordeal. In the end, ragged and hungry, he returned to the orphanage he had run away from in search of a better life. It was only here that he found people who were not completely indifferent to his fate. The mattress, stuffed with rotten straw, was too small for him now, but it was nevertheless his bed. The orphanage workers treated Kazhimurat well and set him up in the local college. Although the food was not great, he was as well fed as everyone else and never went hungry.

The barracks he lived in were stuffy in summer and cold in winter. He would be woken early in the morning, and work from morning to evening, interspersed with classes and study. As the years passed, Kazhimurat increasingly began to sense that the world was a precious place, in which, despite everything, there was a lot of good. The piece of bread that is given to you takes on a precious taste when shared with others who are in the same position as you. You are no better or worse than others and you work together with everyone for the common good. Sometimes you might be allowed to go to a dance, putting on the best clothes that you have and, if necessary, your comrades will lend you something of theirs. And perhaps one day you might see a girl you like and permit yourself to dream... Who can ever forget such things, even those destined to achieve even greater things in their lives?

Slowly but stubbornly, the caravan moved on, like a stream breaking its way through the ice and, thus, it began to enter the *Black Hole*. The high ridge of the mountain obscured the red disk of the sun, and the narrow gorge, full of dusky light, breathed deathly cold right into their faces. To the roar of the water under the ice, was added the rhythmic thud of the sleigh runners as they passed over the ice mounds, the echo only increasing the volume of noise filling the gorge with a racket that was painful to the ears. Strangely enough, it reminded Kazhimurat of the sound of the crowbars and shovels of his distant youth, when he had worked on a labour brigade...

Mine Number Thirteen was well known throughout the whole of the Koktas Region. Only the strongest men worked on it, capable, as they used to say back then, of turning a mountain on its head and shifting the course of a river. They were famous not only for their high production figures but also for their regular scandals and fights. It is rightly said: there is no country where there are no thieves and no mountain on which wolves do not prowl. In any place where many strangers from different places gather together, there will always be the ambitious and talented among them, but also bullies and crooks ready to commit any type of dark deed. Kazhimurat was working as a foreman, and he had plenty of both sorts in his brigade, which was made up largely of young men in their twenties who had been sentenced to various terms of imprisonment. People like these need to be dealt with in a skilled and special way: some listen to practical advice, while others will only react to brute physical strength. When the workforce was replenished with workers of this sort, the mine management would try to make sure they only had the strongest and most reliable men as foremen — the sort of men they could rely upon completely.

In Kazhimurat's brigade, there was one particular character who stood out and not just because of his huge build. He went by the nickname One-Eye on account of his high-cheekboned, pockmarked face and a cataract that had completely covered one of his eyes. The moment Kazhimurat set eyes on him, he knew that One-Eye was going to be a tough nut to crack. This man kept himself to himself and worked reluctantly, doing no more than the minimum required. He was off sick for exactly the maximum prescribed number of days a month, he was quick to answer back, he had a good appetite, never leaving anything on his plate, but he never begged for an extra portion from the kitchen either. One-Eye was extremely worldly-wise, avoiding fights where he could, but giving no quarter either. He exuded an overt coldness and cruelty. He would have happily tried to take over the brigade, but, realising that Kazhimurat himself knew a thing or two, he understood that it wouldn't be so easy to get him singing to his tune. Naturally, it was far from plain sailing between the two of them.

One skirmish followed after another until one day One-Eye got a taste of Kazhimurat's heavy hand and seemed to have resigned himself to the fact that he wasn't going to be calling the shots when it came to running the brigade. He reluctantly kept his head down a bit for the sake of appearances. But everyone sensed that a big fight between Kazhimurat and One-Eye was going to be inevitable and that it would not end well.

One night, the cash register at the mine administration was robbed. However, that evening, Kazhimurat had been out on a date with a girl and only returned very early in the morning. He had barely closed his eyes when three police officers burst into the barracks along with a detective and a trained guard dog on a leash. They got everyone up and began to search the entire place. The dog immediately rushed to Kazhimurat's bunk and began to sniff at a pair of his boots that he had not worn that night. Bundles of money were found sewn into his mattress.

Kazhimurat was sure that One-Eye had pulled this stunt, but did not share his suspicions at the subsequent trial: this was not his way of doing things. He spent six months in remand but by the end of his trial, he was found innocent and returned to Koktas, to rejoin his brigade. One day, One-Eye did not come back from the night shift, and in the morning his body was found under a pile of rubble. The evidence seemed to suggest that a section of the mine shaft had collapsed on top of him, but a rumour nevertheless began to spread through the mine that Kazhimurat was responsible. So, Kazhimurat had to bid farewell to the mine, which had become like a second home to him. Then the war came and he was refused permission to join up and go to the front on medical grounds. Once again, he found himself out of work and with nothing to do. So, sick of his lonely life, Kazhimurat decided to return to his native aul. However, things had not been easy here either ... He had become used to living in large, crowded towns, where life was always busy and there was never a moment of peace, so, the quiet life in his small remote aul took a little getting used to. No matter whether you live in your native village or on the other side of the world, there is always work to be done. You can find the jobs you really enjoy and sometimes you just have to step up to the plate and take on the most difficult ones, assuming, of course, that you are the sort of person who cares about others' suffering. They say that during particularly hard times, it is a man's conscience that decides the measure of his duties and a good man has no time to think about his own well-being...

Way out in the distance, the thin red veil shrouding the mountain top had now dissolved, a sure sign that the sun had set. It would have been nice to get to the watchman's house standing at the exit of the Kurdym Gorge, before nightfall. Even if he had no food to offer, Trofim would at least be able to boil up some water and he would be able warm up and give the horses and oxen some rest, otherwise, they would never reach the district centre. Kazhimurat had just got up to hurry the animals along when suddenly the gorge was filled with a terrible roar. He jumped, thinking that one of the gorge's frequent avalanches was heading his way, but what confronted him was much more terrifying. Four meters behind his sled, the ice had cracked and spread, revealing the black water beneath. With powerful short strokes, Kazhimurat cut the reins with his knife, separating the last three sleds from the convoy and then from each other, and, mercilessly lashing the animals with his whip, led the first two teams away from the crack. By the time he had got back again, a pair of oxen, harnessed to the trailing wagon train, were floundering in the water. Without a second thought, Kazhimurat threw himself into the icy water, pulled the pegs from the yoke, freed the animals and then climbed into the sled, which was miraculously still clinging to the edge of the hole. He began to throw the sacks of grain onto the ice but as bad luck would have it, the sled did not stay where it was but slid back along the tilting ice floe, threatening to fall into the water at any moment.

He did not remember how long the struggle lasted. The unfortunate animals, desperately trying to get out, nevertheless went under the water. Kazhimurat threw off the last sack from the sled and, unable to stay on his feet, fell into the crack that had opened. Grasping the edges of the ice floe with reddened, stiffening fingers, he tried to climb onto its surface, but the water whirled him, pulling him down and his heavy clothes pulled him to the bottom. At the final moment, by some miracle, he managed to reach an ice hummock and crawl onto the ice floe.

Stunned, he sat motionless for a long time. His head was spinning and his chest was burning and bubbling. Still not yet recovered, he began to count the sacks lying on the ice floe: all twenty were there present and correct. Sat there, Kazhimurat looked like a sack of grain himself: he did not even have the strength to move. The bubbling hole in the ice had swallowed both the oxen and the sled. *You've escaped death this time!* he thought to himself, looking around in a daze. *So, you'll live on in this world a little while longer...* The animals had dragged the wagon train to the nearest bank and were now placidly nibbling at the branches of the overhanging bushes. The calm, pastoral scene made him smile. *Hey, get up young man!* he ordered himself. *If you don't, you'll end up freezing!* Kazhimurat got up and brushed himself off. Small globules of ice that had frozen to his sheepskin coat fell with a skitter under his feet. He picked up the sacks, distributing them equally among the remaining sledges, stripped naked, and rubbed his body so hard with the needle-sharp dark snow that he nearly bled. Then he set about sorting his clothes out. He took off his felt boots, poured the water out of them and squeezed out his quilted trousers, then beat his sheepskin coat on the ice and, putting it all back on his naked body, he girded himself tightly with the reins. He ruffled his hair, shaking the icicles out of it and then threw his icy shirt and underwear that was sticking to his skin onto the sled. He chuckled, recalling that Zlikha had given him a new set of clothes for the journey, and although he had been ashamed to be wearing her husband's clothes in public, he was now sorry that the new clothes had been so badly damaged. *You've escaped death this time!* he mentally repeated to himself. *Now get a move on, Kazhimurat, otherwise you'll die before you find safety…*

The slopes of the mountains were covered in an impenetrable black velvet and only the very summit could be made out, shrouded by a red-brown haze, like the faded pattern of a *kimeshek* headdress. The wind picked up. He needed to get a move on.

The oxen were going well: they would eat a little, then rest a little. The road had been hardened by the evening frost and the runners slithered over the ice. Kazhimurat untied his long-handled axe lashed to the front of the sled and tucked it into his belt, remembering that on this side of the gorge, there might be bad people on the lookout for an opportunity on the roads. *Don't even think about getting onto the sled*, he warned himself, feeling the fatigue and cold penetrating his body. *Otherwise, you'll freeze like a piece of dog shit. Keep walking for as long as you have a glimmer of life in you.*

He caught up with the first team. The chestnut stallion, hearing his steps, turned his head, as if questioning where he was walking to, and stopped. Kazhimurat straightened the saddle cloth that had ridden up to the horse's croup, patted his rump with his palm and the animal, as if understanding what his master was asking of him, set off again. The chestnut was one of those horses that would not have sped up even if you'd hit it with an axe but would stop at only the slightest twitch of the reins. With wide and even steps he led the caravan along the icy road. A little while passed and then Kazhimurat checked all nineteen teams' harnesses. To make up for the sled that had sunk to the bottom of the river, shouldering one of the sacks, he joined the sled train himself. It was the final trick he could come up with to stop himself from freezing.

A crescent moon peeked out from behind the hill and everything became flooded with a pale light, reminiscent of a ghostly fog. The savage gorge, devoid of life, oppressed his spirit and he felt that he might never get out of it. Kazhimurat did not remember how many miles he had walked, his head was spinning with fatigue, his ears constantly ringing. On one occasion, he was convinced that the earth was floating away from under his feet. Evidently, he was completely out of breath and beginning to hallucinate. His neck stiffened under the sack, and Kazhimurat lowered his burden to the ground. He looked back and realised that he had moved a considerable distance ahead of the convoy. *One, two, three, four...* He began to count the teams. *Including me — that makes all twenty.* As soon as the frost-covered head of the chestnut leading the caravan appeared from behind the nearest hillock, he took up his sack again.

His quilted trousers and short sheepskin coat had hardened in the frost-like armour and prevented him from walking freely. The sled train was no longer stretched out — the chestnut had clearly slowed the pace. Kazhimurat's hair turned grey in the frost. He continued to walk, no longer feeling the aching pain in the toes of his right foot that had bothered him a few minutes earlier. Sweat poured into his eyes and his head began to spin again. In his mind's eye, Kazhimurat imagined first the dead One-Eye, looking balefully out at him from under the pile of rocks and then Zlikha and Almurat's sad expressions as they looked in at him through a barred window... Then they were obscured by the terrified, bulging eyes and flaring nostrils of the oxen as their heads slid under the water... *No, today is not the day I die!* Kazhimurat thought in his semi-conscious state, not noticing that Trofim's dogs, barking themselves hoarse, were already running towards him. *Keep going, don't stop!*

'Come on you lot! Get back to your places!'

Families living in isolation usually keep a whole pack of dogs. With difficulty, Trofim drove his dogs back into the yard, but only recognised Kazhimurat when he came right up to him. Pale from the frost and ice, he threw the sack back on the sledge, untied the reins, which he had tied around his waist, and flung open his short sheepskin coat with a cracking sound. Trofim recoiled a step when he saw that Kazhimurat didn't even have a shirt on.

'Ah, my friend, you'll die dressed like that out in this!' The old man began to fuss around Kazhimurat, trying to wrap his sheepskin coat around him to cover up his frost-covered chest, but the half-sheepskin was so frozen that he couldn't budge it. 'Mother! Mother, quick!'

Kazhimurat's last reserves of strength left him and he fell onto the sled smashing the icicles hanging from his temples.

'Mother! Have you caught fire in there, or what, damn it woman?! Lukerya, what are you doing there?'

'What are you making such a fuss about?' she replied.

'Give the bench a wash, add another log and increase the steam! Do you hear me? We've got a guest!'

Trofim grabbed Kazhimurat, who was losing consciousness and lifted him from the sled.

'Come on, my friend, let's go! We will steam away all your sorrows and sins and then beat them away with a birch switch! But for now, we need to get these great hooves off you! Come on, stir your stumps! Come on, in you come!'

Kazhimurat barely made it to the changing room next to the sauna. A lamp was burning on an upside-down box and from behind the small greasy door came the sound of a ladle and the hiss of water on hot rocks. Kazhimurat noticed a woman's dress hanging on a nail and looked indecisively at Trofim, but he wasn't listening — with a long knife he cut open the tops of Kazhimurat's frozen felt boots and freed the lifeless, blue legs from them.

'Don't worry. It's so dark in there that you can barely see your own back, let alone someone else's! 'Mother!' Trofim shouted again. 'Put a bit more steam on and cover yourself with a towel! It turns out our guest is the shy type around women!'

Lumbering about on his thick bear-like legs, Trofim undressed Kazhimurat and flung open the small door. Kazhimurat was met with a wave of heat and a rough woman's voice,

'Who are you pushing in here with me, you old fool? Pass me my trousers. My trousers!'

'Put a sock in it, you silly woman! Who wears trousers in the sauna? It's not as if you're going to be sipping tea with him and don't you start preening and showing off!' Trofim pushed Kazhimurat into the steam room and with a hardened edge to his voice, he added, 'Give him a really good steam and rub him well with bear fat!'

It must have been midday — a thin ray of sunlight fell directly on the bench on which he was lying. Kazhimurat woke up from a loud knocking sound and saw the round, squat figure of Lukerya collecting the ashes from the stove. She looked him over with her mocking blue eyes, smiled briefly and furtively and, with a pail in her hand, went outside. The huge stove that filled the middle of the room still breathed warmth. The sour smell of mead emanated from a barrel in the corner, covered with a fur coat. He recalled Lukerya's soft and strong hands, rubbing him with bear fat. The cold that had fettered his body on the journey had seemed to have left him in the steam room along with his sweat and he felt light. Only the aching pain in the toes of the right foot would not give him any rest.

That night, when he finally came to his senses, he recalled Trofim rubbing goose fat into his toes and telling him that he would have to say goodbye to them. 'You can thank your lucky stars that you got off so easy!' the old man barked. 'From now on, you'll be known as *Kazhimurat the Toeless*. Don't worry, you'll get used to it. You've already got so many nicknames, so one more won't do you any harm. You've escaped death, You're not going to die today, my friend!'

Their four-year-old daughter, Nastya, sat huddled in the corner, as frightened as a bird confronted by a snake. That night, she had sat at the same table as this stranger and eaten from the same cup as him, but on that occasion, her parents had been sitting next to her. Now, though, she was all on her own with him. The huge, gloomy man with his shaggy beard and swollen, watery eyes took up almost half of the room. Kazhimurat got up. There was an appetizing smell of onions frying in lard. The table had been wiped clean and the dishes were nowhere to be seen. The washing, which had been hanging on a cord stretched around the room only yesterday, had also been tidied away somewhere. Next to the threshold stood a pair of boots with round, upturned toes. Thankfully, his clothes were nearby; the smell of the bathhouse emanated from his shirt and trousers, but having dried out in the hot steam, they had significantly shrunk and now his arms wouldn't fit into his sleeves and his legs into his trousers. It was quiet outside in the yard as well. Kazhimurat recalled hearing Trofim's angry voice sometime earlier that morning saying,

'It's run away, the wretched animal! Mother, give me my rifle!' Lukerya, who clearly did not want to give him his rifle, sniffed for a long time in her bed, and finally said,

'Why do you need it?'

'Get on with it! If anything, according to the law of the taiga, it should be getting a blast from both my barrels! No trials or investigations!'

Kazhimurat had no idea what happened next. But now that it was already noon and the master of the house had still not returned, he was beginning to worry: *What had happened to the grain, the horses and the oxen? Were they all okay?*

Lukerya rolled into the room like a round spinning wheel, barely perceptibly moving her full lips into a smile, tidied an empty bucket away behind the stove and went up to Kazhimurat. She sat him on the bed, unceremoniously taking him by the shoulders, rubbed his toes with goose fat and tied them tightly with a rag. Then she pulled out his felt boots with the cut tops from under the bench and silently held them out to him as if to say that now he could do as he liked. Her expression was soft, her round blue eyes sparkled with laughter, and her delicate, plump, wrinkled neck peeped out from her unbuttoned collar.

'You, young man, were born under a lucky star!' she pronounced, then added in the tone of a person who knows all there is to know about him, 'A man like you should live for himself and others in pleasure.'

He remembered the hot steam room, the whistle of the birch leaves that struck his body, her soft and strong fingers on his shoulder blades and imagined how her soft white belly swayed as she had bent over him, rubbing his back. He was suddenly seized by that aching, pure and bright feeling that kindred souls have for each other.

'Trofim is in the yard,' said Lukerya. 'Good lord! He's in a mood today!'

Kazhimurat got dressed and went outside.

A bright yellow light spilt across the sky and the air was pure and invigorating. The fog gradually enveloped the ridges of the hills, overgrown with larch and here and there with cedar, but it was not dense and therefore flowed through the gorge, descending and swirling, along the river. The southern slopes began to steam and smoke like heaps of manure, warmed by the hot summer sun.

Trofim had collected the empty sacks that had been eaten by the animals, then he began to harness the chestnut to the sled. The oxen bellowed, greedily eyeing up the selected bags, but the iron halters that clattered against their yoke left them in no doubt their carefree life had come to an end. Trofim finished harnessing the teams, went up to Kazhimurat, sat him down on the sled and sympathetically rested his elbow on his knee, trying to smooth out the dull pain that resided there. The animals sighed heavily as they shifted from foot to foot.

Well, my friend, as they say, if you get a real move on, then the sparks will fly from the heels of your boots! Up you get, it's time to go!'

Trofim took the chestnut by the bridle and led it out onto the road. The rest of the teams followed the lead sled of their own accord; the horses and oxen had long ago learned to live without the whip. Kazhimurat followed the caravan. He could not feel his right leg. His felt boot felt as if it had been stuffed with clay; it would rise of its own accord and fall to the ground like a dead weight. A sharp pain stabbed him in the temples.

Trofim tied the dogs to the gate — apart from making a hullabaloo, they were of little use anyway — and called his wife:

'Mother!' He looked for a minute at Lukerya, who had come out onto the porch, and briefly ordered, 'This time you're going to need to pull your trousers on! This man needs our help.'

'What about Nastya?'

'Our Nastya's not going to go running off into the forest. Tie her legs to the table and pour her out a little bit of milk and she'll be fine!'

The sun was in a hurry to slide down from the crest of Kurdym and the freezing wind remained the absolute master of the *Black Hole*. Kazhimurat stood for a long time at the top of the hill, watching the figures of Trofim and Lukerya, who had come to see him off, get smaller and smaller, eventually turning into black dots and disappearing into the grey haze. He rose to his feet only when he saw the light had been lit in the lonely watchman's house. He began to count the teams: one, two, three, four... nineteen... He brought the sled out onto the road and tried to walk beside it without sitting down, but was unable, and, like a felled tree, collapsed onto the sacks.

The stars, driven by the wind, seemed to float across the dark-blue, fathomless sky. Only during the night, when the freezing cold again began to fetter itself tightly around his body, did Kazhimurat come to his senses. He gazed long and hard at the sky until his eyes filled with tears. In the west, the silhouettes of the tall mountains were barely visible, they seemed to be holding the entire weight of the high heavens, strewn with its countless stars on their shoulders. There, beyond the mountains at the edge of the earth lay the small village by the name of Murat. How many widows and orphans were there in this aul at the very end of the world? And how many of them would be thinking about him now? Kazhimurat recalled the names of the old men and women with dead, lifeless eyes, widows who had lost their youthful beauty before their time and filthy, young children with the permanent gleam of hunger in their eyes.

His chest felt hot as if it had been touched by fire. He also imagined himself like one of the distant mountains on whose shoulders the life of his entire aul rested and, despite its smallness, this village, his village Murat, was also strewn with countless precious stars — each one a living human heart. Ah, the human heart! Sometimes your pride soars higher than the highest mountains and your dreams pierce the horizon and fly off into the distance to warm thousands of other hearts! The sky did not seem as severe and impregnable to Kazhimurat as it had a few minutes earlier, and the stars trembled and shimmered as if they were alive. The creaking of the runners seemed to be accompanied by the sad song of the night, which, as people say, only true travellers can hear. The tiredness that had cramped his shoulders and the pain that throbbed in his foot were now forgotten, and that other pain also subsided, the one that had almost never released its claws from his heart before. He closed his eyes in a sweet, serene slumber, and the last thing he saw at that moment was Zlikha bending over him...

6

Zlikha escorted him to the clayey Sarybulak valley, which had once been a fertile wheat field. One edge of the valley rested against the Bukhtarma, the other three sides were bordered by taiga. Like all the nearby hills, every last section of Sarybulak had been ploughed, even the slopes of Mount Maya or Dromedary Mountain, and now it looked exactly like a camel, from whose sides large strips of skin have been torn off. All over the lowlands, brown columns of smoke rose up to the sky from behind the forest, the scattered migrating auls were evidently grazing their flocks there and trying to get the most out of the last of the autumn grass

The stallion walked restlessly at first, twitching the reins every now and then, but then, seemingly, resigned itself to the fact that the people accompanying it were in no hurry to part with each other, and walked ahead, sleepily bowing its heavy head. It was quiet all around. Kazhimurat even threw its stirrups over the saddle so that they would not knock against the girth buckle. The Bukhtarma had also quietened down, bearing its waters inaudibly and shining in the night, like a polished slope leading down a steep rock face.

Kazhimurat and Zlikha knew every feature of the landscape here, right down to the last rock and hollow on the ground. Distant events that had long been covered by the veil of time, silently came back to life in their memories; hard days, filled with deprivation, now consigned to oblivion. They did not have to look for places where temporary shelters had once stood or small glades which break up the monotonous march of the fields. It was the sort of land on which the traces of old worn-out boots and even crack-heeled bare feet would be forever imprinted, where the soil was soaked with salty sweat and bitter human tears, a blessed and native land that knew everything about their serene childhoods and anxious youth, a land that remembered their words of passionate love, stored up all their joys and absorbed all their sorrows. Kazhimurat and Zlikha had shed more of their bitter-salty sweat than most. And one of them was now walking, cursing himself for not having bothered to make the time to come here at least once in the past twenty years, while the other was walking next to him and also cursing herself for not having found the strength to leave here at one time for the sake of the person who was dearer to her than all others. Life had passed, the years had flown by like river water and there was no returning it. That's the nature of one's native land when it is so dear to the heart...

Zlikha took his hand, letting him know that it was time to say goodbye. Her fingers sank into Kazhimurat's huge palm and she was in no hurry to pull her hand out of his. She didn't want to part. His palm was still hot, which meant that he had not yet given up on life, he had not grown old.

'I'm not asking you to come specially, but if your road passes us, don't forget to pay us a visit,' Zlikha said. Kazhimurat hugged her tightly and again she did not rush to free herself from his embrace. She didn't want to part. Her body was still hot, as it had been before, in her younger years...

He left without looking back, fearing that otherwise, he would be unable to leave her. Zlikha sat down on a large log, knowing that Kazhimurat would not turn around again. Her breast was filled with a cold and empty feeling. Her knees trembled. All the warmth of her soul seemed to have parted with him. Zlikha felt empty and devastated. It seemed to her that nothing now would ever arouse an emotional response in her ever again. She figured that this was much how stagnant water must feel. But what sort of life is a life lived in stagnant water? Everything that had been agitating Zlikha earlier that evening, all her expectations vanished, like that light perspiration that appears on the body of an old horse that has just taken its final steps and will never walk again. *So, it is true when they say that a life lived without love is an empty one*, Zlikha thought. *But what kind of love can it be when the head is covered in grey hair and everyone refers to you as an old woman? Is it possible to rekindle a fire from embers that have long gone out? No, it's probably my past suffering and loss that is possessing me, rather than any true feelings...*

A small black whirlwind rolled down from the top of the hill, creating circles in the grass and disappeared into the river, unable to create an impression on the water. Far behind the hill, the smoke from Murat aul's chimneys stretched up in vertical columns. However, Kazhimurat and Zlikha had built no hearth or home in this aul. The fire of their hearth had gone out before it had ever been allowed to flare up into a bright flame. It had been extinguished before it had even had a chance to overcome the first vital barrier that she, Zlikha, herself had erected in its path. She had only herself to blame...

A lone traveller, leading his horse, disappeared off behind the hill. She needed to catch up with Kazhimurat while he was still in sight. Otherwise, it would be too late, but Zlikha did not have the strength to rise from the cold log, half buried in the sand and continued to sit and bitterly reproach herself. The figure of the lone, swaying traveller disappeared in the space from which the yellow haze emanated, and at that moment, when the last hope seemed to have broken in her heart, the pale sun, as if it had got stuck to the top of Sarybulak, suddenly flared up brightly, spilling an ocean of golden light over the whole of the earth. And the potential for change signalled in nature caused bitter, inconsolable tears to pour from Zlikha's eyes in an unstoppable stream. If the pain of her loss could have been quenched with tears, she might have felt better.

'Maybe it's time you went home?' a voice drawled nearby.

It was her husband.

'No way!' she answered. Zlikha didn't even turn around at the familiar voice. 'What for?'

As if there wasn't plenty of good grass to be had nearby, the clapped-out bay nag reached out with its muzzle to the log on which Zlikha was sitting, and pulled up a clump of mint from almost under her feet. It seemed to Zlikha that it was not the bay gelding plucking the grass, but Kiyakmurt robbing it from her for the very last time. Yet it was not the innocent animal, but the man she hated, and it was only this consideration that stopped her from kicking the horse away from her with her foot.

Kiyakmurt dismounted from his horse and went up to his wife, tightening the laces of his trousers, which hung in two huge bags at his knees. He thrust his whip into one of his boot tops and, folding it in half, took out a bag of tobacco from the other, struck a match, lit a cigarette, then spat directly on the toe of his tarpaulin boot before wiping it on the spray of mint growing in the shade of the log on which Zlikha was still sitting motionless.

She looked at her husband with an uncomprehending look and turned away again. She did not want him to poison her mood with his presence. He reminded her of a dung beetle, concerned only with its own troubles and worries. Kiyakmurt didn't seem to have a care about Zlikha's mental anguish. He had simply thought that his wife had been outside long enough and now it was time for her to go home. Zlikha did not rise from her place, and Kiyakmurt did not leave.

'Maybe, you've sat there long enough? Go home already!'

It was only now when Kiyakmurt caught the furious look in Zlikha's eyes that he realized that something unusual had happened to his wife. Her deathly pale face merged with the white shawl covering her shoulders, which contrasted starkly with her jet-black hair, which had been evenly combed down both sides of her head. His wife's eyes burned with a cold light, like ice floes. It reminded Kiyakmurt of the cold lunatic sheen of Bakhyt's, who once lived in the village of Murat. Had Zlikha gone mad that night? He cautiously went up to the horse, bridled it and, taking the animal by the reins, went off to check the herd.

The huge and round surface of the Sarybulak Valley shone a dark velvet in the sun. The water of the Bukhtarma splashed against the wind. The green forest loomed in from all sides, squeezing the valley, and Mount Sarybulak, circling smoothly, seemed to rise up above it. Lights flickered here and there in the forest thickets, indicating the presence of small shepherd's yurts. The mirage of yellow haze and the vertical columns of morning smoke were scattered by the freshening wind. Zlikha got up.

Not far away, the bay gelding nibbled on some grass. You might have been forgiven for thinking that Kiyakmurt had deliberately left it so that his wife might at least have some living soul for company. He himself went to the house, his trousers, worn to a shine, glistened in the sun, his long birch club tucked into his belt, one ear of his cap stuck up, the other stretched to the ground as if listening out for the worms. His short, crooked legs pattered along, seldom leaving the path. Many times, Zlikha had noticed that her husband would often turn to look back at her like a devoted dog looks at its master and she suddenly felt sorry for him — regardless of what he was like, he was still her husband. She went up to the bay, put her foot in the stirrup and sat on the saddle...

Once again, her heart began to ache; she didn't want to return to the living death that was her home, but she lacked the strength to chase and catch up with Kazhimurat, and for the first time in her life, she understood what it was like to leave something half done. She was suddenly seized by an overwhelming feeling of orphan homelessness. The bay horse didn't care about her suffering either. It sighed heavily and out of habit pulled her in the direction of the farm and the cattle breeding centre. The poor animal, like a living personification of the inevitability of a miserable fate that can neither be conquered nor rejected, took Zlikha further and further away from her recent fond dreams, from the memories of that short, brief, happy period of her life, from her past feelings and joys. The past would now remain only in her memories, which for Zlikha were perhaps the last refuge that remained for her soul in this life...

* * *

In the second half of March nineteen forty-three, a warm wind blew down from the mountains and in a week, the dirty snow on their slopes had melted and receded. This spring had been a peculiar one, the Bukhtarma had broken its banks and did not return to its normal course for a long time. The flood spread far and wide and the entire valley was filled with water. The taiga animals huddled closely together on the higher hills as if Noah's Ark had sailed past and left them there to flourish and provide the world with future generations. For some time, these auls had been living their isolated nomad lives, unable to communicate with the outside world. Some communication was possible via telephone but that was only with the district centre and, therefore, no one knew how their neighbours were getting on.

A whole week had passed since Kazhimurat had left the village, and there was still no word of him. The most terrible news was usually spread by word of mouth of whole caravans ending up under the ice on such and such bend of the river, or travellers being buried in a landslide on the slope of such and such a mountain. Each bit of news increased the level of anxiety in the aul. As soon as the first wave of rumours passed, another, even more terrible, washed up on their doorstep: a sled and the corpses of some oxen that had drowned under the ice had been thrown ashore at the mouth of the Aksu and Bukhtarma rivers. The only person who could verify these rumours was old Zhusup. So, naturally, he immediately set off for Kurdym and, on his return informed everyone that he had recognized the aul's oxen. But apart from the bloated corpses of the animals, the old man had seen nothing else. Zlikha rang everywhere she could, including the district centre, but the answer was the same: Kazhimurat had handed over the grain a long time ago and left for the village. There was little doubt that he, along with the convoy, had been killed on his way back from the district centre.

The collective farm office was humid, hot and stuffy and it was hard to believe how unbearably cold it had been quite recently. Someone had stuffed the stove to capacity with dry larch logs as if they'd been planning to melt sugar, and the firewood burned with such a resounding crack that the red-hot sides of the iron stove buzzed and shuddered.

Zlikha took off her outer layers and moved further away to a small table standing next to the window. She decided to look through the farm's documents, calculate what had been done during the winter and sketch out a plan for the upcoming season, but the ink had dried up in the inkwell, and she had no particular desire to pore over the papers. Suddenly, the phone on the wall gave a long, drawn-out ring. Zlikha was seized with fear and she felt the ring had a sad and mournful tone to it. Before recent events, Zlikha had convinced herself that she only felt pity for Kazhimurat, but in fact, it turned out that her feelings for him were anything but — it appeared that genuine feelings, the sort of feelings a woman feels for a

208

man had awoken in her breast and now he seemed the dearest person to her in the whole wide world. She didn't answer the phone.

The whole aul could be seen from the window. Shoots of grass had just begun to break through the winter snow heralding spring and they would soon cover the entire earth, hiding the heaps of garbage and human detritus from people's eyes. The forest was still bare, only the firs and cedars grew in green islands, and the rest of the trees were yet to produce their leaves. The sheep and goats grazed greedily without raising their heads. Sparrows hopped about on the back of a cow standing near the window, plucking out hairs for their nests.

The village was quiet and peaceful. No one except her, it seemed, was worried about Kazhimurat disappearing without a trace.

Kiyakmurt entered the office with a green field bag dangling from his side and stopped at the threshold to shake the mud from his boots. He then threw down the switch broom that had been leaning against the door jamb, and began to vigorously wipe the dirt off the bottom of his boots with it. The bag dangled like a shovel in front of his groin, a bit like the piece of felt that is tied to the belly of the rams to prevent them from tupping the ewes ahead of time. The broom was left in tatters on the floor. Kiyakmurt took off his coat, straightened his holster and, shifting the weight on his short legs in a self-important manner, walked past Zlikha to the telephone. He picked up the phone and vigorously wound it up.

'Hello! Hello! Is that the district centre? The Head Department, please! The department?! This is the official report from the authorised representative at the Murat Collective Farm! Everything is in order here!'

Zlikha could not help laughing at his pompous, self-important officialese. Kiyakmurt frowned, his eyebrows and his stiff and unruly moustache twitched. He cast a sidelong glance at Zlikha, cleared his throat and, half-turning his back to her, began to speak down the receiver again. Kiyakmurt now tried to speak more calmly and in more detail, especially now that he had switched to Kazakh. However, it is difficult for a person to change their nature and Kiyakmurt was no exception, and he couldn't help ending the conversation with his favourite and incessant 'everything is in order!' Indeed, it is truly said, Zlikha thought, *When there's no dog in the yard, even a pig imagines itself to be a guard dog and when there are no men left in the village even the saddest individual imagines himself to be a warrior.* She almost said it out loud but managed to bite her tongue in the nick of time.

Kiyakmurt wandered around the office for some time, his nail-shod heels clattering against the floor. Not knowing what to do with his hands, he would either thrust them into his trouser pockets or slip his fingers under the belt of his tunic, then, with the pronounced dignity of a person whom nature has deprived of a physique worthy of it, he sat down on a stool. With a slow and deliberate movement, he lowered the tops of his box calf boots, and, throwing his head back, ostentatiously began to comb his hair. He looked around the room, his eyes lingering on the broken twigs of the broom and the mud on the floor, which he himself had brought in from the street, and began to speak in a much more sympathetic tone,

'You do everything yourself, sweeping the floors, chopping the wood, stoking the stove and carrying out the ashes... I would get a cleaner in — let her look after the office.'

'The women have enough on their plates already.

'That's not what I'm getting at... You are, after all, the boss, it's not for you to get your skirts dirty sweeping the office floor.'

Zlikha erupted. 'So, one of your authorised responsibilities is to keep a watch over the women's skirts now, is it? What a hard job you've found for yourself, you poor thing!' She wanted to shout at him. However, this time too, albeit with great difficulty, she managed to restrain herself.

In his own way, Kiyakmurt had understood the real cause of Zlikha's agitation. He straightened up on his stool and, with a self-satisfied air, pushed a home-grown tobacco roll up between his teeth. *How was he finally going to rein in this aloof woman?* he pondered. Although he felt at ease in the village, he was shy when confronted with Zlikha. She never raised her voice and never shouted like the other women, she always behaved in an even and calm manner with others, with that rare restraint that betrays a strong, well-rounded nature. Even the jokes that Kiyakmurt cracked for Zlikha's benefit seemed to hang in the air, ignored.

Zlikha looked at his uneven teeth, his fingers, yellow from his home-grown tobacco, and thought how dark and secretive Kiyakmurt's soul was. He was ugly to look at. His thin, elongated lips, low, almost finger-wide forehead and bristly haircut betrayed not so much obstinacy but rather stubbornness, not so much consistency but rather pettiness, and these qualities did not speak in his favour. It was strange, but Zlikha was still unable to get accustomed to Kiyakmurt's face, although he had been living in the aul for over a year and hadn't missed a single meeting or celebration, no matter where they had taken place — be they in the collective farm office or at someone's house. He would sit there at the presiding table or in his host's place of honour as if constantly trying to assert his power in the aul and his importance in the eyes of the villagers. Nevertheless, he was still the collective farm's authorised representative, appointed by the district committee. Sensing that at some stage in the future she would have to stand up to Kiyakmurt, Zlikha examined and studied him carefully.

'I need to have a word with you,' the authorised representative declared, inhaling his tobacco smoke. 'And it's a serious word.'

'I'm listening.'

'It's regarding a very important matter.'

'Well, I don't come into this office just to drink tea, you know,' Zlikha quipped.

'I want to talk to you about Kazhimurat Yelmuratov...'

Kiyakmurt's expression was giving nothing away, but Zlikha felt her heart skip a beat.

'I understand that he is now living with you.'

At these words, Zlikha gave a deep sigh of relief, and her heart started beating normally again.

'Well, Kazhimurat is the only real man left in the village, so, he could probably choose whichever widow he liked to live with,' Zlikha couldn't resist cracking at least one bitter joke at Kiyakmurt's expense.

'That's not the point,' Kiyakmurt flicked his cigarette end into the stove, 'He still hasn't been registered anywhere. You should have taken this up with the village council. He is not listed as a resident of the village with the executive committee.'

'Well, that's hardly a matter of great importance. The main thing is that his people have accepted him and he has never let us down.'

'This aul would accept a donkey as their own, if they thought it would carry their baggage for it.'

'You have to respect every person regardless, comrade. This is a truth as old as the world we live in.'

'Well, I can't respect criminals!'

'I'm surprised that you would repeat such slanderous nonsense! So far, around here he has shown himself to be the most reliable person in the village. I only wish there were more members of the collective like him!'

'Why was he in jail then? No sooner does he get back here than he starts stealing other people's hay. What do you make of that? That's my first point. His father was a notorious outlaw, was he not? That's my second point! How can the son of a bandit who crossed over the border in 1928 be considered a reliable person?! You know as well as I do that our district lies within the border zone. We have a war going on, you know? And there is a law that states that elements like Yelmuratov should be resident in places that are at least one hundred and fifty miles away from the border zone. So, now do you understand the seriousness of our conversation? We have only left him alone so far because he can't speak and has been helping the collective farm. Things could have taken a very different turn... In general, I wouldn't advise you to rush to his defence every time his name crops up.'

Zlikha let his words go. She was angry that Kiyakmurt, who did not usually dare so much as cross Kazhimurat's path, should have said what he did at a time when Kazhimurat had disappeared while risking his life to deliver the farm's grain to the district centre. And she also considered it beneath herself to be even talking to a man who was unable to see beyond his own petty interests, like a mouse grubbing for sustenance in a heap of manure. There were two things in the world that she could not stand. These were slavish and base hypocrisy and black envy that can destroy even the finest soul. She wanted to end this humiliating conversation, and she began to collect the papers that had been spread out on the table. Kiyakmurt also got up. He had no idea what Zlikha was thinking and was sure that he had finally had the *serious conversation* he had been planning for so long.

'Good, good...' He said, adjusting his belt. 'I'd better go to the farm: I need to check in on the women there. In times like these, you need to keep a personal eye on folks. Our people are conscientious, but there are some among them who you constantly need to keep an eye on. By the way, the district centre was asking for a summary of the spring sowing plans. You'll need to have it ready today.'

Zlikha could barely control herself before the sound of his officious well-shod heels had left the room. She got up and threw the latch on the door, as if afraid that Kiyakmurt might come back into the office again. She sat for a minute, trying to collect her thoughts, all the while pestered by a huge greenbottle that was buzzing around the office. Every creature that grows fat and breeds on dirt flocks to the warmth and reduces everything around it to its own level and likeness. And this was exactly the sort of creature Kiyakmurt was... He had been entrusted with a serious responsibility — to help the collective farmers do their work, but the only duty he could see was to chase them up and urge them on. People like this can never change, no matter what you do. The war had elevated him to a position that required sensitivity and education. But if Kiyakmurt were to suddenly disappear, there would be hundreds of others like him to take his place. His type is hard to kill.

The sun, which until recently had been shining from the south, now made its way through a window cut through the end wall. The cow on the street also moved, following the sun. It chewed the cud incessantly as if it had eaten something indigestible, and didn't have a care about what was going on around it.

Zlikha turned her thoughts once again to the conversation she had had with Kiyakmurt. She now regretted not interrupting him and letting him know that she did not agree with a word he had said about Kazhimurat. The men of the aul were now fighting the evil enemy thousands of miles away, but none of them sensed the distance one iota. They were nearby because they were protecting their auls, their native lands and native peoples. And Kazhimurat was fighting just as hard as any of his countrymen at the front, only his battles were being fought deep in the rear. Enough! There was no point worrying over the foolish words of a man like Kiyakmurt. Similar rumours had been going round the village for a long time, *An evil tongue poisons the people and a fat lazy backside defiles the lake.* It might have been possible to be consoled by these wise words if only Kiyakmurt's evil tongue knew some restraint. She would just have to wait and see.

Old Zhusup tottered his way down the path, angrily stabbing the ground with his cane. Seeing Tazhimurat walking towards him in the distance, the old man crossed to the other side of the street, even though this required him to climb through the dirty quagmire. The two of them had never got along. One had never been in the queue when intelligence had been handed out but was obstinate to the point of idiocy, whereas the other had been, but had also been rewarded with an extra portion of obtuse donkey stubbornness. When two people who belong to the same clan do not get along, why bother getting upset with an outsider like Kiyakmurt? But all the same, it was a great shame that he had been appointed to them as the district centre's authorised representative. Intelligent and honest people had been sent to the other farms and there was no getting away from it, the Murat collective farm had not been lucky.

Old Zhusup turned towards the office. He would wander around the aul every day, seeking the latest news coming from the front, delving into the concerns of every single family and individual in the aul, man, woman or child and then, having looked in on the barns and farm yards where the women were working, he would finally turn into the office where he would provide Zlikha with a meticulous report on who needed help with firewood, who needed an armful of hay and who needed a couple of buckets of water bringing to them. At first, Zlikha thought that the old man behaved this way because the

aul had spoiled him, by conferring the title *Bi-ata*[19] on
him. But later she became convinced that the villagers
really did respect old Zhusup and listened to his every
word. In short, whenever and wherever the *Bi-ata* visited
far fewer crocodile tears would flow, and all kinds of
blockheads and idiots would put up and shut up. The old
man had refused to give up even when the terrible news
came from the front that his three sons, who had gone to
war, had gone missing. He was one of those people who
had integrity in spades. It was for this reason that Zlikha
respected him, and also for the fact that even in his sunset
years, old Zhusup retained a rare masculine beauty and
dignity.

The women who were getting the seed grain ready for
sowing must have been waiting for old Zhusup to finish
his rounds: as soon as he had passed by, they
immediately abandoned their work and hurried home,
like lambs that had finally been freed from the common
leash. The old man would always come to see them at the
very end of the working day. The women were worn out:
some of them were wearing their husbands' oversized
saptama boots, others dragged themselves about in
patched and mended felt boots, despite the spring mud
that stuck to them. Their fur coats and overcoats, which
had been altered and mended for the umpteenth time
during the war, were now being worn by their children.
Blessed is the land that has raised daughters who are so
strong and so forbearing! They seemed to have a
boundless ability to believe that their fathers, husbands

---

[19] *Bi–ata* – a shortened form of 'Biy', which means a 'judge' or 'sage' who
the people of the steppe would go to for advice and adjudication. Aga is
a form of address to an older man, literally meaning 'father'.

and brothers would all return safe and sound, as soon as they had broken the back of the Nazi war machine, and the good life would again be established immediately after their inevitable victory.

Zlikha was not expecting any of her relatives to come back from the front, but she dreamed that as many of the aul's young men who had gone to fight would return as soon as possible so that there would be fewer tears after the long-awaited victory was announced... And then she remembered Kazhimurat, and again her heart was seized with anxiety. Her house could be seen through the window, empty and lifeless — it took her a lot of strength to return there in the evenings. She walked home so unwillingly; it was as if she was being dragged by a lasso. Only those who have drunk fully from the bitter cup of loneliness, bereft of all joys and attention, would have been able to understand her mood. Zlikha did not want to leave the office, but the arrival of old Zhusup made her get up from her seat; she simply didn't have the strength today to listen to the old man's latest instructions and requests.

She had forgotten to unbridle her horse, and it stood there, rattling its bit with irritation and displeasure. It had been a hard day. Lambing had begun and with two flocks of sheep, there was plenty to keep her busy. That morning, it was only with great difficulty that Zlikha had managed to get the specialist lambers and take them out to the shepherds and the flocks. Then she had resolved a few small problems, ordered the shepherds to wait until the lambs had got stronger, and then milked the sheep: the district centre had decided to send salted sheep's cheese to the front. It wasn't much help but at least it was something. 'It's all Kiyakmurt's fault!' she complained to her stallion, untying its tether from the hitching post. 'Otherwise, I would never have forgotten to unbridle you.' Before Zlikha had time to finish, Almurat galloped past on his two-year-old bay gelding, almost knocking her over. She thought he was just being rude and thoughtless and followed the boy rushing headlong the road with a disapproving look. The two-year-old bay flew like a bird up to the hill protruding from the spur of Dromedary Mountain.

Peering up at the hill, Zlikha saw a lone traveller, awkwardly hobbling along the road from the district centre. Behind him stretched a long caravan. *That's strange, the road through the pass hasn't opened yet, so how could he have got through this side?* Zlikha thought. Judging by the way the man was leaning on a crutch, she assumed that he must be someone returning from the front and, without thinking, jumped into the saddle.

The traveller walking down the road was Kazhimurat. Or to be more precise, he was slowly dragging himself along, leaning heavily on his makeshift crutches. He had loaded all the convoy's harnesses and sleds onto two carts and harnessed four oxen to them, which was much easier than dragging them. No sooner had he climbed the hill closest to the village and begun to descend than almost the entire village rushed to meet him, some on horseback, some on foot, and their touching greeting moved Kazhimurat to tears. His chest was bursting with pride: even though he had returned later than planned, he had nevertheless delivered the farm's grain, not losing any on the way, and could look his people in the eye with a clear conscience — his people who had so painstakingly produced every grain for the country's war effort. There was only one thing that upset him: he had set out on the road a healthy man but returned a cripple, thus adding to their already considerable number in the aul.

Everyone who had run out to meet them had gathered together in a crowd at a short distance as if to let him know that they had never doubted that their hero Kazhimurat could ever have drowned in water or been burnt by fire. Only two riders rushed towards him on their horses at a gallop, the two hearts most devoted to him, and Kazhimurat saw another manifestation of that indestructible human love, which is the thing that people have valued the most through all time. Zlikha and Almurat galloped to meet him.

However, Zlikha pulled up on her reins slightly, she felt awkward galloping wildly after Almurat. She looked back, saw the rest of the aul crowded on the road, got off her horse and, to calm her excitement, began to tighten the girths of her horse. Then she sat a young boy in the saddle, who had made it up ahead of the rest of the gang, and remained where she was, not knowing what to do next: return to the crowd and meet Kazhimurat along with the rest of the aul, or continue to meet him on foot. For some reason, she remembered Kiyakmurt's recent words: 'This aul would accept a donkey as their own, if they thought it would carry their baggage for it.' And now these words made her really angry. She stood on the road as if connecting Kazhimurat and his aul kin with an invisible thread, and her eyes were full of tears.

The crimson sun sank behind the mountains; the wisps of mist rising in the west reddened like the glow of a fire. The heavens stretched over the open road and the air was filled with the evening cold, which had been drawn in from the gorge. Oddly, not a single dog barked. It was quiet all around. Kazhimurat took in the whole picture that opened before him with a single glance, reached the fork in the road and turned to the cattle yard, which stood on the outskirts of the village. He walked past Zlikha and did not go up to the people waiting for him on the main road. The cart teams as well as the horses and oxen tethered behind were soon surrounded by the boys. Kazhimurat limped along on one leg amidst the noise and uproar, like a black steppe eagle among a mob of jackdaws.

Zlikha could not summon the courage and overcome her innate female shyness to follow Kazhimurat, but she was even more afraid of the gossip this might engender in the aul, so she turned into a nearby street and, keeping to the outbuildings, headed home. She was annoyed with herself. *You shouldn't have run to meet him*, she reproached herself. *You shouldn't have shown your feelings*.

Shamshinur was burning the manure and scraps of hay that had accumulated during the winter in front of her house. Seeing Zlikha, she stuck her pitchfork into the pile she had made and stepped out in front of her.

'Well, Karagayak-kelin, are you glad that the wagon train has made it back?' She asked, using the nickname *boss's bride* that the aul had coined in her honour. It had stuck to Zlikha ever since she had become chairman of the collective farm. 'Did Kazhimurat return safely from the district centre? Did he lose anything on the way?'

'Why don't you go ask him yourself, seeing as you are so worried about the good of the collective farm?' Zlikha replied, without stopping.

'Well, how was I going to outrun you?' Shamshinur joked after her. 'You're normally one of the boldest among us, but even so, you stopped yourself halfway.'

Zlikha laughed bitterly to herself. Shamshinur was right, she had stopped halfway. Her life had always been like this: she would dash ahead to a certain line and then stop, not knowing what to do next. This incisive thought would not leave Zlikha alone even when she got home. Like a wild animal prowling its cage, she wandered around all four rooms of her house, taking off her clothes as she went and scattering them everywhere, and it was only when she reached the kitchen that she was surprised to discover that she was walking barefoot on the cold floor. Bakhyt was sitting by the bright yellow samovar, talking to herself. She had put on all Zlikha's clothes, which she had found lying around in the house, and now she sat calmly, but the expression in her beautiful alabaster face and the firm gaze of her cold black eyes seemed to say: *has the mistress of the house lost her mind?*

Bakhyt had a habit of going into other people's houses and putting things in order for them: she would clean their rooms, rinse their dishes and wash and darn their clothes. And this time was no different — Zlikha's house was clean and tidy, the table was set and the water in the samovar boiled. Zlikha was still angry with herself and suddenly wanted to smash the dishes. It was good that there was no one except Bakhyt nearby on whom she might have taken out her anger. She stopped in the middle of the room, watching as Bakhyt lit a lamp and placed the whistling pot-bellied samovar on a small tray. The cold floor, on which Zlikha was still standing, gradually drew the heat from her body and she began to feel it with a heavy numbness and weariness.

'Auntie!' Bakhyt called over to her affectionately and poked her in the side with a long finger.

Zlikha jumped as if she'd been stung,

'What's the matter, have you gone mad?'

Bakhyt laughed loudly, but her pure clear eyes remained motionless, only in their depths a dim light. And these lights seemed to pierce right through Zlikha. Without saying a word, Bakhyt brought a pair of felt slippers, threw them at Zlikha's feet and then threw a plush sleeveless jacket over her shoulders. These were the clothes Zlikha had brought back from Semipalatinsk when she was a newly married girl. Or to be more precise, this plush sleeveless jacket and these felt slippers made up the entire contents of the dowry that she'd brought with her from her parents' house. Zlikha's Tartar stepmother had given them to her with a begrudging look that seemed to suggest that even this dowry had consisted of several camels and their calves. As time passed, these things increasingly bore a tinge of miserliness and meanness of spirit for Zlikha, and she tried to wear them as little as possible. So, now was definitely not the time to be flouncing around in such an outfit. She took off her sleeveless jacket and threw it on the back of a chair, but Bakhyt threw it over Zlikha's shoulders again.

'You should not sit around in the evening in a white nightdress.'

'Why's that?' Zlikha smiled.

'A woman in white at night will bear a child but a woman in white in the day will suffer misfortune.'

'Who told you that?'

'Big Zhenge.'

'Who or what is this Big Zhenge?'

'She's *Bi-ata's* wife.'

'So, what misfortune awaits me?'

'No, you're going to have a baby.'

'Me?! But I don't have a husband. Who do you think I am, a hen that can produce chicks without a cockerel?'

'No, you're going to have a baby!' This time, the lights in Bakhyt's eyes flashed. 'Big Zhenge saw you in a dream in a nightdress made out of white silk. You were being carried by a white horse.'

'If I was riding a white horse, then that's a sign of death.'

'No, not death!' Bakhyt corrected her. 'Big Zhenge interpreted the dream in a different way. She said that the white horse was a good angel.'

Zlikha did not want to disappoint the poor girl, who in her heart of hearts really wished her well. She cast aside her troubled thoughts and impulsively embraced and pressed her to her. And it was as if only today, now, at this very moment, that she truly felt herself to be a woman for the first time. Her entire body was suddenly filled with a heavy warmth as if a child's lips had touched her breasts. But at the same time, she fully experienced the weakness of the female character, which is sometimes unable to overcome the most ordinary test set by society, and the fragility of female happiness, which, as often happens, disappears and dissolves in a single short moment, and the inordinate severity of female yearning and anguish, which not all are able to endure.

It was in that moment that Zlikha cursed her lot as a woman and, that like many of them, she would have to go through everything that she was now experiencing in her heart. But what was she meant to feel, she was already living the life she was leading — no matter how unfair it might be! And there was no reason to be upset with old Zhusup's wife just because she had seen her in a dream in a white nightdress. Her intentions had been well-meaning. After all, she had entrusted Zlikha's fate to a good angel. Only a bright shining soul is capable of worrying about another. And how could she be upset by Kazhimurat, who worked so hard both in the winter cold and the summer heat, never sparing himself that he had failed to pay attention to her feelings? It seemed to Zlikha that the lights in Bakhyt's motionless, penetrating gaze shone through with a silent reproach. And this somehow caused her to become dispirited.

The sonorous song of the boiling yellow samovar subsided, and Zlikha asked Bakhyt to put some embers in the samovar and then gave the girl a pack of tea that old Zhusup had brought back from the district centre when he had gone to look for the people who had attacked Kazhimurat. Naturally, the old man never found them, but he had brought back a whole kilogram of tea, dutifully distributing a pack to everyone in the aul.

Once her disappointment had passed, Zlikha suddenly felt very cold. She was chilled to her marrow and now tried to warm herself with the strong aromatic tea. It was a pity that Kazhimurat, who loved tea, hadn't come to see her. The smooth movements of Bakhyt's long thin fingers and the expression on the girl's beautiful face evoked new thoughts in Zlikha.

'Bakhyt, how old are you?'

'Nineteen.'

'But I'm sure you were nineteen the summer before last?'

'No, I'm nineteen!' The girl insisted, her eyes flashing. 'Big Zhenge promised to marry me off as soon as I turned twenty. I'm not married yet, so I must be nineteen.'

'Ah, then you'll just have to wait a little bit longer,' Zlikha reassured her. 'The war will be over, then the men will return from the front, and you will be the first that we see married off.'

What could the rest of the women expect if even Bakhyt was not even admitting that she was twenty? Unfortunately, the flame of intoxicating love that embraces you at twenty is irretrievably extinguished by thirty. But an even worse fate is to embrace your beloved husband at twenty only already to be widowed by the age of thirty and left embracing a cold pillow, wet with tears. What could be more unfair than a fate such as this? It was strange, but Zlikha's memories of her twenties contained neither regret nor great joy. Her girlish years had passed unnoticed as if they had never existed at all. She had grown up in her parents' house, subject to their strict rules, and she had had no time to find and choose a man. The fun and frolics of youth seemed to have passed her by somehow.

Zlikha spent her youth measuring the path from her school to home and then back again, and then repeating the process from home to the technical college, each monotonous journey accompanied by the endless criticism and complaints of her stepmother. Zlikha was certain of only one thing: she was going to have to get married someday — so she married the first man who happened across her path, even though he was much older than her. In cases like these, people say that the bride has been caught by a groom, whose lips are already cold. It was as if the flame that should have intoxicated her in her twenties had never flared up and remained unspent and now it would give her no rest. Someone gently opened the outside door.

'It's Auntie Rapiya's red-haired son,' Bakhyt pronounced. Without fail, she could recognise the footsteps of every member of the aul.

Bekmurat came in, holding a brown bridle in his hands and, sniffling loudly, reached up for the nail and hung it up on it. He then threw a piece of paper folded into four in front of Zlikha and headed for the exit.

'Come in, son, have some tea with us!' Zlikha invited him.

'No, I've had mine.' The boy shifted uneasily from one foot to the other.

'Hark at you! Anyone would think you'd eaten your fill of smoked meat and other dainties.'

'I didn't have any meat, but I did drink my fill of fresh milk.'

'Ah, well, seeing as you've eaten so well, why don't you have your tea without milk,' Zlikha smiled ironically. 'You can catch your breath a bit.'

Bekmurat was ready to take off, but he didn't dare turn down Zlikha's hospitality. She pushed a bowl of dry oatmeal porridge towards him.

'Go on, eat!' she said. 'There's no need to be shy in this house, we don't stand on ceremony here.'

Bekmurat's face stretched into a wide toothless grin. Bakhyt, seeing his hands covered with a large crust of dirt, gasped and dragged the boy to the washstand.

'And the scamp says he's been drinking fresh milk!' she scolded the boy angrily. 'You've been milking the cow, but you haven't even washed your hands! Or did you forget to do the milking today? You'd better watch out or you'll end up losing your nickname *Ginger Housewife* at this rate!'

Zlikha noticed that Bekmurat's legs were black with dirt. Not wanting to embarrass the boy, she took the lamp from the table and moved it to the side dresser. Then she sat down on a chair with her back to her guests and unfolded the document that Bekmurat had brought. It was the receipt from the regional grain reception centre. Zlikha sighed with relief: the collective farm had now fully met its grain delivery quota. The aul's hard work had not been in vain. And Bekmurat's too. His hands and feet, like those of his peers, had become hard and cracked during the harvest, when he, along with the other boys had gleaned all the ears of wheat that had fallen on the fields. It was a pity that all he was receiving today for all this hard work was a small bowl of dried oatmeal porridge. Well, never mind, the war would come to an end, and everyone would be able to live in prosperity and plenty. But what about Kazhimurat, whose shoulders had borne the brunt of the weight of the wheat harvest? How was he feeling? What was wrong with his foot?

'I'd better be off,' Bekmurat said. 'I've got things to do.'

'Where are you in such a rush to get to?' Zlikha looked at him attentively. 'Come on, you can level with me, darling!'

'Mama will have my guts for garters.' Bekmurat said, lowering his eyes.

'Are you on the run from her?' Bakhyt began to interrogate him. 'You probably didn't keep an eye on the calf, is that it?'

'The calf is on its leash,' Bekmurat answered seriously. 'It's just Mama said she wanted to send a warm shirt to the front. She was going to knit it today and ordered me to do the spinning for it and get the threads ready... And I haven't finished doing it yet.'

A melancholy silence settled over the room. *And even this emaciated young lad is only thinking about the front,* Zlikha thought bitterly. *At that time of life, when a boy should be riding about on the back of a yearling, he has to work like an adult, spinning yarn, gleaning ears of wheat, collecting the hay, removing the manure, carrying the water, grazing the cattle and even milking the cow. The damned fascists, they've even stolen our children's childhoods!*

Zlikha went into the bedroom, put on a dress and went back into the kitchen.

'Where is Kazhimurat?

'He was in the cattle yard, and Almurat was with him.'

Zlikha threw the plush sleeveless jacket over her dress and rushed out of the house.

She found Kazhimurat in the office, where he was sitting with old Zhusup and Almurat. He greeted her coldly, and Zlikha detected some hidden resentment in his eyes, which were looking point-blank into hers.

Kazhimurat had not shaved for a long time, his moustache and beard shone a rusty-red, his face was haggard, his eyebrows protruded forward and the skin on his forehead was unhealthily translucent. The fire was roaring in the stove, its red glare flashed on his sharp cheekbones, carving out a deep blush. Kazhimurat sat hunched in his chair, his chin almost touching his knees. Zlikha was not surprised at his thinness. There wasn't a trace of the former friendliness and the childish expression of serenity to be found in the sharpened features of Kazhimurat's face. They had gone, to be replaced by a hardness bordering on extreme unapproachability. For a minute or two, he almost seemed like a complete stranger to her.

A heavy silence hung over the office, similar to that in a house where someone has recently died. Old Zhusup's head was nodding like a horse that has just come back from a long journey. Almurat looked into the mouth of the stove silently and intently, as if he'd lost the gift of speech and was looking for it in the flames. The greenbottle, which had until quite recently been bugging Zlikha, continued to buzz near the ceiling.

Zlikha, who had been running full speed, froze at the threshold for a few seconds, then, stepping gingerly over in her socks, went to the cabinet and shoved the receipt into one of the folders. The sooty teapot's lid clattered and old Zhusup pulled out his teapot with its broken spout from the chest of drawers and the two cracked bowls tied with wire and put them on the table. Zlikha chose the best moment and asked, looking at Kazhimurat's foot wrapped in its rag:

'Did you manage to get away without a break? If so, you're in luck because I'm the best bone setter in the village!'

Zhusup replied on Kazhimurat's behalf.

'I'm afraid I think things are a lot worse than that for our young hero, here. He delivered the grain on time and many thanks for that, but why take all that risk later? Who needs our dray animals the state they're in? You should have left them with Trofim, he would have looked after them. But why did you have to go when you did?!' The old man looked angrily at Kazhimurat. 'You're the type who won't be turned off your path if Allah Himself orders you to...'

Kazhimurat grimaced in anger: he couldn't stand being given advice after the deed has been done. And as if specifically in response to the old man's words, he got up from his chair and, stepping firmly with both feet, sat further away from him and the stove. Zlikha understood that Zhusup's words were directed at her personally, and the expression on the old man's face did not leave any doubt to suggest otherwise. He plunged his fingers into the canvas bag in which he kept the tea, pointedly and angrily threw a pinch of tea into the teapot, pushed it away from him and again assumed his usual position with hands folded on his knees and his eyes closed. Almurat got up ahead of Zlikha and put the kettle on the coals. She realized that she had missed her opportunity to inveigle herself into this male company and Kazhimurat, by all appearances, was not going to leave the office. Feeling a rush of blood to her temples, Zlikha roughly pulled Kazhimurat's oxen-chewed cloth coat from the back of the chair, and barked,

'Get your coat on.'

Then she threw the ragged half sheepskin, which had survived the whole long and dangerous journey with him, over his shoulders.

'Get up this instant!'

Then she threw his birch wood crutch in the direction of the door and pushed her head under Kazhimurat's armpit.

'Let's go!'

And, before Kazhimurat could object, she was already dragging him to the door. Old Zhusup and Almurat were completely taken aback and at a complete loss as to what to say.

It was a moonless night. When it is as dark as this, the bumps and potholes in the road always seem to increase. They walked home, now stuck in a knee-deep quagmire, now stumbling over hardened clods of mud. The road from the office, which was on the hill, to Zlikha's house, which stood on the outskirts of the aul, seemed to be endless. Kazhimurat was not used to showing his outward feelings, little surprise considering he had never experienced any open expression of any feelings from those close to him. He hadn't made a sound in the district hospital when they had cut his toes off without any painkillers. He had no regrets about anything. But he was now worried that he had become crippled and might not be able to walk on his own. He walked, or rather, dragged himself along the street, first drenched in a hot sweat, then filled with a cold chill. Although Kazhimurat could not see Zlikha's face in the pitch darkness, he could tell by the way she tightly held him by the waist and her faltering breathing, that she was crying. Silently, hiding her tears. A strange warm feeling awoke in his chest, a kind of long and hot pain entered his heart, and he gradually forgot about his foot, which had been causing him such grief all this time.

He felt as if Zlikha could have dragged him like this all her life. Although as big as a mountain, Kazhimurat seemed no heavier than a feather to her, and, indeed, how could she have ever considered a man who had borne the brunt of the aul's work for so many months a burden? She walked, tightly clasping Kazhimurat by the waist, breathing in time with him, trying to navigate an even path in the darkness, and felt as if she were carrying the most precious and valuable gift that life had ever given her.

Just before they reached her door, Kazhimurat stopped to catch his breath.

He sat down on a ledge that protruded from the wall. He was sweating all over and breathing heavily. Worried that he might catch cold, Zlikha reached out to cover his chest with the collar of her sheepskin coat, but Kazhimurat managed to intercept her hand with his huge palm and, with a soft but insistent movement, pulled her away from him.

'Does your foot hurt?' Zlikha asked. 'I ended up torturing you...'

Kazhimurat didn't even nod his head this time, as he had before. He stared at her as if trying to remember her image forever. His black eyes shone with a gloomy light, like dark water. Zlikha caught her breath and sank down beside him, wrapping her arms around his knees.

'O, Creator, why am I being punished like this? I did nothing to offend my mother and my father refused to grant me his blessing!' Crying loudly, Zlikha buried her face in Kazhimurat's chest.

A strong cool wind swirled above, spinning a sad song in the tops of the larches and cedars. A flock of birds, frightened by the gusts, flew up from the tree and circled around the dark blue sky for a long time, emitting restless cries. The stars sparkled in the sky as if its dark velvet canopy had been pierced by innumerable burning rods. In the trembling light of the stars, an amorous heart might have interpreted the sweet smile on her girlish lips. And under this huge sky, the small village lay in a sleepy slumber, shrinking like the constellation of the Pleiades. The lights were out in the houses, but the fires still burned in their hearths. The smell of spring was heavy in the air. And it was spring that released Kazhimurat and Zlikha's hopes and dreams...

The faint light of the early morning entered the room and touched her eyelashes. Zlikha sat up in bed. Pale and unsteady, the ghostly light created a sense of unreality. Everything around was unclear, as if the world had been covered in a haze. And Zlikha felt as if she were floating weightlessly, half-drunk. She could not sense her body, her head was spinning and she was tormented by a terrible thirst. But at the same time, a great delight danced in her breast, much as a young child feels, who has been given a new toy the previous evening, has gone to sleep with it and, waking up, experiences a long-awaited reacquaintance with this joy. Zlikha was seized with impatience. Wasn't this the very happiness she had been dreaming of?

Someone was breathing next to her... Her chest responded to this manifestation of life with warmth, a kind of sweet languor took possession of her body, and the memory brought back a distant sensation, which she had first experienced when she was only sixteen years old. She covered her breast with her elbow, then, without opening her eyes, rummaged around with her free hand, trying to find a blanket and cover herself. But where was it? There was a little more light, Zlikha looked around her with a sleepy look, saw a hairy leg sticking out from under the blanket, recognized Kazhimurat, who was lying next to her, and immediately felt at ease.

That night she had made her bed on the floor so that he could lie more freely and the blankets had slipped to the very foot of it. Opposite the bed stood two chairs, with two sets of clothes hanging from their backs, hers and Kazhimurat's, but she mistook them for two people sitting there. Nearby stood a bottle of alcohol, with which she had rubbed Kazhimurat's foot yesterday, and her handkerchief hung from the chair. There were just the two of them, no one else. Zlikha pulled her blanket over her.

In the next room, the wall clock ticked as if in a competition to keep time with the cockerels. She recalled the jobs that awaited her that morning and it was a pity to have to part with her warm bed. Something made her look back and she met Kazhimurat's gaze staring directly at her, and she was taken aback. Her face flushed with shame, and her first thought was to run anywhere, but then she threw herself into the embrace of his mighty arms...

She did not want to think about the jobs that awaited her in the collective farm yard.

Surely, a little happiness might be apportioned to her in this life. And no one was going to drag her away from what she had waited so long for and had gone through such painful suffering for. Even if the Creator himself were to come for her that morning, she would still not have deprived herself of her long-awaited and painful female happiness...

The panes were wet with condensation, the pale rays of the sun weakly penetrated the windows, barely able to break through the white fog, and patterned shadows trembled along the walls of the room. The red satin blankets, the red curtains, the scarf with a red pattern, and a lampshade made of red fabric all created the sensation that the room was engulfed in red flames... To a person uninitiated into Zlikha's life, this excess of red might have led them to think that she was overly attached to luxury but all this opulence was merely a memory of her past. The things that now caught her eye reminded her of her life with her family, nothing more. However, these decorations now evoked strange thoughts in her, a kind of awkwardness, absurdity or even worthlessness. Zlikha's eyes had been definitively opened.

Very early in the morning, a spring bird had climbed under the cornice of the roof and began to shout its challenge to the day and Zlikha recognized the trill of a blackbird. From the front room came the booming blows of an axe, then the loud, ear-piercing grinding of iron tongs on bricks — evidently, Bakhyt, who was lighting the stove, was not in the best of moods. The new moon that marked the unexpected changes in the poor girl's behaviour had yet to rise and it seemed that Bakhyt's heart was clouded with envy.

Kazhimurat was lying motionless, his eyes closed, but it was not clear whether he was sleeping or just lying with his eyes closed. Zlikha looked at him, greedily inhaled the smell of his body and slipped out of his strong embrace. She knew that if Bakhyt was in a bad mood, then the yellow-bellied samovar would not be singing its triumphant song any time soon. When Bakhyt was in her house, Zlikha relinquished the right to interfere in her own kitchen, so it was best to get dressed as soon as possible and sneak out of the house unnoticed. She began to look for her outerwear, but could not find them. However, Kazhimurat's, worn-out boots, threadbare trousers and short ripped half sheepskin hung next to the threshold. Zlikha laughed to herself at Bakhyt's childish revenge and quickly began to dress in these unusual clothes.

A foul-smelling mist rose from the swampy hollow and ascended above the blearily blackening trees. The hoarfrost had not yet melted and the sun's rays barely reached the tops of the hay stooks. The larks dotted the blue sky, shooting up like an arrow from under each bush and freezing in the sky, barely visible from below. Their sonorous, heart-grabbing trills didn't seem to be coming from their tiny throats but the tremulous flapping of their wings.

Zlikha's brown stallion stood next to the well on the pasture, waiting to be brought its oats. Last year's withered grass was, as they say, barely fit for a horse and its flanks sagged, its hair was bristly and its belly distended, like a wolf's. Accustomed to being well and regularly fed in the morning, it was not happy that Zlikha had appeared today without the usual canvas nose bag, and therefore followed her.

Next to the spacious covered paddock, located between the barns and cattle yard, the five or six old men who guarded the collective horse herd were treating each other to home-grown tobacco. Each had a bag under his arm. Holding a thick roll-up between his lips, Kiyakmurt was standing on a log and, gesticulating vigorously, was explaining something to the old men.

With the first warmth of spring, they needed to start sowing, but, before that, the manes and tails of the yearlings and two-year-olds needed to be cut. At the moment, rope was so scarce you couldn't find enough to hang yourself with. So, the horsehair and the remnants of the wool would need to be distributed to those households that knew how to twist lassoes. There wasn't a single piece of rawhide available for shoe thread so that the shoes needed for the spring could be made. People had no shoes, and you can't walk barefoot on a frosty field and sow the fields.

Kiyakmurt would always end up in the very place that Zlikha was heading as if he knew all her plans in advance.

Just like the proverbial all-seeing mother-in-law who constantly has an eye on her daughter-in-law even when the rest of the aul is asleep, Zlikha thought. *This is what he means when he says he likes to be 'out and about' with the people.* Zlikha could not understand why today the old men had still insisted on bringing their saddle bags with them. Only Tazhimurat had not bothered; he was on his horse with the tops of his boots rolled down, and looked at the old men with reproach. Old Zhusup joined them from the side of the barns, in an unbuttoned camel hair *chekmen* tunic. As soon as he appeared, Tazhimurat got up and stalked off to the forge.

The herd, which had been out on the winter pasture all the cold season, looked well-fed. The full-bellied mares and the three- and two-year-old fillies had already managed to shed their winter coats. Zlikha rejoiced that the horses had come out of the blizzard-driven winter well-fed and in good form. Without interrupting the old men's conversation, she made a mental note of the number of mares that looked likely to foal any day now. Kiyakmurt had his own theories on all this and was expounding them now.

'How much milk does a mare give each day?' he asked Zlikha as soon as she approached the herd.

'I've never had to milk them,' she answered evasively. 'So, I don't know exactly.'

'We need to set up a commission to find out.'

'But the mares haven't foaled yet...'

'They will foal and we need to set one up. By the way, each miscarriage will be recorded as the herdsmen's fault.'

'A foal is only a certainty when it's on the tether and kumis, when it's in the flask. And anyway, it's not our custom to sell the mare's milk.'

'How could that have happened?' Kiyakmurt reacted. 'Your collective farmers drink ayran[20]. Why not sell them the mare's milk? And there isn't a Kazakh alive who doesn't like a drop of kumis. Just work out how much extra income the collective farm will make!'

---

[20] A yoghurt–like drink made from milk.

Zlikha was astonished at Kiyakmurt's penny-pinching.

'Have you thought about trimming the fluff from the bird's eggs?'

'Based on the average state value of fluff, I reckon a single ball of it would probably be worth as much as a hundred eggs!' Kiyakmurt retorted, ignoring the irony of Zlika's comment.

It was unclear how the conversation might have ended if old Zhusup had not intervened.

'These are the last remnants of Yelmurat's herds,' he said, admiring the horses. 'Big in the bone and frisky at the gallop — when we went on raids we would always choose horses from his herd. Yelmurat was unlucky that he never produced a famous racehorse that would have glorified the name of its master.'

'That probably happened because he knocked his herd together by stealing other people's...' Kiyakmurt interjected.

'What utter nonsense!' Old Zhusup frowned. 'A stolen herd will have different markings. Just look at all the horses here, they're all dark brown, which tells us that they were all sired from the same pair.'

'Oh, Allah!' one of the old men exclaimed suddenly. 'This dark brown one with the white head markings looks like she isn't pregnant!'

'She doesn't just look like she isn't, she definitely isn't!' old Zhusup confirmed. 'For the whole of the summer they didn't take the collar off her, and if they did, she'd be chased by just about every male, be he a stallion or a gelding. Just you try getting properly knocked up, when you've got every Tom, Dick or Harry trying to climb on top of you!'

'Hee-hee-hee!' the old men giggled, passing the snuff-box around and sniffing their fill of the finely ground tobacco.

'But look at this mare — every hair is shining on her!' another of the old men said. 'Look, how she runs, just like a steppe fox!'

'Not much good for a team, but under the saddle — she'll fly like a bird!' old Zhusup began to explain. 'You'd only ever get couriers or stewards riding on a horse like that.'

At that moment, Auntie Rapiya came running and rushed up to Zlikha.

'It's a disaster, Zlikha, come quickly! The women are about to take the seed grain!'

'What do you mean, take the seed grain?'

'Someone has spread a rumour that you're planning to give all our remaining grain to the Algabas collective.'

'And who spread that?'

'The devil knows!'

At the warehouse that now occupied what used to be the club, an unimaginable scene was unfolding. The gates were wide open and a crowd had formed at the doors. Some had already climbed in and others were forcing their way out. There's a lot of truth to the old saying that *when the women are on the march, they sweep everything before them like a black tornado.* The walls of the dilapidated building were on the verge of falling down. The women were fighting to get into the warehouse, tearing their clothes to shreds and without a thought for the children who were getting trampled under their feet. The air rang with their furious cries, but no one was listening to anyone else. Zlikha tried to get into the warehouse, but then a blood-curdling cry went up,

'Drag the chairman by her hair! We aren't going to sweat our good blood for complete strangers! We've suffered enough from these outsiders who've been put in charge of our collective farm! Drag her away, give her what she deserves!'

Zlikha found herself swirling like a leaf in a whirlpool. The only thing she could recall were the furious, bulging eyes that surrounded her, the faces and eyebrows turned white with flour dust and shaking, greedy fingers plunging into the grain supplies. When Zlikha came to, she found herself lying in the yard, one of her eyes was swollen and she could not see out of it and her mouth was filled with the taste of blood. A moth-eaten hat and a half fur coat with a torn collar lay nearby.

'Oh Allah, these are not human beings, they're savages!' Rapiya shouted angrily, lifting Zlikha to her feet by her armpits. 'You've all gone completely mad, you miserable wretches!'

With difficulty, Zlikha managed to get to the scales and sat down on them. Her head was ringing as if she had been hit with a heavy stone, but more terrible than this was the bitterness she felt at the change she saw in the people around her. The place where her heart should have been felt cold and empty. Zlikha froze to the spot, sitting on the scales like an ancient pagan idol. She found it impossible to recognize the women: their faces distorted into a mass of rough frowns and wrinkles that resembled tree bark, and their hands, like gnarled branches. Indeed, Rapiya was absolutely right — they weren't like human beings but savages.

The dust stood in the air like a large column and the women were pouring the grain into their sacks with such haste and greed, it was as if they were sacking a town and seizing their enemy's goods. *What on earth is going on?* the feverish thought drummed through her brain. *Are these the same women that I shared my last possessions with?! Are these the same people with whom I laboured day and night, never giving myself a moment's rest?! Who would have ever thought that they might have husbands and that they had ever given birth to children? They weren't human beings but animals who had been driven mad on the eve of an earthquake! It's at times like these when the old saying really comes into its own: 'The mind of a woman never rises much further than the hem of her dress'. But what am I to do? If only Kiyakmurt would ride up... Maybe he was right to have such a poor opinion of them.*

For a few seconds, Zlikha was seized by an uncontrollable desire to jump on her horse and fall on the women with her whip in her hands. The blood rushed to her head, her body tensed, preparing for the fight, but a moment later, Zlikha realized that there was no way she could raise her whip against these women, who had simply been driven distraught by their unbearable hardship and decided to bury their snouts in the grain. *O blessed times of peace!* Zlikha thought to herself, wiping away the tears that streamed down her face. *How we failed to fully appreciate you! Who would have thought that the time would come when people would curse their very own lives and leave their children to be trampled underfoot by their fellow madwomen!*

Shamshinur tried to fight her way out of the scrum, dragging a full sack of grain. She tried to lift it onto her shoulders, but she had miscalculated her strength and poured too much into it. After two or three steps, she sank helplessly to the ground. Rapiya prowled next to the gates, trying to scold one woman and putting another to shame, but none of them listened to her. Zlikha caught her pained and suffering gaze and nodded in the direction of Shamshinur:

'Give her a hand, Auntie Rapiya! She clearly has a large family to feed, poor thing, and can't provide for so many mouths! Help her lift that sack onto her shoulders!'

Shamshinur, however, pretended not to hear what she was saying and turned her back on her... However, her defiant look seemed to say: *Just you try taking this from me when I've fought so hard for it.* Gradually, the women went out into the yard, most of them collected their grain in small shopping bags and occasionally in sacks. Only two or three of them ran out and disappeared into the back streets. The rest were in no hurry to go home — they appeared only now to realize the enormity of what they'd done.

Old Zhusup and Kazhimurat now appeared outside on the street. One of them was leaning on a cane, the other, a crutch. On seeing them, the women froze: a deadly silence hung over the yard, which only a minute ago had been the scene of the most unimaginable commotion and caterwauling. The gates were wide open, barely hanging on their hinges, scratched female faces, dishevelled hair, grains of raw wheat laying scattered and trampled in the mud... This terrible and incredible scene seemed to have a depressing effect on the men because for some time they just stared in silence way out towards the mountains. Old Zhusup, the aul's respected elder, walked right up to Shamshinur and sat down next to her on the end of her sack and then just as calmly began to sweep up the grain that had been scattered under her feet with his cane. Kazhimurat limped up to the warehouse, closed the gate and the heavy doors with his shoulder and locked them, throwing the keys at Shamshinur's feet. She completely shrank into herself, not daring to raise her eyes from the ground.

The children stood nearby, their cracked bare feet covered with goosebumps from the cold.

A thin stream of smoke wisped out of the chimney of the *samanka*, which had previously been used to dry the grain. However, ever since the cows had calved, it had been used to boil up a floury liquid mash. Although not the heartiest of dishes, Zlikha reasoned, it gave some strength to those working in the barns and the cattle yard. The women stood rooted to the spot and it didn't look like they'd be coming to their senses soon after what they had done.

'Auntie Rapiya, the children are hungry, and here we are sitting around here like a lot of brides waiting for their bridegrooms,' Zlikha said with malicious irony. 'Give them the hot mash.'

'Come on, kids!' Rapiya's voice sounded gruff. 'Come and get it! After all, it's in your name that certain people around here seem to be ready to sell their souls!'

But the women understood Zlikha's order in their own way. They thought she had called the children over because she didn't want them to hear the tongue-lashing that she was about to deliver them. But Zlikha continued to sit in silence even after the children had followed Rapiya in a great rabble to the *samanka*. She pulled her hat down over her forehead, hiding her swollen eye, and said in a calm tone:

'So, you're going to play dumb, are you? After all, it seems you've taken everything you wanted and said what you wanted to say. So, you can go home and celebrate your victory.'

Nobody uttered a word in response. Sacks and bags were proffered on the end of arms like heavy weights. The women were ready to run back to the barn that moment and pour the grain back into the hopper, but there was a black padlock on the gate. And no one had the strength to come up and take the keys lying at Shamshinur's feet. Kazhimurat dragged the body of a cart from somewhere, turned it over and placed it next to the scales and then handed Zlikha a piece of paper and a pencil stub. Old Zhusup stopped sweeping up the grain with his cane and raised his gaze from the ground.

'Dear Zlikha, did you deliver the grain to the state in accordance with the quotas and plan?' the old man asked Zlikha.

'Yes, I did, *Bi-ata*.'

'And what about the seed grain for next year? Will we have to beg and borrow from our neighbours again?'

'We'll be able to lend a little ourselves. We have enough in the store, so long as there are enough working hands to sow it in the spring and harvest it in the autumn.'

'So, we're doing well.' The old man nodded his head in satisfaction. 'Thank you, my dear Zlikha! In my memory, ever since the Murat Collective Farm was first founded, we've never achieved this. We've always had to go with outstretched hands, begging for grain from our neighbours. That's good, good... We have enough workers.' He pointed his cane at the sullen crowd of women. 'There are enough working hands to feed those who need to eat. How do things stand at the Algabas collective in this regard? They have often come to our aid in the past. And if my memory serves me right, there has never been a time when they ever refused us. That's why we are a collective farm... Soviet collective farms look after each other, for we have a common cause, am I right? Or maybe I've misunderstood something in my old age?'

Old Zhusup had approached the cause of the recent fracas from a cunning, oblique angle. First, he had outlined the situation in the aul's collective farm, then the neighbouring farm and finally reminded everyone that everyone was facing the same challenges. Basically, he had just delivered a master class in political persuasion, a lesson that the collective farmers at this difficult time singularly lacked. *It is precisely this sort of pep talk that the people need, instead of Kiyakmurt's unreasonable shouting and demands,* Zlikha thought, marvelling at the old man's wisdom for the umpteenth time. Old Zhusup closed his eyes, sat, thinking about something, stroked his beard with the palm of his hand, then took out a handkerchief the size of a towel and started brushing away the grains of snuff tobacco that had become lodged in his moustaches. Everyone knew that he wouldn't speak again until he had combed through every hair in his beard. Some of them even smiled imperceptibly, looking at the ground while others breathed a sigh of relief, shifting from foot to foot. Only Shamshinur, whose winnings had been more impressive than the others, suddenly felt annoyed and threw a piercing glance at the old man from under her brows.

Zlikha hung a weight on the scales with a clang, as if drawing a line under this short, hard-hitting discussion. She turned to Kazhimurat.

'Let's start! We'll distribute to the families of front-line soldiers first! First of all, we need to count how many children each family has...'

'But what about those who don't have any children? Since we're all working for the front, that makes us all families of front-line soldiers!' Shamshinur exclaimed, jumping up. 'Everyone has worked hard every month of this year and that means that the grain belongs to everyone. If we hadn't taken our share, it would have all ended up in Algabas's barns!'

'Ah, my dear girl!' old Zhusup chuckled. 'You seem to think that God has given people a tongue simply to say the first bit of nonsense that comes into their head? Well, go on, carry on speaking! But saying that, it would seem that our farm's quota for hot air and chatter has been more than fulfilled.'

'But our husbands are fighting at the front!' Shamshinur shouted, sitting next to the old man and still not backing down. 'She thinks she's the big boss around here — and all she wants to do is let all our hard work go to the four winds. It reeks of thievery to me!'

'What are you like?' the old man said, shaking his head sadly. His eyebrows drew together at the bridge of his nose. 'You're not being accused of anything, my dear child! I had just hoped that you'd come to your senses and realise what you'd done, but it turns out you haven't.'

'Come on, comrades put the grain on the scales!' Zlikha announced, seeing that the argument was in danger of flaring up again. 'Even water has a price, but we are, after all, talking about grain here... Bring up your sack, Shamshinur! Perhaps you'd like to stand next to the scales, otherwise, you might say that we have short-changed you?'

None of the women moved, they just shifted uneasily from one foot to another again. Kazhimurat had to drag their sacks and canvas bags to the scales, weigh them, and then carry back to each woman the booty she had won. Zlikha glanced at the list and made a mental calculation.

'You've only taken a tonne in total,' she summed up calmly. 'If you make good next year, I'm ready to give you another tonne.' Go on then, Shamshinur, open the gate, help yourself! Maybe you think you don't have enough?'

'Leave her be, my dear,' old Zhusup remarked. 'I think she's already heard enough for one day.'

'I know that none of you have spared yourselves, working in the fields,' Zlikha addressed the women, standing next to the scales. 'Your bodies are covered in scars and scabs and there's no flesh on your arms at all — just tendons and bones. But when all's said and done, we all know we're working for the sake of the country, for the sake of victory over the enemy! Thank you for your work, there really is no measure for it. There can be no measure for the tears you've shed and the groans, sleepless nights and sweltering days you've suffered. I wanted to try to free you from the heavy stupor that overcomes you when you come home from the threshing barn at midnight, completely exhausted. As you know, our mill isn't working like it used to in the old days. Without it, you're not going to get much use out of your grain. Today you will eat it, and end up callusing your hands, trying to grind it in your mortars. But tomorrow your pantries will be empty again. When you could have received the shares you've earned in part, if necessary. Then it would have lasted better until times get better. And then there are your own kin living in the next aul, Soviet people like you and me who have handed over their entire harvest to the state and have no seed grain. They have nothing to sow this spring! Perhaps, we should all rejoice in their grief?'

Zlikha's throat constricted, and she paused, continuing even more quietly, 'This war will end with our victory, we all believe it, but this victory will not come in a day. How are we going to survive until next year? And what awaits us after that? You're wrong if you think that I was going to give away our grain to anyone just like that, for the sake of it! They were going to bring us seed potatoes and cabbage in return for our grain, which we will plant in the spring. The most difficult time will be when we have neither meat nor grain. I do not want the children to swell from hunger and you yourselves to fall ill. That's why I've decided to plant vegetable gardens. They probably won't make us rich but there's no denying they're going to help us get through. So, there you have it. That's essentially all that I wanted to say to you. If you think we've talked too much, we won't drag out the meeting any further. Decide for yourselves. If you think I'm wrong, here are the keys to the barns. Go ahead and continue to squander our collective reserves. It ultimately all belongs to you anyway. None of it is mine.'

Zlikha picked up the heavy braids that lay on her chest, tied them tightly around her forehead, and stalked away. The silence that ensued was total and deafening. Old man Zhusup got up from his seat.

'Why am I sitting here with you? The horses need me!'

Listening to him, you'd be forgiven for thinking that the herdsmen would never have been able to cope with cutting the mares' manes and tails without him.

It was already late morning. The warm rays of the sun warmed the earth and a moist steam rose from it. The village children, having eaten their fill of mash, returned back to the warehouse yard and started making a merry hullabaloo next to their mothers, who were still standing there like statues.

'Well girls, you've had your fun and lost half a day in the process,' Rapiya remarked. So, what are you standing around here for? Or are you just having a little rest from your *glorious labours*?'

'If you appoint a crane as a watchman, you'll soon become deafened by its squawking!' Shamshinur snarled, never missing an opportunity to hurl a barb at someone. 'I'm absolutely sick of you today, Auntie Rapiya!'

'*I* would say the same about you, and not just today...'

'Well, go ahead then! We might never get an opportunity like this again! Is it my fault that they threw a stone at that bitch, but they're all having a go at me! So, say what you've got to say here and now, Auntie Rapiya!'

'Just wait a minute, Shamshinur!' an old woman interrupted her. 'We need to decide what we're going to do with the grain.'

'Zlikha is right — we need to put it all back in the warehouse!' Rapiya replied. 'What is there to decide here?'

'God forbid that word of this ever reaches our husbands at the front... How could we ever look them in the eye after that?'

'God grant that we all survive to see that day!' Shamshinur laughed nervously. 'I wouldn't be looking him in the eyes but throwing myself on his neck!'

'Oh no! Kiyakmurt is coming!' one of the women shouted, jumping up in fright and clutching at her hem, just in case she'd have to make a run for it.

'So what, if he's coming?' Shamshinur jumped up again. 'Has a decree been issued that says that every woman has to make a run for it every time Kiyakmurt appears?'

The women huddled together like frightened sheep, then all the same, unable to control themselves, rushed out into the yard. But it was too late. Riding on a foaming bay mare, Kiyakmurt jumped out of a side lane and blocked their way. The cap on his head was tilted at an even more jaunty angle than usual and his eyebrows were knitted into a deep frown.

'So, you're going home already, are you?' he said while calming his horse. 'I see, I see!'

'Yes, we're going home,' Shamshinur retorted. 'We need to get a bit of rest.

So, work's finished a bit early today, has it? I see, I see!'

'Yes. Why shouldn't we be finished? We'll be back after lunch.'

'I know exactly what kind of work you've been up to today!' Kiyakmurt jumped off his mare and looked around at the sacks and bags the women were holding as if taking stock and counting every one of them. 'Come on then, show me what you're carrying in there!'

He examined the contents of each bag, taking a pinch of grain and almost sniffing it as if he were seeing wheat for the first time in his life. Then he clapped his hands together, brushing the dust off them.

'Well, the thing is, my dear ladies! There is a strict directive forbidding collective farm workers to be paid for their work in grain. So, what is this, I ask you?' Kiyakmurt stretched out his hand to Shamshinur's sack and held up a handful of grain from it. 'This is sabotage! You are undermining the war effort, this is a disgrace!'

At that moment, Kazhimurat went up to him and, as if greeting a close relative who he had not seen for a long time, shook Kiyakmurt's hand tightly. Then, with a grin on his face, he motioned him over to one side as if to say, let's go into the warehouse. Unable to free himself from Kazhimurat's iron grip, he meekly followed him. Kazhimurat seated Kiyakmurt on the overturned cart next to the scales, wrote a few lines on a piece of paper and handed him the note. While Kiyakmurt was reading it, Kazhimurat brought him his horse and stopped it in front of him, making it clear that he could now go about his business.

'Hey, who do you think you are to go about distributing grain to the people?!' Kiyakmurt was taken aback. 'Are you actively seeking your own early death? What do you think you're getting involved with here, are you a complete idiot?'

Terrified, the women took to their heels, regretting that they hadn't had time to pour the grain back into the warehouse.

'Now to avoid any more trouble, tell me who has the keys?' Rapiya asked the women cautiously.

'Leave it till later!' Shamshinur interrupted her.

'Oh, I see. I see!' Kiyakmurt now noted something down on the piece of paper he'd been given and began to read aloud, holding the sheet very close to his eyes. 'Listen carefully everyone! You will be my witnesses! *Witness statement! Despite my objections and disregarding the decision of the district executive committee not to give grain to collective farmers for their days worked, I, Kazhimurat Yelmuratov, the watchman at the Murat Collective Farm...'* Kiyakmurt looked up from the document and looked at Kazhimurat: 'Listen, are you the watchman or foreman around here?'

Kazhimurat replied with a vague shrug of his shoulders as if to say,

'Who cares?'

'The watchman at the Murat Collective Farm, Kazhimurat Yelmuratov, gave grain to the collective farm workers or, to be more precise, to the families of front-line soldiers from the surplus grain stored in the collective farm barn... Hmm! I'm going to have to disagree with you on that point. There is currently no surplus of grain. But, all the same... *From the surplus grain stored in the collective farm barn and personally distributed it in the form of a one-off grant to them...* Hey-y, wait a minute... *This declaration was drawn up by the district policeman of the Murat Collective Farm on 15 April 1943.'*

Kiyakmurt finished reading the declaration and, after snatching the stub pencil from Kazhimurat's hands and licking the tip, painstakingly signed the declaration.

'Should I present you with a summons or will you follow me of your own accord?' He said turning towards Kazhimurat.

'He had absolutely nothing to do with it,' Rapiya tried to explain.

'How could he, when he himself has admitted that it was he who distributed grain to the families of front-line soldiers? It's all explained right here!' Kiyakmurt nodded at the piece of paper. 'In writing!'

And then, to everyone's surprise, Shamshinur jumped up, grabbed the piece of paper from Kiyakmurt's hands, tore it up and then put the tiny pieces in her mouth.

'What are you doing?!' Kiyakmurt squealed.

'Open up the barn!' Shamshinur shouted, without deigning to answer him.

Before anyone had time to come to their senses, she had begun to throw the small children who had come running at the commotion at Kiyakmurt's feet.

'You deal with them first, if you're so brave! Judge them and send them to prison first!'

Shamshinur seemed to be mad with fury. Without letting Kiyakmurt even open his mouth, she put her strong arms around him and dragged him towards the warehouse. The other women also helped. A solid scrum of bodies formed around him, and Kiyakmurt only came to his senses when he found himself already in the warehouse.

Seeing the women getting out of hand again, Kazhimurat intervened, forcibly tyring to wrestle the policemen from their grasp. However, stopping Shamshinur was never going to be that easy.

'Here you are if it makes you happy!' And with a powerful push, she knocked Kiyakmurt face first into the grain and then emptied her sack over his head. 'Come on, girls, pour it back in!'

When all the grain had been replaced, Shamshinur deftly locked the gate and, putting her empty bag under her arm, walked away.

* * *

Zlikha was already in bed when Kazhimurat came in. He sat down at the table for a long time. He was evidently in a very bad mood. Shadows thickened in the corners of the room, the stove had gone out and the pot-bellied samovar, still with cold water left over from the morning, gleamed resentfully at the door. Although Kazhimurat was able to find some peace in this beautiful and spacious house, he nevertheless felt constrained, and therefore could not bring himself to kindle a fire. It seemed strange to him that Zlikha had not responded to his arrival, and he did not know what to think. In addition, she was lying with her head covered and turned to the wall, a posture that seemed to question why he had come. The collective-farm office was cramped but he felt free there and able to be himself, and now it seemed to be a little piece of paradise — at least, there was no danger of upsetting anyone there. There is a Kazakh saying that the worst thing in life that can happen is if a mare develops the temper of a camel, or a camel appropriates the qualities of a mare.

His foot ached, and he bandaged his foot. Then he picked up his boots at the door and stood for some time at the entrance, wondering if he would be better off sneaking off somewhere else, but it was a pity to have to part with the blessings of life that he had begun to get a taste for here. Kazhimurat tiptoed over to the table and sat down on the chair again. The photo of Toremurat on the wall was hanging crookedly. He straightened it, thinking again about the fickleness of fate, which one minute might turn its face towards an individual only to turn its back on him another. Maybe he, Kazhimurat, would face a similar fate? He sat for a long time and didn't notice how he had fallen asleep, lulled by the monotonous ticking of the wall clock and the quiet, measured, barely audible song of the cricket, emanating from behind the stove.

'Kazheke[21], is that you?' Zlikha's voice resonated in the darkness. 'I'm sorry, I fell asleep.'

Kazhimurat went up to the bed and stroked Zlikha's hair. The pillow was wet — she must have wept her fill before falling asleep. Zlikha took his hand and put it to her hot face, then pressed it to her breast.

'Sweetheart, you have no one to take care of you!' she sighed.

He felt his palm become hot, leaned over her and hid his face in her breast...

There was a racket in the hallway — the sort that is made by people who are used to unceremoniously making themselves quite at home in someone else's house. Kazhimurat and Zlikha jumped out of bed like

---

[21] *Kazheke* – an informal but respectful form of Kazhimurat

scalded cats and ran to the kitchen to be greeted with the sight of Rapiya and Shamshinur triumphantly placing a can of mead on the table.

'Look, the sun has barely gone down outside and the pair of them are already in the sack!' Shamshinur remarked, shaking her head. 'These people!'

'You're not exactly a blushing wallflower, Shamshinur,' Rapiya interjected in the same tone. 'So, what should they have to be shy about?'

She also knew how to cut a person to the quick with a well-chosen caustic word when the opportunity arose. Apparently satisfied that this bawdy exchange corresponded to something like a suitable greeting to their hosts, Rapiya kicked off her husband's huge *saptama* boots at the threshold with a soft thud and Shamshinur followed her example.

It was clear from the women's expectant looks that they considered themselves already invited in and would not be leaving until they'd enjoyed a proper treat at their hosts' expense. Their behaviour was supremely and defiantly self-confident, as if, with this minimum preamble, they had resolved a matter of extraordinary importance. With Shamshinur it paid to expect the unexpected. There was nothing she might have done that might surprise the aul except, perhaps, bring the dead back to life, and Kazhimurat and Zlikha watched her warily: had she turned up just to create a new scandal or continue the previous one?

'Come off it, Zlikha, you're not still sulking at me?' Shamshinur took off her coat and threw it on the couch. 'A woman is always a woman, she has but two misfortunes: the first are her tears and the second... Well, you know exactly what that is.' She smiled. 'And every woman forgets about both when she is in the arms of a good man. This morning, I didn't even want to look at you, but now, as you can see, I've come of my own accord. But I haven't come here to ask forgiveness and bow and scrape! I've come here with good news! So, you owe me some *suyuinshi*[22]! I wonder, what you'll give me for the good news?'

'Your tongue... Roasted on a platter!' Zlikha smiled radiantly. 'Well, go on then, tell us. You're about as coy as a bride on her wedding night.'

'Oh, Auntie Rapiya will tell you. But first, light the lamp and put on the samovar!'

Once Shamshinur got her teeth into something, there'd be no leaving it until she was completely satisfied. She now resembled a spider that has just sucked every last drop of blood from its victim. The guests set about kindling the stove, put on the samovar and found and lowered the meat into the deep pot. The fire in the stove caught and the house became warmer and came to life. Shamshinur clung to Kazhimurat, hugging him and pressing him to her several times.

'Check this out, you smell completely different now!'

'And you're well acquainted with how he smells, are you?' Zlikha asked, masking the hint of jealousy in her voice. 'Now, leave him alone!'

'No, what I meant to say is that he smells like you, that's all!' Shamshinur ran her hand along Kazhimurat's back and then across his cheek. 'Don't shave off your

---

[22] *Suyunshi* – a Kazakh tradition whereby the bringer of good news is given a present.

259

beard, it suits you! Otherwise, next to this dry mare, you'll end up looking like a yearling that's been driven out of the herd.'

'Oh, the tongue on you!' Rapiya interrupted, desperately trying to find some way to put a stop to Shamshinur's torrent of mischievous invective, and sat down at the table and pulled out a soldier's triangle-shaped letter from her bosom. 'Look, my hubby has sent me some news. He doesn't know how to write Russian but he seems to have asked someone to write it for him. As always, he's up to his usual tricks. He probably thinks that people in the rear only have time to learn Russian. Can you read me his letter?'

'Let's have a glass first!' Shamshinur suggested, grabbing the mead jar. 'Auntie Rapiya's heart is about to burst with joy!'

The mead was strong and after the first glass all four of their foreheads were beaded with sweat. Zlikha skim-read the letter and silently stared at Rapiya as if the mead had stuck in her throat. The others stared at Zlikha, terrified that the news might be bad. Kazhimurat took the letter, read it and smiled.

'Well, speak up, don't torture me!' Rapiya pleaded. 'Don't spare me, I'm used to putting up with anything! What does it say?'

Only now, when Kazhimurat started laughing, did Zlikha begin to get an idea of the thrust of the letter.

'It turns out that it's you who should be paying us *suyunshi*!' Zlikha announced, addressing the guests.

'Yes, it's time, you young love birds were paid your dues? So, here's your *suyunshi*!' With a thud, Shamshinur plonked a full glass of mead in front of Zlikha. 'Don't even think you're going to get any more!'

'Right. Then listen.' Zlikha replied, barely holding back her laughter and took the letter from Kazhimurat. 'Shamshinur, could you take the dishes off the table I'm afraid Auntie Rapiya might start smashing them up in her anger! Ri-ght... *To my thoroughbred wife, the mother of my four blockhead children...* Zlikha started to shake as she repressed her laughter. *...To the mother of my four blockhead children, warm greetings from the working class!'*

'Wait a minute...' Rapiya threw up her hands. 'Did he really write that?'

'Why would I make this up? Listen on... *In the name of everything holy, in the name of the motherland, we eat dates, our bellies are full and our clothes are intact* ... Hmm! Do you want me to read on or is that enough?'

Rapiya pouted. 'You'd better put it into your own words.'

'Okay. So...' Zlikha started to read the letter again: *'I live well, I am warmly dressed and I eat well. Everyone here respects me. The only thing I'm worried about is you. The most difficult thing I've so far had to do is to write this letter. I have had to hire someone to do it for me and pay good money for his services. We eat in the canteen, but, you know, their Russian soups and macaroni-potatoes are barely what I would consider food. I miss our hot thick tea and before now I could never have got through a day without it, therefore, to make up for it, I've taken a younger second wife.'* Zlikha stumbled over her words again, trying not to giggle. *'She is a pure and affectionate creature and her only drawback is that she is not of Kazakh stock. If you can forgive me then maybe the Almighty will. I often dream of our little Bekmurat. I hope you're not*

261

hitting him too hard? You always were a bit heavy-handed! I told them about my old fracture and they sent me to the medical commission, but I'm afraid they're not going to give me a disability pension. What should I do with the new wife, if she's allowed to come home with me? I would never act against your will. If you don't think you could live alongside her — what can I do, I'll just have to stay here. But I feel sorry for you and the children. Say hello to all my kinsmen and countrymen for me. Your Zakhar.'

'Why's he calling himself Zakhar, that's a Russian name?' Rapiya was alarmed when she heard this.

'Well, what were you expecting?' Shamshinur couldn't help sneering. 'Since he's gone and married a Russian, then no wonder Zakhair's become a Zakhar.'

'Well, thank God, he's alive and well!' Rapiya shrugged her shoulders in relief and laughed awkwardly. 'I was worried he might have kicked the bucket.'

'What are you babbling about, Auntie Rapiya?' Shamshinur looked at her, her eyes a-goggle. 'There are women here ready to make a replacement husband out of clay, and you're going to calmly surrender your own, strong, healthy one up to some slut! Get a grip, woman!'

'Just take a look at her!' Rapiya pulled away from her but in a good-natured way. 'The main thing is that he's alive... He is far from his home, why on earth would I forbid him at least a little female affection? That would be unbefitting of a true and loving wife...'

'Oh, Allah!' Shamshinur threw up her hands in horror. 'Then why not slaughter your only cow and organise a feast for the whole village!'

'And that's exactly what I might do!' Rapiya replied. 'They say, the prophet himself had thirteen wives, so what can we say about mere mortals...'

'So, let's start the feasting right here, right now!'

'Instead of talking empty nonsense, you'd do better to pour out some more of my mead!'

'You may now be the elder wife, but I wouldn't go flapping your wings like a cuckoo, just yet.' Shamshinur continued. 'Let's write a letter to your rival first! I have a couple of tender words for her right here, on the tip of my tongue. Let her know who she's dealing with!'

Zlikha did not know what to make of all this. Kazhimurat just sat there grinning. He was pretty sure some joker had written this letter as a prank on Zakhair and his wife. Shamshinur, of course, took every word she'd heard at face value. As for Rapiya herself, she seemed to be extremely pleased with both the letter and all the news that it contained.

While discussing all these things, all four of them failed to notice that they'd stayed up until close to midnight and the mead canister was empty. Rapiya's dark cheeks had flushed red. She had enough trouble both at the collective farm yard and at home with her four growing children. For two years she had worked tirelessly, knowing neither sleep nor rest, and then a letter came from her husband, which gave the poor woman a little relief for at least a while from the hard daily grind of those war years. Rapiya was simply overjoyed that her husband was alive and well — that was the most important thing and, seemingly, she didn't take the rest of the letter seriously.

Kazhimurat softened and visibly changed. At first, he felt awkward — he didn't know how to behave around women, let alone predict their whims and wishes — and had somewhat isolated himself from them, but then he got used to their proximity and even tried to put them at their ease. He wanted to warm their hearts and for them to be free, if only for a short time, of their current cares. Admittedly, he couldn't sing along with them, but he laughed merrily at their jokes. Even Zlikha's frequent jealous glances didn't cause him to withdraw into himself as they used to.

'Zlikha, it's getting late, what shall we do?' Rapiya asked Zlikha when the table was cleared.

'It's time to go home, there's no bed made up for you here!' Shamshinur said. 'And I noticed a while ago that there's only one made up in the bedroom.'

'Oh, Shamshinur, you daft bat! Did you remember to let Kiyakmurt out of the barn?' Rapiya remembered, suddenly alarmed. 'Maybe you should take a look, we don't want him to pop his clogs and end up in trouble!'

Zlikha was alarmed,

'What have you done there now?'

'I haven't done anything!' Shamshinur sulked, pouting. 'I'm not going to unlock that gate today, even if he swears that he was the one who made the mistake and cocked up. And the morning will always come, with or without the cry of the cockerel, and for at least one day we'll have a break from his shouts and orders!'

'Oh, stop it! Do you think he behaves that way because he has nothing better to do?'

'Whatever the case is, it's not his job to boss every woman down to the last detail! He gives us no peace!'

'Ah, that's why you burned all the rubbish that was lying around your house,' Zlikha chuckled. 'So that no one can sneak up on you in the dark?

There was no more kerosene left in the house, so, Zlikha carried the guttering lamp into the mudroom and went back into the kitchen with a bundle of logs. They might have happily spent the remaining half of the night sitting by the light of the fire in the stove, but Rapiya and Shamshinur began to put their coats on.

'You should get yours on too!' Shamshinur turned to her hosts. 'You should grab two or three sacks too!'

'You're not going to steal them, are you?' Zlikha replied warily.

'Ramadan is over, which means people have stopped fasting,' Shamshinur began to explain. 'It's the custom to visit each other to celebrate the end of the fast.'

There were only one or two practising Muslims in the village, and they all understood that Shamshinur had decided to revive this custom for her own amusement. However, Kazhimurat and Zlikha decided to go out for a walk with the women.

The new, knife-blade moon rolled past the tops of the larches and cedars. Higher up in the sky, the calls of the cranes could be heard, heralding warmer weather. Old Zhusup was telling everyone that the grass was already beginning to grow on the southern banks of the Bukhtarma, where, naturally, the earth warmed up earlier than here on the northern banks. It might have been possible to start the ploughing there, but until the river levels subsided, there was little point in even thinking about crossing to the opposite bank. It was strange, but both the arable land and meadows were on the southern banks but the aul itself lay to the north.

This was all due to the fact that this was where Yelmurat had decided to settle. He had chosen this narrow, inconvenient, low-lying hollow because he had taken a liking to the five or six old wooden cabins that had been left there by previous settlers. It was a convenient place for him to conceal the horses that would occasionally appear from out of nowhere before being sold on. And now, an aul of fifty households had grown up in this inconvenient spot, which was cut off from its own fields and meadows and presented new difficulties and challenges to its inhabitants with each passing year, but it never occurred to anyone to move to a more convenient location. However, the people here didn't know how to make the most of the blessings they enjoyed, let alone worry about those that they didn't.

The woodcocks called loudly to each other in the Batpaksay marshes as if trying to outdo each other. The tinkling of a small bell could be heard in the forest, punctuated by the lonely and anxious whinnying of an inexperienced yearling that had strayed from the herd and wandered into the deep forest. Light peeked through the branches. It was unclear whether it was a herder or a traveller who was staying out in this old abandoned forest cabin in the dead of night. Kazhimurat kept a close eye on the herd at this time of year when the mares were due to foal and a lone light in the forest made him suspicious. He led the women to the road, dawdled behind them unnoticed and headed into the forest. Kazhimurat was used to the constant demands of looking after the farm's livestock, and he found it difficult to waste his time listening to the women's idle chatter. And, indeed, living indoors in a warm house, surrounded by four walls was not what he was used to either. The recent bonhomie that had warmed his soul, and the mead that had warmed his body suddenly seemed out of place and inappropriate. There seemed little point in it now until life got back to normal and peace would put everything back on track again.

Over the last week or so, the sun had begun to warm the earth and smooth out its wrinkles, and last year's grass rustled dryly against the tops of his boots. This year, the young shoots of grass were slow to break through the soil but would have been good for the hungry cattle that had become so emaciated that winter, allowing them to gain a little strength before the strenuous spring sowing. It was sufficiently high for the sheep and horses, but still too sparse for the oxen, who prefer taller and lusher vegetation... How many ploughs would they be able to put out into the field this spring?

Kazhimurat made a mental count of the oxen and horses fit to be put in the harness and worked out they would be able to have fifty. But the real problem lay in the fact that the village did not have the necessary workers to do the ploughing. They would have to replace the milkmaids with some of the old women for a while and put the women behind the ploughs. They would also need more drovers to drive the sheep. Kazhimurat mulled the children over in his mind and tried to work out which of them was tough and smart enough to pass muster as a drover. He would have to speak with the teachers to ask if the children might be allowed out into the fields, although their studies couldn't be abandoned indefinitely. The adults could live in temporary shelters, and the schoolchildren could be given a single yurt and that would free up most of the brick quarters in which the collective farm's library and culture room were housed. And that way they would end up with a field school. Zlikha was nominally in charge of everything on the collective farm, but Kazhimurat was used to resolving production and everyday problems on his own without her, although it would turn out that his decisions never ran counter to her plans.

Kazhimurat was passing by the old mill near the lake when he heard the sound of a hammer. The sound surprised him for, as far as he remembered, apart from him, there was no one in the village who could skilfully use a hammer. He turned towards the mill. In the wooden building sat his uncle, Tazhimurat, who, strangely, had not figured at all in any of the lists that Kazhimurat had just now been compiling in his head, which meant he had completely slipped out of his own nephew's reckoning when it came to the life of the village.

Even Tazhimurat's eyelashes were covered in the mill's ubiquitous white dust and he sat, bent low over the millstone hammering away at it with a hammer and chisel in the light of a tallow lamp. His thick neck did not bend and, as was his custom, he turned his entire body around to stare at Kazhimurat from under his brows.

'Doing your evening rounds?' he growled. 'Well, off you go then! After all, a man of property like you needs to keep watch over his cattle...'

No matter the circumstances, he would never change his habit of having a dig at someone. If he felt he had a score to settle, he would inevitably present all his arguments to the person who had offended him and force him to swallow them like a piece of felt concealed in butter so that they would stick in their throat and they'd be unable to say anything in their defence.

'If you don't keep a close eye on your wife, she'll leave you for another, if you don't rein in your son, he'll end up getting out of hand. You are on crutches and my hands are covered in blisters, but, as you can see, neither of us knows any peace. I want to breathe some life into this dilapidated building. Spring has come and along with it — life... People will be needing the mill.'

The millstones, which had lain all winter under the snow, were impossibly frozen, but Tazhimurat beat the stone with such energetic, powerful movements that the cold didn't affect him at all. Kazhimurat couldn't bear standing idle and having to swallow his uncle's insulting words and went up to the iron stove in the corner, opened the door, made a well in the kindling and lit the fire. Tazhimurat was completely absorbed in the job at hand. Whenever he worked, he always did so in a kind of rapture, regardless of whether it was for himself or someone else, as his father had taught him. Kazhimurat took up a hammer and decided to help him, but Tazhimurat did not let him near the millstones.

'Leave them alone! I'll manage on my own. And don't worry, I'm not going to be charging the farm for my work. So, you can get yourself back into the warm bed of that chairwoman of yours.'

Not everyone would have guessed that behind his unsociable mask and even rudeness, Tazhimurat concealed an intense, verging on eccentric, love for any job he was busy with. Which was why he wouldn't let anyone else help him, no matter what it was. His neck was bristling like a wolf guarding its prey. Tazhimurat cast an angry look at his nephew that seemed to say, 'don't even think about challenging my decision'. At that moment, from the direction of the village came the barking of dogs and some indeterminate racket, and Kazhimurat rushed to the door.

The lights in the village flickered here and there and soon, human voices joined those of the dogs, among them Rapiya's — calm and Shamshinur's — loud and shrill, as they went around the houses congratulating everyone with the end of Ramadan. Kazhimurat did not like the women's idea. He would have preferred for everyone to get an extra hour or two of rest because the next day's work wasn't going anywhere. He stood for a minute and, shaking his head disapprovingly, headed off into the forest.

The smell of sap and resin hung heavily in the air. A gentle wind blew, blackening the surface of the lake and rustling the small islands of reeds that confided their hidden thoughts to each other. An unpleasant boggy smell was wafting over from the direction of the marsh in the middle of which a lonely light shone, piercing its way through the dry trunks of the larch trees. Kazhimurat knew exactly where it was coming from — an abandoned Kerzhak cabin. An eagle owl let out its terrifying, mocking cry. Was it an owl or a forest sprite? In the aul, they had been saying that a tree sprite had taken up residence in this cabin... Kazhimurat had wanted to check out these rumours for a long time, and he entered the deep forest with a decisive step. He was immediately surrounded by low-growing larches whose trunks were covered with moss at human-waist height.

Soon, the way became completely impassable, trunks intertwined with branches lay horizontally across the path. The soil underfoot became treacherous, the marsh was covered with a loose layer of silt, rotten branches and moss, and each step was now accompanied by the sound of sucking and wheezing and bubbles as they burst through the surface. The woodcocks fell silent, replaced by the marsh bittern, its booming cries echoing throughout the stunted forest. His ears overwhelmed by these unpleasant sounds, Kazhimurat hiked on without taking his eyes off the light, fearing that it might go out and he would lose his bearings. A strange and incomprehensible rumbling and ringing sound hung over the dense forest in which humans had rarely set foot.

The dwelling was a small log house. Its windows and doors had been torn off long ago and gaped emptily. Kazhimurat looked inside and saw Bakhyt sitting in the middle of the room, combing her hair. On her knees, she held a stump of wood, tightly swaddled in a quilted jacket, and she rocked it like a child. The wall behind her was covered from floor to ceiling with moss and lichen; it was black with dirty, smudged stains caused by the rain.

Sections of an old wooden bed lay scattered in the far corner, and an old icon hung in another. Kazhimurat threw a pebble into the room, but Bakhyt did not turn around at his improvised knock. She did not pay any attention to him even when Kazhimurat entered the room, still nursing her imaginary child. He gently touched the girl on the shoulder and then tried to raise her up, supporting her by her armpits. But Bakhyt looked

at him with an uncomprehending look and pressed the
tree stump closer to her chest,

> *'Hush, little baby, hush you now!*
> *Where's your daddy, where's he gone?*
> *You tell me that he's gone to war?*
> *I'll throw a blanket on his horse...'*

Kazhimurat thought she'd be as light as a feather, but
this was anything but the case: the girl pushed him away
with a short and sharp movement, rather like the strike of
a bird of prey and, surprisingly, her fingers were as hard
as iron. A deep wave of cold emanated from her.
Kazhimurat was seized by an incomprehensible fear. He
moved away from Bakhyt and sat down on a log that had
once served as a door jamb, and was now lying on the
floor. He did not know how he was going to persuade the
unhappy girl back to the village.

Long-tailed wild chickens known as *kezkuyruk* called
from a nearby stand of trees. Moss, like matted wool,
covered the entire floor of the hut and stepping on it felt
like standing on the piles of husks, grains and droppings
that litter the entrance of a mouse hole. Overhead,
somewhere on the roof, the eagle owl flapped its wings
loudly and again let out its eerie call. A wall of dry larches
surrounding the forest hut swayed with a creak. Bakhyt
did not hear the night sounds that filled the marsh. Her
lullaby had turned into a kind of plaintive moaning and
she covered the stump with the quilted jacket and sat
staring into the fire. Her unblinking eyes had turned red
as if they were bloodshot. From the cracks in the walls,

the distant hearths of the village burned like the eyes of a pack of wolves.

Kazhimurat, who was rarely scared by anything, was now seized by a perplexing wave of fear. He snatched the stump of wood from Bakhyt's hands and jumped out of the dilapidated cabin. With a wild cry, Bakhyt rushed after him. Kazhimurat ran pell-mell through the marsh without looking back, the branches whipping his face until he found himself in a clearing.

However, next to the mill, Bakhyt overtook him and clung to his coat. Kazhimurat freed himself from her tenacious grasp with great difficulty and threw the stump into someone's yard. Bakhyt gasped and rushed after it, wailing at the top of her voice. Something clattered, fell and rolled along the ground.

'Who's there?' An old woman cried in fright. 'If you don't go now, I'll knock seven bells out of you!'

Seeing that it was Bakhyt rushing about in the yard, the old woman went back inside. The lights in everyone's houses were alight, the first time they had burned so brightly in a long time. A noisy crowd followed Rapiya and Shamshinur, and people greeted and congratulated each other on the end of the fast. Children galloped around the streets on horseback and oxen, filling the night air with their cries. Shamshinur sang loudly to everyone, praising some and scolding others, making up songs in honour of one person's baldness and another's lack of good looks. People laughed and gave out gifts, but nothing except trifles: a piece of cake, two or three small buns, a spoonful of butter, irimshik and kurt.

'Although our Shamshinur may have lost her sack of grain this morning, she's not going to let that stop her today!' the old men and women joked. 'She's just taking what's hers!'

Bakhyt had now also joined the crowd, spinning and dancing, her dishevelled hair whirling like a black flame. No one, however, noticed the poor girl. Shamshinur, meanwhile, ended up at the collective farm barn and had made up a new song,

> 'Hey, Kiyakmurt, how are you, my friend?
> Have you had time to think of a song for your sweetheart?
> I hope your moustaches did not droop in the night?
> Our life here without them would be boring and dull.
> No heartier food will you find in the village.
> But don't drown yourself in our collective farm bread,
> Fill your greedy belly to your heart's content.
> But, please, stop frightening us girls with your thunderous looks!'

Laughing merrily, the women then led Kiyakmurt out of the barn. He had been chilled right through the night and was a pale shadow of his usual self. He didn't even cheer up when he found himself on the street, not saying a word or looking anyone in the eyes. Shamshinur took him by the shoulder and gave him a big hug and, finally, Kiyakmurt suddenly smiled and walked jauntily alongside her, twirling his moustaches with his fingers. Kazhimurat smiled approvingly — anything is better than a quarrel. He allowed himself to lag behind the crowd again.

The sky over the taiga was thickening, the horizon in the east was lit up with a faint red light and somewhere a rooster crowed. It was still dark outside, the dirt squelched underfoot and the cool pre-morning breeze pleasantly cooled the body. Kazhimurat changed his mind about going back to Zlikha's and climbed up onto his familiar hayloft in Tazhimurat's yard. The hay was damp and his foot began to ache, the pain immediately spreading up to his lower back.

The stars in the dark blue sky had thinned out, glowing pale and lifeless, as if all the hopes contained in them had been extinguished. His body was exhausted, but he didn't feel like sleeping, images of the previous day floated successively in his mind's eye: the dishevelled, screaming women grabbing the grain, the wise exhortations of old Zhusup, Zlikha's angry speech at the warehouse, Kiyakmurt's attempt to concoct a case against him, Bakhyt's red bloodshot eyes, Tazhimurat lonely and unwanted, hammering away at the millstones... *How complicated and difficult life has become!*

Gradually, the women calmed down, and the village became quiet. The light came on in Zlikha's house, where she, of course, was waiting for him. 'That's life for you!' Kazhimurat thought. 'It's harsh on a person one minute, then tender the next. And infinitely precious! Even a single day is like a priceless treasure. And you have to live it, no matter how difficult the trials it sets a person on their journey through it!'

The autumn rain, fine and endless, was a long time coming and when it did it came down not so much in raindrops but as *ramrod rushes*, as old Trofim used to say... The natural world was overwhelmed by a kind of torpor. The slopes of the hills had turned green again, the earth was washed away not only near the cattle barn but also the infertile rocky soil which gurgled and bubbled with the rain. In weather like this, you want to crawl under a thick felt blanket and sleep forever, forgetting all your cares and worries in the world.

But home comforts were only a distant dream for Almurat. This time his wife had kept her word, she had gone back to her mother and father and still not returned home. And he was quite happy without her. There was no one left in the office, except the young girl Kulmayran, who worked as an accountant at the state farm, sitting at her desk all day, doing her endless calculations. Kulmayran loaded a half-typed piece of paper into the typewriter and, shifting the lever, began to tap on the keys, pressing them carefully with the pads of her fingers in an attempt to avoid breaking her finely painted nails. Almurat could not keep his eyes off her finely formed calves and her taut, full hips that could be made out under her short dress. The girl was to his liking, although he did not know why. For some reason, in front of others, he tried to wind her up, teasing her with a sharp word, and then regretting it, would fall silent. Kulmayran seemed to have divined Almurat's feelings and tried to be free and easy with him, defending herself from his attacks with jokes and laughter. People attributed her behaviour to the fact that she'd been left on the shelf.

The girl pulled the hem of her short dress over her knees and threw a coquettish glance in Almurat's direction. It seemed to him that she had put on too much bright red lipstick today and it did not go well with her dark brown eyes and, to compound matters, she had left a careless streak of powder down her beautiful, slightly sloping forehead.

'Kulmayran!'

'Yes!'

'Your parents should have called you Gulmeiram — after the festival of flowers.'

'Well, my parents aren't from the most literate generation. So, they ended up calling me — Kulmayran. And that's how I like it.'

'Who's going to be the lucky man for whom flowers and holidays are an everyday occurrence?'

'I'm interested in one thing only, Almurat. That our lives are a bed of roses all twelve months of the year.'

'But what about the festivals and holidays?'

'These days, there's a holiday almost every other day. Excluding Saturdays and Sundays, of course. I hate it when a holiday falls on a non-working day.'

'Why don't you and I turn today into a holiday?'

'Are you thinking of throwing your wife's saddle cloth over my back now?'

'We could invent our own games, Kulmayran.'

'And how often do you get to invent games?'

'Very rarely.'

'Don't sell yourself short.'

'You know I really do have some big regrets in my life. I have no remarkable memories to draw upon from my past.'

'A man's regrets about his past are no more than the dust that settles on his chest. The dust is easily wiped away when he meets and embraces a woman.'

'And to what would you compare a woman's regrets?'

'I have never met a woman who regrets her past.'

'Oh, really?' Almurat was enchanted by Kulmayran's quick wit.

'Women have to live in the present and can only regret the passing of the day and nothing more.'

'I wouldn't say that, my dear! The past becomes more precious when you regret that which has not come to pass.'

'We don't have regrets, but we do experience sadness,' Kulmayran corrected him. 'But not every woman has this quality either.'

'So, what is this woman like then?'

'She is the sort of person for whom a man would lay down his life.'

Kulmayran removed what she had typed from the typewriter and handed it over to Almurat to be signed. The fragrance of the girl's perfume was pleasant but did not touch or excite Almurat's soul. He felt that it was masking the aroma of her girlish body and that she didn't sufficiently value her youth.

The fingers holding the paper appeared slightly coarse, the palms of her hand plump — the sort of palms that are usually sweaty.

Almurat gave the girl the keys to his house.

'Take my keys,' he said to her. 'You won't be obliged to me for anything. You can treat my home as if it was your own. I just want it to feel the benefit of a woman's hand. I have fresh meat hanging in the larder and wine in the fridge. Why don't you go and prepare us a delicious supper?'

'You might be thrown out on your ear if I'm found in your house...'

'Don't worry, my wife isn't going to show up any time soon.'

The white, vertical, autumn rain sowed itself widely over the earth, the stiff wind spraying the water from the black clouds, which swirled in the distance like a dense misty wall. The green taiga swayed and the aul hid silently in its hollow with the doors of its houses tightly closed. The tractor, which had woken everyone up in the early morning with its clattering diesel, barely crawled over the soggy mire and slowly reached the state farm's garage. From a distance, it looked like a dung beetle immersed in a ball of slurry. Behind the wheel of the tractor was Zakhair's lanky son, who had only recently been responsible for the fight between Almurat's prize bulls and the collective farm's crane truck. *It's clear there's going to be no bringing you to your senses,* Almurat thought gloomily. *And it's true what they say: a son is half the man that his father is. And since Zakhair's your father, there wasn't much to be expected of you in the first place...*

Since the rains had set in, the hay was being transported to the sheep pens using the farm's one and only tractor. And now Almurat regretted that he would have to entrust the supply of the fodder, on which the farm's livestock would depend for the winter, to this lanky young man, whose heart simply wasn't in his work. The sound of an unknown car engine rolled up to the office and behind it a fancy yellow *Moskvich* motor car, its fine wheel arches caked in mud. A bearded man in a smock got out of the car. Almurat winced, recognizing the artist from the city who had recently come to the state farm to see what he could wangle out of its budget for a commission.

'Hey, old chap!' The artist shouted over to Almurat in Russian, spotting him standing at the window. 'Can you help me get to the main road? I'll make it worth your while.'

'Find someone else!' Almurat replied, leaning out the window. *You son of a bitch!* He swore angrily at the artist under his breath. *You've already managed to line your pockets at our expense. Where else, I wonder, have you been earning a bit extra on the side? And I'm not your old chap... The price you've charged just to paint a mural on the farm's social club wall should be enough to send your forefathers and mine spinning in their graves in shame!*

A few minutes later, an old eight-seater *GAZ* jeep drove up to the office, coughing and shaking. Generally, Almurat preferred his motorbike, it was faster and more convenient, but now that the road had turned into a quagmire, he had had to call out a car. He left the office, thanked the driver and let him go home.

The bearded artist was standing right next to it.

'Do you have a tow rope?'

'Of course!' The artist opened the boot of his car and pulled out a thin coiled steel cable.

'No, show me your money first!'

The artist pulled his wallet out and began to rifle through it, counting his banknotes. Almurat initially started haggling with him for the fun of it, but then he was seized by a desire to put one over on the irritating parasite. *After all, he's taken the farm for a ride with his mural, so why not get at least a bit of it back from him?* Almurat decided. *I might even end up returning a bit of the money to its rightful owner.*

'That's not going to be enough!' he said, looking at the crumpled three-rouble note that the bearded man had taken from his wallet.

'But the road's only three kilometres away!'

'Well, then drive there yourself.'

The artist reluctantly took out another rouble and then counted out another twelve kopecks. *What a skinflint! Almurat thought to himself. Is he having a laugh?!*

'That's nothing like enough! You're not in the city here, you know. The mark-up is at least another fifty kopecks.'

The bearded man started counting his money again but still wouldn't give an extra kopeck. Before setting off, he sternly warned Almurat,

'Look, the suspension is not very strong. So, please tow it smoothly. No sudden jerks.'

God forbid, I'd hate your car to fall to pieces on the way! Almurat smirked to himself. *I'll show your suspension enough to turn your beard grey...* With that, Almurat dragged the *Moskvich* behind him with a jerk. He deliberately headed for the bumpiest parts of the road, first plunging into deep ruts and then climbing up out over high ridges. He turned around for a moment to see the bearded artist's face contorted with fury and alarm, desperately trying to turn his steering wheel to avoid the worst of the obstacles in front of him, his eyes nearly popping out of their sockets. Finally, they reached the road. The artist coiled up the cable, threw it into the boot, and only then opened his pale trembling lips:

'You are an utter scoundrel!'

'Out in the taiga, you'd be wiser to watch your tongue... Old chap!' Almurat replied coldly with more than a hint of threat in his voice. 'Now, off you trot, while you're still in one piece!'

He decided to head straight back over the high hill, on which the cemetery stood. It was only a stone's throw from here to the village, but the jeep nevertheless climbed the hill with difficulty. The four roubles and sixty kopecks that Almurat believed he had earned through his honest labour were now burning a hole in his pocket. He wondered who that greedy parasite was going to rip off next. It often works out this way, a man becomes obsessed with getting rich at all costs and kills all that is human within himself with his greed. How can you live by money alone? These days, everyone's bellies seemed to be full, they were shod and dressed, but no, this was still not enough... What remains of a person for himself when he uses all his talents merely to get rich? Who needs your artistic gifts if your only aim in life is simply to stuff your belly? Is there anything more worthy of a man than his deeds that help him to make a good mark on the earth during his short sojourn on it? To do something good, no, even better, to do something beautiful and leave it for future generations... what more can one ask of a man? A person cannot be considered to have lived in terms of the years he has lived, but by the deeds he has wrought...

Almurat drove around the cemetery, on the edge of which a fresh black grave had been sunk, and began to choose a less steep road to descend back down to the aul. Then he stopped the truck. The aul was not visible from the top of the foothill, disappearing beneath the low clouds. They were so thick that it was hard for him to make out the slopes down from the hill. He peered down for a long time and then got into the cab and began his descent.

Kazhimurat was sitting on a red granite stone. Seeing Almurat, he put aside his hammer and chisel and got up. He had pulled the collar of his camel hair sweater up around his neck and thrown a birch-bark cape over his shoulders. His short curly hair was red from granite dust, and his face was dusky and motionless as if he had just risen from one of the graves that hummocked the summit of the foothill and come down to mingle with the living.

'You haven't frozen yourself through there, have you?' Almurat asked him.

Kazhimurat shook his head absently and clicked his tongue. Almurat returned to the truck, brought out a bottle of cognac and a piece of boiled fat tail from the pocket of the seat cover and called over to Kazhimurat,

'Let's go and pay our respects to the poor old man! Today is exactly seven days since he died.'

Trofim had been struck low with a sudden bout of paralysis and had lain in his bed for just three days before he quietly departed into the next world. Ignoring the grumblings of the village elders, Kazhimurat and Almurat had buried him in the Kazakh cemetery, precisely the one that Almurat had just passed by. They measured out two metres of land for Trofim, who had arrived in the Altai from the distant province of Oryol in a rattling old wagon drawn by a stubby horse. He had chosen as much land as he could plough and settled down among the Kazakhs for the rest of his days. During this long life, he had never been in debt to anyone and had never done anyone any harm, and not a single person among the living knew whether his path now lay in the direction of heaven or hell. The brothers had dug Trofim a deep grave. He had sometimes complained that God would never have taken him but it was hard to tell if he was joking or serious. However, when the time came his death was, as he would have put it himself, a kind one because he was only ill for a short time and did not suffer unnecessarily.

Admittedly, Kazhimurat had his doubts that old Trofim would end up in any paradise because he hadn't been a great believer while he had walked the earth. He had died with an enigmatic grin on his lips and although Kazhimurat had not been able to make out his dying words, he guessed that the stubborn old man had been preparing some joke or other that he was going to tell the Almighty when he finally met him. It could not have been otherwise with Trofim.

The old man was strong in spirit, there was no denying that. Neither the death of his two brothers and three sons at the front, nor his wife Lukerya, who had drowned during a flood in the spring of forty-three had bowed him — her body was never found, but her name remained engraved on a large stone in the Kurdym Gorge. Kazhimurat considered it his duty to produce a headstone for Trofim's grave and had begun hewing it from a block of red granite so it might stand for eternity with Trofim's name on it. He had decided to use one of the millstones for it and it had turned out to be very hard-wearing indeed. Kazhimurat had been working on it for a whole week and was nowhere near finishing it.

'That's a fine gravestone,' Almurat nodded approvingly, examining the stone. 'During his lifetime, he lived in nothing grander than his mill and his cabin in the gorge, covered with straw thatch, but in death, he will lie like a sultan... That son of a bitch Bukazhan seems to have disappeared. The district police are searching for him, but nothing so far.'

Bukazhan, which meant *bull*, was the nickname of Trofim's son-in-law. At one time he had worked as a clerk for a cattle import enterprise but then he left and had recently been moonlighting all over the Altai, like many of the other informal workers in the region. There had been no need to contact the police, as Kazhimurat could have found him in no time — he wasn't the sharpest tool in the box. He was bound to be working on the timber rafts floating down the river at Zeretsda and, no doubt, he would end up drinking away his earnings and turn up in one of the surrounding villages. These days, there was nowhere to hide another person's stolen cattle in the taiga, let alone a fugitive on the run...

A distant mist swirled over the dense forest. The roar of the Bukhtarma could be heard from here as if it had cleft the earth into two with a knife. The rain clouds covered the western slopes of the Altai Mountains and drifted east, enveloping the high hills and the sun would flash in the gaps between them, trembling momentarily and then disappearing again behind its dark veil. The shaggy crowns of the larches swayed under the wind in the narrow hollow, stretching down towards the village. The washed-out black road ended at the gorge like a thick dark yarn, threaded into the eye of a huge needle. The clouds blocked out the entire sky and it seemed that the rain would remain for a long time.

Downing his cognac and chasing it with some salted bacon, Almurat went for a wander along the lake, while Kazhimurat took the rest of the cement, using it to smooth any unevenness on the stone, and began to collect his tools.

It had already got dark and the forest's canopy closed in, when Kazhimurat and Almurat climbed into the jeep and it immediately sagged under their weight. They moved with difficulty at first, but then picked up speed, the tyres' worn treads sliding easily and quickly down the hill.

To avoid having to brake too often, Almurat drove in first gear, knowing that this would allow him to have a smoke at the same time.

'What a pile of old junk!' he complained, holding his cigarette between his teeth. 'We should have got it off our books ages ago; it's barely worth half what it used to. There's a whole lot of junk we need to get rid of on the farm... Starting with our current director... I wanted to get a new car, but the acquisitions committee wasn't having any of it, saying that every single one of our managers had a car. Well, you can see for yourself the quality of this motor! We are losing gold coins hand over fist but they insist on pinching the pennies! If I had my way, I would have a big bonfire of all the old and replace it with the new. It's more like torture than a life!'

He slammed his foot down on the pedal angrily. The car lurched forward, fish-tailing from side to side and jumping over the potholes. Kazhimurat remembered the hummocked winter road that he had had to travel all those years ago on the ice of the Bukhtarma. Almurat might be swearing and cursing at this old car now, but did he remember the long procession of sledges that they had had to use during the war and the slow-moving oxen, which never changed their pace, no matter how many times you hit them?

Previously, it had taken the entire spring to plough this valley using a wooden plough drawn by emaciated animals. They hadn't so much ploughed it as scraped and furrowed it with their bare teeth! But now, the tractors would pass up and down it in a matter of hours, as if they were traversing a single oxhide rather than the wide Sarybulak valley. The silvery birch posts showed up here and there against the dark velvet of the arable soil. A noisy mob of crows flew over them like a querulous black cloud and settled on the nearby tree tops, the birds now outnumbering the autumn leaves on the trees. A sign of impending bad weather and more specifically — snow.

'There's no free land left these days,' Almurat continued to complain. Everything has been ripped open and exploited but there's been little benefit had from it. In the fat years, when the weather was good, we would laze around and play the fool, and in the lean years, we would constantly be asking for handouts. Rejoicing at every kopeck's worth of straw we could get, forever in debt to the state. I can tell you, our department is the only one that's turning a profit on the entire farm. And so, we only get out of the hole we've dug for ourselves thanks to our livestock farming. But even this is nothing to brag about. Ten years ago, we had fifty thousand head of sheep. But then, year on year, we've begun to reduce our pastures, and our livestock numbers have now fallen to the levels that we used to have in our most unsuccessful years. No one is rooting for the state farms anymore!

'If I had my way... Instead of sowing two thousand hectares of wheat, I would be pasturing two hundred thousand head of sheep out here! And not the sort we have foisted on us these days, but the old Kazakh fat-tailed breeds, which are not ruffled even when it gets down to minus fifty degrees. Unfortunately, our scientists have flooded the farms with sheep that freeze to death even when they're kept in a roofed enclosure! I don't know what our leaders are thinking. I spent five years at the institute, having my head stuffed with things that can't be put into practice! They don't even know what the farms need. The most important thing is that they need to be entrusted to people with common sense and those who lack it need to be kicked out of their posts and thrown out on their ear!'

Listening to Almurat with his critical but intelligent and heartfelt opinions, Kazhimurat realized that he was failing to keep abreast of modern life. He was pleased that Almurat had taken after his father, for whom the job at hand was the most important thing in life. The only difference was that his father had laboured all his life solely for himself, whereas Almurat tirelessly and totally gave of himself for the good of the country and his people. Admittedly, he could be a bit stern and liked to shoot from the hip. He lacked a certain gravitas and refinement when it came to the way he lived his life because his words and actions had a direct influence on the development and destinies of others. It was no good driving his subordinates like draft animals in much the way that Kiyakmurt had done in his time.

Almurat, it seemed, had inherited a certain element of those bad old habits, when threatening shouted orders and pounding fists on tables were considered an effective way of commanding people. Clearly, it is hard for a person to free himself from the mark that their own times have left upon them. And yet... He could never bring himself to curse those days of long suffering, no matter how cruel and sometimes simply unfair they were; they were nevertheless the steps the country had had to take to climb up towards its great future. Their native country, for which they had been and were now ready to give their lives, should the need arise.

Kazhimurat returned his thoughts to his cousin again. *He knows the farm like the back of his hand but can't get on with his wife and he has estranged himself from his own mother. If you listen to Almurat, you can see that he has immersed himself in his work and has no time for anything else in his life and he is happy to be scolded for his negligence and lack of engagement with his nearest and dearest, but isn't this just another form of apathy and indifference? Half a month has passed since his wife left home, and he hasn't given the break-up of his family a thought. He already has his answer and justification ready: his wife could not stand him spending all his time at work. But he argues that he is too important to spend his whole life tied to his wife's apron strings, he is not destined for such things. No, cousin, you cannot hide behind this sort of argument and reasoning. No one, no matter how important they think they are, is destined to have to destroy their own family or anyone else's for that matter*. During this same half month, Kazhimurat had rebuilt the collapsed mill, met up with Zlikha and accompanied Trofim off on his final journey... However, Almurat, his own flesh and blood, gave him no satisfaction. Perhaps Almurat was happy that Kazhimurat's stay had at least brought some benefit to the aul? The mill was now working again... It wasn't a relative that his modern wheeler-dealer cousin had needed, but his hands and labour to build something that his farm department, and therefore he, Almurat, needed. Kazhimurat's heart and soul began to grow cold from these thoughts.

The dirt road meandered along the slopes of the hills and dived into the gorge. It had been built just before the war when people worked with a shovel and a pick in their hands and was now a shadow of its former self. The side of the road that plunged straight down the gorge consisted largely of patches and repairs — in one place it had been buttressed with logs, but they had already shifted and fallen in on each other, in another it had been shored up with a pile of stones that barely held up. It was the only dirt road that connected the remotest forest places with the district centre, and it was only passable in summer; in winter in the deep snow, it was impossible to drive on. As usual, for the whole of the summer, no one had paid any attention to the condition of the road, and by the autumn, when the road had been practically washed away by the rains, the district authorities at all levels would blow a gasket because the only and most important artery road in the entire area was not being properly looked after.

A long column of timber trucks could be seen backed up along the road from the bridge — a heavily laden timber truck had slid off the bridge, taking off almost half the railing with it, and was now lying upside down in the water with its wheels in the air.

'Damn it!' Almurat swore. '*I* work my fingers to the bone to get this bridge repaired and all they do is smash it to pieces!'

Leaving the jeep at the crossing, Kazhimurat and Almurat went up to the crowd of drivers standing next to the river bank.

'Is the driver still in one piece?' Almurat asked.

'They couldn't give a damn about anything!' The bridge keeper said, pointing to a man with watery, bloodshot eyes who was sitting at the side of the road. 'You're going to love this one! The son of a bitch is still drunk!'

Almurat stalked around the guy. 'Completely smashed!'

'A complete idiot!' The bridge keeper added.

'Whose truck is this?'

'The saw mill's.'

'Write up a report!' Almurat ordered. 'We'll fine him five times his monthly wage.'

Kazhimurat ignored the conversation, although the driver's features seemed strangely familiar to him. The roar of the timber trucks was completely deafening him, and he decided to continue back to the village on foot, keeping to the cliff face. Trofim's old house leaned drunkenly next to the old crossing. It was probably being used by the bridge keeper because there was an antenna sticking out over its dilapidated roof. He was unable to find either the boat or ferry that had previously been stationed next to the house. The two iron landing stages from which the ferry cable traversed were rusted and blackened.

Trofim had moved here from the *Black Hole* in forty-three and got a job as a ferryman. From mid-spring to late autumn, he would transport people, cattle, ploughs and draft animals belonging to the Murat Collective Farm from one bank to the other. Handling a ferry is a difficult task and not everyone, even the strongest person, can manage it. After three years of working here, Trofim's shoulders grew huge callouses much like those you find on the neck of an ox. The hearth in his house, standing on its black piles, like a hut on chicken legs, was always alight and welcoming. Trofim knew every single lake or backwater in the vicinity where the fish were to be had with his trap nets. Shepherds descending from the mountain pastures, ploughmen returning to the aul from the spring fields and mowers from the summer floodplain meadows — all enjoyed fat carp and trout in this house. A lot of people used to visit Trofim, and they all found warmth, hospitality and a hot supper here.

Kazhimurat wandered along the overgrown shore, finding desolation and abandonment everywhere he went. The mint had grown wild and stood as tall as the reeds, and the reeds themselves had rotted and formed a dirty slurry on the water. Everything smelled of sludge and pond scum. His clothes were heavy with the damp and he felt as if he was wearing a suit of thick felt battle armour. His shoulder blades ached with the memory of the fateful trip he had made along this winter road delivering the grain to the district centre. These familiar places brought back memories of events that had taken place twenty years previously, evoking in Kazhimurat's heart both a light sadness and an aching pain. Here, under the red cliff that hung low over the dark water, they had found Bakhyt's poor, unfortunate body, and there, in the hollow, old Zhusup had slaughtered his only three-year-old grey bull... And over there, on the bend of the river, he had pulled the half-drowned Kiyakmurt out of the high waves... No one, but the two of them and Trofim had known anything about this incident. And Trofim knew how to keep his own counsel...

In the heat of the summer, the snow had melted the tops of the mountains, and the Bukhtarma flooded for a second time. Trofim had used this opportunity to keep Kiyakmurt in the village for a whole month and save the mowers from being pestered on the other bank, although the district policeman had tried to get to them on several occasions. In the end, Kiyakmurt lost his patience and decided to make it across the river in a boat, but it had capsized and he found himself in the raging torrent. It was a good thing that Kazhimurat had happened to be nearby the river and managed to pull him out of the water in time. Kazhimurat recalled how Trofim had not been best pleased with the way that he'd rushed to Kiyakmurt's aid, even telling him that he thought he'd made a grave error. The old man had some strange ideas... He believed that the world was better off without the likes of Kiyakmurt, who have no sympathy for human suffering. Kazhimurat did not attach any importance to Trofim's words at the time and it was only later that he realized that the old man might have been right. If it hadn't been for Kiyakmurt, Kazhimurat's whole life might have turned out completely differently.

The cows returning from pasture had turned the street into a quagmire. The querulous cries of the herder could be heard throughout the village and he picked his way through the mud on his gelding with its pendulous belly. He cursed each animal in the herd individually, making remarks about each of their characters, although leaving little doubt that it was the characters of their owners that he was chiding. His whippy long-handled club whistled down on the backs of the cows and came down especially hard on those whose owners still owed him wages for his work.

He takes four roubles from each household, so he must take home two hundred roubles a month, Kazhimurat thought to himself. *The same salary as an average manager. Not bad... No wonder he's got so much to shout about...*

'All well, Kazhimurat? I see you haven't left us yet?'

Kazhimurat did not bother looking up at the old man — he had no great liking for loud mouths — and merely answered the greeting with a barely perceptible nod of his head. But the old man did not seem to notice.

'For fuck's sake! Not that way!' He shouted again, rushing off towards the herd. 'Where's that one gone off to now? I should have left you with the wolves on the mountain pastures!' And with that, his long club whipped down on a young black cow with a stubby tail.

Old Zhusup's abandoned house could just be made out among the thickets of cow parsley and burdock where it had sunk into the soft earth, its window and doorways staring vacantly like empty black eye sockets. There were axe marks on the walls and corners of the house. The local people lived right next to the forest, but why bother going to the taiga when you have a dilapidated old house on your doorstep? Here was another home that had had the life snuffed out of it forever. There was no one left to carry on old Zhusup's family line...

Almurat's car was standing in front of the gate, the water drained from its radiator. The doors of the house appeared to have been locked from the inside, but the doors of the second-floor room had been flung wide open, and the appetizing aroma of freshly fried meat wafted down from them. Kazhimurat was slightly taken aback and hesitated at the door. At that moment, another jeep drove into the yard, and a tall lanky red-haired young man and two girls tumbled out of it. Loud resonating laughter cut through the air. The girls had identical short boyish haircuts and they were both wearing trousers — one in a chequered pattern, the other in bright red. One of them was small with a waspish waist and swarthy face while the other, on the contrary, was tall and light-skinned. The lanky young man turned out to be Bekmurat, Zakhair's son, who used to be known in the aul as *Ginger Housewife*. Seeing Kazhimurat, he rushed up to him and gave him a big hug, which was a far cry from the customary greeting in the aul. Bekmurat reeked of tobacco.

Almurat jumped out of the house.

'Hey, Ginger Housewife, what took you so long? We've been waiting since morning! We had to head out without you!'

'Do me a favour and drop the silly nickname, will you?' Bekmurat muttered to him quietly.

'Well, what are we standing here for?' Almurat smiled warmly.

'The doors are open and the dastarkhan awaits. Let's get some lamb inside you!'

The second-floor room was well ventilated, the steam rising from the kitchen downstairs and the cold outside made the windows drip with condensation. The walls shone, cladded with varnished planks, which for some reason were hung with large sheets of white paper here and there. Everything sparkled with cleanliness and there was no sign that the mistress of the house had been away for the last two weeks. As if trying to enhance the effect, Almurat began to turn on the lights everywhere. But the small dark-skinned girl spotted some candles in the corner of the room.

'Let's eat by candlelight!' she suggested in Russian.

Her voice sounded hoarse, and Kazhimurat assumed that she must have been smoking as well. Her short, red-dyed hair stuck out like porcupine quills. Her tall friend took off her coat, climbed onto the couch and sat next to Kazhimurat, leaning on a foam cushion.

'Let's introduce ourselves.' said the dark-skinned girl.

'What's the folk saying? It's better to see and know a single person by sight than to hear the names of a thousand...'

Bekmurat began to introduce everyone to each other, starting with Kazhimurat.

'Sitting next to you is the very same legendary Kazhimurat, whom I was telling you all about on the journey. And you've probably already guessed that this giant of a man is Almurat.'

The fair-faced girl offered her hand first. Her hands turned out to be soft and supple and a golden ring sparkled on her finger: she was either wearing it for show, or she was married. Her name was Nazym. The dark-skinned girl's hands, on the contrary, were hard and calloused, and her handshake cold and lifeless. Her name was Ukizhan. Both girls were doing an internship with the regional newspaper and had decided to take advantage of Bekmurat's visit to take a look at the aul. They explained that they also had some business of their own here, in the village of Murat.

'Well, our Nazym has chosen the right spot!' Ukizhan laughed. 'We heard that at one time you ended up feeding the whole village, Kazhimurat.'

'Well, it would be an honour for me to be given so much as a lamb's ear from his hands!' Nazym replied. 'However, if you play your cards right, you might end up with the other ear, Ukizhan. So, don't worry yourself too much.'

There is no fettering youthful spirits — freedom and spontaneity are inherent in them. But they made Kazhimurat somewhat ill at ease. As Nazym looked him over appraisingly, Kazhimurat did not know what to do with his powerful hairy hands. He felt out of place among these young people and felt he ought to leave but to do so now would have been awkward. At Ukizhan's insistence, Almurat lit the candles and turned off the electric lights and in the semi-darkness, Kazhimurat began to feel a bit more composed.

Bekmurat carefully examined the room and concluded,

'Fabulous bachelor's pad you've got here! If you could pick it up and transport it to Alma-Ata, that would be the life!'

'I'm not sure whether a country aul house might not look a bit out of place in the capital,' Almurat objected. 'We live as we can here, not as we would like to.'

Kulmayran had already arrived and was playing the role of hostess. Without waiting for the girls to get too settled, she herself started a conversation about this and that, placing the shot and wine glasses on the table and, although the dishes were not particularly luxurious, she had furnished the table with sense and good taste. She had also dressed tastefully in a short, knitted dress with a fringe along the edge of its hem that emphasised the harmony of her beautiful legs and a neckline that was not too low but showed off the striking stone pendant that glittered on its gold chain on her alabaster breast. Nevertheless, she betrayed no sense that she had put her best dress on especially for the guests and she behaved as if their arrival was a complete surprise for her. Whatever the case, Kazhimurat surmised that her effortless female charm was far superior to that of her trouser-clad rivals.

Almurat did not introduce Kulmayran to the guests and the girls mistakenly assumed she was the mistress of the house. *Well, she is worthy of becoming any dashing young man's wife*, Kazhimurat concluded, watching the girl closely and increasingly admiring her. But as far as Kazhimurat could perceive, Almurat seemed to treat her in a casual and unfamiliar manner. The measured tapping of the raindrops on the window panes, the subtle smell of the women's perfume and the dim light of the candles made the room comfortable and cosy. The hot dishes had not yet been served. Bekmurat wandered around the room for some time, drinking his wine and languidly grazing from the cold snacks and dishes laid out on the table. Then he went over to the coffee table, sat down in a deep easy chair and began to leaf through the magazines there.

'You know, Almurat, the aul is a bit run down and has seen better days!' he remarked, sipping his wine and looking at some photographs in a magazine.

'What do you mean, a bit run down?' Almurat replied, not understanding what he was getting at.

'Do you remember as children how we measured out the streets and organised races on the yearlings? Now I look at everything and the houses have become smaller, and the streets — shorter.'

'Have you also noticed how the Altai Mountains seem to have shrunk in the intervening years as well?'

'Well, this is just the law of nature... It's only natural, Almurat.'

'In the same way that those who've moved to the big city seem to think that everything about our life is small and insignificant.'

'I didn't mean to offend you...'

'You came back here to relive your childhood. But the world changes... And it's not only the world but also each individual human soul that ages.'

'All I was trying to say is that there hasn't been a single new household added to the aul in all this time.'

'You're right there. And there's not likely to be either! But, okay, let's talk about this later, we don't want the girls to get bored...'

Kazhimurat could not imagine Nazym being a journalist. She reminded him of those calm and unhurried mothers who settle down next to the yellow pot-bellied samovar at dawn, only rising again at sunset to empty its contents while distributing sweets and sugar throughout the day to their numerous offspring who constantly look to her for attention and love. But Ukizhan didn't seem to be the type of woman who would worry about whether her children and husband were dressed and fed and, in general, whether she would ever have a husband or children at all. She seemed much more interested in learning other people's secrets and gossip. Ukizhan, Kazhimurat decided, was a natural journalist...

Almurat began to fill the vodka and wine glasses. Ukizhan downed her cognac like water, and the fair-skinned Nazym barely took a sip of her champagne.

A whole lamb had been cooked and cut into its traditional twelve constituent parts on the dish and, as befitted distinguished guests, the head had been prepared and brought in separately. Bekmurat refused to accept the honour of carving it, referring to the ancient Kazakh custom that no son is worthy of such an honour while his father is still among the living. Instead, he picked out a rib for himself and, picking off the meat with his fingers, slowly began to eat. As promised, Kazhimurat treated the girls to the lamb's ears. Unlike the local aul folk, they were not accustomed to eating with their hands and tried to pick at the meat with their forks and ended up dropping it on the tablecloth. Nazym placed her glass of champagne next to Kazhimurat's shot glass as if sensing his awkwardness sitting with these young people.

You seem to be one of those women who are endowed with the ability to gladden and illuminate the lives of the lonely and solitary, Kazhimurat thought, suddenly filled with a renewed sense of respect and gratitude to her. *However, sadly, I am not endowed with the ability to engage you in witty and interesting conversation.*

Little by little, the conversation began to replace the clatter of the forks and plates. They talked much and about everything: the latest news from the capital, rising prices, new works by new writers, the fact that art was becoming increasingly empty, that women were now wearing the trousers and men were growing their hair long and becoming feeble in body and mind as a result. Kazhimurat grinned ruefully at the fact that none of them seemed to remember the old folk saying that 'a fine fellow has much in common with a beautiful girl, and a beautiful girl has much in common with a fine fellow'. Is there really so much bad in people now that it is no longer possible to meet a good person? No, the truth of the matter is that people have simply become pettier and more prone to gossip and conversation these days is a cause of irritation instead of pleasure and satisfaction. In much the same way that even in the auls now, people preferred to drink factory-made kefir over freshly-strained kumis... It was not that life had become bad but that people had diminished the value of the word. Human tongues had become too accustomed and too easily inclined to slander.

Kazhimurat began to feel out of place at this table. The company seemed to fade from the meagreness of the conversation. Nazym also seemed to sense this and did not know where to put herself. Kulmayran tried to spice up the conversation but her two or three well-meaning jokes seemed to hang awkwardly in the air. In the end, Kazhimurat resigned himself to the fact that the talk that evening was not going to amount to very much. The young people laughed at the parochial backwardness of the young men living in the aul, and Kazhimurat listed in his memory those of his generation who at their age had gone to war and never returned. Then, they began to do the same to the older generation and Kazhimurat likewise recalled the legendary old people who still survived and seemed to him to tower over the influx of riff raff that had flooded the region in recent times.

Someone else in this sparkling clean and smoothly varnished room mocked the elders for their stinginess, and Kazhimurat recalled the wisdom of the aul's old men and women, who were now no longer with them. Another praised the qualities of these young carefree girls, and Kazhimurat recalled the young women who, during the difficult hungry years during and after the war, had been left bereft of their husbands and their youth and in charge of the small orphans in their arms to whom they devoted their entire lives, turning them into responsible adults. Someone else waved a glass of cognac and sentimentally mused about their homeland, and Kazhimurat thought about this village of fifty households, which had never abandoned its basic human dignity even when it had been pushed to its very limit...

'Kazhimurat, have another drink!'

Concise words, wisely spoken Kazhimurat thought, surprised at Kulmayran's intuitiveness. *You can read people's minds, it seems.*

Kulmayran had chilled the kumis and was now straining it into the large *tegene*[23] before pouring it into the small drinking bowls. Halfway through the process, Nazym picked up a blue-white drinking bowl full of kumis and, with a tender respectful movement, placed it in front of Kazhimurat. And once again this simple action warmed his heart.

There's little point in getting offended like this, Kazhimurat! He began to reproach himself. *She clearly retains the best inherent qualities that have always existed in our Kazakh womenfolk. And who could rightly condemn or speak badly of Nazym's character or behaviour? There is something indestructible in this world, the good that is inherent in people never exhausts itself — this is the nature of human life. You are just jealously defending what your past stood for and have become a grumpy, quarrelsome old man as a result... When you were young, your life had plenty of both good and bad in it as well. It's just that back then you didn't have the experience you have now and probably didn't notice it as much...*

'Would you like some tea?' Kulmayran asked Nazym.

'Thank you!' The girl smiled. 'You can't beat a good kumis. Kumis, in my opinion, is the very manifestation of desire itself, it is constantly luring you in to drink it...'

She faltered and blushed, not knowing how the others sitting at the table might understand her words. Or more specifically, how Kazhimurat might perceive them. Kazakhs have a tradition of defining certain foods as the manifestation of desire itself when a woman is in the first days of her pregnancy. Kazhimurat pretended not to have heard her turn of phrase, raised the bowl to his lips

---

[23] *Tegene* – a large wooden bowl usually carved out of birch wood.

and drained it to the bottom, the bowl was a large one and it was not an easy task.

The room was full of cigarette and candle smoke and in the resulting bluish fog the faces of the company became blurred and the colour of their skin painfully sallow.

'Let's turn the lights on,' Bekmurat suggested to his host. 'Your bachelor's pad is beginning to smell like a church. We're going to suffocate ourselves at this rate.'

The wall clock chimed melodiously.

'They turn off the electricity at midnight,' Almurat answered, rising from the table. No matter how much I bang my head against a brick wall... There's still no way I can persuade the authorities to extend the power line on to us from the Bukhtarma hydroelectric power station. And good-naturedly he remarked to his guest, 'Just because you've forgotten everything else, Bekmurat, there's no reason to have a go at our good old aul kerosene lamps.'

'But my forgetfulness of my roots is no reason for you to suffocate the lot of us,' Bekmurat also joked.

Almurat opened the windows, returned to the table and continued to jest,

'One frosty January night, there was once an old Kazakh who, having filled his belly in his warm house with *kazy* horse sausages and *karta* tripe and washed it all down with a delicious *sorpa* broth, to which dried kurt cheese had been added, turned to his wife and said, "I think you should take the blanket off the black cow in the stable, I reckon she's probably too warm now!"'

'That wasn't your father by any chance, was it? It certainly sounds like him!' Bekmurat laughed. 'But the trouble was, we didn't have *kazy* or *karta* in our house. We had to scrape by with thin gruel. You always had plenty of meat in your house. After all, wealth is not passed on to those whose parents have frittered it away in the previous generation. As you can see, you seem to be referring to the wrong person, Almurat...'

'Who knows, who knows, my friend... Do you think that fifty years ago, a poor but eloquent man would ever have thought that his son might one day become a journalist? He himself selflessly helped all sorts of people around the aul with his gift for words: he would strengthen someone's faith here, console someone there, and now his son earns his daily bread using the same gift. But enough of this, we should leave the souls of our ancestors in peace — this is neither the time nor place to be discussing them.'

Kazhimurat grew pensive again. How easy and simple everything seemed to be for them! Who could possibly know the real truth about their forebears? As if it wasn't bad enough that these hasty young people were so quick to speak and to judge their ancestors, but even the most respected people in the aul still had no idea where many of their kin were living, who had been scattered to the four winds and, indeed, whether they were even alive. At one time, he had heard that he and Almurat had cousins and nephews living abroad but then these rumours died out and then spluttered into life once more. Kazhimurat wondered whether perhaps their relatives had returned to their homeland and were too ashamed to get back in touch with their kith and kin again. He had tried to make inquiries about them and search for them, but none of these efforts had yielded any results. Kazhimurat was not the sort of person to forget his family ties, even if they had been severed by political borders and historical events... And in those difficult times, their relatives had not emigrated because they were opposed to the new way of life but because of their ignorance and lack of literacy... How could he feel anything other than pity for them?

The rain had subsided and the wind died down. Large drops of collected rainwater fell noisily from the window frames with a sound reminiscent of the soft smacking of the lips of a sweetly sleeping child. A refreshing chill spread across the floor and pleasantly cooled the legs. As ever after the rain, the booming roar of the Bukhtarma could clearly be heard, as if large rocks and a whole hailstorm of smaller stones were smashing against each other.

'They say that the sound of water calms the nerves,' Ukizhan remarked. 'So, you all must have pretty strong nerves here!'

Almurat agreed with Ukizhan. 'You can say that again, my dear guest.'

It's paradise around here! The only thing is that it gets dark so early and the sun rises so late.'

'But is that altogether a bad thing?' Almurat picked up again. 'When you lock your doors and close your windows early, you have more time to lie in your warm bed. And that, incidentally, is why we have such big families around here... And we're going to need a lot more children with strong nerves in the future, I think!' His laugh was loud and resonant.

'That's very true,' Ukizhan replied. 'Whenever you go into any house around here, you are met by a horde of children!'

'Yes, our womenfolk have a hard time of it up here!' Almurat replied getting more and more flirtatious. 'There's only one maternity hospital in the entire district and that's over a hundred kilometres from here.'

'Kazhimurat, with your blessing, I'll clear the table now, if you don't mind!' Kulmayran felt the need to interrupt Almurat's train of conversation, which was in danger of crossing all the boundaries of decency.

Kazhimurat held his hands in front of his face in a sign of blessing. The women got up to help Kulmayran, but she insisted that they remained seated and soon had the dishes finished. She left the sweets on the dastarkhan and, having washed the glasses, placed them on the table along with replacements for the bottles that had been finished. She also tidied up the coffee table, making it clear to the guests that they could make themselves comfortable and stay as long as they liked.

Nazym and Ukizhan went out into the yard.

'Who are they?' Almurat nodded after the girls.

'Didn't I introduce them to you?' Bekmurat answered in surprise.

'It's not their names I'm interested in but who *they* are, Ginger Housewife.'

'Well, they are young women, as you can see. And very pleasing on the eye they are too.'

'Thank God, I can still tell the difference between men and women. I was actually talking about something else.'

'Well, you're a strange one, Almurat! Why don't you just ask me directly what my relation to them is?'

'Well, if it's difficult for you to say, you don't have to.'

'Why? Have you taken a fancy to one of them?' Bekmurat smirked.

'I thought that you'd brought them all this way to present them as possible brides to your parents?'

'And which of them do you prefer? Go on, don't be shy!'

'Well, which of them is yours?' Almurat squinted questioningly.

'You'll have to ask them that yourself! I'm not close to either of them. They just came along for the ride and they wanted to see where I'd come from. So, I brought them along with me. After all, guests are and always have been sacred around here.'

Taking a long sip from the glass in his hand, Almurat walked over to the shelves on the wall and, muttering under his breath, turned over a couple of sheets of paper. They had some diagrams drawn on them. Then he sat down in a deep chair and called Bekmurat over.

'Do you understand these plans? I'd be interested to hear what you make of them.'

'Well, I understand a little bit. Let's have a look.'

Bekmurat carefully examined the sheets, stopping to take in each one. He didn't appear to have found anything of particular interest in them. Kazhimurat also had a look but couldn't make head nor tail of them, although he peered at the drawings and diagrams for a long time. Almurat was clearly not happy with Bekmurat's reaction, who had now taken a seat next to the coffee table and, with an indifferent expression, was finishing the contents of his glass and putting his cigarette out in the ashtray.

'Well, if that's how you feel, let's not waste any more time with this,' he muttered gloomily. 'We're not used to staying up all hours with guests and in the morning we're all going to be up to our necks with work.'

'What are you so upset about? You explained to me what these plans are about, but I haven't understood you right, is that the problem?'

'Is there anything in this village that might remain a secret to you?'

'You're being the same as you ever were! Everyone has to double-guess what you're thinking!'

'You yourself said that the houses here seem to have shrunk, to become smaller, which means that I have also become worn out and diminished... And all you two have ever done is run away from this aul! You can see for yourself how things are with Kazhimurat... I came up with the idea of asking him to repair the mill and it's barely kept him in the village for a week. The mill! But to be brutally honest, who needs a mill, these days? It's not worth a pinch of tea. I only asked him so that he'd stay in the aul a little longer, do you understand?'

'I can see you're upset about something. But I don't see what I've got to do with it, can you at least explain that to me? What are you talking about?'

Kazhimurat was deeply wounded by Almurat's words. He had put all his heart into his work, believing that he had done a good deed for the people of his aul, and it was as if Almurat had spat right in his face... And yet... He made a mental note of all the days he had spent back here in his native aul as if he was reviewing his entire life, both past and present and it seemed to him that he was beginning to understand Almurat's resentment.

His house, its furnishings, the table settings — they were strikingly and deliberately different from the world as it existed in the village of Murat, as if someone had thrown a gilded saddle over the back of an ox, but this was not about any desire on Almurat's part for the trappings of wealth or luxury. Whatever the case, it was quite clear that this wealth brought him no spiritual satisfaction. No, Almurat's mind was set on something completely different: how to change the life of the village for the better and make it more fulfilled. And, albeit in his own way, he had been desperately trying to draw the attention of everyone who had a stake in this aul, Kazhimurat and Bekmurat included, to this problem...

The sound of footsteps could be heard coming from the floor below, and the young women appeared on the spiral staircase. Kulmayran, who was following them, suggested to the girls that they might want to go to bed if they were tired. 'If you want to sleep, I've already made up the beds.'

Without waiting for them to answer, Almurat declared,

'Men's talk makes for dull company. You'd better open the champagne for the girls, so they can sit with us for a little while longer. It won't be the end of the world if you don't get to sleep through the night.'

'We're very interested to hear what you've got to say,' Ukizhan replied. 'Unless, of course, we are in your way.'

Kazhimurat surmised that she had just been smoking. Nazym sat down in her former place. Kazhimurat wanted something to lean on — it had been uncomfortable sitting in one position all this time — but the back of the wide settee was too far away. Kulmayran, with her characteristic tact, noticed her guest's discomfort and gave everyone a satin cushion and then quietly uncorked the champagne, carefully filling the glasses. Almurat waited until Kulmayran had finished her duties as the hostess and seemed pleased with how naturally and gracefully she looked after her guests, unobtrusively showing them every attention.

'Do you see that hill to the east? They're going to build a highway there that will go all the way to Buryatia.' Almurat continued, nodding at one of the plans in front of Bekmurat, 'Construction will begin next year. Who knows, perhaps the next time you come back to your native parts you'll be doing so on this new road. It will significantly shorten the journey.'

'But what good is this road going to bring everyone here? Surely, it's just going to bring every profit monger from all around to plunder the region's natural wealth and the taiga along with it? After all, if it's suddenly available — they'll take it whether they need it or not.'

'That's true. But I would probably put a different spin on it, Bekmurat. This road project will be a relatively inexpensive one for the Ministry of Road Construction and it will provide the Timber Ministry with the means to reach the very heart of the taiga. But what it means for us is that we will end up losing our pastures and hay meadows.'

'So, what are you going to do, then?'

'Well, this is the whole point. I've been in touch with the local district bosses and written to even higher authorities, pointing out that the choice of route for this road is going to cost us and other farms dearly. I've already received their answer and it looks like things might work out to our benefit.'

'And what benefit is that going to be?'

Well, I'm hoping that we'll be able to kill two birds with one stone. You see, the main thing is that the road is going to pass through Mount Maya.'

'But that's where other farms are, not ours?' Bekmurat objected again. It would appear to me that you're only thinking of yourself.'

'It's not the road that I need. According to the geologist's report, there are huge underground water reserves under Mt. Maya. And when the mountain is blown up, these waters will be dislodged, turning where we're located now into a reservoir.'

'That doesn't sound much like a benefit at all!'

'Ah! But that's where you're wrong! We will have to move the location of the aul, which means a new village will have to be built. In addition, each household will be given compensation and the farm itself will receive a considerable subsidy from the state. The new reservoir will end up being a benefit, allowing us to open fish and aquatic bird breeding enterprises. But that's not all! As soon as the road is built, we will be able to fence in our entire district and turn it into a nature reserve, which will automatically be protected by the state. Then we will be able to set up a deer farm. In fact, I've already received the permissions for this. And that's how we'll be able to protect the land from the timber industry.'

'Wow! Listen to you! You've turned into a real wheeler-dealer!'

'I'm not just thinking about myself,' Almurat smiled contentedly. 'The idea is mine, but it's the people and the

312

country as a whole that will benefit. And this is where I need your help. Assuming, of course, you still have a place in your heart for your native aul.'

'So, how can I help? Do you want me to become the head of the local the district committee...'

'I wouldn't want you to get ideas above your station!' Almurat laughed. 'The only thing I'd need from you is for you to write some articles in the local papers about the benefit that these changes will bring! And leave the rest to me!'

'But surely the rest of the collective farm's management is involved as well, isn't it? Why are you taking everything upon yourself? Are you planning to get a promotion for yourself out of this?'

'No, it's not any post or position that I want. I have enough on my plate worrying about the fifty households here.'

'What are you going to achieve with your fifty households?'

'Great things can be done here! We could move mountains if only we had the machines to do the work... But what would I need all that for? I am in charge of a department that consists of fifty households, yet the entire collective farm relies on us. As I mentioned before, our department is the only one on the entire farm that is turning a profit. And that's the whole point of my plan. If everything works out, then we'll be able to separate our aul away from the larger collective farm and set up an independent one. Its main purpose will be deer and sheep breeding and the cows and horses will be an extra side enterprise. There's no profit to be had in sowing grain here, the soil is not fertile enough to justify the costs and effort involved.'

'So, in short, you're looking to get yourself a medal? Is that what your plans are all about?'

'I wouldn't say no to a medal if they give me one. But there isn't much honour in being one of the many with a medal on their chest, I'd much rather be one of the rare few without. The main motivation for me is to inject new life into these parts. Otherwise, everyone and everything around here will soon fall into an eternal and irrevocable torpor.'

'Very often that's because their bellies are full.'

'And people whose bellies are full become no better than lazy and docile animals! My dear Bekmurat, you need to express yourself more precisely! A journalist's words need to be precise and concise. The easy life isn't for me!'

'How amazingly similar you and my old man are! I haven't been back to my native village for years, and you won't let me relax and catch my breath for even a minute: it's all do this, do that, and do the other. You won't let up until you've made me listen to every last one of your ideas. Can you explain to me why you need this so much?'

'Even animals have the ability to feel anxious and ill at ease, so what can you expect of sentient people, my dear Bekmurat? If you don't give people a kick up the backside from time to time, they'll happily drown under the garbage they create. People should not be allowed to remain indifferent to their lives! I've heard that you've been collecting material for an article about our aul. Our fifty households! And this material is probably very interesting to you as a journalist, but isn't it more important to be looking out for these very same people's current needs? It is not enough just to honour and chase the shadows of the past. The past isn't going anywhere, it has lived its life, but the question is, how should we live now? We must participate in the life that we need to live today.'

Kulmayran effortlessly served everyone coffee from the long-necked coffee pot. The wall clock chimed again — it was already twelve. The lights went out, but it was bright outside. Kulmayran cut the guttering wicks of the candles burning near the table with a pair of scissors and then parted the window curtains. The room was quiet except for the sound of coffee spoons stirring in their cups. The two candles perched on their fretwork candlesticks next to the door burned faintly and looked as if they were about to go out. However, lounging in their armchairs on either side of the coffee table, there wasn't a trace of fatigue on Almurat and Bekmurat's faces.

Almurat placed a deer antler candlestick on the table and then took a thick notebook from one of his drawers and tossed it down in front of Bekmurat.

'I can see that you're not very excited about what I've just had to say. So, here, read this at your leisure. All the calculations and finer details are in there. Kulmayran will help if you have any questions.'

Bekmurat did not know how to pacify Almurat: it would have been awkward not to pick up the notebook, but he did not want to read it either. Almurat closed the windows and drew the curtains. Thinking that the men were about to take up their serious conversation again, the young women went downstairs to the guest room. Kazhimurat also got up. He had never had coffee before, and there was a bitter taste in his mouth and his throat tickled, as if he had eaten something that had been burnt on the fire and, besides, he felt his heart quickening and beating unevenly.

The street was filled with a milky-murky white light. The aroma of juniper and creeping coniferous shrubs wafted in from the forest. The trees and houses had been washed clean by the rain.

Scooping up a handful of rainwater from a wooden bowl, Kazhimurat rinsed his face. The water was soft and as quick as mercury, and it smelled of young larch leaves and fresh snow. His drowsiness left him in an instant.

The door creaked, and Kulmayran appeared on the threshold with a towel in her hands. She had anticipated that Kazhimurat was quietly about to take his leave.

'Kazhimurat-agai[24], I made a bed for you on the folding sofa,' she said, holding the towel out to him. Then she turned to Nazym and, noticing that she had come out, dressed warmly, like a person about to hit the road, said to her, 'And you, Nazym, you should also rest. The cockerels will be crowing soon. True, tomorrow is Sunday... I do need to get back to my place. Renting a room in someone else's house is never much fun. If you arrive home early, you don't know what to do with yourself, it's so boring, and if you arrive late, instead of asking after you, your landlady is immediately giving you the once over to assess your state of undress... My old

---

[24] The suffix *agai* is a term of respect to an older man. It literally means 'uncle'.

landlady probably hasn't gone to bed yet, so, I'd better be getting back to my room.'

A shadow of sadness flickered across her recently animated face. When a woman has not yet had the opportunity to kindle the hearth in her own house, she is always plagued by some sense of guilt or other that she is somehow herself to blame for this state of affairs and it is very difficult to cast off. Until a few minutes ago, Kulmayran had been the epitome of the hospitable hostess, but now she sensed that she was superfluous to requirements in this very same house. Kazhimurat was well aware that the landlady where Kulmayran was staying had gone to bed long ago and that it was going to be awkward for the girl to have to disturb her at such a late hour. But for some reason, she hadn't been asked to stay the night here. He was disappointed at Almurat's tactlessness.

He really is just a big-shot wheeler dealer! he muttered to himself in irritation, thinking again about the conversation in which Almurat was no doubt deeply engaged. *It's not the collective farm that you're thinking about but yourself. You were just using Kulmayran to create a suitable impression on your guests and show your hospitality off in the most advantageous light...*

Kazhimurat had no desire to go back into the house. He wiped his forehead absentmindedly and hung the towel over the railing. The light still burned in the second-floor room, the long shadows of the two men could be made out behind the white silk curtains and, from their energetic gestures, it was clear that they no longer entertained the slightest thought about the people who had only just now been sitting with them at the same table.

'Kazhimurat-agai?' Nazym called quietly. 'I wanted to have a word with you.'

Not expecting to be addressed in this way, Kazhimurat tensed. Hearing his name uttered in the middle of the night by an attractive young woman would have been enough to set any man's pulse racing, let alone Kazhimurat, who couldn't remember the last time he had had a one-to-one conversation with a young girl. Nazym descended down from the porch and went up to him.

'Kazhimurat-agai, please forgive me, but would you object if I took a little walk with you?' she asked. 'I don't know the place very well and would be so grateful if you could keep me company.'

No, it was not so much a request as a demand. And what was more, sensing that he might say no, Nazym had couched it in terms that could not be so easily refused. No, this was not some girlish whim: while sitting at the table her eyes had been observing him artlessly, with that pure look that betrays an honest, open nature. Her long white face was bright and clear. Kazhimurat looked uneasily at the door, but no one else looked like they were planning to leave that night. He was confused and didn't know what to do.

It was so light out on the street that you could have easily spotted a needle on the road, let alone a couple out for a stroll around the aul. The dirt road, descending like an arrow from the nearby mountain, seemed to have been doused with *ayran* and the rain-filled lake glittered in the moonlight right up to the darkening horizon. Silence reigned. The Bukhtarma quietly splashed and gurgled beyond the aul. The larches looked like strange monsters that had crawled out of the lake and were now frozen motionless, not yet able to shake the water from their shaggy fur.

Kazhimurat and Nazym walked Kulmayran back to her lonely lodgings, standing next to the cliff. A light came on in the window as soon as the gate creaked. Kulmayran bid her companions goodnight without inviting them into the courtyard.

'My old landlady is very lonely and worries about me as if I were her own daughter,' she smiled softly. 'She's probably not had her dinner yet and been waiting up for me. She gives me a hard time if I don't eat regularly three times a day.'

Kazhimurat did not ask what the old woman's name was, although the steep-roofed house seemed familiar. There was a time here, in the aul, when there wasn't a single old woman for whom he hadn't done chores in return for a ladle of gruel and he was sure that this house was no different. The house's old dog saw him and Nazym off with a hoarse and toothless bark.

'Let's go to the river,' Nazym suggested to Kazhimurat.

Well, there could be no harm in taking a stroll with a young girl along the banks of the Bukhtarma, although he felt slightly uncomfortable he was after all a bit long in the tooth for these types of adventures... Nazym seemed to guess his thoughts and went up to him, confidently presenting the elbow of her right arm for him to support...

Happy the man who ends up marrying you! Kazhimurat thought. *How thoughtful and solicitous you are...*

'Kazhimurat-agai, I think you should know that I have come all the way from Alma-Ata specially to meet you,' Nazym declared after they had gone a few steps. 'I have been dreaming of meeting you for a long time, and it's a really happy stroke of luck that I met you so soon after my arrival.'

He could sense how hot and flushed she was through the thin sleeve of her jacket.

Whatever was she going to say next? He didn't want her to say any more, and Nazym seemed to sense his secret wish and fell silent for a long time.

It seemed to Kazhimurat that Kulmayran and Nazym had a lot in common. Although Kulmayran was more talkative, she chose her words wisely and concisely, understanding whoever she talked to so subtly that whatever she might say would resemble the first two lines of a poetic stanza putting her interlocutor at their ease and drawing them further into the conversation. Nazym, on the other hand, seemed taciturn, but always seemed to know exactly what her interlocutor was thinking while addressing them with the utmost care, as if they were something precious. Both of them had the gift of being able to win people over.

The Bukhtarma shone brightly, competing with the moonlight as if it had collected all the night's stars and threaded them on a string. Not far off, the bridge hunched over it like a heavily laden pack animal. The lonely watchman's house glowered in the dark where Trofim's house had once stood. Two cars passed by on the road, their headlights blazing, and then it was quiet again.

'You know, we girls are a funny bunch,' Nazym continued. 'We are attracted by those qualities that we ourselves do not possess and by those things that are distant and beautiful. You could say that I know your life off by heart.'

Indeed, you are a funny bunch, Kazhimurat agreed with her. *How otherwise, could anyone be so fascinated by my life...?*

His life seemed to him like a quiet autumn day, the silence of which has much in common with the experience of being a mute. There might be some rare joys to be had in it, but it was generally filled with an unrelenting and heavy grief. And the fact that there might be someone who understood him did not make things any easier for him. Even Almurat, the person who was probably closest to him, could say nothing that really touched Kazhimurat's heart. But, who was he, with the life he had led, to expect to hear any great words of praise or gratitude from anyone else? People say that *when a person is not revered by those around him, it is because they do not perceive his mind but only hear his voice.* But no one had ever heard his voice. But on the other hand, it's no bad thing to go through life without ever having disgraced yourself or those near to you...

'The land here is blessed,' Nazym continued, developing her thoughts. 'The air is like some miraculous wonder-working elixir. You have no idea how wonderful this dense green forest and this broad constantly flowing river are! I come from a place where the smallest amount of water is worth its weight in gold. Have you heard of the dry deserts of Mangystau?'

Kazhimurat had never seen the beauty of his native land in the same light that Nazym now admired it. It had always been a familiar sight to him and he had taken it for granted. And yet he found himself agreeing with Nazym's words wholeheartedly.

Your admiration is understandable because you are still young and have seen so little in your life. You have your whole life ahead of you, my dear sweet girl. It has yet to show you what it contains — both that which is beautiful and repellent, it contains an abundance of everything. And in due course, it will demand what it is owed. But I am someone who has already crossed that boundary beyond which there is little room for wonder. Beyond this line, lies a world of regret. Although you might be from a land that knows no water, there is much about the depths of human life that you do understand. You would be better off not wasting your feelings on me. It would be like trying to plumb the wells of the hot valleys of your homeland that conceal their precious water at such great depths. You must always remember never to be too hard on life, even when you find that times are hard...

They stood for a long time, looking over the railing of the bridge that had been destroyed earlier that day by the timber truck. Until just now, it had seemed that the river had been flowing with milk rather than water, but as they drew closer the eddies whirling in uneven ridges revealed the dark cold depths below. It's often the same in life: beauty seen from afar often disappears when viewed up close. The water was seething around the huge truck that was wedged hard against the bridge as if it was trying to drag it away and suck it down into the bottomless abyss of a nearby whirlpool. There was something ominous about this furious onslaught. The sight made Nazym feel dizzy — she gasped and wrapped her arms tightly around Kazhimurat's waist.

'My mother always told me never to look down at the raging current of a river and especially at night!' she muttered in dismay. 'Look, the glittering reflection of the moon on the surface makes it look like human faces!'

Kazhimurat had been ready to stand next to the river until dawn but suddenly thought he also saw a face in the waves: the pale and unearthly beautiful face that had once belonged to the ill-fated and unhappy Bakhyt... Confused and dazed, he stumbled away from the river. Nazym, it seemed, was also shaken and walked with him, hugging him around the waist like a child. Kazhimurat was still unable to rid himself of the vision that had appeared to him when a hoarse cry rang out,

'Hey! Who's there?'

Both Kazhimurat and Nazym shuddered and stopped still as if they had hit an invisible wall.

'Stop right there! Do you hear me?' Someone was rushing down towards them from the old watchman's house, running, clumsily, like a bear tumbling down a mountain. He seemed to be waving something long and thin in the air like a pipe or a gun. It was the watchman. He caught up with Kazhimurat and Nazym from the side of the road as if trying to prevent them from escaping and stopped right in front of them. The watchman was wearing a half-length fur coat that had been turned inside out and its collar hid his face. His eyes shone out from under a three-flapped fur hat, like the wary eyes of a jerboa.

'What are you doing here?'

'We're just taking a stroll,' Nazym replied, coming to her senses first.

'Who are you?'

'We're visitors.'

'Well, what's it to me if you're visitors?'

'Well, we weren't asking for you to put us up for the night?' Nazym smiled.

'Oh thank goodness. For a moment, I thought you were a man but it turns out you're a girl.' The watchman stared at Nazym's trousers in amazement. 'Ah! I'd heard that Zakhair's fly-by-night son had brought a gaggle of half-men-half-women with him from the city to visit. I'm guessing you're one of them?'

Nazym laughed softly and merrily.

The watchman slung the double-barrelled shotgun back over his shoulder and tightened his belt by wrapping a hemp rope around his waist several times. Then he brought his face right next to Kazhimurat's, as if he was almost sniffing him.

'Is that you, Kazhimurat?' he murmured. 'They're right when they say there's more of the lone wolf than a man about you. What are you doing, wandering about at this time of night? You don't have a light, do you?'

'You're out of luck, I don't smoke and neither does he,' Nazym interjected.

'As if you don't have enough on your plate already, by the look of you, darling!' The watchman replied. 'Ri-ight... you've come to visit, you say? Well, they've left me here to keep an eye on the truck that tumbled off the bridge today. As if anyone is going to steal that pile of scrap! The driver had finished a whole bottle of vodka and was three sheets to the wind. He's still sleeping it off in my lodge up there! Nothing seems to bother him! Well, I'll be off — I was worried about the truck.'

The watchman had put on his winter felt boots as if he was expecting a freak blizzard on this warm autumn day. Too big for his feet, they slapped against the stones but then stopped on a huge rock, as flat as a table.

'Oh yes, and has Almurat's wife come back from her relatives yet?' the watchman suddenly asked turning to Kazhimurat, as if Almurat's solitude was a subject of personal torment for him. But then, seeing that no answer was going to be forthcoming, he waved his hand and said, 'Ah well, he's never long without a woman! There's been more than one girl from around here in his bed! He's a fast worker, that one!'

Blundering through the shrubs and bushes as he went, the watchman headed straight back up to the hut. He had clearly been bored out here all on his own and had only run out to exchange a few words with them. Kazhimurat and Nazym did not take his malicious gossip seriously. Nazym understood that while openly having a go at Almurat, the watchman had also been trying to wind up Kazhimurat. But she could not understand why he had compared Kazhimurat with a lone wolf. Maybe it was because Kazhimurat was out walking with a young girl late at night. She smiled, remembering the old Kazakh proverb, *The wolf is always on the prowl for fresh blood*. A mature man out with a young girl is always going to be a target for a caustic joke. Well, she was quite capable of bearing the brunt of these sorts of jokes herself. Nazym glanced at Kazhimurat, saw that his eyebrows were gloomily drawn together into a frown on the bridge of his nose, and placed her thin soft fingers into his huge hand, wordlessly reassuring him not to pay attention to the old man's rough, clumsy words. Kazhimurat's palm was slightly sweaty, he did not squeeze her hand but did not withdraw it either: it was as if his life had left him.

Ten days had passed since he had returned to his native village, and during all this time Kazhimurat had not met a single man, young or old, who could talk to him openly and without some ulterior motive. Everyone seemed so supremely self-confident and swaggering that they would say the first thing that came into their heads, without attaching any importance to whom they were talking: be they kinsmen, strangers, countrymen or visitors. They were strangely intolerant to their own, but for some reason familiar with strangers.

'I met Bekmurat's father and it turns out he's an extraordinary man,' Nazym declared, glad to change the topic of the conversation. 'More like a performer playing a part than an ordinary man! Compared to him, his son seems almost mediocre and two-dimensional.'

Kazhimurat understood that Nazym was taking up the thread of the conversation that the watchman had started on the bridge.

A fool's wisdom is stored on the tip of his tongue, so I wouldn't worry too much if I were you... You just need to understand that in this aul, people neither gossip about nor envy each other. Even the most worthless person here is equally frank to everyone, no matter who they are and regardless of whether they are being friendly or hostile...

But it was not these thoughts that occupied Kazhimurat's mind but the image of the long-drowned Bakhyt's beautiful alabaster face, with her motionless burning eyes, which he had just imagined he'd seen in the water. Twenty years must have passed since that day... The spring of forty-five brought with it a huge sense of relief when many of the terrible hardships they had been bearing were lifted from their shoulders, a feeling that only befalls a people once a century, if ever...

'I saw Auntie Zlikha,' Nazym said. 'She's not the sort of woman to entrust her thoughts to the first person she meets. Besides, she wasn't in the mood particularly. They say her husband left her yesterday.'

The unexpected news did not surprise Kazhimurat — he had half expected this might happen, only for some reason he felt not so much sorry for Zlikha as Kiyakmurt. What would he do with himself now, the poor fellow? His son had his own family, his daughter had only just managed to marry off her own daughter and his first wife was unlikely to want him back after he had brought her so much shame. The years had passed and his strength wasn't what it used to be and he would never enjoy the standing he had once taken for granted... But, perhaps, for the first time in his life, Kiyakmurt had acted like a real man. It was hard to know whether to pity or curse him. Maybe it's better to live in solitude than to be in a constant state of apprehension in your own house, to lie down in the same bed with your wife only to have her turn her back on you and leave her early in the morning like some chance stranger, knowing that this is how you would live out the rest of your days. Surely it is better to take the bitter path of loneliness and freedom than to be tied to your home and hearth with a lasso around your neck and heavy fetters on your legs. Even though he sometimes cursed his lonely life, Kazhimurat would never have exchanged it for another, even a better and more beautiful one.

The first cockerel crowed, signalling that it must already be midnight. The full lunar disk was covered with a dark yellow light. The chains of mountain peaks, piling up on top of each other, rose silently and impregnably in the distance as if they had been cast from lead. The aul was fast asleep. Only the second-floor windows of Almurat's house still shone where he and Bekmurat were still putting the world to rights.

The water of the irrigation canal tinkled with a crystal ring against the thin crust of ice that had formed during the night. Kazhimurat and Nazym did not enter the village; they decided to skirt the house and, keeping to the banks of the canal, climbed the nearest hill. A lonely house stood there at the very edge of the forest, looking like a cow that's strayed from the herd. They reached the spring, plucked a handful of grass each, and began to wash the thick mud that was stuck to their boots. The water was icy and the cold pounded in their temples. Nazym hummed a tune. She felt so light and carefree it was as if she had grown wings.

Kazhimurat, supporting her by the elbow, led her into the spacious yard that was cluttered with outbuildings. An iron hook banged, the gate creaked, and somewhere from the depths of the house, a light flashed. Old Batikha was not yet asleep but she did not call out and ask who Kazhimurat had brought back with him. Although Nazym soon realised that Kazhimurat was no stranger to this courtyard, she had no idea that this was Almurat's parents' house.

His ears rang from the silence that hung over the house. Kazhimurat had always found it difficult to get to sleep in the dark and his pillow felt as if it had been stuffed with rocks. Kazhimurat got up several times to plump it up but still sleep would not come. It is never hot in the Altai, but from the very beginning of every summer, Batikha, with her morbid fear of flies and midges, would always have her windows and doors tightly sealed. After tossing and turning, Kazhimurat finally got up, went over to the windows and with a single movement tore off the newspapers that had been stretched over the panes. The paper was dry and the dust that flew up like weightless smoke made his throat tickle and he sneezed loudly. The bed in the next room, where Batikha was sleeping, creaked and he became worried that he might have woken Nazym, but she was sleeping peacefully on the couch. Kazhimurat opened the window, flung open both doors leading to the kitchen and, pulling the felt mat and blankets off the bed, spread them on the floor.

Oh, how good it is to lie, stretched out freely on the floor! What a pain to have to squeeze yourself into a cramped bed. It's like being buried alive in a coffin!

His back had become completely numb lying on the sagging mesh of the bedstead, but on the floor, he luxuriated in seventh heaven. A breeze was sucked in from the window through the open doors and pleasantly tickled his chest. Of all the inconveniences that settled life had to offer, Kazhimurat disliked stuffy, hot rooms above all others. Whenever he found himself in one, he would twitch and lash out like a horse that has been attacked by gadflies. As soon as the palms of his hands or the soles of his feet became even slightly sweaty, he would lose all appetite for food or work. At times like this, he was not himself and he would become lethargic and drowsy. However, on the contrary, he saw the cold Altai autumn as a time of cleansing purification, with its crackling winter frost cleanly slicing through the torpor of summer. There was no place in Kazhimurat's memory for wonderful, warm, spring days. Evidently, the universal joy that the warmth brings most humans was not for him. However, he recalled the cruel, severe frosts when he had to complete mountains of work all on his own with a quiet reverence. He missed those 'hot' days and nights. But this time too had passed, sunk into oblivion.

The first thing he could make out in the pale morning light were two pairs of shoes standing by the door. Nazym's elegant boots leaned against Kazhimurat's huge agricultural ones. He glanced up at the sofa. Nazym was sleeping quietly, her face half buried in her pillow. Her soft short hair, hiding her high forehead, barely perceptibly moved in the breeze blowing through the window. Her face wrinkled comically at the tickling of her hair, and an indistinct smile hovered on her lips. She must have been dreaming... Let her have her dream, he hoped it was a good one. There is nothing that can beat a good night's sleep, especially when you are still young. As you get older, even your dreams become vague and foggy, barely like a dream at all but more like a ghostly shadow. As you get older, you only usually dream at night about those things that you have experienced during the day, and they are not always a pleasure.

The age of twenty is a happy time in a person's life, a naïve and trusting time. How else could he explain why this girl had come all the way from the capital to a lonely aul lost in the remote taiga just to meet a stranger? Who knew what was going on in her mind, but if you looked into the expression of her eyes, listened to her voice and thought about the ideas she expressed, then you might have thought that she had only been motivated by journalistic considerations. She had taken Kazhimurat's life too much to heart, she had reached out to him without considering whether it might appear shameful for her to remain so close to him for the whole night. If Kazhimurat had been young, if he had been endowed with the gift of speech, maybe he would have told her about his sufferings. And, most importantly of all, he had been planning to entrust them to the person who had been closer to him than any other in his life but, unfortunately, had been unable to do so. There was no limit to his grief. What else was there to expect from life, when he was already well in advance of forty?

The rays of the moon's light drew closer and closer to Nazym's bed. Her cheeks were puffed out, as if she had hidden some sweets in them, her straight thin nose with their slightly concave nostrils flared. The girl's face was striking in its purity. As if he was almost jealous of the moon's rays, Kazhimurat placed a chair hung with his clothes at the head of Nazym's bed.

He didn't have the strength to look at her face. *She's still a child,* he muttered to himself. *Still a child, a child...*

A person who has been treated harshly by life from their childhood and who himself has grown harsh and unsociable could, it turned out, easily be broken in their later years. He had once lived, believing that if his head ever became broken then he could cover it with his hat or if it was his arm then he could always hide it inside his sleeve, but now he was ready to completely revise these convictions.

The cockerels crowed for a third time. Kazhimurat had no regrets that he had been unable to sleep that night. For a person who has become accustomed only to confiding in himself, a sleepless night like this one was no great loss as long as there is a living soul nearby who, despite not being able to hear you, is able to put you in the mood for a deep meditative journey just by their very presence. He was glad he hadn't lost this night to fruitless sleep. Kazhimurat turned over on his side and glanced at the girl for the last time. The pale moon's rays had failed to reach the bed on which Nazym was sleeping and had dispersed and disappeared into the semi-darkness. The unexpected thought occurred to Kazhimurat that Nazym reminded him of the old Zlikha he had known during the war. Although admittedly, Zlikha had been slightly older back then... It seemed strange that a girl of Nazym's age should seem so young now, almost like a child when, only two decades earlier, twenty-year-old girls had borne all manner of hardships to keep the country clothed and fed while the men had been fighting at the front...

* * *

In the east, the sky had been torn open by a bright streak of light. Kazhimurat rose with the first trills of the larks. That early morning, everyone in the temporary shelters with their pointed roofs was sleeping soundly.

The young teacher made a quick dash to a nearby bush from the yurt, which housed the children in the middle of the temporary village, and quickly returned back to her warm bunk. The morning was cold, a grey mist shrouded the hollow next to the river bank, the ground was frozen and the sticky buds on the birch trees were icily translucent. Kazhimurat left the hut lightly dressed, just in his shirt. He wanted to go back to get his warm quilted sleeveless jacket, but then remembered that he had placed it under Zlikha's head. All night, Zlikha had been tossing, turning and groaning. She had evidently caught a cold during the day, and he had not been able to come up with any better way of showing her his attention.

Not long ago, the aul had moved to the left bank of the Bukhtarma in time for the sowing season. Every year in April, as soon as the water levels subsided, all the inhabitants of the village of Murat, young and old alike, would move to the southern bank with their cattle teams and ploughs. The primary school children had been brought along to help drive the horses and oxen and they would do their studies while at the same time working alongside the adults in the field. They managed here with the minimal amenities: the children lived in a covered cart while the adults had settled in the ten temporary shelters surrounding the yurt. Each shelter had been equipped with rounded plank bunks attached to the poles holding the structure up, which were then covered on top with a thick layer of pine branches and then felt mats. In the middle of each shelter was a place for a fireplace. Anything is better than living in the open air and on the dank, damp earth. But this nomadic aul had been moving from one spot to another for three years during the spring sowing, the summer mowing and the autumn harvesting and had now become universally known as *Kazhimurat's camp*.

The people of the aul could see that he cared about them, and tried not to complain too much about the inconveniences of their lives out in the field. In their heart of hearts, they were all extremely grateful to Kazhimurat, who gave of himself tirelessly and was continually coming up with new ideas to help the collective farm survive. Nevertheless, that spring, everyone was in good spirits, and when the people were in a good mood, Kazhimurat's strength seemed to double. He would walk everywhere with his head held high, he smiled at everybody and was livelier, more responsive than before. What's more, the front had now crossed the border into fascist Germany and our army was approaching the wolves' lair itself. People who had lived through four extremely hard years were expecting news of victory any day now. Even those unfortunate mothers who had lost their sons to the war or wives who had resigned themselves to remaining a widow for the rest of their lives found their spirits beginning to perk up. And Kazhimurat had his own special reasons to be joyful these days...

But for now, he was going to look in on the horses in their night shelter, and on the way, he worried about Zlikha. He had done his utmost to convince her that it would make much more sense for her to stay in the village for the cold season. After all, the old men and women who had been left behind would need looking after, but Zlikha insisted that she'd be setting a bad example staying at home in the village during the sowing season. Ploughing the land was a difficult enough job even for a healthy young man and not everyone could do it, and even the strongest might stumble when it became difficult, let alone a woman in her third month of pregnancy. Kazhimurat was extremely worried about Zlikha's restlessness the previous night and the stomach pain she had been complaining about. If only it would pass, he was now thinking as he walked between the quiet slumbering pointy-roofed huts. Kazhimurat and Zlikha had started living together just so — without a wedding ceremony or words of love, which he neither knew nor was able to utter. No one condemned them for quietly starting a family, no one reproached Zlikha as a woman for marrying a homeless man who had served time in prison and no one reproached Kazhimurat as a man for moving into a house that was the property of his wife. Not that either of them cared what anyone else had to say. For Kazhimurat, there was no woman more precious than Zlikha — his first love, and for Zlikha, who had lost her first love early in life, there was no man who would ever provide the support and protection that Kazhimurat did.

Kazhimurat felt that his life had finally acquired meaning, even if he believed himself to be an inferior sort of person. He gradually forgot about his lonely and difficult past and his constant doubts associated with his own unsettled life gradually disappeared. He was ready to move mountains for and devote his life to the people of this aul and saw that this was where his happiness lay.

From the very first day, he learned that Zlikha was pregnant, he was overcome with a feeling of tender compassion for her. His love for this unborn child turned out to be stronger than all the other feelings he was experiencing combined and he overflowed with hopes and dreams of a bright and meaningful future.

Having covered a distance of about fifty metres, he stopped at the banks of the Bukhtarma but could find no horses there. The short-tailed bay horse that he usually rode was resting that day. It had been purchased from a Russian village at one time and, having given its all for the entire week, every seventh day it would disappear off to pasture to recoup its strength and there was no way he was going to find it today. However, the faithful animal would appear of its own free will the next day, ready once again to unquestioningly submit to Kazhimurat's bridle and command. Kazhimurat regretted that he hadn't put the animal out to graze on the halter — there was plenty of grass here and the stallion would have happily eaten its fill by morning. He had a long list of things to do, but he would have to remain on foot.

The Bukhtarma was deep in these parts and had laid a winding channel, turning sharply to the left and right and its banks were so densely overgrown that a dog would have found it hard to find a way through it. A carrion buzzard was circling above the dusty shrubs, its discontented cry making it clear to anyone listening that it had been scared away from its find. Kazhimurat walked along the bank towards the bushes, kicking some animal's sun-bleached bones into the water on the way. He had had to insist that Rapiya did not entrust the children with the job of herding the cattle. Whatever misfortune had happened, this wretched bird had been circling over these bushes for a reason.

As he got closer to the bushes, there was a noise and some animal — either a fox or a corsac had scuttled off into the undergrowth. About four years before, wild deer had roamed here in large numbers, but now every manner of vermin stalked these parts. At the next bend in the river, he saw the shreds of a familiar hide that had been ripped to pieces by some wild animal's razor-sharp fangs about a week previously. Kazhimurat had slaughtered a well-fed three-year-old heifer and wrapped the meat in the hide to keep it fresh, and then given it to Rapiya to cook for the collective. Evidently, Rapiya had not hidden the remains of the meat well enough and they'd been stolen by the foxes. The day before, she had had to serve a thin gruel for dinner! Kazhimurat angrily pulled out the piece of hide from under the stones and threw it into the seething water.

There were plenty of people that needed to be fed in *Kazhimurat's camp*, about a hundred people for the five dozen teams. It was a good job that Rapiya was so resourceful and had been able to feed them with the beef for a whole week. But what was he going to feed everyone with now? Carrying his trap net over his shoulder, he turned around and climbed back up the hill.

The jagged edge of the sun appeared from behind the mountains. In the fog, it seemed like a dimly glowing piece of copper covered with soot. Clearly, the next two or three days were going to be cold, otherwise, the sun would have been adorned with a rainbow necklace. The earth had not warmed up at all, if it had, they would already be walking ankle-deep in mud, but it wasn't too cold to start ploughing. They had been at it for quite a while now, only a few small clearings next to the edge of the forest and a round promontory right on the bend of the river remained. However, besides the ploughing and sowing, Kazhimurat had more than enough other things to keep his mind occupied.

The fog was thickening in the valley. The cranes feeding in the marshes began to ascend into the sky. Zakhair approached, leading the horses and oxen to the watering place.

'Your camp has been on the move,' he said, surveying the area. 'But by the time my dear wife serves the morning tea, it'll be noon before you know it. She's become very sleepy lately, who knows she might be up the duff! Hee-hee-hee!'

The shelters surrounded the only wagon in a dark ring as if they were protecting it from invisible enemies. Thick puffs of smoke rose up. Rapiya stood next to the cooking fire wielding a large pair of tongs in her hand. It was still cold. Feeling sorry for the children, the women had not woken them up early and, throwing a halter over their shoulders, had come out to meet the oxen returning from the watering hole.

'So, your short-tailed gelding has got the *day off* again?' Zakhair nodded at the silver bridle hanging over Kazhimurat's shoulder. 'Well, you've got a strong-headed one on your hands there! You'd have thought he could give up at least one Sunday to help us?' Zakhair looked up at the sun, squinted and then pulled his *Kirov* pocket watch on its chain out of his pocket and handed it to Kazhimurat. 'You know I can't get the hang of these things. What time does my golden watch say it is?'

Zakhair would usually take out his watch with an air of self-importance — watches were a rare sight in the aul — but now he was moving sluggishly, he was evidently tired having been up all night grazing the cattle. His thin moustaches, which had not been trimmed for a long time, hung lifelessly down his face, like the icicles hanging from the roof of the shelters. Kazhimurat first put the watch to his ear, then looked at the hands and showed Zakhair seven fingers and smiled. Zakhair knew perfectly what Kazhimurat was smiling about, but pretended not to notice, cleared his throat and said,

'It's still too early. Let's sit here for a while and leave the women to get breakfast ready.'

Breakfast, they both knew, was going to be a pretty meagre affair: tea brewed from willow herb and dried viburnum berries for the adults and the same for the children with a handful of oatmeal added. Kazhimurat followed Zakhair and sat cross-legged on a heap of rotten straw. They had done this every morning as if they were about to settle some long-held dispute until the women were ready to lead the teams out into the fields.

Half a year had passed since Zakhair had returned from the Labour Battalions. On learning that he was about to return, the village had been seething with gossip and rumour, convinced that he was going to bring back a second wife with him, and a Russian one to boot, but in the end, he came with no more than his pocket watch and a medal for his service. Admittedly, no one believed that he had been given the medal personally by Kalinin[25] himself or that his pocket watch had belonged to the director of the plant where he had worked and had been

---

[25] Mikhail Kalinin was a Soviet politician and Bolshevik revolutionary. He served as head of the Soviet Union from 1919 to 1946. Kalinin remained the titular head of state of the Soviet Union after the rise of Joseph Stalin, but held little real power or influence. He retired in 1946 and died in the same year.

given for his excellent service. Indeed, some of his fellow villagers were even upset that Zakhair could have pulled their legs in this way. But the aul's elder statesman Zhusup settled the matter by thanking Zakhair for not dragging the aul's reputation through the dirt by completing his service and returning home still riding 'high on his horse' as they say. Zakhair was not to blame for the fact that he had been taken into the Labour Battalions and not sent on active service, where he had sworn blind that he would have been more than a match for the long-legged fascists. From that time on, for the last six months, listening neither to those who wished him well or ill, Zakhair had been proudly wearing his medal on his chest and his watch on its chain — the only example of either in the entire village.

When anyone either jokingly or in all seriousness asked Zakhair the time, he would first take a fix on the position of the sun in the sky and then, looking at his watch, tell them the time. Except for a couple of occasions, Zakhair had been absolutely right, although his watch had had little to do with the process.

Kazhimurat crumbled a piece of clay in his fingers, it was damp and smeared all over his fingers.

'We'll need to wait a bit,' Zakhair nodded in agreement. 'It's too early to start throwing the seed grain into the ground. It will end up baking in the soil as soon as the sun warms up and all our work will have been in vain. We'll just have to be patient, it's the same every time.'

Kazhimurat had never previously held so much as a hoe in his hands, but in recent years he had learned many of the secrets of agricultural labour. A man can learn everything if life pins him up against the wall and forces him to. He can learn the secrets of all four of the seasons, each of their features, and comprehend the whims of nature and the fertile power of the earth. He was pleased that Zakhair, who was old enough to be his father, felt able to talk to him on an equal footing. This was also no mean achievement. Kazhimurat looked at the smoke stretching over the aul and his heart was warmed at the thought that all this had been his idea and was the work of his hands. And the world that had been created was as old as human life itself.

Women's cries could be heard near the temporary shelters.

'Just look at that rascal!' Zakhair exclaimed. 'The devil himself must have taken possession of him!'

A four-year-old grey bull that was still unused to the halter was dragging two women along behind him who in turn were trying in vain to control the animal.

'Damn it, if I had my way, I'd have nipped your sacks in the bud and that would have calmed you down quickly enough!' Shamshinur shouted at him. 'I hope they dry up and fall off! It's high time he was gelded once and for all! And just look at our men sitting on their hill and enjoying our discomfort!' She shouted at Zakhair and Kazhimurat. 'I'd like to see how this bull would cover them given half the chance?!'

Zakhair burst out laughing. Shamshinur's crude and biting abuse tickled his sense of humour. But Kazhimurat, on the contrary, squirmed at her words, pronounced well within earshot of young and old alike.

You wait until this evening I'll have a rope threaded through your nostrils and then you'll know what it is to rage! he silently threatened the grey bull.

Mist rose from the surface of the marshes. A metallic clang rang out from the direction of the main camp — it was Rapiya letting the aul know that the tea was ready and it was time to get their breakfast. Zakhair did not react: as long as Rapiya remained his wife, his breakfast wasn't going anywhere. He straightened his back in pride, exposing it to the sun's rays.

'In the early years of the collective farm, our aul used to be called the felt village,' Zakhair reminisced, returning to the idea he had been expounding at the beginning of the conversation. 'We were living in the middle of the taiga, but were too set in our nomadic ways and didn't know how to lean two tree trunks against each other to make wooden houses for ourselves. We continued to live in our old-fashioned *kibitka* covered carts. But this made little sense. We planned to settle together in one place and establish a collective farm making felt, but the next morning we looked outside and all the wagons had gone and in their place were the still warm embers of their campfires. It turned out that your father had forced the people to leave and took them over the border. He frightened them with stories about the collective farm... And no one among us was able to open these steppe-dwellers' eyes to the advantages that this new business had to offer. Your father made a big mistake... He went over the border to foreign lands, but what was there waiting for him there? He simply disappeared from the world...'

Zakhair looked into Kazhimurat's face, saw that he was frowning and picking at the ground with a sprig of *kurai*, and regretted what he had said. He shouldn't have touched upon an old wound. He immediately backtracked to make amends for his oversight,

'A son who sells his labour is more precious than a father who sells his beard, they say. But that's not important, even if our aul doesn't look great with its people living in temporary shelters. Thank God you can take great pride in the fact that they call it Kazhimurat's camp. So, it turns out that after Yelmurat left, his son remained to gather the new aul around him and, unlike his father, lead it to a brighter life. You have done a great thing, son! May God grant you a long life.'

The teams of oxen came out of the aul, dragging their ploughs behind them, on which a gaggle of sleepy young boys huddled like hawks on a hunter's perch. Behind the ploughs walked the women, tucking up the hems of their dresses with hemp ropes, which they then used to tighten their belts. They were shod for the most part in felt boots with wooden soles. This footwear, that Kazhimurat had come up with himself was ungainly and uncomfortable — two or three kilogrammes of mud would stick to them, but on the other hand, at least people's feet didn't freeze in the mornings.

'Hey, Kazhimurat, I left the grey bull especially for you, so you can go milk it yourself!' Shamshinur shouted, pointing to Apmuraga, who was now struggling with the restive beast. 'Did you think that just because I don't have a husband that I lacked a stubborn bull in my life? Well, as luck would have it, you've gone and found me the wildest of the bunch!'

343

Kazhimurat said nothing in reply, but when Almurat drew level with him, he tore the halter out of the young boy's hands, whipped the bull's snout with it and jumped on the back of the animal with one great leap. The bull danced under him like a mad thing, making huge leaps, first in one direction and then the other, but it was beyond its power to throw off the huge, powerful young man who sat astride him. Then, raising his tail upright, he rushed out into the steppe. Behind the bull the plough skipped like a tin can tied to the tail of a cat, hitting the hillocks on the way and flying into the air.

'Watch out, he'll end up breaking his neck!' Shamshinur yelled out.

'For the love of God, what are you doing sitting there?' Rapiya shouted at her husband. 'Chase after him or he'll be trampled to death!'

Everything had happened so quickly that Zakhair had no time to react. He chased after the grey bull for a minute, which was rushing through the marsh like a whirlwind, and laughed out loud. Before the huge bull could even reach the middle of the swamp, it stopped, trembling all over, and everyone could see how Kazhimurat instantly jumped off him, clinging onto his muzzle. The pair of them were immediately transformed into a whirling ball and disappeared into the thick bushes nearby.

After a little while, Kazhimurat came out of the marsh, leading the subdued bull behind him.

'Kazhimurat, what have you done?' Zlikha gasped, running up to him.

The bull's tongue was lolling out of its mouth, and bright crimson blood flowed foaming out of its nostrils.

Kazhimurat had pierced the bull's nostrils with his long knife and he had threaded a horsehair lasso through the hole he had created. Kazhimurat was a terrible sight to look at: his face was bruised, blackened and covered in scratches and his jaw and cheekbones were set tight. His teeth were gritted in anger, and his gaze was so fierce and piercing that he seemed like a complete stranger to Zlikha. Without saying a word, Kazhimurat lifted Zlikha as if she were a piece of down, sat her on the grey bull and, leading the beast by its halter, walked on. The bull, which until recently had been ready to crush anything that crossed its path, now meekly swayed behind Kazhimurat. A large crowd had gathered around the edge of the marsh, loudly discussing what had happened and staring at Kazhimurat, Zlikha and the bull. Zlikha felt embarrassed — traditionally when a woman is made to ride a bull, especially one without a saddle, it is done to humiliate her in the eyes of people — she was about to get off and walk, but Kazhimurat turned around and gave her such a fierce look that she shrank back and seemed to have become transfixed on the broad back of the trembling animal.

That day, Kazhimurat ploughed the land with the grey bull from morning until evening, having yoked it up with a more experienced ox. Zlikha worked with him as his driver. Kazhimurat worked without a single break, except on those occasions when he went off to help the other teams repair their broken harnesses, or hook up their shafts to the base of their plough. Leaning his entire body weight onto the plough handles, he pushed so hard that the ploughshare entered the ground right up to the mud board. For the first time in her life, Zlikha actually felt sorry for the unfortunate lot of the draught animals. Sweat rolled off the grey bull in streams, it staggered from fatigue, but the moment it stepped back from the furrow, fell behind its partner, or tried to rest its hoof on the hard ground, it would immediately feel the full force of Kazhimurat's long whippy club. The beast's entire body would shudder with the pain, gathering itself into a ball, and then continue to meekly pull the plough along the line of the furrow again. When the mud board became stuck with soil, Kazhimurat would pull it out of the furrow, knock off the clods of mud with a few blows of his iron rod, and, without giving anyone a moment's rest, plunge the ploughshare back into the ground again.

He didn't seem to know the meaning of fatigue. The muscles on his mighty shoulders bulged when the blade of the ploughshare went too deep into the ground. The more he worked, the spikier and angrier the expression in his eyes became. His face, eyebrows and lashes turned white from the dust, sweat streamed down his forehead and his ears became pinned back to his head like a wolf's. His short curly hair, which had barely ever been covered, seemed to have been carved onto his head out of stone. It seemed to Zlikha that he was behaving like this to frighten her, or even, perhaps, put her in her place once and for all. She sensed something cruel and merciless in his movements. That day both the grey bull and Zlikha felt the full brunt of it. At noon, when the clanging from the main camp sounded out, Zlikha's legs were ready to give way under her. She threw the reins over the necks of the oxen and staggered back to the camp, barely able to see what was in front of her. *What have I done to displease him?* Zlikha thought bitterly, wearily dragging her feet. *Why is he behaving like this?*

Kazhimurat himself could barely keep to his feet. He let the animals head off to pasture and collapsed on a pile of rotten straw that lay by the side of the road. The stubble had stuck together in the clay into a hard lump, but this seemed to him as soft as down. He gazed up at the clear sky for a long time. How nice to lie on the ground and look up at the sky! Is there any better feeling than lying exhausted after a hard day's work, lacking the strength to even move your arm or leg? You can forget everything both good and bad...

His toeless foot ached. Kazhimurat took off his shoes and calfskin footcloths and laid them under his head. At the edge of the marsh stood the grey bull, its head bowed dejectedly, unable to take in what had happened to it that day. And yet, who knows, perhaps it was precisely on that day that it had finally learned the true meaning of its life if this is something a brute animal is ever given to learn.

Well, well, you can stand there and ponder your life a little, Kazhimurat chuckled. *You've become used to being a burden to others, well now it's time you learned what it is to carry them yourself! So, you just stand there and think about that for a little...* He laughed soundlessly.

When he thought about it, there was a lot that he and the bull had in common — one was lagging behind his peers, while the other had been deprived of his herd. His mouth was still full of dust, no matter how much he spat his saliva was claggy and his tongue could barely move. He unbuttoned his shirt collar. The cool breeze brought relief. He relaxed his shattered body, staring up at the sky again.

The midday silence hung in the air and filled his ears as if he had plunged deep under heavy still water. An eagle soared slowly and smoothly in the sky like the paper kites that young boys launch into the sky and then stooped down like an arrow, leaving the sky to shine again in its original purity. The larks, which had been competing with the scraping of the plough since early morning, had now ceased to shout their challenge to the day with their silvery trills. It was clear to Kazhimurat that there are no wings in the world that do not eventually tire and no songs that do not eventually cease.

The horizon receded, and the earth seemed boundless and spacious. And he wondered how such surprisingly different people could live under this same clear blue sky and on this wide and beautiful land. Some lose their heads and, sowing evil, rush through life at full gallop; others, lose their spirit and, without heart, droop sadly under their loads like pilgrims; others still rejoice at every little thing, brightening the world with their smiles and joy. Apparently, there is no permanent and rigid river channel down which everyone can be squeezed so that they end up perceiving the world in the same way and breathing as one being. And having come to this simple and clear conclusion, Kazhimurat regretted that he had been so unfair and harsh towards Zlikha that day, who lived entirely for the sake of others, and so cruel towards the poor grey bull, who had simply not wanted to have its freedom curtailed. He began to reproach himself, only now realising all the injustice of his behaviour.

A marmot whistled from a hillock on the south side of the hill, and Kazhimurat stirred with interest. If a marmot pulls up the stores of grain it has left over from the winter to dry them in the sun, then that means it's time to start sowing. The evocative cries of the partridges, gathering for the breeding season at the bottom of the hill, seemed to back this supposition up. Admittedly, only today, Zakhair had warned him about the cold winds coming down from the Kuralai, which any day could bring snow with them. But, so what, the winds might suddenly rise but they would also subside, like Kazhimurat's and the grey bull's sudden flash of fury, and the snow would melt and evaporate, like the excess sweat leaving his body after his exertions. Hurricane winds would pass and they would still cope with the sowing. They had, after all, survived four unimaginably difficult years of war. The aul's spirits would pick up with the arrival of summer and they would gather their strength in time for the autumn harvest.

Kazhimurat calculated in his head the number of men in each of the aul's households and worked out that one-hundred-and-twenty young men had left for the war. *Imagine what the aul would become if they all returned alive and well!* Kazhimurat thought. *And imagine what would happen if this were repeated in every village throughout the country!* But then he recalled that over half of them had already been buried and many others had died on the field of battle or disappeared without a trace... How many of them would return home safe and sound, to which of the aul's houses would happiness return, in how many of the women's eyes would the light flash once again?

Many of the houses had become empty... All four of old Zhusup's sons, Trofim's two sons and now Shamshinur's husband were all gone... The poor woman was still doing the work of ten others and yet she still did not know that she was destined to live the life of a widow... She was loud, sharp-tongued and would sometimes shoot from the hip, but when she wasn't treating them with her constant tongue lashings and jokes, people would often get bored and look around, as if something was missing in their lives. Every Kazakh aul has a woman like this who holds a special place in the hearts of its people... Shamshinur's husband had left the village at the very beginning of the war and more than a year had passed since the arrival of the letter notifying of his death. Zlikha could not find the strength to tell her the terrible news and she had recently turned to Kazhimurat to gather the elders and inform poor Shamshinur of her husband's death through them. But Kazhimurat could not bear to undertake this task either and he had been carrying the official notification around in the pocket of his tunic for so long that the envelope was beginning to get worn. The letter was not just burning a hole in his pocket but his soul as well. Once they had dealt with the sowing, maybe then would be the time to inform Shamshinur of her irreparable loss...

And so, our joys and sorrows are inextricably tied with our unending hard work, Kazhimurat thought to himself as he stared up into the bright blue sky until his eyes hurt. *We connect everything to what we do and those things that make up our lives...*

Kazhimurat unbuttoned the button of the breast pocket of his tunic. Zlikha had insisted that he wore her late husband's old clothes, and Kazhimurat now regretted that he had yielded to her insistence. It's not that he believed in superstition, it was more just feeling out of sorts because ever since he had worn this tunic he had been carrying Shamshinur's letter around in its pocket...

But that was strange, the notification was no longer there in his pocket! Where could it have got to? Kazhimurat sat up with a jerk and quickly checked all his other pockets.

Heavy footsteps approached from behind, like the tread of a horse's hooves on soft ground. Kazhimurat did not look around, thinking that someone was passing by on horseback.

'You don't need to look for it anymore!' a voice said from behind him.

It was Shamshinur. Breathing heavily, she was almost standing over him in her faded dress, barefoot, its hem tucked into her belt. She picked up a clump of straw and began to wipe the mud stuck to her perfectly formed marble-white calves. The young woman's powerful and healthy body radiated strength. Kazhimurat felt awkward and began to cover up his frostbitten foot with his footcloths.

'You don't need to look for it anymore!' Shamshinur repeated. 'Just because you've hidden the piece of paper, it doesn't mean the person will come back from the dead. I already guessed that he'd died a long time ago, my dear. I could see it in your eyes... And then, that time when I washed your tunic, I finally found the official notification in your pocket. I have got over his death, Kazhimurat.'

It was only now that Kazhimurat realised his mistake: two weeks ago, Shamshinur had offered to wash his tunic and he'd forgotten to take the letter out of his pocket.

Shamshinur sat down next to Kazhimurat,

'What are you doing lying here? Pleased with yourself that you've broken in the grey bull? And what would happen to you now if you fell into the hands of our women? You wouldn't have the strength left to see to them, I suppose?'

Kazhimurat stirred anxiously, not fully realizing that Shamshinur was hitting on him. She was breathing heavily, her full breast was trembling, her thin face was pale, and her eyes shone brightly as if at any moment they would fill with tears.

'Kiyakmurt has finally showed up,' she announced, moving a bit closer to him. 'He's looking for you, he says we need to hold a meeting. But don't rush, the meeting isn't going anywhere. Or maybe you're worried about Zlikha?'

She suddenly tore Kazhimurat's footcloths out of his hands and pressed them to her chest. Only now did he notice that she had unbuttoned her dress, exposing her breasts.

'Have you gone blind as well, you unfortunate man?!' Shamshinur's voice trembled. 'What are you finding so difficult to understand? Do you think that now I'm going to give up the tenderness that a man can give me... Are you going to make me beg you for it?'

Shamshinur embraced him tightly and then pulling him towards her, threw him onto the straw. Kazhimurat tried to throw her hot heavy body off his but Shamshinur was almost strangling him in her strong embrace. He saw the blood pulsing in a swollen vein in her neck...

Later, when it was all over, Kazhimurat dragged himself to his feet and, staggering, walked off towards the field, inspecting each plough. A passerby might have mistaken him for a drunk. But he was not drunk, he was just stumbling around, seeing nothing before him except the black velvet earth that had just been ripped open by the ploughshares. He was extremely uneasy and embarrassed at what had just happened. He found a bucket of grease and, mechanically hooking his finger around the handle, began to lubricate the bearings of the cartwheels. In another place, he found some upturned harnesses lying on the ground that had been left to dry in the sun and, noticing that a bolt on one of them was loose, he fixed and tightened the strap for good measure.

Looking behind him, he discovered that he was the only person next to the shelters and noticed Shamshinur lying motionless in shock, curled up in a ball on the pile of straw. She had begun to weep bitterly after he had gone. Kazhimurat felt sorry for Shamshinur. He wanted to go back and comfort her with a warm word. But he was incapable of uttering a single word, let alone a warm one... He knew that what had passed was not just some whim on Shamshinur's part. He understood full well the mystery and power behind their brief encounter... Human grief seeks and finds solace in many different ways...

Some boys were playing under the aspen tree and Kazhimurat could guess from the tone of their voices that their game was in danger of turning into a quarrel. The leader of the gang was broad-shouldered Almurat and it was Zakhair's youngest son — Ginger Housewife who he was arguing with.

'You can shut up the lot of you!' Almurat shouted at his subordinates. 'What I say — goes! Ginger Housewife is going to be Kiyakmurt and the rest of you are going to be the aul's women. Got it? The rest of you are going to be the women!'

'I'm not going to be Kiyakmurt.' Ginger Housewife whined again.

'Then you can be one of the women as well!'

'And I don't want to be one of the women!'

'Then who do you want to be?'

'Kazhimurat.'

'No, I'm going to be Kazhimurat!' Almurat, it seemed, was not going to cede his birthright to anyone else.

'We're going to run out of time and miss lunch!' one of the boys observed. 'Let's play without anyone being Kazhimurat.'

'And what sort of game would that be?' Almurat asked in amazement.

'We can pretend that Kazhimurat is not here and has gone off out into the fields.'

'Well, all right! But who's going to be Kiyakmurt then?'

None of the boys wanted to be Kiyakmurt. In the end, Almurat gave in and magnanimously took on the role of the district police officer. He climbed up on a stump and began his speech.

'Women, I mean, comrade women!' he addressed the crowd of boys, doing a surprisingly good impression of Kiyakmurt. 'As you can see, the war is in full swing! And you need to protect the farm's goods with your lives! If so much as a grain of wheat is lost, you'll answer for it with your heads!'

Don't go pushing your luck and taking it too far, Kazhimurat had wanted to interrupt him. *Kiyakmurt still has the well-being of the country at heart and doesn't just care about himself.'*

However, seeing that the boys had begun to glance suspiciously towards the bushes where he was observing them, Kazhimurat decided to quietly move on. Let them play their games for half an hour or so. They'll soon be trudging next to the ploughs for the rest of the day, driving the dawdling oxen and exhausted horses.

Kiyakmurt had gathered everyone in front of the only wagon and Zlikha was sitting at the table next to him. Not wanting to catch Zlikha's gaze, Kazhimurat settled down at the back behind the bulk of the women.

'Comrade foreman, could I ask you to come up to the praesidium,' Kiyakmurt announced, spotting him.

Kazhimurat did not move, pretending not to hear the invitation. Everyone turned to look at him and then at Kiyakmurt. They knew full well that the latter had only invited Kazhimurat to the praesidium as a formality. And that was how things turned out. Believing that he had observed the rules, he proceeded to open the meeting.

'Women! I mean to say, comrade women! You are all well aware that the war is in full swing!'

Kazhimurat couldn't stop himself from bursting out laughing. The women had long been accustomed to Kiyakmurt starting his meetings in this way and looked at Kazhimurat with surprise as if to ask him what he thought was so funny. Kiyakmurt lost his bearings and wanted to pull Kazhimurat down a peg or two with a stern word, but seeing the icy cold expression on the foreman's face he sensed that he would do well to leave him well alone that day.

'Wome... I mean, comrade women! You know as well as I do that there are only two weeks left until the First of May, the international day of solidarity with the workers of the world!'

Unable to sit idly by, Kazhimurat moved over into the shade of the wagon and began to sort through the yokes, halter straps and other tackle that was lying there. Having examined them, he gathered those in need of repair into one pile and those that passed muster into another. The gear for the oxen was easier to sort out — they didn't need any traces, but the horse teams were a different story: although there were only a few of them, their tackle was in a bad way. It was extremely old and was constantly breaking and in need of patching up. Keeping half an ear open to Kiyakmurt's speech — on the very off chance that it might contain something of import — Kazhimurat began to cut some thin strips from a piece of rawhide. Despite there being no flies around, for some reason, the animals had moved closer to the aul, spreading out underneath the shade of the trees and the shelters. They should have been driven away so that they could graze a little longer, but the children were completely immersed in their game, and it hadn't occurred to any of the adults to do anything about it.

'Comrade women! You know as well as I do that our army is hitting the fascists hard and driving them away from the borders of our Motherland.'

'Yeah, but where are they fighting now?' Zakhair piped up.

It was possible that Kiyakmurt did not know exactly where the front line was because he answered the question with a question of his own:

'Comrade Zakhair, I could tell you, of course, but it's unlikely that you'd get the whole picture. After all, which places have you been to in your life?'

'Blimey! Where have I not been!' Zakhair exclaimed. 'When I took Rapiya as my wife, I had even been to visit Markakol! And if you want me to tell you about places closer to home, you know as well as I do that I recently returned from Koktas.'

'Yes, but these places are all nearby, Comrade Zakhair!'

'Well, that my dear chap, depends on how you measure things! After all, have you travelled anywhere further than the district centre? That, for example, is only sixty kilometres away.'

The crowd shifted and a titter could be heard here and there. Kiyakmurt realized that he had fallen into yet another of Zakhair's traps. He frowned in annoyance and turned to Zlikha so that she might call the workers to order, but, seeing the sarcastic smile on her face, he decided to take the initiative and reins of government into his own hands.

'Now, that's enough, comrades! We can't allow an empty word to distract us... Let's not waste any more time and carry on with our meeting. At this moment, we need to focus all our attention on the sowing. I'm sure you yourselves have heard the slogan that's been going the length and breadth of the district: *Late with sowing – late to the battle!* So, how do you plan to respond to this call, Comrade Shamshinur? How do you plan to fulfil your social obligations? How many hectares have you ploughed?'

Kazhimurat had not noticed when Shamshinur had joined the meeting. She was sitting next to an old woman, her thick black hair tied back in a knot on her head. There was nothing to suggest that she was feeling any awkwardness about having to sit with the older women without her headscarf on. She had a friendly expression on her face and her eyes looked clear, except for a slight puffiness beneath them. Indeed, it had been a long time since she had looked so radiant and beautiful.

'We are neither sparing ourselves nor our labour,' Shamshinur answered. 'We are working harder than ever!'

'We all know how tired you are. But we are all working towards the same aim. Everyone in the administration is in the saddle all day as well...'

'Yes, we know only too well that you never leave your saddle day or night,' Zakhair butted in and causing the women to laugh. 'I just hope God can work out what good it does!'

'Now that's enough, comrades!' Kiyakmurt angrily interrupted the laughter. 'I must insist that everyone takes this meeting more seriously. Who else would like to speak?'

'Dinner is getting cold,' Rapiya piped up. 'It's time to wrap up the meeting.'

'Your thin and runny stew isn't going anywhere. We'd be much better off listening to Kiyakmurt's wise and inspiring speeches!' Shamshinur answered her.

'Don't you be hard on the food, she's trying her best!' one of the women objected.

'Look at you, you shameless glutton with your face so fat that you can barely open your eyes. You're just trying to get into her good books so she'll give you an extra ladleful!' Shamshinur joked, drawing Kiyakmurt's attention to the poor woman who was as skinny as a rake.

Zakhair's leg had gone numb, so, he got up and then squatted down again.

'Comrade Zakhair, did you want to say something?'

'No, what have I got to say about anything?' Zakhair waved him away, adding more quietly, 'I only got up because my legs have gone to sleep... Wait till you get to my old age. It's no joke, you know!'

The meeting had lost all semblance of control or an agenda.

'Well, then we'll just have to wish everyone good luck and every success and close the meeting on that note.' Kiyakmurt looked at those still listening with a stern gaze and then turned to Zlikha and finished firmly, 'However, we do need to record the social obligations expected of each member of the collective in the minutes!'

Hearing the clanging of the ladle on the cauldron, the children rushed into the tent, and the women, who had not had any rest since early that morning, headed for the shelters.

Zlikha called Zakhair and Kazhimurat over to her.

'Let's start the sowing in the morning!' she said to the men. 'It's a little early, but we should do it ourselves rather than waiting for the district management to upbraid and give us a hard time about it. Zakhair, you need to go to the village immediately. Take Trofim with you on the way back and the two of you can bring the seed grain in the carts.'

'That means that I'm going to have that waxed moustache following my every step.' Zakhair complained.

'Well, it is his duty to see that nothing happens to the grain. You don't need to be too hard on him... And you, Kazheke, can you measure out how many acres we've ploughed and provide Kiyakmurt with a summary in the morning.'

Zakhair saw Kiyakmurt saddling up his horse and shouted to him,

'Where do you think you're going? You need to follow me now!' Zakhair gave an ox that was lying nearby in the shade a kick with his boot. 'From now on, we'll be following each other like shadows!'

Kiyakmurt did not respond to Zakhair and continued to saddle his bay mare with its drooping belly.

Zlikha was out of sorts. At first, she thought that it was because Kazhimurat was very tired, but when he came closer and, avoiding her eyes, sat down next to her, Zlikha saw the real reason for his low spirits.

'Get yourself to the shelter and put on the shirt with the high collar!' She said in an angry whisper, trying hard to sound indifferent. 'Your whole neck... Are they bites? Oh, the shame of it!'

Kazhimurat came out in a cold sweat and wanted the earth to swallow him up. He wanted to run away and escape, but instead, he obediently trudged after Zlikha towards the shelter.

While Kazhimurat was measuring the land that had been ploughed, Kiyakmurt kept following him from a distance but avoided approaching him. At one time, Kazhimurat would have happily knocked him off his high horse and given him a good hiding, but the trouble it would have caused was not worth the pleasure it would have given him. Men like Kiyakmurt would always get up again and continue to plague him and try to get him into trouble.

And this Kiyakmurt can put up with a lot, Kazhimurat thought to himself, giving him the benefit of the doubt because this was a quality that he valued in people. *He is busy about his business from dawn till dusk, never closing his eyes for a minute. He knows everything that is going on in the village. If only he could learn to trust people, he would have become an invaluable member of the aul...*

Down in the hollow, Kiyakmurt suddenly rode up to Kazhimurat, jumped down, hobbled his mare with a bit of rope he had handy and let her graze on the grass. Then he walked up and sat down next to Kazhimurat, who was calculating the area of the ploughed field they were sitting on on a piece of paper.

'Well, the ploughing is over,' he said with a satisfied look, 'and we've managed to get a lot ploughed this year, both fallow and virgin soil. If only we had enough seeds. We've ended up helping our neighbours, but landing ourselves in a hole. Let me write down the figures you've got for me.'

Kiyakmurt took out a battered notepad and, looking at Kazhimurat's notes, transferred the numbers to it. Then he took out his tobacco pouch, but it turned out that he had run out and there wasn't enough to make himself a roll-up. So, he picked out the last pinch from the corners of his pouch and placed it under his tongue.

'You and I have squared up to each other on more than one occasion,' Kiyakmurt remarked quietly, looking steadily into Kazhimurat's eyes. 'It's the nature of my job to give advice here and to shout at people there. If I've ever gone too far, I hope you won't hold it against me.'

Kazhimurat, however, pretended not to hear him. Kiyakmurt spat and wrote something down in his notebook.

'The district authorities are demanding that we finish the spring sowing as soon as possible,' he continued. 'It would be good to start sowing in the next two or three days and be able to report to the district committee that we've finished it earlier than the other farms. This isn't about you and me. You and I are giving our all because that's in our nature, but the reputation of the entire collective farm would rise in the eyes of the entire district.'

Kazhimurat wrote something on a piece of paper and threw it down in front of Kiyakmurt: *It all depends on the aul, but, as you can see, they are completely exhausted.*

The policeman did not pick it up, instead reading it from where it lay on the ground, but he added,

'A bear is taught by the stick, but a man is led by his sense of duty. Women, however, as you know, need to be forced into doing things. I'll take on the role of doing the shouting — there's nothing to be done about that — but I'll need you to do the leading.'

The sun was setting. In the west, the sky was ablaze with a red glow. The wind was picking up. The steppe seemed to have become completely dead and deserted, and only the handles of the ploughs sticking out on the fields belied any sign of life.

So, you'll do the shouting, and I will have to lead the people? Kazhimurat thought wearily. *A leopard really doesn't change its spots.*

And for some reason, he remembered Trofim's words, *If in doubt, stick to the law of the taiga: stick a slug in him and be done with him, without trial or investigation.* At least, Kazhimurat was pretty sure that was what he had said if he was not mistaken. He glanced askance at Kiyakmurt as if searching his true thoughts with his gaze. And sensing that his words had irritated Kazhimurat, Kiyakmurt grinned and carried on sharing his thoughts with him.

'Yours isn't such a simple case you know, Kazhimurat. There is a law for people like you: you should be living no closer than one-hundred-and-fifty kilometres from the border... This all depends on what you decide to do... Let's get the sowing done as soon as possible — it'll stand in your favour. When a person gets a reputation for being reliable that will always outweigh any laws governing where he should or shouldn't be living!'

Kazhimurat got up, pulled the measuring stick out of the ground and placed it over his shoulder. Kiyakmurt hawked, spat and licked his lips, like a hungry puppy.

'Have a think about it,' he advised, glancing cautiously at Kazhimurat. 'And another thing, I'd stop these nighttime raids of yours, as well. You believe you're stealing for the sake of the people in the aul to help them through these difficult times. But remember, better times will come, and those very same people will think nothing of dragging you through the mud... Why invite fresh troubles down on your head? All the good things that you ever did for them will be forgotten, scum always floats to the top. But, basically, just have a good think about everything I've said!'

It was impossible not to be constantly surprised by Kiyakmurt's cunning but simultaneously highly practical mind — ultimately, he understood people. But at the end of the day, it's every person's right to arrange his life as he sees fit, right? *So, thank you, Kiyakmurt, for your advice.* Kazhimurat knew only too well that people often mistake extreme unselfishness for stupidity. He knew this truth, but could not let himself live in any other way. You have to do good to people, you have to help them as long as you have the strength, and what happens afterwards is not your concern. There was just no way that people could survive such a terrible war and then become worse...

Kiyakmurt and Kazhimurat parted and went their different ways across the fields. For the first time, they had parted on peaceful terms. One had left at ease with himself, believing that he had won an important victory. The other walked away dejected, unable to believe that bad luck and failure would haunt him his whole life through.

In all the low-lying areas of these parts, every sunset heralds the arrival of a blue misty haze. Kazhimurat was afraid that tomorrow would be rainy, but now he was more at ease, seeing that the grey cumulus clouds had parted, the sky had cleared and the waning moon had floated out from behind the trees, illuminating the air with its pure light. Some large curlews rustled on the river bank. Grey cranes cried in the marshes. Everything seemed to indicate that tomorrow would be a clear, fine day.

In the rightmost shelter, a small fire burned. Kazhimurat slowed his pace, remembering the tired women and hungry boys waiting for their thin gruel. He was also ashamed about what he was going to say to Zlikha when he saw her again. He would have liked to have disappeared for a week and come back later when her anger and his own sense of guilt had subsided.

Never again! he swore to himself. *That was the last time! If she has any real feelings for me, she will forgive me this once! She has to forgive me for the sake of our future family and the unborn child...*

He glanced at the opposite bank of the Bukhtarma. The slopes of the Altai Mountains were completely lit up with camp fires and the evening wind seemed to carry the smell of fresh meat and singed wool. For several days now, the *Skotimport*[26] herders had been driving their herds along the paths and roads. Immediately after the snow melts, the herds of cows and buffalo are the first to head up the mountains, followed by the innumerable flocks of black-headed white sheep as things get hotter and the conditions drier. The livestock then stays up there all summer and autumn, until the very first snows, turning the roads and the surrounding area into a dusty, overgrazed dustbowl on the way. Now, at the end of winter, the cows were still thin and unfit for slaughter, but the buffaloes were fat, although their meat was on the tough side. Kazhimurat stole only cattle, he could not be bothered with sheep, which he did not believe were

---

[26] A typical Soviet enterprise abbreviation. Literally meaning *Cattle import*.

worth the fuss. The herders never looked to make good their losses, they knew they would never pass through the aul's lands without paying a small fee of one or two heads of horses or cattle. Sometimes they showed up at the camp in hot pursuit but left with a full can of strong mead. This was the unspoken rule in those years when Kazhimurat lived in the village.

Never again! he repeated to himself. *I will never deceive her again. I swear by the Almighty! If Zlikha is an intelligent woman and loves me, she will forgive me... But now I need to head to the herds...*

Kazhimurat was in a hurry: he needed to find the chestnut pacer before the moonlight had gone. Buffalo meat is tough, but it might be possible to get a younger and fatter animal... It wasn't always possible to get hold of a heifer every day. Even if Kiyakmurt didn't approve, Kazhimurat could not sit back and watch the women and children scraping their bowls with their spoons, fishing out the lumps of dough at the bottom of their thin stew. And tomorrow the hard work would begin, and they wouldn't have the strength to do it on an empty stomach...

The leaves were unfurling on the trees and the ground was covered with vibrant green grass. With the beginning of May, the warm days would set in, and today it had been so humid that it had been difficult to breathe. The air seemed infused with the scent of flowers and herbs. And there was no dewfall. The forest was silent and the aul made no sound.

Murat Aul had been celebrating the end of the war for several days now and seemed to have gone unnaturally quiet in anticipation. The spring ploughing and sowing had been completed in good time and the aul was allowing itself a small breather.

Kazhimurat stretched himself, shook the sleep from his body and headed towards the river. His head was ringing and his body felt as if it had been given a beating. Near the house stood the short-tailed bay tethered to a stake, wildly whisking away the pestilent flies with its tail. Today was a Sunday and the horse had not been allowed out to graze in the pasture, which had not happened to it for a long time. Numerous welts could be seen on his flanks and blood had dried black on its haunches. The animal squinted at Kazhimurat with displeasure. In response, he spread his hands guiltily and slapped a large gadfly that was clinging to the horse's chest. Then he untied the animal, led him out of the village, patted him on the rump and walked away. The intelligent horse realised that it was free for the day, and, clattered away on its broken horseshoe in the direction of the forest. Watching the bay stallion leave before its inevitable return on the morrow, Kazhimurat remembered his life and sighed sadly.

He crossed the hollow diagonally towards the mill pond, undressed and bathed for a long time in the running water there. The water was as cold as ice and his body was covered in goosebumps. By the time he returned to the banks he was completely chilled and his fatigue had vanished. Kazhimurat went up the hill, sat down on the stones of an old ruined house, picked himself a bunch of juicy horse sorrel and with a crunch began to chew the herbs with gusto.

With the arrival of peace, the aul had become exceptionally lazy and was just waking up. No women could be seen making themselves busy around the village and the children had disappeared off somewhere. There was no sign of Zakhair either, who would usually be driving the cows out to pasture at first light. The bulls and heifers, taking advantage of their unusual freedom, spread out along the lanes of the village. Two boys ran out from behind the school and ran towards the mill. Kazhimurat recalled that the school had a leak and that he'd have to have a meeting with the village elders to organise a repair party while there was a brief lull in the collective farm work.

Almurat and Ginger Housewife ran up, talking over each other:

'Zhusup says... They're lacking a seventh elder... And asked you to come!'

What do you mean, they're missing a seventh elder? Kazhimurat frowned interrogatively at the boys.

'How do we know?' Almurat replied, divining his expression. Ginger Housewife wiped his perpetually running nose with his sleeve. 'Zhusup has led his grey three-year-old down to the river and taken my father with him!' Almurat added. 'And the women have all set their cauldrons on their hearths! Several of them at once!'

Then the boys ran back to where they had come from. Kazhimurat got up, dusted off his trousers and followed them.

Old Zhusup is organising some feast again. He's already slaughtered several of his goats and now he's decided to give his only three-year-old grey ox the chop. There's no stopping, our Bi-ata...

On the banks of the Bukhtarma sat all six of the aul's elders, motionless and cross-legged like granite steppe

368

idols. Old Zhusup sat in the very centre of them in his skullcap and quilted *shekpen*[27], tightly girded with a fine belt. Next to him sat the spindly mullah Myryk and alongside him were Tazhimurat and Zakhair. Old Zhusup waited for Kazhimurat to sit down, then gathered the skirts of his *shekpen* tunic under his knees, and gave a significant sigh, running his hand over his chin. The others followed suit as if removing something that had become lodged in their beards. Then old Zhusup turned his gaze to the sky and his face became solemn and motionless.

On the river bank, seven camp fires had been dug into the earth and seven cauldrons placed over them.

'Well, what are we waiting for?' old Zhusup exclaimed suddenly.

'Indeed, what are we waiting for?' Zakhair burst out laughing, always seeing the funny side of everything. 'No one seems to be descending down to us from out of the heavens.'

'Our most esteemed Zhusup has decided to celebrate the end of the war by arranging a feast for us all,' Mullah Myryk began to explain, pronouncing every syllable that he spoke like someone with a terrible stutter. 'He has decided to kill his three-year-old bull for a feast to remember the dead and bless the living.'

The grey bull, tethered to a nearby tree, roared loudly and was trying to break free. It seemed to sense that

---

[27] *Shekpen* – A type of fairly tight-fitting tunic that reaches down to just above the knees. A standard type of clothing by men of all ranks throughout Russia, the Caucasus and Central Asia in the 19th and early 20th centuries.

something was amiss. An indistinct song could be heard and then Bakhyt, appeared from out of nowhere, rushed up towards them and sat down right in front of Mullah Myryk. The girl's thick raven hair was scattered over her shoulders, with two crimson flamed flowers behind each ear, she fixed her eyes on the mullah and froze still in front of him as if her life had left her.

'Oh, Allah!' The mullah pulled up his collar in fear and moved closer to Old Zhusup. 'Take this evil spirit away from me!'

'Come here, poor child!' Rapiya quickly approached. 'Come with me!' She took the girl by the hand and led her away.

The mullah calmed down a little and turned to Zhusup.

'As the elder, you should give your blessing for the feast!'

'It's not for the host to give the blessing!' the elder answered curtly. 'And it's not my job to say the prayers either,'

In the end, Mullah Myryk began to intone a prayer in his mournful voice.

'Oh Allah, before our bull finally gives up his soul to Allah, the sun will probably have already set!'

Zakhair smirked and looked up at the sky but seeing Zhusup's shaggy eyebrows furrowed into a frown, refrained from laughing.

Myryk finished the prayer and gave the assembled people the chance to pass their hands over their faces again in a sign of respect. Zhusup, Myryk and Kazhimurat remained seated in their places, while the other four elders set about the grey bull. They were completely exhausted before they had barely been able to knock it to the ground.

'You can't bless a poor animal and then subject it to prolonged torture,' Zhusup exclaimed.

Realising that these words were addressed in his direction, Kazhimurat gestured the old men away from the bull and tied the animal's muzzle tight with three turns of a horse hair lasso. Then he hooked the bull's hind leg with the other end of the rope, pulled it up to its groin, drew the lasso between its haunches and tied it in a knot to his bicep which was as thick as a log. Before the elders were even able to blink, the young bull's head was turned towards sacred Mecca, and Kazhimurat's long knife with its yellow bone handle was sticking out of its throat.

Kazhimurat's eyes gleamed like a wolf astride its prey. Five minutes later he untied the bull's legs: the beast had already given up its spirit.

'Oh Allah, what a heavy hand he has!' the mullah muttered, turning pale. He had heard about Kazhimurat's strength, but this was the first time he'd seen him with a knife in his hand. Kazhimurat cast a piercing glance in his direction, and Myryk, without taking his eyes off the long knife, shuffled closer to old Zhusup again. In less than half an hour, Kazhimurat had skinned and butchered the carcass. The elders then set about *loading up* the huge Kazan cauldrons.

All the inhabitants of the aul had gathered on the banks of the river. The fires were burning under the cauldrons and the samovars were boiling. The young women rolled the dough while the older ones talked quietly among themselves and the children capered about in the distance. Kazhimurat washed his hands next to the most outlying hearth, pouring water over his hand from a long-necked *kumgan*[28] jug, then he looked for Zlikha among the women. She was sitting on the edge of the carpet, laid out for the honoured guests, where the six aul elders were sitting. Their eyes met, and Kazhimurat caught a smile in her eyes. Zlikha had come on foot but, as always, she held her *kamcha* riding whip in her hands. Kazhimurat took a long time washing the blood from his knife, holding its tip in her direction.

'One, two, three... five, six, seven... Dear Kazhimurat, please try this blessed food!' Zhusup's old woman addressed, placing a tin bowl with seven thin flat breads fried in butter in front of him.

One of the young women placed a wooden tray with a pile of fluffy baursak buns in front of the old men while another dragged a steaming pot-bellied samovar over towards them. Kazhimurat remained next to the old women like a restless orphan. Nobody invited him up to the dastarkhan of honour. He had been needed when they lacked the traditional seventh man to bless the sacrificial animal, but now there were enough hungry mouths sitting at the honorary spread without him. There was an empty seat next to Zlikha, just big enough for him, but Kazhimurat believed it would have been humiliating to come up and sit down without being invited by the elders.

Kazhimurat tried the flatbreads and was about to leave, but Shamshinur, her ripe full body swaying, came

---

[28] *Kumgan* – A tall pitcher with a long spout, often made out of metal used for washing hands and other similar jobs.

up and threw a whetstone and a dozen knives next to the fire at his feet.

'There is no one in the aul who knows how to sharpen knives!' she said. 'Can you sharpen the blades, please? I've been collecting them from everyone in the village!'

She smelled of fried baursaks and butter, her face had turned pink and her lips were smeared with butter and glistened in the sun. Kazhimurat averted his eyes from her, gathered up the knives and went over to the rocks next to the river bank.

Everyone had let everything go to pot. No one cared whether their houses were in order or whether the cattle had been put out to pasture. A hot samovar and seven thin flatbreads served for each dastarkhan had obscured all that was important in the big wide world to them.

The water of the Bukhtarma still lapped the banks and small fish played in the shallows, crowding densely together and then scattering in different directions like a shower of arrows. Smoke poured from the chimney of Trofim's hut and he himself was sitting with his trousers rolled up on the landing stage of the ferry, fishing. He usually used his trap net, but now that the ferry was no longer needed, Trofim had plenty of free time and was passing it in the company of his fishing rods. Seeing Kazhimurat, he waved his long rod in his direction several times, either in greeting or inviting him to share in the fish soup he was preparing.

The strum of a tuneless *dombra*[29] was added to the clatter of the ladles being wielded by the women next to the cooking fires. The instrument had seen better days

---

[29] *Dombra* – A Turkic long-necked lute that can be played by plucking or strumming.

and rattled like a wooden bucket that has lost its iron hoops. A scrawny, snub-nosed, old man enthusiastically strummed the withered strings, as if he were playing the famous tune *Kokeikesti* by the great steppe composer Tattimbet himself[30], and the old people listened to him, with their eyes closed, evidently yearning for the sound of the *dombra* played by a true master. The women and children devoured the liver, lungs and offal that had been cooked and served before the meat. Even if the legendary Tattimbet himself had appeared on the river bank and started playing, he would not have been able to distract them from the food and their hunger. The snub-nosed old man suddenly stopped playing and with it, the tortured strumming of the *dombra* ceased.

'Where's Kazhimurat got to?' Zhusup's voice rang out in the silence.

'How long does he plan to wander about the aul unmarried?' Mullah Myryk piped up. 'Although he may look like the devil himself, you still can't help feeling sorry for him. Why not marry him off to that half-crazed Bakhyt? A demon and a half-crazed woman — I've seen worse marriages?'

The elders laughed, thinking that the mullah's words were in jest. But Kazhimurat tensed at them, staring blankly into the river. A sharp pain brought him back to his senses: he had inadvertently squeezed the knife he was holding in his hand, and the sharp blade had cleft the flesh of his palm into two. With an effort, he unclenched his fingers. All the knives in front of him flashed before his eyes... One with a bone handle, another with a

---

30 *Tattimbet* – a legendary Kazakh steppe composer.

wooden one, a blue shimmering blade with no handle, a cleaver, a long knife with a yellow deer horn handle... Blood flowed from the palm of his hand. He began to grab the knives lying nearby, and one after another, he hurled them into the ground. At that moment, only the earth could have withstood his indomitable rage. The knives shuddered as they sank into the soft soil right up to the hilt. At the next moment, it seemed to him that the earth itself was trembling from the pain that had been inflicted upon it.

Kazhimurat came to his senses, having waded out a long way from the river bank. He felt like a fish that has been stunned by the spring ice floes and been washed ashore.

'Oh no! Bakhyt has drowned herself in the river!' one of the young women screamed.

The women rushed as a single crowd towards the Bukhtarma. Kazhimurat ran back, then turned towards the river, sensing that he had missed the opportunity and was too late to save Bakhyt. The long locks of her raven hair were fluttering like a fan on the surface of the water as if they had a life of their own and were trying to crawl back onto the shore. Bakhyt's pale face peeped out from under the water as if it had been carved from white marble and now looked more like a reflection in a mirror. Kazhimurat pushed through the crowd who dared not approach the drowned woman and lifted Bakhyt in his arms. The girl's body was cold and rigid.

The women drew back in horror and someone ran to the elders who were still sitting at the dastarkhan. Kazhimurat did not know where to go, or where to carry the corpse, so he stalked off towards the aul. Nobody followed him. After taking a few steps, he came to his senses. Only now did Kazhimurat understand why the elders had not got up from the dastarkhan. It was because they did not want the corpse of the drowned woman to defile the village. Kazhimurat turned towards Trofim's hut.

After that, he could not recall what happened. His soul had frozen into a lump of ice. It was as if he had been wandering about between the houses of the aul in a dream. The mullah had stubbornly refused to say a prayer for the dead woman and his reasoning for not doing so struck Kazhimurat as being deeply blasphemous.

'An evil spirit has taken possession of her soul and Allah will not accept her up to heaven,' Myryk had muttered.

After that, Kazhimurat had taken Trofim and Zakhair with him and committed Bakhyt's body to the ground himself. For a whole week after that, he had simply lain in front of Trofim's hut. Not long after that, news came to him that Zlikha had gone to an old healer who had induced a miscarriage... This was the last straw for Kazhimurat and he was never seen in the aul again...

9

The taiga merged into the vast autumn sky, marching into the distance in mighty yellow-green waves. After the long hard rain, the world sparkled with purity and cleanliness. The earth had not been able to withstand the onslaught of the warm rain and young green vegetation was beginning to force its way up through the stubble. The air was clear, the rain softening the scent of the battered mint. Yellow-brown leaves lay in a thick carpet on the forest floor. The aul had surrendered and gone silent in anticipation of the upcoming autumn winds. Kazhimurat surveyed Trofim's grave which he had built out of red brick and the mill that nestled next to the pond. He himself had breathed life into this mill, and it stood like a living monument to his tireless hands and his love for the people of this aul who had at one time failed to appreciate and acknowledge his sincere disposition towards them. The telegraph wires hummed, and their song echoed the bitter song that burst forth from his soul. It was a melody that would probably never cease.

Evening drew in. It had been a long time since Kazhimurat had been out to the dirt road. The bus that passed the village every day at this hour was late today. Bored, Almurat had wandered off to one side, made a turn, sat silently for a while and said,

'Even if it's only occasionally, do come and visit us.'

Twenty years earlier, in the very same place and at exactly the same hour, Almurat had said goodbye to his brother with tears in his eyes, asking him:

'When will you come back, Uncle Kazhimurat?'

He recalled that back then, none of the aul's adults had come out to say goodbye to him either. Now, Almurat himself was the head of the aul and, of course, could not help but say:

'Even if it's only occasionally, do come and visit us.'

This time, he was saying goodbye with a cold indifference, accompanied by these polite, perfunctory words. Times had changed. On his previous departure, one-hundred-and-fifty kilometres had seemed like a journey to the ends of the earth. Today, the same distance seemed little more than one-hundred-and-fifty paces. If only the heart did not harden to stone in the human breast. If only human strength was inexhaustible, and his love for his native land and people remained the same. Then he might have been able to return to the village of Murat.

'Oh yes, I almost forgot. Nazym asked me to pass this on to you.' Almurat handed an envelope to his cousin.

Kazhimurat remembered the fair-faced girl. It must have been because they had only said goodbye yesterday that Nazym seemed to block out everything else that was now endlessly processing in his mind's eye. He understood that the reason for this was precisely because she had shown him compassion. He was pretty sure that she had written something like: *Kazhimurat-agai, I look forward to hearing your news, write to me soon.* And because he didn't want Almurat to see his impatience to read the letter he divined its contents instead.

A small bus with a blue line along the length of its chassis trundled down the hill.

Almurat had wanted to see him all the way home, but Kazhimurat had said no. Almurat shook his hand.

I've always found my way even in the most difficult times, I'm not likely to get lost now! Kazhimurat had wanted to say in mitigation.

He had wanted to make things easier between him and his younger cousin, the only soul in the world who held him dear, but he did not know how to speak these words out loud.

THE BACKWOODS

1

Mountains. Forest. A thick grey mist snaked along the bottom of the deep and narrow gorge; the pointed tops of the blue spruces and withered pines poked up through it, and the muffled roar of the river was barely audible. The world breathed in peace and silence; the taiga was covered with abundant dew and, in its heavy half-slumber, seemed to have forgotten everything. Only the light breeze that plucked the crimson leaves from the trees with a quiet rustle as they whirled to the ground and the quiet, monotonous waters that gurgled and splashed showed any sign of life. The mournful, protracted cry of a deer floated in from afar.

The night dew and white mist enveloped a lonely little cabin, nestled on the river bank as if swallowing it up; its windows were dark, the plank fence and high wooden gates were closed and silent. Near the house was a modest vegetable garden and a small bathhouse, its doors and windows caked with smoke and soot. Behind the bathhouse, on the bank of the river, lay a blackened, upturned old boat, waterproofed with tar and mended with numerous patches. Only one living creature made itself felt in this blanketed and sleepy world — a dock-tailed bay gelding with fresh weals on its back, standing by a feeble spring. The horse's legs had been hobbled, and it had also been tied to a tree with a lasso. The animal reached out with its lips to the fronds of dry saltwort that grew tantalisingly out of reach. To make things worse, the water bubbling out of the spring was muddy and the horse was being plagued by a magpie that was pecking at the wounds on its back. It lashed its sides with a thin, mangy tail, kicked out at its belly and pulled its skin tight, spreading it over its thin ribs, but the magpie stuck to it like a leech, occasionally taking off only to immediately alight on its back again. The unhappy creature was only finally relieved when the gate opened with a creak.

Through it came a stocky old man of about sixty with a bushy beard and a bald head covered with dry, yellowing skin, set with sparse, greying hair that stuck out at his temples and on the back of his head. With a slight shiver, he straightened his canvas poncho, which had been slipping from his shoulders, and looked up at the sun, which was slowly rising from behind a mountain range covered with spreading pines. His small clear eyes squinted at the bright morning rays breaking through the dense trees, and his face creased into a network of deep wrinkles. His gaze surveyed the trees and bushes surrounding the house and settled on the forlorn bay gelding next to the spring. The horse met the old man's eyes, drew in its belly and yawned, baring its teeth; the old man yawned contagiously, covering his mouth with his hand. Then the man turned his head and looked up at the wide, gravel-covered road that led into the mountains, writhing like a snake and disappearing behind a distant ridge. The road was deserted and smoking under the sun. The old man stared at the road for a long time, as if he were expecting someone, then, taking a cage net from the fence post and slouching in his boots, which were too big for him, wandered down the overgrown narrow path towards the river. When he reached the boat, he paused, studying the numerous pock marks and cracks blackening on its bottom, and, shaking his head sadly, walked on, dragging his feet in his worn-out boots.

The water in the river was dark and lumpy. A thick streak of sunshine that had broken through the trees lay across it like a long yellow log. Countless droplets of spray flew up from the crests of the white foam, flashing like red beads in the rays of the morning sun. The strip of yellow sunlight widened over the river towards the shore and rested on a buoy, which seesawed on the waves

The old man stopped at a gentle slope in the bank, where the driftwood had piled up in heaps, checked the cage net and, putting it to one side, pulled another out of the water, which splashed between two flat stones that resembled the gills of a giant fish. The trawl net was full of trout but the impressive catch did not arouse much enthusiasm in the old man. He hauled the cage net a bit further up the bank, slapping it down onto the large pebbles, then sat down on a stone, threw off his shoes, turned up his trousers and scratched his hairy calves with pleasure. He noticed how his toenails had grown, clicked his tongue disapprovingly and shook his head again in dismay. Somewhere not far away a crow called out harshly, and then again, but now noticeably further away, signalling that someone was approaching the river. The rumble of an engine was the next thing to be heard, and the old man wrinkled his nose in disgust, as if he could already smell the gasoline, and spat on the grass. But the truck didn't give a hoot what the old man thought, its chassis rattling obliviously as it moved off into the distance taking its racket and noise away with it. The truck must have been passing along the road. The old man wasn't too bothered about it either. Without even glancing at the road, he got to his feet, took the empty net and went down to the river. Dipping one foot into the water, the old man shuddered all over from the intense cold, then dipped in the other and grunted loudly. The water was freezing, and he quickly fixed his net between the stones and hurriedly jumped back onto the bank.

'Hello there, old man!'

Busy with his own affairs, the old man hadn't noticed the log raft that had appeared around the bend in the river. It was controlled by four men. Two were stood at the bow and with long poles kept the raft in the middle of the river, preventing it from getting too close to the banks, while the other two — at the stern — guided it with their long rudders, evidently using all their strength to do so. All four were built like hyperbolic folk heroes, with thick moustaches and bushy beards.

'Having a sit-down?'

The old man sighed silently in response. The fast-flowing river water swept the long raft away in the blink of an eye and it disappeared around the bend with a flash of its log-ribbed stern. The dark waves once again swelled over the river surface, running up to the bank and splashing tree bark and flotsam against the pebbles. The old man sighed again, then, as if remembering some urgent business of his own, struck his boots several times against a nearby stone, knocking the dust out of them, and began to pull them on. Near the house a hen squawked loudly and flapped its wings noisily. The old man turned his attention from his boots and looked around. The speckled hen clucked loudly as it swayed on the fence and the old man stared at it as if he was looking at it for the first time in his life. His lower lip drooped in surprise, revealing sparse yellow teeth. When the chicken desperately flapped its wings and flew up into the hazel tree with a plaintive squawk, the old man suddenly let out a roar as if he'd been poked in the side with a large needle,

'Dunya!'

The gates remained motionless and the old man also froze for an instant, looking expectantly at the house. Quite a long time passed before the gate reluctantly opened with a creak and a girl with sleepy eyes and dishevelled red hair emerged from it. She was about seventeen years old, barefoot and in a long sundress.

'Look!' The old man pointed somewhere behind the house.

The girl silently dashed off in the direction he was pointing at. A loud and plaintive clucking could be heard and then Dunya appeared out of the hazel tree, carrying the hen under her arm. She scratched her plump finely shaped calves with her free hand and then, spitting out a nutshell, turned the hen round and lifted her tail so that her father could see for himself.

'You see, nothing!'

'She must have been laying her eggs in a secret hiding place again!' the old man growled.

'Without a cockerel, she's not going to lay any eggs — even for you!' Dunya exclaimed and disappeared back behind the gate.

'Cockerel... cockerel...' The old man muttered unhappily under his breath as he slowly got to his feet.

2

The day was approaching noon. In the depths of the forest, the breeze had no way of penetrating the dense mass of the leaves and it was stifling. The glade was filled with the buzz of bees flying from flower to flower, the drone of the horseflies and the random fluttering of the vibrant, multi-coloured butterflies. Among the trees, the bay gelding whisked at the bothersome flies with its short, stumpy tail.

Two or three trucks with trailers were driving away having left their loads and in an instant a large pile of felled timber grew up near the lonely little house. Trucks were now moving in a long serpentine line along the dirt road, some climbing up towards the mountains with a strained roar of their engines, others, with a continuous honking of their horns, descending into the gorge. The cries of the drivers could be heard as they headed around the sharpest turns.

The old man sat hunched over the upturned boat. In one hand he held a hammer while with the other he rummaged through a box full of rusty nails. He was absorbed with the delicate job of mending the holes in the bottom of his boat, nailing narrow, thin planks over them. From time to time, he would wave his arms at the pestilent mosquitoes and midges that swirled in clouds over his head. He carefully sank another nail into the boat and removed that drop of sweat hanging off the tip of his nose with a deft movement of his finger. His trousers were made of a coarse fabric and his scrawny wrinkled neck and hairy chest peeped out from the open collar of his white linen shirt. The old man had just taken a nail from between his teeth and was expertly driving it into the bottom of the boat, when the roar of an engine echoed out behind him. He had assumed it was one of the countless trucks scurrying up and down the road, but it turned out he was mistaken: there was a shrill squeak of brakes and then a hiss. He hunched his shoulders and pursed his lips in displeasure.

'Here he comes again!'

The motor continued to tick a little, quietened, and then the door opened with a thud and slammed shut again.

'Hey, Yegor!' The old man missed the nail and, groaning, put his bruised finger in his mouth.

'Son of a bitch!' he cursed angrily.

'Hey, Yegor, you gone deaf?'

The old man unhurriedly drove another nail into the boat and only then turned around in the direction of the voice. Next to his mighty *ZIL-155* with its trailer loaded to the gunwales with logs, stood Ayan — a swarthy, stocky guy with a bristling moustache. He had already lifted the bonnet of the overheated truck and hot water bubbled and gurgled out of the top of the radiator.

'Your delivery's here!' The driver called over.

'Well, you'd better unload it!'

'Maybe you could help me? I'll pay three roubles seven kopecks.'

'I spit on your three-rouble note!' The old man was offended by Ayan's offer and turned away from him, letting him know that he wanted nothing to do with him.

'Well, at least take a look and see how many cubic metres I have here?'

'What do I care how much you've brought.'

'Ugh!' Ayan spat angrily and added in Kazakh, 'Bloody Kerzhak!'

The old man only understood the word *Kerzhak* and, although he knew that strong words had been spoken about him, he pretended not to hear. A match struck — Ayan had evidently just lit a cigarette. Then a chain rattled and heavy logs began to fall onto the ground with a dull thud.

By the time he'd finished the unloading, Ayan was completely exhausted — working in thick overalls in this heat was no easy task. When the last log rolled off the trailer, he threw the long wooden pole he had been using as a lever to one side, jumped to the ground and wiped his face with a handkerchief. Then he walked around the truck, kicked the rear wheel a couple of times and, having satisfied himself that the tyres were in order, lit up again and wearily sat down on a log. They were surrounded by the usual sounds: the rumble of the trucks on the road, the hum of the taiga and the splash and gurgling of the river. From the direction of the house, looking out onto the dense forest, came a strange soft tapping sound like the knocking of a woodpecker. Behind the hazel tree, the edge of the vegetable garden could be made out where the heads of sunflowers shone a bright yellow and potatoes bloomed with their pink flowers. This was where the sound was coming from, someone must have been hoeing potatoes.

'Hey, birdie!' Ayan shouted, craning his neck to try to see who was there.

The young man's cry remained unanswered. The old man, who had been sitting next to the boat, bristling and ruffled as a vulture over a grave, got up and began to collect his tools. He straightened up and looked at Ayan, who also gazed straight back at the old man. The former's gaze was filled with distaste while the latter's was creased with sneering laughter. The old man went up to the gate and called out sharply,

'Dunya! Come and sign this goggle-eyed cretin's delivery docket, will you?'

Ayan spat out his cigarette butt and also got up from his log. The gate creaked open and closed behind the old man again.

Ayan stuck his head under the bonnet. He was busy fiddling with the engine when someone slapped him hard on the backside with the palm of their hand. The young man straightened up in surprise, hitting his forehead on the bonnet and, clutching it with his hand, squatted down. A loud laugh rang out from behind him.

'Ah, it's you, little bird! Is that how you greet everyone you know?'

'Everyone!'

'And how many people do you know?' Ayan asked curiously.

'That's none of your business! And you've grown as fat as a badger!'

Ayan's face cracked into a smile. 'It's time you found yourself a husband!'

'Right. Then I'll have you...'

Ayan jumped off the bumper of his truck and landed right next to Dunya. He looked into her clear blue eyes, then glanced down her high open neck and stared at the pert girlish breasts protruding under her tight sundress. He sighed and stroked his black moustache.

'Your overalls look like they've been torn to shreds by

a pack of rabid dogs.' Said the girl straightening the strap of her sundress in embarrassment.

'It's all the strain they're under,' he joked clumsily.

'You idiot!' Dunya snapped.

'Well, I 'don't have any great objections...'

'To what exactly?'

'To getting married...'

'You're too fat.'

'It's not that hard losing weight. Once we're married, the excess fat will melt off me in an instant, and so will your headstrong spirit.'

'What spirit?'

'Your Kerzhak spirit.'

'You idiot!'

'There you go, immediately giving me an earful!'

'How else am I supposed to get through to you?'

'Once we're married, I can assure you, you'll have plenty of time to give me an earful. But there's no need now.'

He lit a cigarette but couldn't help looking at the girl's bare legs. Pretending to wave the smoke away, Dunya took a step back.

'In theory, I wouldn't have anything against marrying in church. But I don't know how we'd be able to reconcile that with a classic Komsomol wedding!'

'You've got a gob on you, Ayan!'

'You see, a Komsomol wedding would be an immediate plus. First of all, they're giving flats to newlyweds these days. Although, admittedly we do already have one...' Ayan went up to the girl, took her by the chin and looked into her blue eyes.

'Get your hand off me!'

'I wonder if the head of the timber mill or someone from the local Komsomol committee would agree to officiate at the wedding, what do you think?'

'Give it here!' Dunya's voice sounded very demanding.

'Give what here?' Ayan frowned incomprehensibly.

'The delivery docket!'

'Aaah, there was me thinking that you wanted us to go straight to the village authorities to tie the knot...

'It's in Srobel, isn't it?' Dunya couldn't help smiling.

'You're a right one!' Ayan began looking for the docket in his pockets, fishing out bits of old broken cigarettes and scraps of newspaper in the process. 'That's weird, where could it have gone?'

'Dunya!' A loud voice thundered from the river.

The youngsters jumped at the unexpected shout and simultaneously turned in the direction of the house. The old man was nowhere to be seen. The planked fence, the tightly shut gates and the low, sagging, soot-blackened bathhouse were all as they had been...

But the old man was now sitting on a big log stump at the far end of the back yard. A battered, dirty bucket was hanging from a log, in which pine resin was boiling. Beyond the gates, trucks scurried back and forth along the road with a rumble, the wind whistled along the gorge and the drivers shouted at each other on the tight turns, but here in the yard, the boiling resin bubbled and gurgled, and the old man was utterly absorbed in the work at hand, requiring skills that he had been taught by his father and grandfather before him and which had now already been forgotten by most folk. At the entrance to a small shed that had been built into the corner of the yard lay a piglet. Its small watery eyes attentively followed every movement the old man made. The smell of the resin evidently seemed to please the animal because its pink snout twitched, sniffing the air, and it grunted contentedly. At the other end of the yard, five hens restlessly darted about, kept in by an old fishing net that had been specially stretched out for the purpose. Every now and then, they would stick their cox-combed heads into the holes, trying to get out, get stuck, raise a hullaballoo, and then, with difficulty, free themselves from the net and start the whole process again. A beehive stood under the only tree in the yard — a stunted low-growing hazel, the bees industriously crawled in and out of a notch in the trunk and flew away on the hunt for nectar and, returning again laden, lethargically crawled back inside. On the veranda attached to the house, an axe, a plane and planed boards were scattered over the floor, a large-toothed saw hung from a couple of nails on the wall and next to it a small hand saw, chisels and various other woodworking and carpentry tools. At the back of the yard a crude washstand had been set up and water permanently dripped from its spout into an old enamel bucket that had been attached to a rickety stool.

The old man glanced once more at the boiling pine resin, pulled the burning logs out from underneath the bucket, and put them out one by one in the ashes. Avoiding the acrid smoke, he removed the bucket from the tripod and set it to one side. Voices could be heard coming from the direction of the river and then a friendly laugh rang out. The old man curled his lip and yelled at the top of his lungs:

'Dunya!'

The young couple were sitting in the cabin of the truck. Ayan was rummaging through the glove compartment, and Dunya was looking inquisitively at a photograph of the movie star Monica Vitti, which was attached to his mirror. Ayan took out a pile of *Soviet Screen* magazines and newspaper clippings and bent over the glove compartment again.

'And who's this?' Dunya asked.

Ayan looked up, and seeing Dunya pointing accusingly at the picture of Monica Vitti, he could barely stop himself laughing.

'It's... Well, how can I put it...' he hesitated, as he sorted through the magazines. 'Well, she's my fiancée.'

'Liar!' Dunya was upset.

'Have I ever lied to you before?'

'Well, who is she?' There was a hint of jealousy in Dunya's voice. 'What does she do?'

'What does she do? She works in our timber mill. In the canteen.'

'Liar!'

'You only just said that, you're repeating yourself now... Don't believe me, if you don't want to! Now where did that docket go?'

'I don't like the look of her!' Dunya declared.

'Why?'

'They say that all beautiful women are loose and disreputable.'

'But she's a wonderful person. Damn it, where did I put it?'

'Then why don't you marry her?'

'Why don't I get married? The skinny ones' bones stick into you... And she smells like a stale beer barrel.'

Ayan started checking his pockets again. 'Now, where did I put it?'

'What?'

'That wretched docket!'

'Ah, it's fallen down there!'

'Where?'

'Under your feet.'

Ayan picked up the sheet of paper that was lying right next to the accelerator and remarked to Dunya with displeasure,

'Couldn't you have told me earlier? I've been doing my head in trying to find it.'

'How was I to know what you were looking for!'

'Go on, sign it!' Ayan placed a small cushion on the girl's knees, the docket on top of that and then handed her a pen.

Dunya awkwardly took hold of the pen and drew a small bird on the docket.

'Oh, birdie, birdie!' Ayan sighed. 'Haven't you learned to write yet?'

'Well, you teach me then!'

'By all means! If you'd like me to!'

'It's difficult, I guess. Tell me, is it difficult?'

'Nothing is difficult at the end of the day.' Ayan picked up his magazines and newspaper clippings and stuffed them back into the glove compartment. A fashion magazine fell out onto the seat.

'Why are there only pictures of women here?' Dunya peered over Ayan's shoulder, looking at the colourful pictures.

'To attract the attention of men. It's all advertising, you see, Dunya?' He wrote the word KERZHAK in large capital letters on an image of a girl in a dress with a plunging neckline, and handed the magazine to Dunya. 'Copy this word several times — and you'll soon be writing your name on the delivery dockets. And as for these girls — some of them, not all, of course, but the best — will eventually make it into the movies.' He noticed Dunya growing gloomy, and added, suddenly blushing, 'By God, you've turned into a beauty!'

Dunya's cheeks turned pink and, gazing trustingly at Ayan, she asked quietly,

'Tell me, do you... Do you know this girl?'

'It was all a long time ago.'

'But what about now?'

'She went off to the movies.'

The gate opened with a creak and the old man came out with the bucket of pine resin in his hand. The young couple jumped out of the truck, and Dunya quickly moved away from Ayan. The old man walked towards the river bank, his boots slapping. Dunya looked angrily at the magazine in her hand, then bent down and swatted a mosquito that had landed on her calf.

Ayan put his hand on the small of her back and then slowly slid his palm downwards. Dunya jumped back and shot him an angry look.

'You idiot! Do you really think I know nothing?' She straightened her sundress and then buttoned up the collar. 'I see and understand everything...'

The old man began to coat the boat with the resin. He cleared his throat loudly, making it clear that it was time for the young man to be on his way.

Seeing no in point pushing his luck, Ayan jumped into the cab, turned over the engine, hit the gas several times, and the truck set off, its trailer rattling deafeningly behind it. Having driven a respectable distance from the house, Ayan blew the horn to Dunya several times, just as he always did every time they parted.

Dunya noticed him leaning out of the cab, trying to catch a sight of her again. The truck drove out onto the dirt road and joined the rest of the traffic, followed by two more trucks loaded with timber that were slowly wending their way down to the river.

3

The heavy hoe, which her grandfather had made, hit the ground with a jarring scraping sound. She didn't particularly feel like working today, and the hoe, and the scraping sound, and the potatoes that had to be weeded were all hateful to Dunya. But there's no getting away from work! She weeded a few more potato bushes and, unable to bear the torment, hurled the hoe into the ditch and sat down on the lush grass. The cool northern breeze plucked up the mosquitoes and midges that had just been swirling in a cloud around her head and scattered them over the river. She immediately felt the cold of the earth rising up through the grass. The callused soles of her feet burned as if she had been stepping on coals. She plunged them into the soil and piled damp sand on top. The thud of an axe rang out from the yard. *How does he not get bored?* the girl wondered irritated to herself. She couldn't work out why, but after dinner her mood had slumped and she moped around pouting like a child who has been offered a treat she doesn't like. And she had no one to sulk at except herself. Normally, her work around the house and garden never bothered her, but today she didn't feel like doing anything and to make matters worse nothing she turned her hand to seemed to go right. An incredibly heavy weight oppressed her soul. Even her favourite scarlet poppies, which she had planted herself and spent whole days tending, failed to lift her spirits. She could have pulled the lot of them up by their roots! She glanced up at the sun — it was time to get dinner ready. *How nice it would be if people didn't have to eat!* Dunya thought. *I could do whatever I liked... I could wander over the fields or take a walk in the forest. And then what?* She was suddenly frightened by her own thoughts, which seemed somehow seemed sinful to her and quickly crossed herself. Then she pulled up a large bunch of spring onions and a whole clump of potatoes by the stems, something she had never done before, and began, one by one, to throw the tubers into her bucket.

She sat by the river for a long time, washing the young, thin-skinned potatoes. The chill water froze and cramped her hands and, for the first time, it seemed to her she noticed how coarse and hard her recently childish plump palms and fingers had become. Her hands seemed to swell from the cold and became even larger and almost indistinguishable from the ugly tubers they held. Once again, she began to wash the potatoes and threw one whose skin was particularly deeply ingrained with the earth and dirt far out into the river.

The river bank was deserted and dreary. The shadows lengthened and the trees seemed to stretch out and climb to the very top of the bare cliff face. The waters darkened. Dunya sensed the rapids revealing their bottomless depths. She shuddered, stepped back from the river and felt a stab of cold run right up between her shoulder blades. Near a grey boulder mottled with dark spots, the buoy bobbed and swayed on the waves. How many years had it been floating on the water like this? It danced on the waves as if it had a life of its own, showing the raftsmen the way and revealing no sign of wear or impermanence, as living things do.

Twice a year, in spring and autumn, when the water in the river would rise, she and her grandfather would row out to the buoy on their old boat and free it of any stray branches or accumulated silt. Likewise, twice a year, Dunya and her grandfather would cross over to the opposite bank, where the village houses were scattered and dispersed. The girl could not understand the force that tied her grandfather to this buoy. From the very first days of spring, he would constantly worry whether it had been torn from its mooring or carried away by the waves, and with the onset of winter, he would spend days on end breaking the ice around it and catching it and catching the fish under it. The old man was totally oblivious to the fact that from her earliest years, Dunya had been dreaming of one day living on the other shore, among other people. In those early years, the buoy seemed to be showing her the way to people and society, but her dreams, it seemed, would never come to fruition. These days, she saw little difference between her situation and that of the buoy that was tightly moored to the grey boulder with its mottled dark spots. There had been a time when there had been no dirt road out here. In those days, the forest was dense and untouched, the mountains seemed impossibly high, propping up the sky itself, and the Bukhtarma river amazed and delighted her childish imagination with the breadth of its banks and depth of its waters. She had thought there could be no place on earth more beautiful than this spot, where she lived with her grandfather. She would never tire of sitting on the shore of the river from morning till evening, observing the buoy, playing games and throwing pebbles into the water. But most of all, she liked to keep watch over the buoy, and then run to her grandfather and joyfully let him know that it was where it should be and doing its duty by the river's raftsmen. Sometimes, she would return home when the dusk was already falling, and her grandfather — which seemed very strange to her — was still awake: he would be lying on his bunk, thinking his own thoughts.

'Grandfather, the water is rising!' she would report excitedly, flying into the house, sometimes well after midnight.

'But the buoy hasn't been washed away, has it?' he would ask, lying on his plank bed, his eyes wide open.

In those distant childhood years, Dunya never once thought about why he was so obsessed and worried about this buoy. She lay down on her bed and listened for a long time to the dull roar of the river water. In her mind's eye, the buoy swayed and bobbed on the waves, long rafts raced towards it each guided with long poles and rudders by mighty raftsmen, each and every one of them with bristling moustaches and bushy beards. Dunya did not like them because they were usually so silent and taciturn. Sometimes she even thought they were incapable of speech, but as soon as the first glass of alcohol passed their lips they would begin to prattle about the first thing that came into their heads. Then they would light up their homegrown rolling tobacco and smoke it so unceasingly that it was impossible to go anywhere near them without coughing. To Dunya, the truck drivers almost seemed angelic in comparison.

Dunya glanced in the direction of the buoy: it swayed sadly in the dark water. For some reason, she recalled Ayan and felt her heart reverberate in her breast and her cheeks burned.

They had only known each other for a year. It was thanks to Ayan that the nickname *Birdie* had stuck. He had given it to her when he found out that she couldn't sign his delivery dockets. At first, Dunya had been offended, but then she got used to it, and now she was more upset when he addressed her with her real name — Dunya. Their lonely house was visited by many drivers, she didn't remember them all by sight, let alone by name, but Ayan had caught her attention the very first day she saw him. He wasn't very attractive to look at and wasn't particularly bright, except for his quick wit and jokes, but still Dunya remembered him. It was just that he was somehow different from the other men, but Dunya couldn't say how. And she was glad that he wasn't like the other drivers. But, again, she didn't know why this made her happy. She was not quite seventeen, but for her there were three different types of people: the first were people like her grandfather, the second were stupid, and the third were holy fools. Naturally, she considered people like her grandfather wise and intelligent but everyone else was either a sinner or a blasphemer. Dunya was tormented by the fact that she didn't yet know which group Ayan belonged to...

Dunya lowered her feet into the river and felt how the cold water made her soul feel lighter. As if a weight had been lifted from her shoulders. Her only regret was that the water made her toes seem short, stubby and much larger than they really were. Suddenly, she remembered Ayan's words: 'My God, you've become beautiful!' and laughed joyfully. Dunya did not believe his words, but it was nice to hear them said about her. She did not think that anyone would call her beautiful, but in her heart, she lived, hoping for someone to admit as much. Dunya peered at her reflection in the water, but the ripples distorted the features of her face: her nose would become long, then short and then suddenly crooked, while her mouth stretched like a rag floating on the water, or would suddenly twist into a sneer, as if mocking her thoughts. Dunya slapped her foot on the water and clambered back up the river bank. Then she took out the magazine that she had hidden under her sundress and peered intently at the image of the girl in the dress with the plunging neckline. It seemed to Dunya that this unknown beauty was also mocking her. She counted the number of letters in the word that Ayan had written on the photo and looked around her, seeing if she could find something to write her last name with, then she took a twig and drew the letter K in the sand, followed by the letter A, followed by a Zh and in this way scratched out the word KERZHAK on the sand, but starting from the end of the word backwards. For a moment, she wondered if Ayan had been playing a joke on her — his eyes had been painfully mocking — but then she cast her doubts aside.

From the bushes came the rhythmic chirping of the grasshoppers. Dunya looked in the direction of the road: it stretched from the bottom of the gorge up into the mountains, wriggling its way like a small intestine. The road was deserted and the dust hung over it. It was quiet all around. The sun barely made it over the horizon. Orchestra music could be heard coming from afar, they must have been playing it in the timber mill.

'Dunya!' Her grandfather's cry echoed and dispersed over the river.

4

The old man was always busy doing something, he couldn't get by without keeping his hands busy. Very early in the morning he would begin tinkering with something or other and by noon — by the time the summer air had warmed up — he had usually sorted it out. He was also tormented by insomnia in his old age. All night he would be constantly wandering outside and with the first glimpses of dawn he would already be on his feet. However, the house and holding didn't require a great deal of attention. Dunya, his granddaughter, took care of the only piglet, the five hens and the small kitchen garden. And the old man was supposed to look after the forest and the short-tailed bay gelding, which, as their watchman, the timber mill had allocated to him.

The raftsmen would collect the timber tomorrow and float it further downstream. *And the sooner the better!* the old man thought to himself. *What are they waiting for? They're probably scattered around the local bars and taverns. You could never round them up...* He cursed the raftsmen and concluded indignantly, *How can they be allowed to work like that?!*

Over the last two or three years, the felling of the forest had not been quite as shocking as it had in previous years. Yes, the forest had certainly become much more impoverished, you could say that it was almost gone. There were rumours that the timber mill was about to be closed, moved to another place where the timber grew more densely and the people working at it would move on either to the collective deer farm or the gold mines. But the demand for wood was growing, the numerous local mines, factories and mills were swallowing up ever greater mountains of logs and planks with each day and it appeared that there would never be enough to satisfy them, but local workers had already moved away and there was no one left to cut down and raft the remaining timber. As always in such circumstances, a ragtag rabble had taken advantage of the situation: lovers of easy money from the city had taken jobs at the timber mill, ripping off the business by charging three times the going rate for their services. The old man used to call them leeches. But they were of little use: after they had floated the latest batch of timber down the river, they would take off to the bars in the local town and stay there until they had drunk everything they had earned — right down to the last penny. They weren't great workers, but they could all talk the hind leg off a donkey. They let their beards grow, smoked homegrown tobacco like seasoned raftsmen and littered their speech with a weird mixture of Russian and Kazakh with a liberal sprinkling of outlandish foreign words. 'Ugh!' The old man spat on the ground. *Nothing but leeches — the lot of them. Sucking the lifeblood out of the local communities and taiga, damn it!*

Out of habit, the old man glanced up at the sun; it had risen the length of a lasso, shining palely through the smoky clouds that shrouded it and encircling them with rainbow-coloured rings. Under the heavy wet branches that drooped after the morning storm, stood the bay gelding, its legs trembling, its back arched like a wheel, and its short tail tucked in between its legs. It met the old man with an unfriendly gaze.

The old man couldn't bear the sight of the old bay nag. As soon as he saw the horse, he would be overwhelmed by a wave of irritation and resentment. Resentment at the people who, in his opinion, were not living as they should, letting the business slide, squandering the people's property and rapaciously devouring the rich resources of his native land. And resentment at life, which he was convinced was increasingly losing its time-honoured values and meaning with each passing day. His forehead tightened and he felt a headache coming on as he began to criticise and curse everyone and everything around him. Here, for example, was this horse. He had never asked for it from the timber mill, but, as the official buoy keeper, they had sent him one anyway, and it had become for him a living symbol of all the troubles in life that now pressed in on him from all sides. In his anger, Yegor had tied it to an iron stake and left it to pasture. 'Here's some grass for you, now eat it and go make your way in the world.' The gelding was also one of nature's more stubborn creatures. They hated each other with a passion and both seemed to be waiting to see who would stumble and kick the bucket first.

The morning mist covered the land. The silence was to the old man's liking and his mood improved a little. It would have suited him even better if all the machines that so disfigure the earth were to suddenly fall silent. He went to the river and bent down to pick up his net, but as he pulled it up, he looked back and nearly jumped on the spot, as if he had been bitten by a snake. His small watery eyes were fixed on the gate of the house, which had been inscribed in black resin with the word: KERZHAK.

'Dunya!' His cry rolled over the river.

The gate slowly creaked open, and a sleepy barefoot Dunya appeared in the gap. The old man did not begin to

407

explain the reason for his unspoken agitation, and the girl did not even try to find out why her grandfather was in such a foul mood. She tucked a tousle of red hair behind her ear and stared expectantly at her grandfather. Silently, the old man jabbed his finger at the inscription on the gate. Dunya laughed gleefully, recognizing the familiar word, written by some unknown hand on their gate.

'But Grandpa, that's our last name, isn't it?' she said with a distinct note of satisfaction.

'Do you even know your last name?' the old man asked, but his voice now contained neither indignation nor reproach. He waited, looking inquiringly at his granddaughter, whose face was lit up with a joyful smile, then he bent down to the water, pulled out the net and walked away. Something broke in the old man's soul. For the first time, it seemed, he had fully understood to what their secluded taiga life had doomed them. He felt much like the bay nag that he had tied to the stake.

Dunya still stood at the gate, wrinkling her forehead intensely, as if painfully trying to recall her surname. Her blue eyes darkened with the effort and she bit her childishly plump lips resentfully. Any outsider might have thought that it was not she who had inflicted a heavy blow on her grandfather but her grandfather who had upset her. She looked at her grandfather for some time as he walked along the river bank, stooping and dragging his feet in his worn-out old boots, then turned abruptly and disappeared back into the yard.

The old man spat angrily on the ground. His indignation had subsided, but a disturbing feeling of alarm would not leave his soul. He did not doubt his granddaughter's innocence and purity, but if today people felt emboldened enough to daub pitch over their gate, then tomorrow a filthy hand might decide to tar them and then there would be no ridding themselves of the shame. Any one of these leeches was capable of making fun of honest, hard-working people. The old man looked around involuntarily, as if someone was watching him unseen, preparing to inflict another insidious blow. 'Don't be such an old fool!' He scolded himself immediately. 'Do you want to jinx yourself with these thoughts and bring a whole lot of trouble down on your stupid head?'

The old man went up to the overturned boat and slowly walked around it, touching the recently tarred patches with his fingers to make sure that the resin was smooth and had dried out overnight, then he tramped to the gently sloping bank, where he usually set his cage net. The water had risen noticeably and the boulders, which only yesterday had half protruded out of the water, were today submerged under the seething stream. The bank had even been washed away in places. The old man did not like the unseasonably high water. He generally didn't like it when natural events happened before they were meant to, he couldn't stand it when something was born or died prematurely and he despised people who arrived ahead of schedule or left without waiting for their hour to come. He took all this as a bad omen, a harbinger of trouble. This year, the summer had come early, the intense heat melting the snow on the Altai peaks, and the melt water filled the lakes, ravines and lowlands below, disrupting the habitual course and flow of life. 'The main thing is that no real misfortune sneaks up on the back of this mischief nature seems to be playing on us.'

But then the old man turned cold with horror — the buoy was no longer in its usual place. It had disappeared! In the spot where the old buoy had always bobbed and swayed, a sediment of silt and branches now protruded and muddy water bubbled over some unknown obstacle. He turned towards the house and gave a heart-rending shout to his granddaughter, who was scraping away with a plane at the inscription on the gate,

'Dunya!'

Then he threw his canvas coat onto the grass, rolled up his sleeves and tried to turn the boat over, but the vessel, swollen with moisture and covered with a thick new layer of tar, would not budge under the old man's frail efforts. He took a deep breath and tried to turn it over again, but at that moment he could hear the sound of Dunya's voice and steps behind him. As she approached, she was singing a song, '*The road, the road to far-away places is calling us...*' and then handed her grandfather the long pole.

'Fetch me the axe as well!' he ordered.

He would never have asked for help if he thought he could have handled the matter on his own. He was strong enough for his age, but time had taken its toll. He didn't want to admit it to himself, being so busy with his chores around the holding from morning to evening, but if you looked closely at everything — the wooden house, the shed, the beehive and the vegetable garden — then none of them looked quite as good as they had before. Everything had gradually become more and more dilapidated, but he was proud that he had never had to turn to anyone for help, did not have to show his

410

weakness. In any case, he had always considered himself a cut above the countless people who had filled the forest in recent years. No, they hadn't so much filled the great taiga, as flooded it.

He wrestled with the boat for a long time, angry at his impotence. However, he finally managed to turn it over and sat down on the thwart, gasping for air and sensing his temples prickle from the effort. In the place where the boat had just been lying, a mound of fat earthworms stirred among the sickly yellow stalks of grass; they writhed desperately, climbing all over each other like Dungan noodles in a boiling cauldron. The old man felt sick and felt his head spinning. He slowly got up and took a step back.

At that moment, Dunya arrived with the axe and two battered buckets, which she had grabbed just in case. The old man threw the axe into the bottom of the boat and left the buckets to one side.

Together they climbed into the boat and, as soon as they pushed off from the shore, the seething white water immediately picked the vessel up and carried it away. The old man tried to steer and steady the boat with the pole but a wave lifted it up, and he couldn't reach the bottom and they were carried even further downstream. Dunya tried to help her grandfather, but he shouted at her to sit tight.

The strong current tossed the boat onto a sandbar a long way downstream of the spot where the buoy had been attached. The old man muttered under his breath. It was clear that he was angry with himself, the recalcitrant river and the whole wide world. Dunya jumped out onto the bank after him, but the old man shouted at her again, this time more angrily,

'Where are you going? Get back on the boat!'

He rolled up his trousers, handed the pole to his granddaughter and, stumbling over the slippery stones, dragged the boat upstream along the river bank.

The buoy was still in place, held under the water in the fork of a small, gnarled, uprooted birch tree. The old man crossed himself briefly, as if he was standing in front of someone's grave, and barked to his granddaughter,

'Pass me the axe!'

Dunya gave him the axe and moved to the stern of the boat. This time, she did not even try to help her grandfather, knowing that he would not tolerate any help on her part! But Dunya herself didn't know for sure why he was being so tetchy. Maybe her grandfather was afraid that she would catch a chill in the cold water, or maybe he thought it inappropriate for a woman to be engaged in heavy man's work. Dunya looked at the high, clear sky that spread over her head. A white cloud the size of a blanket hung over the mountain range. It looked like some living being, but Dunya could not figure out what it was. Maybe she had seen something similar in a dream, or maybe no such animal or beast existed in nature at all. As a child, she could remember seeing the most fabulous creatures in her dreams and witnessing the most incredible events, soaring like a huge bird in the sky. But Dunya hadn't had such vivid beautiful dreams for a long time: it seemed that even human dreams change as people get older.

The hum of an engine could be heard coming from the direction of the dirt road. A small blue bus passed by. Today was Sunday, and there were almost no trucks on the road. The bus's windows flashed in the sun and it disappeared around the corner, leaving a cloud of dust behind it. And once again the permanent mountains, the hushed, drowsy forest and the dark, deserted road came back into view...

'T-h-e, r-o-a-d... m-m-m... has but one turn...' These were the only words she could remember from the song that Ayan liked to sing. It always sprung into Dunya's mind when she was daydreaming. Some days, she would sing this tune from morning till evening. And now she thought of Ayan. She pictured his face — his thin aquiline nose, the whiskers of his moustache that stuck out like a cat's — and she began to laugh merrily. She was seized by an overwhelming desire to set off and follow this road somewhere, anywhere far away. 'T-h-e, r-o-a-d...' The old man coughed. Dunya came back down to earth. Her grandfather was swinging at the snag with all his might, but the waterlogged branch would not budge. Wood chips flew but he barely made an impression. The water had risen above his knees and streamed from the folds of his trousers. His thin sinewy legs trembled from the cold.

Dunya jumped out of the boat, tucked the hem of her sundress into her belt and joined her grandfather. She studied the branch for a couple of minutes then, wading around her grandfather, approached it from the other side, grabbed it and, bracing herself, pulled it free and threw it to one side.

'Who asked you to help?' the old man barked. Dunya pretended not to hear his reproach.

'There's another buoy just downriver from here at Kzylzhar!' The old man muttered. 'I wonder if the high water has dragged it away?'

413

In truth, the old man did not really care about the buoy at Kzylzhar, because he was not responsible for it. He was more upset that his fuss and effort had all been in vain and come to nothing. The gnarled birch branch rotated slowly in the water and floated on downstream, dragging its long wiry branches behind it. The buoy jumped out from under the water and danced merrily on the waves. The old man threw the axe into the bottom of the boat and, muttering something to himself, quickly crossed himself.

The sun had not yet reached its zenith and the air was hot and stuffy. The mosquitoes and midges whirled and billowed in a cloud.

Old Yegor always honoured and revered Sundays. On Sundays he would pay his respects to God and then without fail cleanse his body in the bathhouse. Back at the house, he had changed into some dry clothes and was beginning to chop the wood for the sauna. The old man recalled how in his youth, that no sooner had he heard that someone was heating the stove in their bathhouse, he would be there eager not to miss the chance to enjoy another sauna. What could be better than a sauna, where you can lie on the high bench for as long as you like, banish the world from your head, whip yourself into sweat with fresh birch leaves and then wash it all away afterwards? For Yegor, the steam bath was the closest thing in this life to paradise on earth. He had already chopped enough dry firewood for the stove when the door creaked and Dunya came out of the house. She was wearing a colourful cotton dress, a blue scarf around her head and a pair of unfashionable thick-heeled shoes on her feet. The old man looked at his granddaughter with a surprised look,

'Where are you going?'

'To the timber mill.'

'What did you forget there?'

'I'm going to bring back a cockerel. The hens aren't laying...'

'I know what sort of cockerel you're after!' The old man split a log with a flourish and turned away.

The old man did not overtly forbid his granddaughter from going to the timber mill, and Dunya did not directly ask his permission to leave the house. A minute later, the old man was back chopping his firewood, while Dunya rushed to get away as quickly as she could on the forest path. She walked briskly, afraid that her grandfather might yet change his mind and shout out, 'Dunya!' to the whole forest and she would have to return home. She did not dare disobey him. Her heart pounded in her chest. Thus, she reached the dirt road, anticipating the imminent and inevitable shout, 'Dunya!'. But strangely, the further she made her way from the house, the more anxious the feeling in her breast grew. Her heart was pounding harder. Her heavy heels resounded even louder on the asphalt, like rocks rolling down a mountain, and the small stones in the road kicked over the edge by her shoes fell into the ravine with an ever-increasing reverberating echo. In an attempt to raise her spirits, she began to sing to herself as she walked,

'T-h-e, r-o-a-d... m-m-m...' But her voice trembled and quavered with anxiety, '*has but one turn...*'

She reached the turn in the road, took a breath and looked back. The trees already obstructed the lonely log house from her sight.

All she could now see were a part of the clearing, a corner of the small bathhouse and the stubby tail of the bay gelding, twitching from side to side. She suddenly felt a pang of sorrow for her grandfather left all alone, and she stood for a long time at the turn in the road, not knowing what to do next: go back or go on.

Yegor knelt down on one knee and, crooking his arm at the elbow, picked up the logs he had split and looked around him as if unable to believe that he was all alone. There was nothing but silence except for the whining of the mosquitoes and the buzzing of the horseflies. He could not see his granddaughter in the yard or by the river and looked up at the dirt road. His eyes followed the contours of its curves as it climbed higher and higher and then onto the pass itself until he finally saw Dunya's slender figure. Her head swayed in time with her quick step and her blue head scarf flickered among the trees. Her figure was getting smaller and smaller, disappearing over the horizon. The old man remained on one knee and continued to gaze after his granddaughter, expecting her to at least look back. However, when the figure turned into a tiny dot and finally disappeared, the old man's arm dropped limply to his side, the logs clattered to the floor and he heaved himself up onto his feet. He glanced once more at the road leading out beyond the mountain range. A sultry yellow haze trembled over the winding ribbon of road. Swaying as if he was drunk, old Yegor wandered back into the house.

5

A yard. The very same yard. Five hens, one piglet and a beehive. The old man sat hunched up on a log. His faded eyes and wrinkled face expressed a hopeless, deep sadness. It seemed only now that it had fully dawned on him that he really had been left all on his own in this empty world in his lonely, forlorn, little house. The water dripped monotonously from the washstand into the bucket attached to the rickety stool, as if counting down the days that Yegor had to live. He knocked the basin off the washstand, catching himself thinking that right now he could send the whole thing flying with one kick. It wasn't just the washstand he wanted to destroy but everything else around him, all his possessions that he had collected piece by piece, believing at one time that they might come in useful... Useful? Useful for what? What did he have that was useful? It was all a dead weight on his shoulders... The old man thought he could smell the damp earth. The silence the old man had always longed for, now seemed monotonous and heavy. And no matter how the smell of the exhaust from the traffic passing by the house usually irritated him, he would have been happy to have them for company with him right now. But, as always, the very things that you wait and crave for the most happen all too rarely. The steady tumbling splash of the river filled the air. It was joined by the staccato tapping of a woodpecker. After a little while, there was another pecking sound, but also familiar — this time a nutcracker breaking open pine nuts with its beak. Tap, tap, knock... The stabbing pain assailed the old man's temples again.

Evidently, I'm going to end up dying out in this wilderness as well! He thought sadly. Before now, Yegor had never taken the possibility of death seriously, life had always seemed endless to him, but in recent years the thought of death had occupied him more and more and even scared him. The old man was not remotely afraid that he had no one at hand to commit his remains back to the earth in the proper manner, what frightened him was this force he had never known before that was weighing down on his shoulders, his heart and his soul, pressing him ever closer to the ground. The old man looked back over his life, which had had its fair share of events, and tormented himself with doubts and belated regrets, for he knew only too well what debts he owed and what his sins were. He raked over his past, weighing up everything he had done as if on a pair of scales. He and he alone knew what he had achieved in his life and whether it contained more good than evil.

'It would seem that death itself has driven me into this wilderness,' the old man muttered to himself thoughtfully. However, he still wasn't sure what it was that had driven him here: death or people? And again, for the first time in his life, he regretted these twenty long years that he had lived away from other folk. But now it was too late — regardless of whether he regretted it or not. Once again, he made a mental note of his life and began railing against the people who had once inhabited it with him. It seemed to him that they were to blame for everything that had happened. Over the past forty years, Yegor had tried no less than three times to build and feather a safe nest for himself and three times he had been forced to up sticks and move. And all in vain. Each time, everything he had built had trickled away and evaporated, like the rain that waters the desert. No, he had no regret about the riches he had lost, to hell with them! A man cannot live by wealth alone, but he regretted the sweat he had shed, and the disappointed hopes that had inspired him. But this insight did nothing to relieve his soul and the bitterness only grew.

The old man was convinced that his troubles had started back in the twenties that had been filled with one military campaign after another. Various bands of soldiers roamed all over the country: some headed for China, others to Mongolia. They did whatever they pleased — thievery, murder and violence of all sorts became commonplace. Everyone suffered: Russians and Kazakhs alike and honest ordinary folk most of all. Some profited from the turmoil, some went bankrupt, one man saw his business shoot skywards while another lost the head from his shoulders. Peace and tranquillity were consigned to oblivion, people cursed life as they buried their loved ones and found themselves permanently in mourning. Thank God, Yegor was not directly affected, it was all the same to him whether it was the Whites, Greens or Reds who found themselves temporarily in power. And there was a good reason they left him well alone. His personal patron was none other than Krivonosov himself, who kept a whole detachment of White Guards on his estate. And if it hadn't been for the Reds, who later set about picking on the kulaks and the wealthy, Yegor might have kept his holdings, which were doing relatively well for those times. At first, he thought his luck would never run out. Back then, Krivonosov was firmly established, he was known not only in Quldja and

Urumqi, but even in far-away inland China. In the north his influence extended as far as Ridder and Koktas and his strong business ties connected him with many of the cities of central Russia.

Yegor was not interested in how Krivonosov had taken possession of all his lands and forests in Altai and the region's countless coal and mineral mines, or the miraculous fortunes that came his way, or his ability to squeeze the last drop of oil out of a barren stone or the unceasing rivers of gold that continuously seemed to end up flowing into his pockets. Yegor was much more impressed by the thousand-strong herds of Maral deer and the boundless stretches of arable land and forest that had come into Krivonosov's possession. He guarded Krivonosov's wealth as if it were his own and served him day and night, ensuring that the people working under him did not spare themselves or their labour. Yegor did much to increase Krivonosov's fortune, but he didn't do badly by himself and lacked for nothing. Krivonosov was not mean and didn't waste time on trifles when it came to looking after his stewards and lieutenants. As long as the torrents of gold kept flowing into his coffers, then if there was a little bit left over, they could help themselves. Yegor felt no shame and even a measure of pride serving such a master and spared neither himself nor others. And he was greatly upset when he learned that Krivonosov had had to flee to China. But the fact that Krivonosov had cunningly managed to take his immeasurable fortune with him without leaving even a single copper kopeck behind didn't bother Yegor in the slightest.

The very rich escaped to foreign climes with their fortunes, those who stayed behind lost theirs. The Soviet authorities confiscated their lands and livestock, and resettled them to other places. Yegor moved deeper into the taiga, grabbed a chunk of Krivonosov's land for himself, cobbled together a decent estate for himself, hired a dozen farm labourers and lived quite happily without having to deny himself anything. The only bad thing was that he lived in constant fear that one day the authorities might take away both his land and his herds. And that was how things turned out. Yegor ended up on a list of rich peasant kulaks, and soon he was forced to part with both his land and livestock. But he did not despair because of his losses, he was quick-witted and knew how to work, and he had no doubt that his acumen and strength would be of use to the new government as well.

The poor began to unite into artels and collective farms, some things worked out for them but others did not. The kulaks marched with pitchforks and axes against the men who had been their hired labourers only yesterday, while the latter stood their ground against them like a solid wall. Yegor kept aloof from these struggles, he knew they would eventually grind each other down and someday his day would come anyway. He calmly watched as the Kerzhaks from Korobikha killed peasant activists and put their children to death for joining the Komsomol. Yegor could never have taken such a sin upon his soul. He looked at the battles that flared up between the old and the new and shook his head...

The thirties came and a drought struck, the newly created collective farms were unable to cope with it, and there was no bread in the villages. Famine gripped the entire region. Once again, Yegor took over land that its owners had abandoned, he cobbled together a decent little holding and hired labourers. This was a mistake on his part. And so was the decision to trade openly at the local market because a man of his acumen always sticks out in the crowd. But how could he resist the opportunity, when a small pot of potatoes had become more valuable than a fine overseas carpet, and people were willing to part with a sack load of money for a piece of bread? In a word, the day soon arrived when Yegor was utterly ruined for the second time in his life. Once again, he had to console himself that at least he hadn't inherited the holding from his parents, that it wasn't something passed down through family and blood but acquired and that he was innocent before both his fellow man and the Soviet government. After all, he had only been doing the best he could by the starving and barefoot peasants whom he had hired by giving them clothes and food and coming to their aid in what was an extremely difficult time for them. And that's how he tried to convince the various commissions he was forced to appear before, but he was nevertheless left without a kopeck to his name and that was exactly how he left those parts. And where was he to go this time, what out-of-the-way place could he could escape to where he would be allowed to live in peace, but with the level of prosperity that he had dreamed of all his life? With a bitter sense of resentment at his fate and shattered dreams of bettering himself, Yegor went to an even more remote, almost deserted place, in the very heart of the taiga.

This time, he found himself on the empty bank of a taiga river, where five small farm holdings belonging to the state deer-breeding farm had been forgotten and abandoned. He lived in this new place on his own, reflecting on the past, but also mulling over the future. It seemed to him that there was absolutely no point in striving to better himself and, moreover, that it was a fool's errand to fuss and fret in this disorderly and badly managed world. He needed to to make sure that his wife Agafya, son Fyodor and daughter Nastya had a roof over their heads and were properly fed and shod. This idea seemed to sap him of the last of his strength and he never again bothered to lift a finger to try to put another holding together or get rich again. However, he became extremely irritable and difficult to live with and this affected his wife and children too. He didn't bother working at the collective farm either, although he was offered various jobs there. He got by with the occasional bit of work cutting timber in the forest and the rest of the time pottering around his small plot of land and the mill. His heart was no longer in his work, it seemed to him that everything he had ever turned his hand to had been for nothing and it made little sense to do the same again. In the end, he got the job as the buoy-keeper and watchman with the timber mill. It was a cushy number, they paid regularly, you could make your own honey, turn it into mead and drink as much as you liked. But his liking for the drink led him to misfortune...

It had been a cold rainy autumn. Getting the hay and the deer herds in from the summer pasture and the annual job of cutting, sorting and dispatching the deer antlers had taken a lot longer than usual, and the collective farm had failed to get the wheat harvest in. The rains had started, the earth was being washed away and the unharvested wheat was rotting in the fields while the grain in the threshing barn was beginning to sprout. The problems that befell the workers on the collective farm were no business of Yegor's. But there was still a disastrous lack of hands in the fields, and the farm's managers came to him almost every day asking him if he could help. Yegor flatly refused to go to the threshing barn, and instead sent his wife Agafya to work there, despite her being heavily pregnant and barely able to make it around the house. During these rainy days, Yegor would constantly suffer from headaches and end up getting drunk on homemade vodka and mead. On one occasion, he was drunk for a whole week, he lay on his bunk for a long time and then, finally coming to his senses and feeling peckish, he began to rummage around the kitchen to find something to eat. Unable to find anything, he made a mental note to scold his wife for leaving him hungry. His head was buzzing, his stomach was empty and his wife had gone swanning off to the threshing barn at the collective farm. Yegor climbed back into his bunk again. *The stupid woman! She's forgotten her God-given duty to her husband and gone off to be a do-gooder at the collective farm!* By the time the exhausted Agafya had returned from work, Yegor was consumed with rage. She looked at her husband with displeasure and opened the doors wide open to air the room, which stank of vodka.

'Are you trying to freeze me to death?' he yelled at his wife. 'Well, close the doors, it's like a tomb in here!'

'You foul smelling pig, do you want us all to choke on your vodka fumes?' Agafya exploded, who up until this moment had always been quiet and submissive and never said a cross word to her husband.

Yegor never thought he'd hear the like. At first, he was so taken aback by his wife's words that he remained silent, but then he jumped down from his bunk and kneed her in the stomach with all his might. Agafya did not even have time to gasp, the breath was knocked out of her, she trembled all over as if she was having a fit and she collapsed on the floor, her eyes rolling back in her head.

Yegor rushed outside and ran headlong into the taiga. He did not know where he was going or what he was looking for on this cold rainy night. He finally stopped, far away from home. The world had become an utterly hateful place to him and the windows of the five small houses shone pathetically in the night. Yegor stood where he was for a little and, feeling unable to return home, wandered further into the forest. Not remembering how long he had been blundering through the taiga or how many miles he had walked, tired and drunk, he finally collapsed under an old cedar and fell asleep. He woke up from the cold. He was no longer drunk and his teeth were chattering. His thin, damp, homespun coat was useless. All around him the night was as black as the grave, the wild, unwelcoming forest was roaring loudly and a cold heavy rain was falling... With their thick gnarled branches and deformed growths of moss on their trunks, the trees now appeared terrifying and monstrous... No one was around. Yegor wept in bitter resentment.

He wept for a long time, howling like a beast and felt that the tears brought him a little relief, although his breast was still empty. He looked back at his life again and it seemed to him that it was empty and wasted. Nobody needed him. He wanted to die, to put an end to his rotten, worthless life. With a certain spiteful satisfaction, he imagined how his wife and children, who had failed to sufficiently appreciate and love him during his lifetime, would be mortified at his death and punish themselves for not doing more to save him. Then he remembered how his wife Agafya had fallen to the floor as if dead, clutching her huge pregnant stomach. He then imagined his son Fyodor and daughter Nastya now weeping next to her and, again, he was overwhelmed with a wave of fear and despair. He felt himself simultaneously shivering and shaking from the cold and then burning up with a fever. And the night was getting darker, swirling and closing around him like a deep eddy of water. The old cedar gave him no protection from the piercing wind and cold slanting rain. A solitary wolf howled mournfully and then an eagle owl hooted softly and mockingly. A shiver ran right through Yegor's body. Lord, what was he looking for here? He didn't want to die, he could not find the strength to cut his life short. Home! He had a house, a warm stove, a soft bed... He had a wife and children... He needed to get home! To hurry home!

Yegor jumped up from the ground and ran headlong through the thick forest like a madman, crashing through bushes and colliding with trees as he did so. He was accompanied the whole way by an ominous moaning sound, vague shadows running nearby and someone grabbing at his tattered clothes. Then he was confronted with the image of his wife, her face distorted in pain, her eyes darkening in her agony and torment...

For two days Agafya suffered, coming round for short periods and then losing consciousness again. On the third day she died. People thought she had died of premature childbirth. Yegor saw off his wife with full honours: after all, they had lived together for twenty years. This latest fateful blow was so heavy that Yegor was left totally bewildered and confused, he closed up in on himself and completely retreated into his shell. He stopped talking to people and couldn't eat or sleep. He did not even register his neighbours who came round to share in his grief. He looked at his children with empty, expressionless eyes as they sat huddled forlornly in the corner of the room. To anyone who didn't know him, he seemed to have lost his wits, incapable of understanding the meaning and purpose of life. And indeed, his mind and thoughts were completely empty. Henceforth, he made no effort to try to untangle the problems that confronted him in his life, he blamed neither God nor himself for his misfortune, he lost the ability to laugh and get upset about anything. He felt like an empty living shell, nothing more.

The days flew by and the years passed, and it seemed as if the time had come when a person might recover from even the most terrible blows of fate and gradually find himself again. They say time is the best healer, but it did not heal Yegor's devastated soul. He remained closed and diffident for the rest of his life. Admittedly, Yegor could not remain idle for long. He worked like an ox and, within a few years, had built up a strong and solid holding without any sign of excessive wealth or prosperity. The children grew up. Yegor was just about to shift the responsibilities for this simple and uncomplicated household onto their shoulders to take a well-earned break and see a bit of the world about him when the war started, which put paid to the very last plan he ever made in his life.

At first, he believed that the war had nothing to do with him: let those who started it fight it out among themselves. When the whites and reds had clashed, people persecuted and killed each other, rivers of blood had flowed, but there were also those who had never stopped tending the earth, they had continued to sow and harvest the bread that provided everyone with sustenance and there were those who had fallen in love and got married, started families and gave birth to and raised children. Yegor had never taken up arms; he believed that everyone could and should fight — just not him and his family. However, this war had stirred up the whole country and wouldn't leave anyone in peace. Every single man, young or old, who was able to bear arms, was going off to the war. You'd be forgiven for thinking that the enemy was standing at the gates of every single household. Even the most fanatical Old Believers, who had always ignored any call to war and considered it a mortal sin to bear arms, had sent their children to the front. And when the call up papers came for his son Fyodor, Yegor didn't know whether to be surprised or angry at this turn of events. He looked at it from every possible angle, and couldn't come up with anything. He would just have to say goodbye to his son and bid him farewell. For as long as Yegor could remember, being the undisputed head of the family, he had never once consulted his family about anything. He had always decided everything himself and they had never once contradicted him, but now it turned out there was nothing for it but to ask his son's opinion.

'You decide, father, if you say that I should go and

fight — that's what I'll do!' Fyodor said. 'Everyone else is going to the war.'

His son had been brought up to be obedient and his father had never had to tell him to do anything twice.

But this time, his answer made Yegor bristle. *You son of a bitch!* He mentally upbraided his son. *Don't you have an opinion of your own! You'll probably end up asking me to choose and take your wife for you as well!* Up until now, Yegor had always been delighted that his children had not grown up spoiled and never pestered and angered him with constant demands. They had always obediently worn whatever they'd been bought, meekly ate the chicken that was served at table and unquestioningly performed the work and chores that they were entrusted with. But this had evidently led to no good. He was now more convinced than ever that his son was far too trusting and lacked the backbone and wiliness needed to get on in the world and his daughter, it seemed, was not that different either... However, Yegor did not betray his displeasure and disappointment in his son out loud. And it was clear he would never have understood him anyway. *Let him go, if that's what he's like!* he thought, growing increasingly angry, *I'll leave it in God's hands, and that'll be the end of it!* However, after a while he had a change of heart. *Even the viper pities its own offspring,* he thought to himself. *I have witnessed nothing but evil and injustice on the part of the Soviet authorities, so why should I risk the life of my only son for their sake? If Fyodor dies, there will be no successor to the family line...* And it was with these thoughts that he drew a line under the deliberations that had been tormenting him for several days and nights. Yegor prepared his son for the road, gave him a good

429

horse and accompanied him out to the taiga where he could wait out the war without being bothered. However, they didn't leave him alone for long. Soon a delegation came from the enlistment office and then from the NKVD[31], but Yegor managed to put them off the scent by telling them that he had no idea where his son was now. He assured them that Fyodor had left on horseback for the local town with his call up papers in his pocket and that he couldn't be held responsible for what might have happened to him on the way. For a long time, Yegor was afraid that the authorities might guess that Fyodor had deserted and would deal with him accordingly. But he was lucky that all their immediate neighbours had moved to the village once their menfolk had left, leaving him and his daughter all alone in their isolated spot by the river...

The old man got to his feet. His lower back ached and he felt a stabbing pain in his knee joints. It was clear that that his long dip in the ice-cold water that morning had taken its toll, or maybe his rheumatism was taking a turn for the worse. It was still hot, but his bones ached as badly as if it was about to rain. *No, today, there's going to be no getting by without a sauna,* Yegor decided. *It's time I lit the stove...*

Silence reigned. The water drops reverberated as they hit the dented bucket under the washbasin. He had been meaning to throw this junk into the tall grass for ages and replace it with a new washbasin, but had never had the time, and now he didn't have the inclination either. The bees buzzed under their solitary tree. The old man lingered next to the hive. The swarm was getting too big

---

[31] NKVD - the Stalinist forerunner to the Soviet KGB and current FSB

and it was high time that he separated it into two, but he hadn't got round to finishing the new hive. And what did he need these bees for anyway? He chuckled to himself, remembering that in former days he wouldn't have allowed a single bee go astray. He clearly didn't have the strength he used to. The bees rose up into the air in a huge cloud, which swirled around for a bit, was carried up by a gust of wind and then fell back to the ground in a single ball. The old man silently watched the swarm of bees. It became quiet for a moment, then shot back up into the sky, as if it had been hurled up there by someone with an extremely strong arm. It then made two circles over the yard and flew off in the direction of the timber mill. The dark cloud disappeared beyond the trees, and only then did it dawn on Yegor that he was now left without any bees.

The sound of hooves came from the direction of the road, followed by the creak of a cart. It was none of his business but, out of curiosity, he went to the gate and, on the way, stumbled over the piglet, which had followed him in the hope of some food. The old man almost fell over it and, in his anger, kicked it in the snout. The piglet squealed desperately, as if it had had its throat cut, and scampered off to hide in the barn, and the old man suddenly began to feel sorry for the poor dumb animal. It was wrong of him to take it out on the piglet, for it was, after all, his last remaining yard animal.

The cart laden with freshly mown hay made its way along the road. On it sat a stocky old Kazakh man in a fox fur hat, an old woman's white *kimeshek* scarf peeking out from behind his shoulder. Shaking its head, the mare effortlessly kept the wagon rolling, while its foal trotted alongside on its spindly legs. The old man pulled lazily at the reins and hummed a song.

'Look at the state of that cart!' Yegor muttered and shook his head.

He did not really have anything to do with the neighbouring Kazakh village and in his heart had no great liking for its inhabitants, but he was always surprised by their way of life and even envied it. The Kazakhs were never idle, they were always busy with something or other and appeared supremely calm and self-sufficient, and when they were saddled up on their horses and on their way off somewhere, you'd be forgiven for thinking that there was no happier people on earth. But there had been a time when Yegor mistook their calm for carelessness and their happiness for foolishness. Back in those days, he had owned huge pastures that spread further than the eye could see and herds that would take more than a day just to count. The Kazakhs had never lost a sense of themselves or their world, but he, Yegor, had eked out a lonely and miserable life.

The cart swayed off into the distance, the figure of the old man diminished and his wife's white *kimeshek* was now barely visible. The clatter of the horse's hooves subsided, and silence again hung over the lonely house. Yegor took his buckets and went down to the river.

It was quite a long time before the old man had filled the water butt and the black cauldron, standing next to the stove in the bathhouse. He felt a sharp pain in his arm, his shoulders were overcome with a strange fatigue and he had to take a seat in the shade to catch his breath. He found himself dropping off. But as bad luck would have it, a large *MAZ* truck drove past with a roar, its unpleasant fumes wafted through the air, and the old man grimaced in annoyance. All at once, an avalanche of bad memories swept down, resurrecting some of the saddest pages of his life...

Living on the banks of this small river in the taiga, Yegor had failed to experience even the smallest human joy. First, his only son Fyodor had gone off to live in the forest, then Nastya had had a baby by someone and left him with her little daughter while she swanned off goodness knew where. At one time, Yegor had been glad that he had found a small quiet fertile piece of land where he could be left undisturbed to look after his river buoys and guard his tranquillity, hearth and home. But over time, he was even at risk of losing his buoys...

Rumours began to circulate that a man-made reservoir was going to be built further down the river and that many people would be settled along its banks. At first, Yegor attached little importance to these rumours. After all, it wasn't clear when or if this reservoir would ever be built, and if it was then it's overflow would go downstream and not here, where his house was standing. And anyway, who would want to go and live next to a reservoir when it was already pleasant enough here. Folks rightly say that, 'The earth seems cramped and small to the man who migrates from one place to another, but the man who is settled in one place, looks after the land he lives on.' But things turned out much worse than Yegor anticipated. The river was completely sealed off downstream, the boats and barges stopped travelling upriver, the buoys became surplus to requirements and naturally, the river authorities began to ask themselves whether the buoy keeper was also. The river became empty of people and traffic, except for the occasional raftsmen, but as everyone knows, they only work seasonally. A part of the famous Eastern Ring Road was submerged under the reservoir, so a replacement section was built up in the mountains. And, as bad luck would have it, the road now ran right past Yegor's lonely, isolated house, and vehicles and lorries would drive past day and night, announcing their presence to everything and everyone around with their permanent roar and foul-smelling fumes that poisoned the clean forest air. Human life in all its trivial bustling vanity had found him again, no matter how hard he tried to hide from it. Yegor was convinced that both the reservoir and the dirt road had been invented by humankind simply to irritate him and prevent him from living his own simple life. Then he was offered a job keeping an eye on the forest, and the buoy turned out to be needed by the raftsmen, after all.

'Are you all right there, old man?'

The raft careered around the bend upstream and continued down, spinning and curving along the river.

'Still alive, I see?'

One of the raftsmen called out and started laughing loudly. The old man sighed silently. The fast river carried the long raft, that was almost a quarter the width of the river, and its four wiry, bearded helmsmen further downstream, until at the next turn it disappeared with a flash of its stern. Its wake spread out along the river and made the buoy bob and jump. The old man let out another sigh.

6

Normally, the market would have been very noisy at this time, but today there were not many people about. Under the awning of a wooden lean-to, several Russian women were sitting on sacks stuffed with pine nuts while next to them, Kazakh women had set up shop with their kumis and were pouring it into their tegenes. Every now and then, someone would try a glass of the tart, mildly alcoholic drink and a little further away, out of earshot, the old folk would gather in a circle, talking quietly among themselves.

'Your kumis hasn't fermented properly,' one of the old men remarked to a plump seller who was sitting next to the shop window. 'That kumis isn't fit to be rubbed on a sheep with scabies!'

A saddled piebald mare and chestnut stallion were tethered to a post. The young mare neighed, shifting its legs, swivelling its quick eyes in all directions. The stately golden-chestnut stallion became agitated, snorted and pulled at its reins, trying to free itself, then it froze to the spot, arched its back and began trembling all over.

'What the devil's got into you, Kairakpai!' The old man in a thick quilted robe immediately put the tegene back on the counter and ran to the tethering post. 'Why the hell did you tie your mare upwind of him?' He took handfuls of water from the ditch and sprinkled them on the stallion's groin. 'Do you want him to lose all his potency, just like that?'

Dunya laughed, watching the old man's troubles, caught Ayan's cheerful glance and, embarrassed, changed the topic of the conversation.

'Look how much they can drink!' She exclaimed in surprise, nodding at the old men, 'I'm surprised they don't burst!'

'To my knowledge, there has never been a Kazakh who has ever burst from drinking too much kumis,' Ayan replied. 'Do you know who that old man with that stallion is?'

'Who?'

'He's my father.'

'He looks strict.'

'He's more friendly than yours.'

Ayan had said it as a joke, but Dunya pouted her lips in resentment. Her shoes were pinching and she rubbed her feet. Ayan noticed that she was keeping a close eye on the fat, red-haired waitress as she carried out the plates. They were sitting in the *Dorstroi* highway construction canteen, which was already beginning to fill up. Although, the only thing it had in common with a canteen was its name. It basically comprised several improvised tables under a small round canopy that barely protected its patrons from the scorching sun. The waitress finally brought them two helpings of some pretty anaemic-looking cutlets, thumped a bottle of wine on the table, and turned on the old radio on her way back to the service hatch.

Mishka, Mishka, flash me your smile, a feisty female voice rang out, accompanied by the crackle of a blunt needle.

'So, where is your blonde bombshell?' Dunya asked.

'What blonde bombshell?' said Ayan, mystified.

'Your fiancée.'

'Ah! I told you, she went off to work in the movies!'

Ayan giggled as he remembered his joke.

Dunya did not touch her cutlet. Ayan poured their glasses full with dark vermouth, but Dunya didn't even look at the wine.

'Let's drink!' Ayan proposed. 'This wine is drunk all over the world. It's a hundred times better than your mead. Probably, a thousand times.'

A middle-aged man came up to their table and sat down in an empty chair. A second later, the waitress appeared.

'What would you like?'

'Well, what have you got?'

'Macaroni soup, macaroni with cutlets, meat with a macaroni garnish, liver and macaroni, and macaroni navy style,' The waitress listed.

'Then I'll have three glasses of tea without sugar. But only if you've got hot tea.'

'No, we've only got cold tea.'

'Then three glasses of white coffee. And it would be nice if they could be hot.'

'So, you like it hot?' The waitress asked with an ambiguous smile.

'As much as the next man,' he smiled back.

Mishka, Mishka... Tsss... Tsss...

The large waitress rolled up to the old radio and yanked the cord out of the plug. The canteen became quiet again.

Two bearded hunters, a Russian and a Kazakh, were deep in conversation at the corner table. On the floor near their feet lay two dogs: one a black-and-white spaniel, the other a large, sandy-coloured Great Dane the size of a small calf.

'Is she a bitch?' the Kazakh asked, pointing at the spaniel.

'A bitch,' the Russian replied. 'A wonderful bitch!'

'Yeah, but bitches get restless. Three times a year you need to find a dog for her and three times a year you have to take care of her puppies. And when you need her for an actual hunt, you'll be left without any dog at all.'

'You don't know what you're talking about!' his companion objected. 'Bitches make the keenest and hardiest hunting dogs. Just look at her reactions.' He broke off a piece of bread and threw it to the spaniel, but the Great Dane intercepted the bread on the fly. 'And is this your hunting dog?' the Russian chuckled. 'It doesn't look like one.'

'My son brought him from the city,' the Kazakh replied, in his turn trying to justify himself. 'They say that you can even go hunting after bears with them.'

'And have you?'

'So far, I'm still only training him,' the Kazakh answered evasively.

The Russian threw another piece of bread to the spaniel but again, the Great Dane intercepted it.

'Hmm, I find it hard to believe that he'd take on a bear!' the Russian concluded. 'Gluttons like him don't make good hunters. And then he is a bit too silent.'

'What do you mean, silent?'

'Oh, that's just the term for it... No, you're better off with a spaniel, or even a mongrel. It doesn't matter what sort of dog you hunt bear with. If it's not a purebred then you won't feel so bad if it gets mauled in a fight.'

'Never mind, I'll bring him along anyway. Although, I have to admit, he's become a bit of a coward after a badger bit him on the leg once.'

Ayan listened to the hunters and laughed,

'So, you're bear hunters are you?'

The old Kazakh immediately reacted,

'Who asked your opinion, snub-nose?'

'All I'm saying is that this year the taiga is full of bears and wolves,' Ayan replied, trying to calm him down. 'If it's bears that you're after, there's loads of them around at the moment.'

'Bears are gentle and harmless creatures,' the old man softened his tone. 'But the wolves are a pest. Only last week, they took one of my father-in-law's cows, right in his back yard. I followed their trail but couldn't find their lair. But I'll find them and deal with them, if it kills me.'

Once again, Ayan interrupted their conversation,

'They say that wolves are nature's orderlies.'

'You'll be telling me they're nature's doctors next!' The old man frowned again.

'But you've heard of natural selection?'

'The fact that wolves are so smart is of no benefit to ordinary folks, that's all I can tell you, young man.'

'Well, you see, the wolf only kills the sick and the weak,' Ayan began to explain, 'but they leave the strong and the healthy alone. And this is called natural...'

But now, it was the Russian who angrily interrupted him, keen to stand up for his hunter friend.

'Since when did you become such a smart Alec, eh? You'll end up feeding the wolves with all the wildlife we have left because these days they're all either lame or sick. You go on about natural selection but you're nothing more than an overblown wind bag!'

Everyone nearby laughed. But Dunya wasn't listening

to their argument, she was captivated by the fly-blown picture on the wall. It depicted an idyllic summer pasture with a snow-white yurt at the foot of a mountain, with a flock of sheep grazing nearby. Several old women in their white *kimesheks* were sitting next to the hearth and some young guy, probably some agit-prop type from the party was making a speech to a circle of old men sitting around him. Behind them an antenna could be made out. Someone poked her in the side and she flinched.

'Have you had enough to eat?' Ayan asked her. 'Shall we go, then?'

They set off along a narrow paved street littered on either side with random log-built houses, each with a heap of dung and garbage blackening next to them. The rotting manure smoked in the sun, giving off a fuggy, stifling smell and their smoke-blackened bathhouses leaned crookedly in the yards. Here and there, lone saddled horses stood tethered on the street, their heads bowed. It seemed that the old men from the market had had more than their fill of kumis and decided to visit their friends and relatives. A huge pig with large sagging teats jumped out of a nearby yard with a desperate squeal, followed by a small, stocky old Kazakh man. Seeing Ayan, he shouted,

'Hey Ayan, stop that smelly critter! I'll have her guts for garters!'

There hadn't even been time to even think of catching it.

'What a shame! I'd have had her guts for garters...' The old man stopped and stared at Dunya. 'And who's this?'

'Just an acquaintance.'

'Oh, that's all right, then... I thought she might be your

fiancée.' And then he turned around again, 'I would have had her guts for garters!'

'What did he say to you?' Dunya asked once the old man had gone back into his yard. 'I could see he was talking about me.'

He was threatening to have your guts for garters,' Ayan laughed.

'Don't talk nonsense!'

'Don't worry, as long as you're with me, no one would dare to say a cross word to you.'

'Idiot!'

'Shall we go to the movies?' Ayan suggested.

'No, I need to drop in on the Tsybins.'

'Are you going to spend the night with them?'

'I want to buy a cockerel from them. Our chickens have stopped laying, and my grandfather keeps yelling at me about it.'

'A-ah...' Ayan drawled sympathetically and then suddenly lunged for a young cockerel scratching around on one of the dung heaps. The cockerel rushed away with a loud squawk, but in a matter of seconds Ayan had him in his tenacious hands. 'Here, take this one. He's more than a match for your hens.'

'Are you out of your mind?' Dunya stepped away, hiding her hands behind her back.

'Go on, take it!' Ayan insisted. 'In this village, chickens are barely considered living creatures, so there's nothing to worry about and you certainly don't need to pay for this scrawny brute. And as for these Tsybins...' Ayan averted his eyes. 'Well, you won't need to go and see them now, will you?'

Ayan accompanied Dunya to the dirt road and then

turned back. Once beyond the village, Dunya sat down, took off her shoes, and began to massage her swollen toes. Then she broke off a branch of leaves from a roadside bush and walked along the road, whisking away the irritating whining mosquitoes with it. At the turn, she looked back and, not seeing Ayan, she let out a sigh. The houses trembled in the sultry haze, grey puffs of smoke stretched up to the sky and a gang of children noisily chased after a ball on the green meadow next to the river. Dunya rarely visited the village — it deafened her with its constant and pointless racket and the people there seemed overly talkative and slightly frivolous. Dunya thought her grandfather was right not to let her come here — she both disliked and was simultaneously slightly afraid of the locals. However, she didn't want to return home either, it was boring her to death living in that lonely forest cabin. She looked back again and felt a sadness in her heart, as if she had lost something important. Suddenly, a cloud of dust rose up from the edge of the village, and her heart skipped a beat. The engine's hum now reached her and then the familiar rattle of the trailer could be heard through the trees. Dunya moved to the side of the road to let the truck through, her heart beating loudly, hoping that Ayan might be behind the wheel. She carried on walking, afraid to look back and have her hopes dashed. The truck clattered to a halt behind her, and the door creaked opened.

'Dunya!' It was Ayan.

He had even managed to change into his oily overalls and tarpaulin boots, and had become the usual Ayan again, the one who she saw every day. Dunya smiled happily and involuntarily reached out to him.

'It's not a working day today, is it?' she asked. 'And here you are in your truck.'

'No, it's not a working day, it's going to be our day, Birdie.'

'Birdie, birdie, that's all you ever say!'

'And what's wrong with that?' He also had a wide joyful smile on his face.

'You're not taking me seriously!' She whisked a mosquito away from him with her branch.

'So, tell me, do you have a sweetheart in your life?'

'I have to go.'

'Wait... Let's sit on the grass and talk heart to heart. Seriously, as you put it.'

'We can talk on the way.' She continued to walk along the path.

'All right then, get in the truck!'

He drove slowly. The dust swirled nearby, covering the stunted roadside bushes and sparse, occasional trees. Ayan stretched past Dunya and opened and slammed the door on her side again, blowing a strand of her hair out of his face as he did so.

'Tell me the truth, why did you really come to the village?'

'I wanted to see you.'

'Get away with you!' he said, squinting at her in disbelief.

'It's true.' She looked away.

'No girl has ever come looking for me before. Not a single one.'

'Us girls have short wings, you see.'

'So, you must be crazy about me, then?'

'When are you going to learn to speak like a normal human being?'

Usually, he turned these sorts of conversations into a joke, but this time he couldn't. *Why have I taken such a shine to her?* he asked himself. *You really are soft in the head and your own worst enemy. What a fool you are, Ayan! That's because there's no one around to knock any sense into you...* He just didn't have a serious bone in his body, and therefore, even when he was at his most sincere, everyone thought he was just making another one of his wisecracks, as the red-haired waitress from the canteen was always telling him. Ayan often got frustrated at not being able to do himself justice in company. He was an honest guy who always wore his heart on his sleeve — everyone recognized that about him. But for some reason he always ended up talking too much and had earned himself a bit of a reputation as a joker, a lightweight who couldn't be taken seriously. He was, after all, twenty years old, and he'd never declared his intentions to any of the girls, he'd never even been on a date with any of them and he'd never let anyone down, in even the most insignificant matter. And now he'd taken the bait, hook, line and sinker... Dunya couldn't resist playing with him. And all because of his obliging nature and cheerful disposition. *I'm not going to say another word to her!* he decided to himself. *I'm not going to talk to her and that's that!* Ayan involuntarily glanced at the hushed and silent Dunya.

The motor hummed steadily. Ayan did not take his eyes off the road, although he could have driven along it with them closed. A road sign appeared: *Drivers! Beware! Steep descent!* Ayan hit the horn several times as a warning. The road cut through a densely forested hill and began to climb steeply. Something moved under Ayan's feet — it was the bag with the cockerel. He moved the sack closer to Dunya. *She could at least say something,* he thought to himself grumpily, but the cat seemed to have got Dunya's tongue. He stepped on the accelerator and the truck picked up speed. Down below the deep gorge glowered darkly, the river glittering at its bottom. Dunya gazed into the gorge for a while, then leaned back,

'Mamma mia! It makes your head spin!'

At the next turn, Ayan blew his horn again and slowed down.

'So, where is your mum?'

'She left,' Dunya answered briefly.

'Where did she go?'

'To the city.'

'And your father?'

'I never had a father.'

'What do you mean, never had one?'

'I don't know anything about him. They didn't tell me.'

The conversation stalled again. The truck came out onto the pass. Ayan straightened up, leaned back in his seat, took a pack of cigarettes that had been tucked in behind the light shield, and lit up. There was sadness in the girl's pure blue eyes, she sat lost in thought, unaware of Ayan's presence. She recalled her childhood, which had passed without any parental affection... In fact, she didn't even know where her mother had gone when she left home. She had heard that she'd gone to the city downstream, where many people from the quiet taiga villages used to go in search of work. She vaguely remembered that her mother had left with some unknown bearded raftsman, taking advantage of the fact that her grandfather was not at home. She had put a bar of chocolate into Dunya's hand, promised that she would come back for her and closed the creaking gate behind her. She never returned home. For a long time, Dunya relived that scene in her memory, when, with tears in her eyes, her mother had left with the bearded man, looking back at her, but never taking her hand out of the raftsman's. Then it would occasionally return to her in her dreams, but over time the picture faded and was erased and now Dunya could remember her mother without any regret. Perhaps it was because her mother had never caressed or spoiled her, that every morning in the house always began with complaints, and ended in the evening with a quarrel, and Dunya was always terrified of the endless fights. She remembered how her grandfather had often beat his daughter, calling her the most awful things. For Dunya, she was a mother, but for grandfather, she was a daughter and he had every right to punish her, but all the same it was all so sordid and sickening, and, as soon as the screaming started up in the house, Dunya would run away into the forest. Sometimes, she would go out onto the dirt road, thinking that her mother had gone to live in the nearby village — in her imagination there was no separating the village from the city. She would then peer into the distance, expecting her to appear over the brow of the road, but all in vain. Over time, she really did forget her mother. Ever since then, she stopped remembering her mother, but she continued to hold a grudge against all the bearded raftsmen who passed through. And as for her father... Well, God had not given her a father, and that was that.

It wasn't her fault that she didn't have a father. Dunya pondered bitterly that of all people, Ayan, her only kindred spirit, should have reminded her of all this.

'Dunya, why don't you leave?'

She glanced warily at Ayan.

'What do I need to leave for?'

'Well, to get away from that nasty old man, for one.'

'You're nasty yourself!'

'We're not talking about me... I'm thinking about you. What's the point of living in that lonely old place? You live like a recluse. Why don't you move to the village.'

'What's so good about the village?'

'Well, life is completely different in the village... It's always more interesting when there are people about. Whatever happened, you wouldn't miss your lonely, boring life.'

'All right, but can you tell what I'd do in this village of yours?'

'What do you mean, what would you do? You'd live just like everyone else does. You'd get by after a fashion, as your grandfather always says. Compared with your forest cabin, life in the village would be like paradise on earth.'

'Well, you can keep your paradise to yourself, and I live well enough in my forest cabin.'

Ayan gently pushed the sack with the cockerel away from the pedals again.

'I've heard they're going to close the saw mill down soon,' he remarked, if nothing else, just to keep the conversation going,

'Really?'

'There's no timber left, you can see that for yourself.'

'So, what are you going to do?' The news seemed to agitate Dunya.

'They're going to set up a new collective farm for deer and horses. What would you think if I became a deer or horse wrangler?'

'They say that wranglers don't sleep at home much.'

'Well, you will come and visit — they say men need to be kept on a short leash. At least, that's what they say in our village.'

'I won't come and visit you!'

'Why?'

'Because you should come to visit me and, to be honest, you shouldn't leave your home at all!'

'Oh, Dunya, it's as if you were born a captive in a prison!'

'Have you been to prison? You seem to know a lot about it.'

'God forbid, as your grandfather would say! Although, I would happily go for kidnapping you, for example. One guy in our village ended up getting eight years for it.'

'For kidnapping a girl?'

'His bride!'

'But it's wrong to send someone to prison for that!'

'And I think it's wrong as well. But, on the other hand, it's also not very good when a girl just goes off with the first person she meets.'

'No, that's not true.' Dunya stamped her foot.

'Do you know what love is? It's a long road of two hearts journeying towards each other, but people understand it all in their own way as best they can. How can I explain it to you? Do you remember that silly song in the cafe, *Mishka, Mishka, flash me your smile*? We need to put those flirtatious smiles behind us, Dunya, because true lovers have to fight for the right to make their own choices and sing their own song. Especially around here, in our parts. And the song that they sing isn't always just going to be about love but about making a life together. We have chosen each other — and that means we're already on a road and roads aren't always easy. The road we've travelled towards each other so far is a much easier one than the one that faces us. Because, you know, it's going to be harder...'

'You're serious, aren't you? I kind of understand you, but I'm scared, this is all so frightening! My mother cried when she left. It's possible she didn't want to leave, but she probably had to. When a fish swims back to its spawning grounds, there are all sorts of things in its way — predators, nets, dynamite and weirs — but it still returns anyway! I don't know how to explain this to you, but you see... I came to the village to see you today.'

'I'm listening.' Ayan dropped his speed. 'I think I always understand you.'

'Don't laugh at me!'

'No, no I'm not!' The truck almost stalled.

'You turn everything into a joke and I won't be able to tell you what I want to... You say that it's a long road, but, you see, I need to know one thing! I absolutely must know! You're not the sort of person that people say you are, are you?'

'Wait a minute, the radiator's boiling over!' Ayan stopped the truck and, jumping out of the cab, pointed towards an enamelled water can. 'Can you help me? With any luck you won't end up getting your hands too dirty.'

Dunya couldn't find the words she wanted to say because Ayan had once again abruptly changed the subject of the conversation, or rather, confused it with one of his usual jokes. It seemed to her that he would never understand her. Ayan screwed off the radiator cap but Dunya refused to leave the cab. He started pumping the petrol suction lever, climbed off the bonnet, and lit a cigarette.

'Dunya, what are you doing in there?'

His question was met with silence.

'Maybe the cockerel laid an egg?'

Still silence.

'Well, what are you still sitting in there for?'

'I'm just sitting,' was all the response she gave him.

'So, you've just decided to sit there, have you?' Ayan teased.

Dunya got out of the cab, set off down to the river and then sat on the grass. Ayan took off his overalls and sat down beside her. She looked at him and noticed a triangular talisman on his chest.

'An amulet?' Dunya asked in surprise. 'So, you have them as well, do you?'

'My mother gave it to me for good luck.'

She tensed at his words.

'Do you believe in supernatural powers?'

'I wouldn't say so. A lot of the drivers believe in superstitions and omens. I can't bear loneliness. I always like to have something in the truck with me: whether it's a talisman, a poster or a pin up. There's one driver who even brings a bird with him. A real one. In a cage.'

She glanced at the river and smiled.

'In a cage, did you say? And does it bring him good

fortune?'

'Everyone's fortune is different!' He smiled and brushed her shoulder with his. 'For example, someone's carved on the wall of my cab that whoever drives it will end up getting married three times.'

'Idiot!'

'You know what I was thinking just now? It looks like you're going to be the first, straight up!'

She tried to reply with a joke:

'I'd be better off being the third.'

Ayan didn't know how to answer: her voice sounded broken somehow, and in her words there was that feminine truth, which a man perceives more with his heart than understands with his mind. He was confused, smiled foolishly and, unable to master himself, threw off his striped navy vest and threw himself into the river from the high bank. He splashed in the water for a long time, sensing that from now on he would have to behave with Dunya in a completely different way than he had before. He would become different and think more about how not to upset her. He climbed the high bank and found Dunya on a small green clearing near a spring. She lay on her back, looking up at the high, cloudless sky. Ayan pulled on his vest, approached her, and looked into her eyes. Then he sat down next to her, leaned over and kissed her on the lips. Dunya looked into his eyes and quietly wiped her lips with her hand.

Horns blared from the direction of the road, and a truck drove past, the roar of its engine dissipating into the sound of the water trilling over the shallows.

451

7

Old Yegor had probably been down to the river and back with his buckets five times before he finally filled the second cauldron, that had been set on the stove. He was thoroughly exhausted and angry. Usually by this time, having already steamed himself to his heart's content, Yegor would be lying on his bunk drinking his tea, but today he hadn't even fired up the stove. Wretched girl! She'd ruined his whole day.

Yegor removed the ashes from the stove with his tongs and lit the furnace. The firewood would not light immediately, which made him even more angry. He waited a while, dipped his hand into the water to make sure that it was hot enough, filled a large basin with water and placed his whisk of dried birch leaves to soak and soften in it. The bathhouse filled with acrid smoke. Yegor coughed and opened the small window that had been plugged with a rag, and then the doors. He splashed water onto the benches and spotted a fish that he'd smoked the week before and forgotten to take down and went back to the house with it. Then he noticed that there was almost no mead left in the wooden cask and he grew gloomy again. The little harlot had left for the village and now there would be no one to bring the mead.

He got undressed and was just climbing up onto the upper bench, when the roar of an engine reached his ears, then voices could be heard in the yard, someone was laughing loudly and then he heard the agitated clucking of the hens. He got dressed again and stalked out of the bathhouse.

At the gate, a logging truck was still rumbling away.

Yegor pulled the axe out of a log on the way and carried it with him. There was no one near the truck. The old man walked around it, recognized that it was Ayan's, whom he had never liked, and then went back into the yard. The old man would have given the snub-nosed young man what-for ages ago, but he had considered it beneath his dignity to have any dealings with someone he considered as stupid as Ayan. The old man especially detested Ayan's bristly mustache that stuck out like a cat's whiskers. *He never dared come into the yard before, but now he comes and goes as he pleases! The insolent half-wit!* the old man thought to himself, feeling his resentment sweep over him like a wave. *I'd set the dogs on him, if I only knew where to get my hands on one!*

Ayan and Dunya were laughing merrily as they watched the five hens chasing the unfortunate cockerel to the four corners of coop. Ayan noticed Yegor.

'Your hens are very frisky, old man!' he remarked jokingly.

'Sling your hook and go cast your nets elsewhere, while you're still in one piece!' The old man's voice was heavy with menace.

Ayan became confused. He glanced at the axe in the old man's hands, shrugged his shoulders in bewilderment, silently closed the gate and carefully locked the iron bolt.

'What are you doing just standing there?' Yegor barked at his granddaughter. 'Bring me the horse reins!'

He sliced open the netting of the coop with his axe, grabbed the cockerel and, placing it on a log, cut the bird's head off with one fell stroke. Warm blood spattered his face, and immediately a throbbing pain radiated out from the back of his head. His eyes grew hot. He threw the still half-dead cockerel onto the rubbish pile.

Dunya was already standing beside him, with the reins in her hands.

'Are you going beat me with these?' the girl asked.

'I'm going to kill you!' the old man answered curtly.

He wasn't able to kill her, although he whipped her for so long, he did not recall how many times he hit her. Exhausted, he almost fell onto the log pile and Dunya, groaning, lay motionless on the ground. It took a while before Dunya came to her senses.

'Is that everything?' she asked, covering her body with her dress.

'God will make you pay for the rest that you owe!'

He fell silent again. Silence reigned.

'The sauna's gone cold,' Dunya said.

The old man didn't answer. 'I said, the sauna's gone cold!' Dunya repeated.

The old man got to his feet with great difficulty. He didn't dare look into his granddaughter's eyes. Only at the very door of the bathhouse did he force himself to say,

'Bring me the mead cask.'

It wasn't Ayan's lucky day either. His truck's back wheel hit a rut hidden under a layer of mud and his attempts to get out ended up with it buried right up to its axle shaft. Ayan put the truck into reverse gear, gave it some gas and tried to rock the heavy truck out of the hole, but nothing came of that either.

Very soon, it got dark. The sky completely clouded over and it began to rain. Ayan peered up the road for some time, hoping that a passing truck might be able to give his truck a tow, but it was already late, and the rain had evidently set in for a long time, which meant that the experienced drivers would probably now choose to avoid the dangers of the wet road in favour of the warmth of the canteen. *You idiot, Ayan!* he scolded himself. *Why did you have to come out to this forest cabin in this weather? Well you've made your bed and you're going to have to sleep in it all night long now!*

Somewhere in the distance, a horse whinnied. Having sensed a person nearby, the intelligent animal let him know his whereabouts. Ayan climbed the hill and saw the bay horse tied, as always, with its long halter to the stake. Even from here it was clear that all the available grass had long been trampled down and that the horse had nothing to eat. The roof of old Yegor's lonely house loomed darkly beyond the poor bay nag. A light shone in the single window facing the road. Ayan left the road and walked straight towards the house. What was Dunya doing now? Did she know that he hadn't stopped thinking about her for a single minute? Did she have any idea that he had got bogged down and was rushing to see her again? The heavy rain intermittently blocked out the halo of light trembling behind the window. Someone's shadow blotted out the window for a minute, and the halo diminished. Ayan picked up his pace.

At first, he politely knocked on the gate but since that would evidently not be heard in the house, he struck it hard with his fist a couple of times. Several long minutes passed before the door of the house creaked and Yegor's familiar cough could be heard, followed by the familiar shuffling of his boots as he walked up to the gate.

'What do you want?'

'Open up!'

The gate opened a crack, and half a beard-covered face, one eye, and a red bald head appeared through the crack.

'What do you want?' Yegor repeated.

'I need an axe and a shovel... The truck's stuck.'

Shuffling in his boots again, the old man hobbled off towards the barn, then trampled about near the bathhouse and returned to the gate. He handed Ayan a shovel and said hoarsely:

'That'll be a rouble!' Then he showed him the axe and added: 'That'll be another rouble! Come on, show us your silver.'

Ayan counted out two roubles in coins and handed them over. The old man unhurriedly picked them out of his palm, went over to the outdoor basin, washed the coins, rubbed each one dry with his towel and dropped them into a canvas bag hanging under the eaves. Ayan glanced regretfully at the window and Yegor headed back into the house.

Dunya jumped back from the window and pretended to be concentrating on the borders of the linen towel she was embroidering. She looked up at her grandfather, put down her embroidery and began to clear the table — her grandfather always liked to have supper at the same time. She placed a cast-iron pot of jacket-boiled potatoes on the table, a bunch of spring onions, three or four lightly smoked fish, and half a loaf of grey bread. The old man was already sitting on his stool. He looked at her gloomily, and Dunya placed the tuyesok[32] of mead on the table. He frowned at her again, and she, immediately

---

32 Tuyesok - a traditional cylindrical lidded container made out of birch bark - common throughout Russia, Siberia and Altai.

realising what the matter was, filled the birch bark cask to the brim.

Raindrops ran down the windows, it was already dark outside. Dunya glanced at the window, saw her own reflection in it, and behind her, the reflection of her grandfather, who was removing a spider's web from the side of the tuyesok with his finger. The sound of an axe penetrated the pattering of the rain on the roof and windows. Evidently, Ayan was chopping branches to put under the wheel of his truck. Dunya wanted to run out to him and help. For a whole hour, she listened to him trying unsuccessfully to get the truck out of its rut, but she dared not leave the house. The room, it seemed to her, had become even smaller, the ceiling seemed to have sunk lower. There, beyond the door of the house, the whole world was waiting — free and boundless — and in it Ayan, her one and only kindred spirit. Dunya had been waiting for him and Ayan had returned, but there was no way for them now to see each other. The truck roared again. Dunya ran up to the window, pressing up against it. The beams of its headlights cut through the darkness, sweeping up and across the night sky, shimmering through the myriad raindrops, then the semi-circular sheaf of light fell back to the ground and, having described an arc, shone off into the distance. Dunya sighed.

'Dunya!'

Ayan got behind the wheel again, cursing the evil, misanthropic old man for not allowing him to see Dunya. The rubber blades of the wipers tirelessly swept the raindrops from the windscreen. Someone was driving down the road in the opposite direction. Ayan flashed his headlights several times, but the oncoming truck didn't reply and disappeared around the corner. Ayan turned off the windscreen wipers. It was black as pitch, the top of the ridge was glowing a vague red and, over the quiet hum of the engine, the sound of the wind came blowing down through the forest. He shivered — while he'd been faffing around with the truck, his back and legs had become as cold as ice. His wet clothes clung uncomfortably to his body. His mouth felt dry and acrid from the bitter tobacco smoke and he was hungry.

Ayan pictured his mother waiting for him to get back for his dinner. Having put the samovar on, she would have gone out into the street several times in the hope of seeing him return. His father, as usual, would probably be sitting sullenly and silently on his bed, staring intently at the photograph of his four older sons in their uniforms, hanging on the wall opposite. None of them had returned from the war and the old man had never been able to come to terms with the fact that they were no more. Maybe that's why Ayan, born at the beginning of the war, had never experienced his father's affection. Generally speaking, his father was cold and strict with everyone, he refused to have anything to do with the running of the house, didn't even talk to the neighbours and was surprisingly neat and clean. Ayan did not take after his father and perhaps this was why his father was so aloof with him. The old man often left home, and when he was with his family, all he would do was sit on his bed and offer up his prayers five times a day. Four of them would be dedicated to each of his dead sons and the fifth to God alone knew who. He also very touchingly looked after his swift footed, red-bellied stallion. The old man didn't care in the slightest where Ayan was — whether he was at home or on duty, whether he had eaten or was hungry or whether he was in a good mood or bad. Sometimes, Ayan felt that his father would have even greeted the news of his death indifferently if some misfortune had befallen him.

Ayan sat in the cab of the truck, acutely aware of just how lonely he was.

Then he began to bitterly berate himself. *Father is right, there's nothing to love about me!* he thought, once again trying to drive out of the rut. *And what was the point of coming to this wretched forest cabin on a night like this? Driving into a rut, spending the night in the rain... Now I'm cold and hungry... Is this how people with at least an ounce of sense live?*

Back at home, no one reproached or gave him a hard time. He was in no hurry to marry, especially as his parents weren't rushing him either. And anyway, he still hadn't felt true love for any girl yet. And chasing after every piece of skirt he met wasn't in his nature either. Except that he wasn't indifferent to Dunya. But it seemed to him that what he felt for her was more pity than love.

Ayan turned off the engine, convinced there was no way he was going to get the truck out now. A faint spot of light loomed in the window of the solitary cabin. He took a small transistor from the glove compartment and placed it on the seat beside him. Rummaging through the pile of magazines and newspaper clippings there, he found a dried-up crust of bread and chewed it. He turned on the transistor and twisted the tuning knob. A familiar male voice came on: *You are listening to the Voice of America!* then the voice disappeared, and the melodious jingle of the *Mayak* classical station could be heard. *At the request of all symphonic music lovers...* Up ahead, another trembling semi-circular sheaf of light from the headlights of an oncoming truck lit up the brow of the hill. Iridescent droplets glittered briefly on the windscreen and then disappeared...

Ayan felt tired, his lower back ached. He opened the door facing away from the wind, put his legs out of the cab and lay down on the seat, propping his head on the pillow that he always brought with him. The cold air made him feel a little better. The wind roared in the mountains, the rain rustled the leaves and the river beat against the boulders at the bottom of the gorge. And the music of Grieg sounded out...

My life is deserted, hurry, my son, hurry.
Playing melodies on the golden dombra...
The sounds of the strings will touch the yearning soul,
And the wind of death will suddenly reach us from paradise...'

He read Abai's poem for some time. It seemed as if these lines, so full of melancholy, had been dedicated by the poet personally to him, Ayan. He seemed the most miserable and unhappy person he knew. He remembered his school mates, who had all gone off to different places to study. But he had failed to get into the university. Twice he had travelled to Alma-Ata to get into the literature department and both times failed to pass the exam. And why on earth did he fill his head with ideas that he might one day become a writer? His friends were studying at veterinary or agricultural college, but for some reason he stubbornly wanted to become a writer. It might have been alright, if he wrote poetry, but no — it was prose that he was obsessed with. Poems immediately get you into the limelight, but prose is a long, painstaking process. So far, his passion for literature had only resulted in financial losses. Each of his trips to the capital had required considerable outlay and the two journeys had entailed the sale of two cows. But being stuck behind the wheel of a truck was certainly not what he wanted to be doing for the rest of his life. It was strange, he loved poetry but wrote prose. He was always playing the fool and joking around so that no one might guess about his true passion for literature. And all because he was afraid of becoming a laughing stock in the eyes of his fellow villagers. It was stupid!

Water, water! Water all around! the song suddenly broke in, interrupting Grieg's music.

'What a load of rubbish!' Ayan grunted, retuning the transistor to catch Grieg again. He couldn't stand these lightweight pop songs. When he was in Alma-Ata, he had bought classical records by the Kazakh composer Tattimbet. *Water, water!* barged in again over the airwaves and he tried to readjust the transistor, but Grieg's divine music disappeared in a chaos of ethereal noise. Ayan returned to his thoughts: *It's a pity, I shouldn't have told my father to sell the heifer. Some day, I'm going to go away again... It would be good if I have more luck this time...'*

The wind had quietened down. The river continued to run loudly over the shallows and the rain continued to pound the truck. Yes, he was stuck good and proper, damn it!

461

Suddenly, he could hear the sound of someone's footsteps approaching. Ayan lowered the window and stared into the darkness. A few minutes later, old Yegor's stooped, thick-set figure appeared without a hat on his head, shuffling along in his worn felt boots. *Has he gone out of his mind?* Ayan thought to himself and suddenly slapped his forehead. *How could I have forgotten?* He jumped out of the cab, found the shovel and axe he'd thrown in the back of the truck, and placed them at the old man's feet.

'I didn't come for them,' the old man said in a dull voice. 'I don't need them anymore.'

'Ah, is it one of your Old Believer's customs? You won't take them back after I've touched them, is that it? I can pay you extra for them.'

'I couldn't give a damn about your money!'

From the truck, the jingle for the *Mayak* radio station rang out followed by the voice of a female newsreader who solemnly announced, *Today the Soviet Union launched another satellite into space...*

Ayan knocked his mud-caked boots against the running board and climbed into the cab. *The announcement made by the TASS news agency has been republished by all the main overseas newspapers...*

The bay snorted in the forest. Ayan felt sorry for the poor, neglected animal.

'Why don't you let the horse go. It's just dying there for nothing.'

'It's none of your business and you wouldn't understand anyway!' The old man shifted uneasily from one foot to the other. 'So, don't go sticking your snub nose into my affairs!'

'How do you know? Maybe it is precisely my business!'

'What do you care about horses? Come into the house and warm yourself with something hot.'

Shuffling along in his galosh-clad felt boots, the old man set off for home. In the dim light thrown into the darkness by the solitary window, his shadow seemed monstrous and huge.

8

Ayan stopped in the wet room, not quite believing that he had been allowed into Yegor's house. He then he took off his shoes, pushing his wet footcloths deep into his boots. The old man had asked Ayan into the house, but treated him as if he was an uninvited guest. Yegor followed him warily, as if noting his every move. He left a trail of wet footprints on the floor. Ayan passed through the room and sat down at the bench. The old man immediately turned the lamp up, increasing the light, then hid the birch bark dishes and containers in the drawer, covered the wooden ladle and pail with its lid, and drew the curtains closer.

On the bunk lay a feather pillow and a blanket in a cotton cover, from which hung the sleeve of an old linen shirt.

Yegor slowly climbed the ladder to the upper bunk, fluffed the feather pillow with his fist, turned it over several times and out of habit called out to his granddaughter,

'Dunya!'

Ayan involuntarily glanced at the doors: on the threshold lay the old man's worn-out deerskin boots and his mud-stained work boots. He cast a bewildered glance at the old man, who had already laid down in his bunk. His bald patch could be seen from below, illuminated red by the warm light of the lamp.

There was a rustle, the short curtain stretched next to the stove twitched and a pair of full round calves and the hem of a blue sundress appeared, followed by Dunya herself. With a sidelong glance at Ayan, she placed several boiled potatoes on the table, a couple of slices of grey bread, the birch bark cask of mead and a glass with a chipped rim.

The old man raised his head, watched how Dunya served the food to the guest and then leaned back down again on his pillow.

The mead, drunk on an empty stomach, immediately went to Ayan's head and he felt the blood rush to his face. He ate a little. He wanted to exchange a word or two with Dunya, but the presence of the old man intruded. Of course, he would have immediately put a stop to their conversation. He just sat there and looked at the girl. He wanted to smoke, but there was no way this was going to be allowed in Yegor's house with its strict, harsh rules. Dunya was as quiet as a mouse and meek as a lamb. After exchanging eloquent glances with Ayan, she climbed back up onto her bed above the stove and fell silent. Sleep weighed heavily on Ayan, he rested his chin on his hand and closed his eyes. The wind died down and the rain subsided. A solitary cricket chirped behind the stove and fat drops of water fell noisily from the roof onto the porch. From time to time, Dunya sighed and tossed from side to side. *How do they live here? All on their own...* Ayan thought. *What sort of life is this? What do they do, what do*

they think about all day long, what do they dream of? And after all, it's not just a single day or a month, not even a single year that they live like this in complete solitude. If they'd had a dog, at least it would have barked! But this house is utterly dead...'
He used to come here every day, but somehow it had never occurred to him to think about the life they led in this lonely house. In any case, it had seemed natural to him that old Yegor should live here far from other people. After all, someone had to guard the forest and keep an eye on the buoy. He had lived his life, it was peaceful here and there was plenty of food to be had. But it was Dunya he was sorry for. What was she going to do here? Well, she'd probably get married, have children, and then what? Although would any husband want to live here? And would the children stay with her?

Ayan lay down on the bench, placing his hands behind his head. The wretched old man might at least have given him a blanket or a pillow! Ayan got up and put out the lamp, but the acrid smoke kept him awake for a long time. He really wanted a smoke. Ayan's thoughts turned back to the inhabitants of this lonely place. Now he felt a real sense of pity for both the old man and his granddaughter, huddled here in this godforsaken cabin in the taiga. The boards in the upper bunk creaked, the old man turned on his side. Then he sighed loudly.

How long had it been since a stranger had last set foot in this house. Let alone an outsider, he hadn't even allowed acquaintances and fellow Old Believers over the threshold before. Old Yegor even surprised himself with his decision today. He couldn't sleep and kept trying to understand why he had suddenly violated his own solitude, broken his own rules, deviated from the unshakable Kerzhak Old Believer laws, which he had always considered to be the most godly. The old man felt hot in his bunk, the palms and soles of his feet were on fire; he turned over onto one side and then the other. His heart was pounding, there didn't seem to be enough air, he threw off his heavy blanket, but it was still too hot. He'd evidently had one too many. *I really ought to know my limits by now*, he began to reproach himself. *I'm not as young as I used to be, which means I should know when to stop but still I show no restraint just like I used to before...*

Then he climbed down the ladder, found a stool in the dark, dragged it to the table and sat down on it. His throat was dry. He immediately found the tuyesok.

'Grandpa, you've had enough, stop drinking!' Dunya's voice came from behind the curtain.

'Don't go poking your nose into other people's business.'

It was not as stuffy at the table as it had been up on the bunk, but his mouth was so dry that his tongue felt like it had been turned into wood. 'It's going to need the hair of the dog,' Yegor decided. But he didn't have the heart to drink straight away. Or to be more precise, the smell of the mead unmanned him. Anyway, he didn't want to be drinking on his own at night.

'Hey guest, wake up!' Ayan got up and sat down on the bench. He didn't feel much like drinking either, but took a sip from the chipped glass and silently watched the old man, who gleamed a vague white in his undershirt in the semi-darkness.

'Maybe we should light the lamp?'

'What, are you afraid the mead will miss your lips in the dark?' the old man growled.

Ayan ignored the old man's caustic reply, fearing that he might explode if he made any more remarks. *I'm better off keeping my mouth shut,* he decided. Then he drew the window curtains a little and sat back down on the bench again.

'They say the saw mill is going to be liquidated? Or is that just more tittle tattle coming out of your village again?'

Ayan chuckled to himself. Wow, check out the word he'd managed to insert into the conversation: *liquidate* no less.

'Looks like they're going to organise a collective livestock farm.'

'Can't you people get by without your livestock? Oh well... Maybe that's the idea. So, you've not managed to take everything from the land, yet. You've torn up just about everything else around here. You've destroyed the entire forest: first with your road, then the saw mill and then the mine... Keep going the way you are... You lot will probably flood the place after you've gone — that's just the way you live.'

'We need a state farm. It'll be profitable both for the country and for the people.'

'But of course! You literate and educated folks know better. We are a dark ignorant people, we don't understand anything about these things.'

The small birch bark cask was already empty. Yegor wanted some more mead but didn't dare go and fill the cask, fearing that Dunya would reprimand him again.

'So, what are you going to breed on this state farm of yours?' he asked. 'Donkeys probably?'

'Why donkeys? There are Maral deer and reindeer.'

467

'So, are you going to take them out to pasture? Not everyone is up to herding deer, you know.'

'So, you teach us!' Ayan replied, touched to the quick. 'You probably haven't forgotten how they used to take Krivonosov's herds out to pasture.'

'Learn from your father. He wasn't that poor either. By my calculations, he must have had at least a thousand horses.'

'Grandfather!' Dunya spoke up again. 'That's enough!'

'And are you the one putting food on the table?' the old man shouted at his granddaughter. 'Pipe down and tend to the marks my reins left on you. It's about the most useful thing you young girls can do, anyway!'

Everyone fell silent. The niche above the stove darkened. Ayan turned away in disgust. Dunya seemed to have gone back to sleep. The old man sat, furious. He had only just warmed to his theme and they'd interrupted him, making him lose his temper. *Look how they stand up for each other, like a pair of mountains!* Yegor thought to himself. His daughter had been no good, so there was no point expecting anything good to come from the granddaughter. Both of them had been spoiled by the outside world. *Just you wait, Dunya will soon bring shame down on my head as well... That little fool Nastya had played the field and left her daughter to be looked after... Like a hen without a cock... A cock! And this one also wants to go off to the village!'* He felt his entire body boiling over with anger. Right now, he really was ready to throw both his granddaughter and that idiot Ayan out onto the street, on this dark cold rainy night. *Just look at him, lying there as if he was in his own house!* he snarled to himself.

The old man's head began to spin, multi-coloured sparks flashed before his eyes and there was a ringing in his ears. He glanced across the table and vaguely made out a striped sailor's vest on the bench opposite and a pair of hefty arms folded across its chest. *I should give him a good kick up the backside and send him packing!* But then he suddenly remembered his only son Fyodor. The old man tried to remember his face, but could not recall it. His son's features appeared in his mind's eye — blurry, barely visible. Evidently, a person's memory does not retain even those faces that are dearest to us...

It had been exactly twenty years ago, during a cold winter riven with blizzards and snowstorms. Yegor had spent many nights at the window, peering into the taiga, now and then venturing out into the courtyard, hoping to see his son striding back to his family porch. It had long been time for Fyodor to pay a visit to the house and see his father. It had been three years since the war had ended, but none of the four families who had moved to the village at the beginning of the war bothered returning to their old homes and Yegor and his daughter Nastya still lived all alone on the deserted bank of the river.

The winter that year had turned out to be particularly severe, the snow came early, then the winds blew and unprecedented snowstorms and whirlwinds struck the region for six whole months. The snow only began to melt at the beginning of May. No one, except Fyodor, ever visited the lonely cabin that the people in the surrounding villages had long forgotten ever existed. Fyodor rarely came back and when he did, he was like a feral animal. He brought a real sense of unease and the cold with him into the house and he was increasingly impudent, always demanding something, bleeding his father and sister dry of nearly everything by the time he left. A human being can endure almost anything except loneliness and Fyodor had been living alone in the forest like a wolf for several years. And his nature had become as savage as a wolf's — ready to pounce with his knife at the slightest provocation. Everyone was his enemy. After these rare visits from his son, Yegor would look back with bitterness at the path he had travelled and recall the old Kazakh proverb: *Woe to the traveller whose horse falls beneath him in the middle of a journey and woe to the man whose wife dies in the prime of life.* Well, now he bitterly regretted Agafya's death. The time had come when illness and old age were now knocking at the door, but he had no wife around to take care of him. His daughter had no time for him, she was still living in her parents' house for now but tomorrow she would run away to someone else's. His son was even worse — tramping around the forest: today he might find the trail of his footprints in the grass but tomorrow his mauled remains left in the bushes. God himself was in no fit position to judge him. How long would the unfortunate boy have to continue wandering through the most empty and deserted places in fear of all living things? Yegor was worried about Fyodor: after all, he was his son, his own flesh and blood. These thoughts only made him all the more bitter and he blamed and scolded himself.

And then one particularly dark and stormy night, it happened... The wind was howling like a wolf, pulling up the thatch covering the roof of the shed, furiously roaring down the chimney and whistling and blowing in the snow through a small broken corner of the window.

Suddenly, the creak of sleigh runners or skis passing over snow could be heard in the yard, followed by a loud knock on the door. Just moments before, everyone in the house had been arguing and fighting, blaming each other for their personal misfortunes and Yegor had a presentiment that their quarrel boded no good. But with the knock at the door, they all rushed about in a panic, forgetting their quarrel in the blink of an eye. Completely forgetting about the cellar, Fyodor climbed onto the upper bunk and huddled in the farthest corner.

Their visitor turned out to be Zhakup, the gamekeeper, a powerful and experienced old hunter with a bushy beard.

'It's no joke out there, today!' Zhakup entered the house, talking animatedly. 'I thought I'd lost the path and wouldn't be able to find your house. Are you still up?'

With difficulty, he took off his frozen fur coat, hat and felt boots and sat down next to Yegor and Nastya. While the old man enjoyed the warmth, Yegor ran around the house, finding him warm dog fur mittens and fresh footcloths — he wanted the old man out of the house as soon as possible. But the gamekeeper thawed out in the warmth and, recovering himself, began to pass on the latest news from the village. Gamekeepers are quick on the uptake and glancing around the room, Zhakup immediately noticed the old Berdan rifle leaning against the wall next to the felt boots that were two sizes too big for Yegor.

'Do you have a guest?' Zhakup remarked glancing up at the upper bunk. 'It looks like I wasn't the only one who's ended up at your door today.'

Yegor broke into a sweat. How could he have been

such a fool to have failed to at least hide his son's clothes and rifle! *No matter what trouble befalls us, forgive me, Lord!* he thought, inwardly growing cold. 'Ah, how stupid of me, I forgot! Those belong to my late Agafya's only nephew, God rest her soul... He's decided to pay us visit...' He pushed the cask of mead towards his guest. 'Why don't you have a drink, warm yourself up before you get back on the road!'

The old man stared at Yegor in surprise: the old Kerzhak had never offered anything to anyone before. He stroked his bushy beard thoughtfully, cast a sidelong glance at Yegor, and pushed the cask away. Then he bent down and fished out a snuff-box from the top of his boots. Zhakup's quick glance around the room and the bed with its pillows and blankets piled up in a heap, did not escape Yegor's attention.

'Have you come across a hunter over these last few days, my friend?' he asked Yegor   .

'How could I?' Yegor pretended to be surprised by the gamekeeper's question. 'I've barely stuck my nose outside recently. Are you after a hunter?'

'Yes, some bastard's been shooting the deer all winter! You know, it's against the law to go hunting in the reserve and he's been tormenting them like a savage lone wolf! I managed to follow his trail, but got lost in the blizzard. But he was headed towards these parts.'

Yegor was at a complete loss, not knowing whether Zhakup was testing him or telling the truth. But what if Zhakup really had tracked Fyodor down and decided to have it out with him directly, relying on his famed and remarkable strength? And he really was remarkably strong — even three healthy strong men couldn't have dealt with him, let alone a half-starved vagabond like Fyodor. *It's clear that the Lord has turned his back on me this time as well!* Yegor thought to himself ruefully. *Damn it all! It's more like torture than having a son! Oh, to hell with it all!*

'And what about your guest, won't he drink with us?' Zhakup asked again. 'Food tastes better when it's eaten in company.'

'He caught a chill on his way here and has taken to his bed...' Then Yegor sternly shouted to Nastya, 'What are you shilly-shallying there for? When will supper be ready?'

Nastya rushed about, not knowing what to put on the table. She hadn't cooked anything hot, so she quickly filled the cask with mead and sliced the bread. Meanwhile, gazing at the fire blazing in the stove, Yegor tried to decide what to do next. *What, if I manage to hit him over the head with an axe and then burn him in the stove?* he thought. *Who would ever find out how he had gone missing? You might as well go and chase the wind in the fields.* But he shrank back in fear at his thoughts. The hair on the back of his neck rose in horror.

Zhakup seemed to guess what he was thinking and stretched out for his double-barrelled shotgun, which — he knew — was already loaded in both barrels with heavy slugs. Yegor shrank back. He waited to see what Fyodor would do, but he remained hidden like a mouse. *The filthy swine!* he raged to himself at his son. *He's just lying there, playing dead...*

'Well, thank you, my friend, for the bread and salt[33],

---

[33] In Russian and Old Believer tradition - bread and salt is offered to visitors as a sign of hospitality.

as your people like to say. The blizzard seems to be subsiding. I'd better be off.'

Zhakup dressed slowly, never letting go of the double-barrelled shotgun, and left the house. There was the creak of ski on snow and then silence. The storm continued to howl outside. Fyodor jumped off the high bunk, dressed in silence, and dashed out into the darkness with the Berdan rifle in his hands.

From that moment, Yegor knew no peace. Every single day, he waited in agitation for the police to arrive.

He didn't eat or sleep, drank heavily, and constantly snapped at Nastya. But the police did not show up. Neither hide nor hair was heard of Fyodor. In the spring, when the snow melted, a rumour spread through the villages that Zhakup's body had been found in a lake in the forest. People said that he'd drowned while doing his rounds around the reserve. And only Yegor guessed what had really happened in the taiga. For a long time, Yegor suffered from the most appalling nightmares. At night, he was convinced that the huge old gamekeeper was sitting on his chest and trying to strangle him, or that he was about to appear at the door pointing his double-barrelled shotgun at him, or even worse — that Zhakup was pushing him into his own roaring stove. Yegor would wake up covered in sweat, devoutly make the sign of the cross, get down from his bunk, and repeatedly empty the cask of mead. But no matter how much mead he drank, the nightmare visions would still not leave him.

Fyodor finally came back to visit his father's house in the middle of summer. Yegor knew he would come eventually: the taiga is a big place but a person cannot hide in it forever. There was also the fact that Fyodor totally lacked spirit — he had grown up small-minded and weak-willed and people like this are doomed if left to their own devices in the taiga. Six years of life on the run had not made him a strong man, capable of relying on his own strength. Just as before, in his youth and childhood, he relied on the support of his father, on his resourcefulness. It did not occur to him to go abroad and cover his tracks, but instead he circled around the family home like a whining pup, waiting for a handout from his master. After six years, Fyodor had finally let himself go completely and now he was more animal than human.

Yegor didn't know what to do with his son. He thought long and hard and ended up advising him to cross the frontier and go abroad, but Fyodor, who was cowardly by nature, became more stubborn than ever. On top of that, he shifted all the blame for his misfortunes onto his father. As luck would have it, that summer the authorities began to build the dirt road and a lot more people moved into the surrounding settlements, which meant Fyodor might be spotted by anyone at any moment. From that fateful winter, Yegor had begun to imagine that his house was being watched. So, with Fyodor's arrival, the quarrels and arguments began to spring up again in the house. The whole affair came to a head when Yegor told his son to give himself up to the authorities: the most they would give him was ten years, no more. In response, Fyodor threatened to kill the old man and rushed at him with his fists. It was a good thing, Nastya was in the house, otherwise who knows how things might have turned out.

As it was, the old man lay in bed for a whole week after the fight. His entire body was bruised and his head was buzzing. He had only gotten up that morning because the raftsmen were due to travel down the river the next day and the buoys needed to be checked. It was still dark, the river had swollen after the recent showers, and there was a chance that the high water might drag the buoy from its moorings. The deserted shore was covered with monstrous looking roots and branches that had been carried there by the river; a dark, cold sky hung low over the gorge. The forest was silent, sullen and menacing. The fierce wind had broken the trees, exposing their gnarled trunks and thick stumps. They resembled terrible furry trolls guarding their prey, dead fish blackened the shallow bank. It was clear there had been a serious mudslide upriver. Crows croaked and cawed loudly over the fish that reeked of rot and decay. The old boat was hard to lift and got stuck on the boulders. With difficulty, Yegor lowered it into the water and sighed with relief as he pushed off. The water seemed cleaner and safer to him than the littered shoreline. He caught himself thinking that it wouldn't be long before senility and dementia overtook him completely.

In a matter of minutes, the fast current had carried the boat to the familiar, grey, moss-covered boulder. The buoy was lower in the water than usual and bobbing heavily. Yegor poked around it with his boat-hook but could find no branches or weed weighing it down. It was strange: nothing seemed to be snagged around the buoy and yet it was almost being dragged under the water. Unexpectedly, he hooked up a length of rope and, pulling on it, realized that one end was tied to the buoy. Yegor pulled the rope hard and saw something black and bulky float to the surface in the middle of the stream and then go under again. *Who could have tied a cage trap to the buoy?* Yegor wondered. *What sort of idiot could have come up with an idea like this!* The end of the boat-hook hit something soft like dough and, directed by some instinctive heavy foreboding, the old man pulled his hand away. He lit a lantern and pointed it mid-stream. Then he waited a little and again jabbed the unfamiliar object with his hook: a swollen corpse slowly rose to the water's surface. Yegor recognised his son's jacket and let out a desperate scream...

By the time the dawn had broken, Yegor and his daughter Nastya had already buried Fyodor's body. It was raining. His son had passed from life as secretively as he had lived it those last six years...

The old man sat wearily at the table. The room was still dark. The chimney hummed, a cricket chirped behind the stove and there was a terrible pounding in his temples. Ayan and Dunya were silent: he lay on the bench, she on the alcove above the stove. Of course, they were waiting for him to leave. Maybe he shouldn't interfere? All his life, Yegor had insisted on having his own way in this world, but nothing had come of it. Maybe it was time for him to calm down and take things easier? He sighed deeply but instead a strangled sob escaped. His chest felt as if it was being squeezed with an iron hoop. Yegor went to the door, found his felt boots, put on his short fur coat and quietly left the house. Without stopping on the porch, he wandered to the river bank, stepping on his long moonlit shadow as he went. The north wind roared in the tops of the trees, the waves splashed in the river. A familiar world that had almost swallowed up his entire life... He exposed his chest to the wind and froze to the spot like one of the many stone pillars that litter the Altai mountains. The clouds were beginning to part, lightening up the sky. The waning moon peeped out over the mountain range. At one time, he had loved this season... When had that been? Back in the days when he had been out on his rounds, checking up on his deer herds grazing out on his pastures... A cold wind blew under his half-length sheepskin coat and down his trousers. The spray hissed angrily as it was torn from the crests of the white-foamed waves. There had been a time when he had loved to row his boat against the swift current, pulling at the oars with all his might... Good Lord, what times those had been? In those days, he had delivered furs and grain to the town and sold them for a handy profit...

He stood for a long time, staring at the roaring river. Then he went to look for his boat and found it downstream, lying upside down. The mudslide seemed much more powerful than he'd initially imagined: the water was as high as the spring flood. The old man and the river had never been on easy terms. The trap nets were nowhere to be seen. They had evidently been carried away in the night.

He stopped again next to the boat, looking at the water. The river was as fathomless as his melancholy thoughts. Then he walked along the bank to check the buoy. The same buoy that had witnessed the final minutes of his only son Fyodor's life. The buoy was not on its mooring: the waves had dragged it away. He felt as if something had been torn from his chest. *Why didn't you drag me away with you last night?* he silently raged at the furious river. Yegor covered his face with his hands and

sat down on a boulder. The palms of his hands seemed to
him to smell of blood.

'Birdie!'

Dunya shuddered and froze, holding her breath.

'Are you asleep?'

She wasn't asleep. What's more, she hadn't closed her eyes all night, indulging instead in the sweetest of daydreams. Ayan's arrival and his perseverance and patience had touched her deeply and she felt so happy. Only a man who felt strongly about her could have come out to see her in such appalling weather and put up with his truck breaking down on the road and her grandfather's malicious words. Dunya's imagination transported her back to the village, where she had spent the whole of the previous day, then she remembered their journey back, the conversation they had had and the clearing next to the river... Suddenly she felt ashamed of the docile acquiescence she had shown at the spring, babbling away like a child. She had let herself get carried away... She shouldn't have let him caress her like that. She shouldn't have! That was why Ayan hadn't kissed her and had become all silent and cold when they got back to the truck. Of course, he didn't need her anymore! But then he'd come back to her, three or four hours later! Dunya remembered how her heart had missed a beat when he entered the house. As if in a dream, she had served him his food and mead, and climbed back up onto her bed above the stove. And she hadn't been able to close her eyes all night. Dunya was afraid that her grandfather might guess what she had been up to with Ayan, and then she'd be on the receiving end of a flogging that would make the previous one seem like a picnic. She dreamed of the day when her life might change, when it might become full, interesting and beautiful, when she would feel Ayan's caring touch, have him next to her all the time. She felt certain that she would spend her whole life in the arms of her beloved. But what if she were to meet someone else, someone gentler and more serious than Ayan? Maybe she would end up marrying someone like that instead? But no matter how much she tried to drive Ayan out of her head, he resolutely remained in her mind's eye — bristling cat's whiskers and all. And anyway, she thought, blushing, how could she dream of anyone else after they had been together at the spring? No, it could only be Ayan, she would marry him and love only him alone! There is no controlling your dreams — they whisk you off your feet and carry you away as if they had wings. Dunya imagined herself in her own house, waiting for her husband to come home from work, and he, too, would be hurrying to get back home to find out how she was feeling — after all, they would definitely be having a child. How happy those people must be whose homes are full of life! Would her and Ayan's home be the same?

'Birdie! Why don't you answer?'

Ayan had sensed that Dunya wasn't asleep. As soon as the old man had left the house, Dunya began tossing and turning in her bed, as if deliberately giving Ayan a sign that she was awake.

'Why won't you say anything?'

'I don't know.'

Silence fell once again. Ayan could hear his own heart pounding in his chest, and felt the heat spreading across his face.

'What are you going to do today?'

'What's it to you?'

'I don't know,' he replied, repeating her recent words back to her.

'I'll wash the floors, clean the house and then cook some food.'

'Dunya, leave this lonely old place!' he implored. 'Come with me to the village. You could get a job in the local textile factory. You could become a seamstress. Then you could go to night school and get an education. You'll have nothing to fear, no one will dare lay a finger on you. I'll always be right next to you.'

'There you go with your textile factory again!' Her recent dreams seemed to have faded somehow. But her heart was pounding uncontrollably in her breast.

The curtain covering the alcove over the stove parted slightly, and Ayan's smiling face appeared.

'Where do you think you're going?' Dunya covered her breast shyly. 'You can't come in here!'

Ayan hesitated.

'Dunya, what I told you was the absolute truth... Everything that I hold in my heart...'

'But what kind of student would I make?' Dunya hesitated. 'I'll never get the hang of my letters. But it doesn't matter where I live to take care of my husband and have our children, does it?'

'Anywhere, but just not here, Dunya! I will always love you, do you hear? And you will have my children!'

'Idiot!' She leaned back and closed her eyes.

The ladder creaked. Dunya felt him place his warm broad palm on her breast and his hot breath and lips on hers. She pulled away from his embrace and wrinkled her nose in disgust.

'Good grief, you could at least take your stinky overalls off!'

'But what about the old man?' Ayan asked in a whisper.

'He's gone to check up on the buoy. He won't be back until late morning...'

Dunya was woken up by a loud clucking and squawking down below. The door was wide open, and one of the speckled hens was pacing around the room looking for food. But where was Ayan? When did he leave? She peaked out from behind the stove and saw her grandfather on the floorboards, lying in a ball under a thin blanket. Of all the bad luck! The young girl was horrified. How had she contrived to fall asleep? What was going to happen now? She had no idea when her grandfather had got back home. And why was the door open? There was something wrong here.

Outside, she could hear the roar of an engine. Dunya quickly pulled on her sundress and jumped down from the stove, then, throwing her dishevelled hair over her shoulder, she ran barefoot out towards the gate. Mist rose from the ground, and the hollow was full of thick fog. The rumble of the engine was coming from the valley. *How could he have left me without saying a single warm word in parting?* Dunya thought resentfully. She bit her lips, trying to hold back her tears. She leaned against the upright of the gate for a second and then ran out into the valley, splashing her way through the puddles.

Two lumber trucks stood right opposite each other, their bumpers almost touching, and two men were busy trying to attach a thick cable between them.

'Hello gorgeous!' the unknown driver — a swarthy broad-faced guy with a shaven head — shouted over to her. 'Have you come over to invite us in for tea?'

Ayan was taken aback when he saw Dunya running over the field and rushed over to meet her.

'What's happened?'

Dunya stopped abruptly and froze to the spot, looking at him with her eyes full of tears.

'Did that old man hurt you again? Tell me, did he hurt you?'

She shook her head. Ayan's agitation calmed her a little, and his appearance made her laugh out loud. Once again, he was covered from head to toe in mud. She laughed, turned abruptly, and ran for home.

'Is she your girlfriend?' the shaven-headed man asked Ayan.

'Yes, she's mine!'

'She doesn't seem all there, you haven't hooked yourself a crazy have you? Half-girl, half-gazelle.'

Ayan laughed merrily and climbed into his cab.

'Well, let's give it another try,' he said, turning to his colleague. 'Wow, that's some hole you drove into yesterday, I landed in one myself only recently. Just don't pull too hard or the cable will break and then I'll be stuck here all day.'

With difficulty, they managed to pull Ayan's truck out of the pothole. The door of the house opened with a creak, Dunya came out with the large wooden pail and poured out its contents. She stared at Ayan and disappeared back into the house again. The two drivers sat down on a log and lit a cigarette.

'It's very beautiful around here,' the shaven-headed

driver remarked. 'Paradise! You've got everything you could want right under your nose — honey, fish, the village nearby. That Kerzhak knows where to put down his roots.'

'Well, I don't like it here. The solitude and boredom would probably kill me.'

'Where did you sleep yesterday?'

'At theirs.' Ayan nodded towards the house.

'Did they give you a bite to eat?

'I made do with what God sent my way.'

'The old man must have kept his eyes peeled on you, eh?' The shaven-headed driver laughed. 'I know their type well. I expect he lay down between the two of you?'

'You guessed it in one!' Ayan laughed too.

'You and that girl were exchanging such eloquent looks that you might be forgiven for thinking... Listen, you're not going to marry her, are you?'

'I don't know yet.'

'Take your time,' the older man advised. 'You don't have to bind yourself hand and foot straight away. I got married early and now I'm really regretting it. A woman is always a woman. I spent five years building us a five-room house, completely exhausted myself in the process, and now we're dividing it up into two parts.'

'Why's that?' Ayan asked in surprise.

'You'd understand if you had my mother-in-law growling at you all day! Sometimes I'd happily throttle her. Okay, I'd better be on my way! Shall I leave you my smokes?' The shaven-headed driver pushed his pack of cigarettes towards Ayan. 'You'll need them, you've still got plenty to do. And think carefully before coming to any important decisions.' He got up and added with a smile: 'Mind you, the girl doesn't look half bad. Very nicely built. A real gazelle, I tell you!'

Ayan removed the heavy wheel, took the tyre off and, with difficulty, found the puncture. He then glued the patch to the tyre, using the jack to squeeze it tight, and waited for it to dry. He stopped for a cigarette. Then he put the tyre back on the mount and began to tighten the nuts. It took him an hour to replace the wheel. Then he finally started pumping it back up. The sun struck the back of his head, his hands had gone numb and he was covered in sweat. He was extremely thirsty and hungry to boot. Ayan kicked the wheel angrily with his boot and lay down in the shade. But, as luck would have it, a river gull hovered right in front of him with a sharp cry. He cursed the stupid bird and turned on his side to get a better view of the green gate. The yard was empty: Dunya did not venture from the house and the old man had disappeared somewhere. Normally at this time, he would be shuffling along in his broken-backed boots between the black soot-filled bathhouse to the river with his nets. With a rumble and a roar, the heavily laden trucks rushed headlong up and down the road, playing on everyone's nerves. He recalled Dunya's hot embrace, the warm stove and the soft bed. And suddenly he laughed at his fond reverie. Things very much looked like he would be marrying Dunya. *So, what am I doing lying around here, as if I were the buoy keeper's watchman?* he thought. *I need to get up and get going. I expect the saw mill will be sending out a search party for me...*

Ayan did not notice how he had managed to fall asleep. He woke up in the evening, bitten all over by the mosquitoes. His face was swollen and his body numb from the awkward position he'd been sleeping in. He got to his feet and walked towards the house. Cautiously he entered the yard and stealthily approached Dunya, who was busy with something by the hearth. Suddenly, from somewhere to one side, Yegor's heavy voice rang out,

'Hey, young man!' The old man's faded watery eyes glared at the young man angrily. 'We gave you shelter for the night, fed you with what we had, maybe it's time to show a little respect, eh? Now, sling your hook and be off with you out of my house! Dunya, see to your guest! And make sure I never set eyes on him again!'

Ayan waited for Dunya and accompanied her out to the yard. There were tears in the girl's eyes and he didn't know how to console her. Tender words arose in his heart, but he couldn't find any way to verbalise them and was furious that his future happiness should depend on the whim of some pitiful old man. But did it really depend on him?

They stopped next to the truck. He needed to tell Dunya what his final decision was and be done with it! Dunya looked down in silence, waiting for him to speak, not daring to raise her eyes from the ground. Ayan took the girl by the hand and pulled her towards him. Her palms were hot, and he shivered. He quickly kissed her on the lips and, lifting her up in his arms, placed her in the cab. Dunya let out a whimper and then, from happiness, buried herself in his chest and, sobbing like a child, burst into tears.

Ayan slammed the door, started the truck and stepped sharply on the accelerator. *Well, that's that then!* he thought with relief as he steered the truck in the direction of the dirt road.

10

Old Yegor was not surprised that Dunya had left with Ayan. You can't run away from destiny, like mother, like daughter — the apple never falls far from the tree. He hadn't been offended at Nastya when she had left him with her small baby, and there was absolutely no point in sulking over his granddaughter.

And yet for a long time he couldn't believe that he had now been left all on his own. For a whole week the old man wandered around the house, shuffling along in his broken-backed boots, all the time thinking that Dunya would return to the house at any moment.

The rumours that the saw mill would close turned out to be true. Within a month, the raftsmen had floated the last of the forest's logs down the river and then a representative from the saw mill arrived and took away the bay horse. It was as if all activity on the riverbank died that day. Only the trucks continued to thunder unceasingly along the dirt road, as before, some climbing up the mountain with a laboured roar, others cautiously descending into the gorge.

The old man now spent whole days, or even weeks, lying in bed. The last two days, he had been feeling particularly bad. He had caught a fever and his bones had begun to ache. He just put it down to old age and did nothing about it. Each man has to accept his fate when it comes to him, he thought to himself. He had abandoned his bitterness about the past, it no longer tormented him, he did not regret anything and his chores and jobs around the household no longer interested him. The pig broke out of its sty and ran away, the chickens wandered about on their own in the yard and the buoy was long gone. His memories of the past were also gone. He couldn't believe that he had spent his life, bullying and fighting certain people, making up with others, begging something from someone else and fussing and worrying about other things. He was no longer tormented by pride, his heart was no longer oppressed with resentment towards his loved ones, there was not a single soul left about whom he might have any regrets. Yegor did not care what lay in store for him, be it heaven or hell. He felt he had finally gained the freedom he had always desired.

His body was hot, it was drenched in sweat and his hands and feet were cold, as if life had already left them. Lying in his bed, Yegor crossed himself, gathered his strength, and got to his feet. He desperately wanted some fresh air. Shuffling along on his weakened legs, he reached the stove, picked up the poker and, leaning heavily on it, went out into the yard.

The red sun was sinking behind the mountains. The clouds gathered around, the mountain peaks were illuminated with a bloody glow and the twilight shadows gathered in the gorge. Somewhere an eagle owl hooted amiably.

Shuffling slowly, Yegor dragged himself up a hill, where a lonely grave lay. All the way, he never once looked back at his house. At the top of the hill, he stopped and, leaning on the poker, looked around. Twilight had enveloped the cabin and the river's roar could barely be heard through the dense mist. Everything swirled before his eyes. Then he knelt down, pressed his hot wet forehead to Agafya's grave and wept inconsolably. He wept for the last time in his life.

The sky was clear and fathomless, and a bright new-born moon hung in the pure night air.

Made in the USA
Columbia, SC
25 March 2023

14040368R00270